Reborn

THE BATTLEMAGE TRILOGY

BOOK ONE

James Blackwood

Reborn: The Battlemage Trilogy

Copyright © 2019 by James Blackwood

All rights reserved. No part of this book may be reproduced or transmitted in any form or by any means without written permission from the author.

ISBN 13: 978-1-7345718-0-6

This is a work of fiction. Any refrences to historical events, real people, or real places are used fictitiously. Names, characters, and places are products of the author's imagination.

Book cover design by germancreative.

Amplified Magic Publishing
47 County Road 751
Hollywood, AL 35752

www.jamesblackwoodbooks.com

SIXTEEN	163
SEVENTEEN	177
EIGHTEEN	189
NINETEEN	205
TWENTY	219
TWENTY-ONE	238
TWENTY-TWO	253
TWENTY-THREE	266
TWENTY-FOUR	280
TWENTY-FIVE	291
TWENTY-SIX	306
TWENTY-SEVEN	319
TWENTY-EIGHT	340
TWENTY-NINE	350
THIRTY	361
THIRTY-ONE	369
ACKNOWLEDGEMENTS	384
ABOUT THE AUTHOR	386

Contents

PROLOGUE	*1*
ONE	*11*
TWO	*22*
THREE	*30*
FOUR	*37*
FIVE	*47*
SIX	*59*
SEVEN	*71*
EIGHT	*77*
NINE	*85*
TEN	*92*
ELEVEN	*101*
TWELVE	*109*
THIRTEEN	*120*
FOURTEEN	*138*
FIFTEEN	*152*

For my daughters:

Addelynn and Avery, this book is dedicated to you. You reawakened in me the importance of imagination. When you are finally able to read this book, I hope it sparks the same imagination in you all over again. I love you both. You will always be my baby girls.

GLOSSARY OF WORDS OF POWER   *387*

PROLOGUE

King Riehner stared out the window, engrossed in the mixture of purple and orange as the sun rose over Lake Aleesia. The King enjoyed starting his mornings this way. He had spent much of his time of late admiring the beauty of the countryside while at Rhys Castle, though he could not remain much longer. Spring was his favorite time of year. It was almost upon them and soon he would become a father. The announcement was to take place in the capital as soon as he returned. Ribbons and streamers were being placed this morning throughout the streets.

Riehner was the embodiment of a king; tall, strong, handsome, adored by his subjects. He had become the first Battlemage, combined the kingdoms, and held peace for an unprecedented one hundred years. He ruled beside his beautiful elven wife, Beltia. Despite all their years together, he could still get lost in her emerald green eyes.

Riehner, immersed in thoughts of his wife and upcoming child, nearly missed the subtle creak of the door as Iwan slipped into the room. Iwan was tall and broad but could move with the grace and stealth of a rogue. He kept his hair cut short to keep it from being grabbed in battle. His gray eyes could pierce even the hardiest of soldiers while melting the heart of the local ladies.

Iwan cleared his throat to announce his entrance. Riehner took a deep breath without looking away from the window. "Tis a beautiful country, is it not? I am hard-pressed not to make Aleesia the capital after the child is born."

"Aye, it is a beautiful place, Sire," Iwan said. "But we must make way to Cèrhin. Preparations have been made to depart after you break your fast. The horses are saddled and await your command."

"If you rise early, before the sun, you can see the smoke start to settle above the water just as the sun begins to paint the sky," Riehner said. "The flowers are just beginning to bloom, and the trees hunger for the sun's rays. Spring is the grandest time of year. It brings new life from death and gives us hope of a better tomorrow."

"Your Highness," Iwan interrupted, "your wife could deliver at any time. The servants are preparing the celebration and announcement in the capital as we speak. We must not delay."

The King turned from the window, looking at his old friend, his eyes almost sad at the thought of departing the small fishing village. "Ah, see now. That is why you are my most trusted adviser."

Iwan gave the King a mischievous grin. "There is no use for a general when we have been at peace for so long. You had to have some use for me."

Riehner smiled back at him. He slapped his friend on the back as he walked away from the window, gesturing to the door with his other hand. "Shall we? My wife is not known for her patience, especially in her current condition."

Before they could reach the door, a commotion could be heard outside and a young soldier stumbled into the room. He was gasping for breath and held a wound over his left arm. "Raiders… in the castle! Hundreds of them!"

Iwan leaped into action. He had not been in a true battle in decades, but that had not dulled his reflexes in the least. Before the young man could finish, Iwan had already drawn his sword and dagger and began gathering information and giving orders.

"Hundreds, you say? Are you sure? Alert the rest of the men. Tell them to assemble in the throne room. There are not enough of us to withstand their advance for long. We must protect the King and Queen at all costs. As soon as you have rallied the men, make way to the town and warn the villagers. Once you have completed that task, make all haste to Cèrhin and notify the rest of the war band. They will need to be prepared. Tell them we come quickly. Do you understand? Speak, man! Do you understand your duty?"

"Yes, sir!" he said and sped out of the room.

Riehner straightened to his full height and drew his sword, an amazing sight in its own right. The blade was completely clear, forged by the elves from diamond and mythril. The silver handle was braided with gold thread, and a diamond was fixed upon the pommel. He was an astounding warrior, receiving training from humans, elves, and dwarves. His abilities in magic were without rival, even among the elves. He looked at Iwan, his blue eyes betraying his disappointment. "One more time, my old friend?"

Iwan squinted as the light from the window reflected off the King's sword. He crossed his fist over his heart. "My life for yours!"

Riehner and his general raced through the castle, dispatching enemies as they went. They burst into the throne room. Queen Beltia stood in the middle of the room with a dagger in her hand, poised to attack at any sight of an intruder. Two young soldiers stood at her side, guarding her. The rest of the guards had yet to arrive in the throne room. Riehner hoped that the soldier that alerted him to the attack had lived long enough to sound the warning.

Riehner rushed to embrace his pregnant wife. She trembled in his arms. He held her tight, reassuring her with his touch. He whispered and the crystal pendant around his neck began to glow, the anxiety disappearing from Beltia's face. "We must get you to safety," he told her, brushing her jet-black hair from her eyes. "Iwan, the horses are prepared to depart?"

"Yes, my lord," Iwan said, scanning the entrances to the room.

He ushered Beltia closer to Iwan and toward a hidden passage that lay beneath a statue of an armored warrior. His eyes flitted between Iwan, Beltia, and the door. "Iwan, you must take Beltia and flee. I will hold them off to give you safe passage."

"But Sire," Iwan said. He was met with a stern glare that advised him not to test the subject further. "Aye, I will guard her with my life."

"You cannot stay," Beltia said, running up to his side. "I will not leave without you."

He wrapped her in his arms and squeezed her tight, forcing the tears from welling up in his eyes. "I love you with all that I am. I can serve you better by ensuring you have plenty of distance between you and our attackers. Iwan, give me your satchel."

Iwan did as the King asked. Riehner shoved his crown in the bag and ordered Iwan to take the Queen to Arebel Forest. "Once inside the forest, she can lead you to Gaer Alon. It is an ancient elven city. Her people will look after you both." He paused, placing a strong hand on Iwan's shoulder and handing him the satchel with the other. "If something should happen to me, present this crown to my child. They will be the new ruler of this land, not these scum that seek to take it by force."

Iwan stared up at his grieving King and emotion almost overtook him. "I will do as you command. If I do not see you by the morrow, I will return for you. On that, you have my word."

Riehner kissed his wife's forehead, wiping a tear from her eye.

"I will await your safe return to me, my love," Beltia told him. "I love you."

"More," he whispered to her. "Go, now. With all haste, go."

They turned to flee through a hidden chamber below the statue just as raiders began to pummel the door. With one last glance back at his beloved King and friend, Iwan nodded, his brow furrowed. Riehner returned his look, sorrowful for only a moment, and crossed his arm over his chest. "My life for yours." Iwan returned the sign and led the Queen away to safety.

The King turned to the door, a determined look in his eye, gripping his sword at the ready. There was a loud crack and then an explosion as the door gave way to the might of the raiders. The enemy, at least twenty strong, fanned out in the room, wielding swords, daggers, and bows. The King and the remaining two soldiers stood their ground, ready to attack at the slightest movement.

As the debris settled, a man dressed in all black armor strode into the room with an air of confidence, glancing around the room slowly. Around his neck hung a polished black stone fixed in a silver necklace, and in his right hand, he carried a hand-and-a-half sword. The blade appeared to be made of pure obsidian, the handle solid black, with a bright red ruby in the pommel. The way he held the sword made it easy to see that he was a master of the blade, all but an extension of his arm. Riehner could not see the man's face but something seemed familiar about him. He stared at the pendant around the man's neck. A Battlemage but whom?

A hearty laugh rolled from behind the man's helmet as he glared at Riehner through the slit. "What old man? Don't you remember me? Surely it is not that difficult". The man removed his helmet and tossed it aside, steel clattering against the stone floor. "Now?"

Riehner's eyes widened in shock, but he shook away the look. It was Tzelder, a prior student, but he had never completed the training needed to earn his medallion "How? Why?" asked Riehner.

Tzelder cackled as he crept closer to Riehner. "You fool! I have studied magic that you could only hope to comprehend. You are nothing in my presence. You shunned me before, but now you will bow to me!"

"You have much to learn if you think to defeat me, Tzelder!"

Tzelder snarled at him as he hoisted the black sword to the ready. "I will enjoy watching you die!"

Tzelder lunged at the King, striking at his head, followed by a thrust to the gut. Riehner deflected the strikes without effort. He could tell that the man in black was toying with him. Riehner unleashed a flurry of blows, and Tzelder danced around the room, avoiding each strike. The two soldiers of the royal guard leaped into the fray with reckless abandon, daggers spinning, slicing into enemy flesh. The raiders responded with counter-attacks against the soldiers.

As the two Battlemages circled each other, Tzelder raised his hand and sent a bolt of lightning coursing toward Riehner. He leaped to the side, countering with a radiant flash of light that temporarily blinded everyone in the room except himself. Tzelder began to whisper, the jewel around his neck pulsing a smoky gray color, and his sight was restored. He picked up the attack with a frenzied pace. The Battlemages exchanged blow for blow until Tzelder feigned a strike to the King's knee followed by a blow to his shoulder, slicing deep into the muscle. Riehner grasped the wound, wishing he was wearing his armor. Tzelder rushed forward and kicked him in the chest, sending Riehner soaring across the room. He moaned and twitched as he landed hard, sprawled out on the floor.

The Queen dashed back into the room from the hidden exit followed by Iwan and two other soldiers of the King's guard. The battle in the room came to an abrupt halt as Beltia entered. Tzelder's eyebrows arched, and he smiled mischievously as he approached the Queen. The two soldiers that escorted her rushed into action, attempting to draw attention away from the Queen. Riehner tried to regain his footing and make his way to his wife, but his injured arm did not want to support the weight of his body. One of the other soldiers seized the opportunity to surprise Tzelder. He grabbed a spear from a nearby suit of armor and launched it at Tzelder's blindside. The dart should have caught the warlock unaware, killing him immediately and bringing the battle to an end. To Riehner's surprise, Tzelder simply raised a hand, while fighting off the other two soldiers, stopping the spear in mid-air. A cruel smile curled across his lips for a brief moment, then, with a flick of his wrist, he sent the spear barreling toward the Queen, where it found a home firmly in her chest.

Beltia stood in disbelief as she stared up at her husband, a tear rolling down her face and blood pooling on her blouse where the spear shaft protruded. Riehner rushed to her side, catching her before she fell to the ground. She tried to speak, the words caught in her throat. The fighting stopped, and Tzelder stood by, relishing in Riehner's torment. A low chuckle escaped his throat as he sheathed the sword over his shoulder and sauntered to the throne, sitting sideways with his legs draped across the armrest.

Riehner held Beltia close as tears fell down his face. "Iwan," he said. "We must leave if I am to try to heal her. The elves will assist. Quickly!"

Iwan grabbed a sword and cut the spear so that the Queen could be transported. Riehner picked her up and scrambled to the hidden exit. The remaining guardsmen made a line between him and the raiders, but Tzelder made no attempt to stop them, unable to control his laughter.

Riehner looked at his wife, her beautiful face becoming ashen. "You would have... made a...wonderful father," she whispered.

"Do not speak of it, my love. I will make this right," Riehner whispered, calling upon the magic to heal her wounds to no avail.

Beltia's breaths became shallow and rapid. "My time has come, my love. Oh, to have seen our son…"

"A son, a proper king," Riehner said. "I love you, my dear, forever."

"More," she whispered and closed her eyes forever.

ONE

Tammuz rose before the first hints of sunlight could slip through his bedroom window and ran his fingers through his shaggy, dark hair. He was shorter than most other young men his age, athletic but not as broad as his peers either. Most men in his village were tall and broad-shouldered. His people were not native to this land. They were conquerors from across the sea who settled in Iradell hundreds of years ago.

He slid out of bed and slipped into the kitchen as quiet as a mouse. He enjoyed getting up early to watch the sunrise before beginning his morning chores. His father, Kèlris, was the town blacksmith and it was Tammuz's personal duty to ensure that the fires were started in the shop before his father arrived.

He had lived in Aleesia for all of his short fifteen years and believed the small-town life to be quite dull. He longed for adventure, to see the world. He had heard stories about the warriors of old, traveling here and there, conquering cities and he desired more than his quaint, small-town life.

After a few bites of bread and jam, he donned his cloak and headed out to watch the sunrise. He jogged down the well-known game trails of the forest until he came to the foothills of the mountains. He climbed high in the hills to a bluff that overlooked the lake. His fingers grasped the dusty rock as he scurried to his perch. He wiped the sweat from his brow before nibbling on a few scraps of meat he pulled from his satchel. The sun was just beginning to peak over the lake and smoke hovered over the water, slowly rising with the sun. A cool breeze blew in off the lake, and a shiver went up his back.

He could see the whole town from here, nestled between the mountains and the lake. The village of Aleesia was small, consisting of a central square surrounded by shops with barns and houses scattered along the outskirts. Several long piers stretched from the town's eastern edge into the lake. People were beginning to move about the small fishing village; some headed to the lake to prepare their boats for the day, while others left southward to work on small farms outlying the town. In that moment, he was at peace with his little piece of paradise.

REBORN

He lost track of time as his mind wandered, imagining what it would be like if his people still traveled the oceans and if the stories of elves and dwarves were real. He grew up listening to the lore of his people, how the humans were exiled from their homeland but found a place in Iradell among the elves and dwarves after one human earned their respect, became the High King, and led them to unprecedented peace after defeating the Kapre. All of that changed nearly one hundred years ago when Tzelder usurped Riehner and took control of the kingdom.

Tamm had heard of Tzelder's ruthlessness, but other than the laws that directly affected him, such as not being able to own a weapon or to speak of King Riehner, his reign did not affect him much. That was both an advantage and disadvantage of being in Aleesia. The lake separated him from the rest of the kingdom. He longed for a more exciting life, one full of adventure and sword fights, of elves, dwarves, and damsels needing to be rescued.

The sun glimmered off the lake, and he shielded his eyes from the glare. He yawned as he reclined against the stone, enjoying the view, and wondered what else lay beyond the shores of Lake Aleesia.

Satisfied that he had seen enough, he slid back down the cliff and rushed to the blacksmith's shop to start the fires. He entered the shop with his arms full of firewood and set to work readying the forge. He worried that he might have spent too much time on the bluff before returning, but the shop appeared empty when he entered.

He froze as someone cleared their throat behind him just as he struck a piece of steel with the flint. He recognized the sound immediately and turned to face his father. Kèlris was a large man, muscles bulging from years at the forge. His hair was dark with flecks of silver showing, his eyes a deep gray, like clouds before a storm.

"Tamm," his father said, "You are late again. This cannot keep happening."

"I know," he said, shrugging his shoulders. "I like watching the sunrise; I like exploring. It helps me to clear my mind. The forge is so…contained."

Kèlris sighed. "It helps you to daydream and show up late. You will be sixteen in a few weeks. You and your brother. It's almost time to choose a profession. No one will allow you to be their apprentice if you continue to disregard your duties here. Have you given it any thought?"

Tamm paused a moment, looking around the shop. "Being a smithy is an honorable profession, Father. It's just not for me. I want adventure, to know what's outside this village. I haven't even been across the lake to Delocia, and you travel there twice a year."

"I know it is not a glamorous life," Kèlris said, "but it provides for my family. If you have not solicited a master by your sixteenth birthday, then I must choose for you."

"I understand," Tamm said, his eyes downcast. He noticed a new sword lying on a table and slid it from the scabbard. He flourished it around the shop fighting an imaginary foe.

REBORN

"Put that away," Kèlris ordered. "That is for Alred, commissioned by his father in celebration of selecting his apprenticeship. He'll be here any minute to retrieve it."

"Oh, and what will he be training for?" Tamm asked, sardonically. "Town guard? So that he can flaunt his authority?"

Alred and Tamm did not get along. Alred was a bully and generally got away with it because his father was the sheriff. He made it his priority to persecute Tamm at every opportunity.

"Yes," Kèlris said, taking the sword from Tamm. "And you would do well to mind your tongue. You never know who is listening."

"Could be anyone," a voice said from just inside the door. Tamm jumped as his brother Echao poked him in the ribs. Echao was tall and athletic with brown hair and gray-blue eyes. He was agile and could sneak up on just about anyone.

"You little rogue!" Tamm huffed, barreling toward Echao, ramming a shoulder into his side.

Regaining his balance, Echao laughed and lifted an eyebrow. "Someone is fussy this morning. I could have slipped a dagger between your ribs, and you would have been none the wiser."

"I'll show you a dagger during training today," Tamm said, laughing and shoving his brother.

"There will be plenty of time for that later. We have plenty of work today," Kèlris cried over the boys' horseplay.

"Speaking of work, Father, I have good news," Echao said.

"Do tell, son, do tell."

"I have solicited an apprenticeship," Echao told them. "I have been speaking with Anryn Tanner, and he has agreed to train me. I start after the Spring Festival. With any luck, in two years, I will be a Journeyman tanner."

"Anryn? Lily's father?" Kèlris asked.

"The very one," Echao said.

"Good. Very good. Tonight, we celebrate. Take this," he said, tossing Echao a small coin purse. "Go to the butcher and fetch some meat, maybe a whole hog. Tonight, we feast in celebration!"

Tamm and Echao walked through town toward the butcher's while joking and talking. The late winter morning was still cool and crisp but not cold enough to see their breath. Tamm rubbed his arms as he nodded a greeting to one of his neighbors before turning his attention back to Echao. "A tanner?" he asked. "Is this because you are interested in leather or because you are interested in Lily?"

"I don't know what you're insinuating," Echao said. "It's a good profession. It will provide for a family."

"That it will and possibly a family with Lily," Tamm said. "I know that you are smitten with the girl. She will make a fine wife one day. Working for her father and being in his good graces will ensure that." He nudged Echao in the side with his elbow.

Echao blushed, a smile tugging at the corner of his mouth. "Aye, she is a fine woman."

They weaved between the wooden buildings as they ambled further into town. They passed by the tanner's, the apothecary, and the healer. The healer seemed an odd man to

REBORN

Tamm. He did not speak much to the villagers and minded his own business for the most part. He was tall with long white hair past his shoulders and a beard that hung past his thin belly. Tamm thought him rude because he would frequently notice him staring, but he rarely ever spoke, and his deep blue eyes seemed to pierce the soul as if he could read your thoughts. The healer was standing in front of his shop that doubled as his home, and he was staring as usual. "He makes me nervous," Tamm said, a shiver jolting down his spine. "The way he stares all the time, it's unsettling."

"I agree," Echao replied. "He could at least say hello. He's a good healer, though."

Tamm agreed on that part. He had only had one encounter with the healer many years ago after falling from a tree. The healer explained to him that he had a small break in the bone but that it would mend over time. His arm was in a sling for nearly a month. Not being able to explore the woods and caves like he was accustomed to had irritated him almost as much as the old man's stares.

"Good morning, Linsyn," Tamm cried out while waving wildly. The healer raised his eyebrows in a confused look. He gave a quick, awkward wave before retreating into his home, causing the boys to giggle.

After meandering through the village, they arrived at the butcher's shop. Holden was a kind man who had always seemed fond of the blacksmith and his family. The two had been good friends since childhood. He was a squat man, quite obese, with a thick, oily complexion. Tamm figured that it was easy to come by when you had fatty meat in your face all day long.

"Welcome boys," Holden said. "What brings you in today?"

"We come for meat," Echao said. "I have been awarded an apprenticeship with the tanner, so tonight we celebrate."

Holden clapped his hands and guffawed. "Ah, well done, lad. And what of you, Tamm? Have you made a decision on your future yet?"

Tamm shook his head. "Not yet. There's still time."

"You procrastinate. Why do today what you can put off until tomorrow, no?" Holden said, chuckling to himself. "That reminds me of a joke." The butcher loved to tell jokes. Most of them were not very good, but Tamm entertained them anyway and even laughed at them, for Holden's sake.

As Holden was preparing his joke, the door opened behind them. Tamm turned to see Alred, the sheriff's son, striding in. Alred gave a wry smirk as he saw Tamm and Echao. Neither of the young men cared much for Alred. It seemed that he was always searching for a way to bully those around him. Alred was arrogant but had the looks and physique to warrant it. He was the epitome of a warrior; strong, agile, and an expert swordsman for one who had just come of age. He had sandy blond hair and hazel eyes. Many of the young ladies in town thought him to be very handsome and went out of their way to catch his attention.

"Holden, my good man," Alred said, "I come for the best cut of meat you can offer. I have selected an apprenticeship with the town guard. My commission begins immediately."

REBORN

He cut his eyes from the butcher to Tamm and Echao, his left hand resting on the pommel of his sword.

Tamm understood the boast and his face flushed red with anger. More than anger, though; Tamm felt jealousy. The sword that Kèlris had designed for Alred was magnificent. The blade remained sheathed, but Tamm remembered drawing it in the shop before his father took it from him. The sword was perfectly balanced with a silver handle and cross-guard. The guard had intricate designs stamped into the steel. The grip was wrapped with delicate black leather that had been smooth in Tamm's hand with a silver diamond-shaped pommel to match the guards and handle.

What bothered Tamm the most was the simple fact that Alred could openly carry the blade and train with it. Regular citizens were not allowed to carry weapons. The king believed that the guards needed weapons to protect and police the people but that the people did not need weapons to protect themselves. Tamm thought that the king might have been afraid to let the citizens be armed. He was known to rule with an iron fist.

Each male was allowed to carry a hunting knife but nothing more. You could get away with owning a bow for hunting, as long as you did not carry it openly or hunt the king's land.

Kèlris trained his sons in swordsmanship, illegally, a few times a week. He said that this was a tradition of their ancestors that could not be forgotten. Tamm did not argue; he enjoyed every minute of the training. His father had taught him to wield a sword, dagger, and bow. He was proficient with the sword and bow, but his brother wielded double daggers as if he were bred to cleave flesh from bone.

"Congratulations, Master Alred," Holden said. "Young Echao has chosen a profession also. Many feasts are to be had tonight. Wait here while I prepare the meat."

The butcher slipped through a curtain to the back of the store, and a cleaver could be heard cutting through marrow and bone. "Another smithy, huh?" Alred asked, glancing over his shoulder.

Tamm's face burned with anger at the guard's mocking tone. "Where are your lackeys?" Tamm asked. "Cyris and Zaech usually follow you around like lost puppies."

Alred glanced at Tammuz in annoyance before turning his attention back to Echao, awaiting an answer.

"A tanner," Echao answered. "Anryn will be my master."

Alred's face contorted into full hatred, veins bulging in his neck and forehead. It was well known that Alred was also in love with Lily, and he had voiced his disgust many times regarding Echao spending time with her. Of all the girls in the village that adored Alred, Lily was not one of them. Her heart belonged to someone else.

Alred, his hand clenching against the handle of his sword, marched over to Echao until his nose was touching Echao's face. "You think I'm stupid?" he asked. "I know what you are trying to do. If you so much as speak to her, I will find a way to have you arrested. I have that authority now. Or, I may take the pleasure of beating you senseless myself."

Echao's hand reached for his hunting knife, and Tamm slid between them. "You will do nothing of the sort," Tamm said, the sarcasm thick in his voice. "We wouldn't want you abusing your power so soon, would we? Besides, what would dear old daddy say?"

Alred sneered at him. "You had better watch your mouth, boy. I have a good mind to cut you where you stand for disrespecting an officer of the law."

Holden returned to the room, carrying a large portion of beef wrapped in linen cloth. His face showed his confusion at the hostility in the room. Echao hurriedly paid for the meat and slid it into his satchel, cutting a glance over his shoulder at Alred before making his way towards the door, Tamm trailing behind him.

"Mind my words, peasant," Alred whispered as they walked by.

Tamm shoved his shoulder into Alred's chest as he pushed through to the door, knocking him back momentarily. Tamm knew Alred would not dare lash out in the presence of the butcher. "You'll pay for that, fool," Alred said in a hushed tone to Tamm as the door closed behind him.

TWO

Tamm and Echao did not speak after leaving the butcher's shop. Both of them were furious and, with Alred now a town guard, the chance that the situation would improve did not seem hopeful. Life nearing sixteen years old was bringing changes faster than he was able to adapt to.

Tamm kicked a small stone, sending it rolling down the road. He wished that Alred would follow him to the training yard one day so he could give him a good thrashing, but that would be foolish. It would expose that he, Echao, and Kèlris had been illegally training for years. Tamm sighed and looked up to see two young ladies approaching them from a trader's shop. Lily and Adina hurried across the road toward them, smiling as they came. Lily had long, brown hair that flowed behind her as she walked and big brown eyes. She had dimples that formed when she smiled and a natural blush at all times. Adina, on the other hand, had hair that was strawberry blond, with eyes the color of the ocean. She had a fair complexion with little freckles around her nose. She was taller than other girls her age and thin, a bit too thin, according to Tamm. She was always smiling and never had a harsh word to say to anyone. She spent most of her free time sitting by the lake reading.

"Good morning, Tamm," Adina called out as they drew closer. Tamm and Echao continued walking without looking back. Lily called out to Echao, and he slowed his pace. Tamm glanced back at him but maintained his stride, his anger still seething. Echao stopped to talk with Lily, his face softening as the conversation continued. Adina jogged to catch up with Tamm.

"Tammuz," she said. "Will I see you at the festival this year?"

"Not now, Adina," Tamm huffed, extending his stride. He wanted to get away to the woods, to the small practice field he, Echao, and their father had constructed. It was nothing special, just a few burlap sacks stuffed with hay to resemble a man's torso. He was angry and wanted to relieve that anger but not on sweet Adina. He did not fancy the girl as more than a friend; however, she was very nice, and he did enjoy her company. The last person's feelings that he wanted to injure was hers. He doubled his pace as she continued to probe at him about the upcoming festival. He glanced back at her disappointed face. "Maybe later, alright?"

Adina nodded, flashing a small smile of hope. Tamm ran the rest of the way through town until he entered the tree line of the forest just past his house. A sharp pain in his side slowed him to a walk. He found the winding game trail shortly after entering the woods and followed it.

Tamm's anger quelled as he walked through the woods. There was something calming about being in the wild, seeing the trees begin to flower and the squirrels and rabbits dart about. He looked forward to spring, and it would be here before long. It reminded him that no matter how cold and dead the winter had been, spring would breathe new life into the countryside. *So it is in life*, he thought.

He finally reached the practice field. It was hidden well, deep into the forest, in the middle of a copse of trees. The family had done well to conceal it. It took nearly a full cycle of the moon to clear the area of trees and brush without being noticed. Tamm stopped to stare at the site with pride.

Once inside, he reached deep into an old tree stump until his hand closed securely around the hilt of a sword. It was an old weapon he had created when first learning to use the forge. The edges of the blade were dull, which ensured that the risk of injury while sparring was quite low. He and his brother were pretty evenly matched in swordplay; although, Echao had mastered using dual daggers and was very fast and equally agile. Tamm had recently begun to practice with his sword and a dagger in his off-hand. This benefited him well when countering his brother's dual blades.

Tamm drew the blade and approached the dummy. He started with basic slashing and thrusting techniques his father had taught him. Between his assaults, he would practice parrying and blocking as if his opponent was countering his attacks. He lost himself in his thoughts as he ran through the sequences which were second nature after years of practice. He wondered what it would have been like to have lived in the old kingdom, where humans, elves, and dwarves co-existed. How different life would have been if he had grown up under the rule of a just High King and not the tyrant he was subject to now. What would it have been like to travel the countryside with a sword at his belt, brushing shoulders with Battlemages, and seeing gryffons soar through the air, in a world where honor and integrity mattered?

None of that mattered since Tzelder had taken the throne. He had usurped Riehner long before Tamm was even born. No one had seen an elf or a dwarf in nearly a decade. Tamm wished he could have seen Iradell in its prime, but he was born at the wrong time.

He practiced late into the afternoon, oblivious of the time. His anger ebbed, along with his strength. He paused to take a breath, dripping sweat, and realized that it was getting dark. He did not have a torch and could not make it home before he would be unable to see to guide himself. More importantly, he was late for his brother's celebration. He wiped the sweat from his brow, dreading what his father would say when he arrived home.

Hiding the blade again where he had found it, he set out towards home. The night closed in without warning in the woods, and Tamm squinted to be able to find even the faintest hint of the game trail. The forest took on a whole new appearance in the dark. He knew for sure that he was lost and had almost settled on the idea of finding shelter and continuing his journey in the morning.

He decided that his father would be even more furious if he did not return home at all, and so continued stumbling through the trees. Getting home took much longer than getting to the training yard, but he could see the faint glimmer of lanterns posted outside his home. Relieved, he slowed his pace, took a deep breath, and prepared himself for the coming chastening from his father.

With his nerves calm, he took a step forward when he heard a twig snap behind him. He spun around but could not see into the dark forest. His hand found the handle of his hunting knife as he crept backward toward the house, not taking his eyes off of the tree line. It flashed in his mind that Alred was trying to ambush him, but that did not make any sense. Alred knew nothing of the woods behind his home. Or, at least he hoped he did not. He stared for several moments but did not hear another sound and, once halfway to the house, bolted for the door.

Tamm entered the house a little more loudly than he had planned, his body stiffening in regret. He made for the stairs, tip-toeing, in an attempt to make it to his room before anyone noticed that he was there.

"Where have you been?" Kèlris asked from the kitchen, his voice stern. "You missed the entire celebration. Everyone else left almost an hour ago. You had your mother worried sick."

Tamm stiffened and turned toward the voice to find Kèlris propped up on the door frame, arms folded across his chest.

"I went to the grove," he answered. "I lost track of time. I apologize. It won't happen again."

Kèlris huffed and walked over to the base of the steps, staring up at Tamm, making sure their eyes met. "The time for apologies has passed. You carry on like nothing else around here matters. You spend so much time exploring and spending time on things that matter to you that you are neglecting your duties at the forge and now your family. This ends tonight. No more. Do you understand me?" He slammed his fist onto the rail.

Tamm had never seen his father so angry. "Yes, Sir," Tamm said, his shoulders slumped in defeat. He climbed three steps when he heard a knock at the door. "Who could that be?" he whispered to himself.

Kèlris answered the door as Tamm looked on from the top of the stairs. Kèlris seemed puzzled at whoever was on the other side of the door. "Greetings," he said to the man across the threshold. "What brings you calling at this late hour?"

"There was an issue that occurred with your son this afternoon that I would like to discuss with you," the man said gruffly.

Tamm tried to get a better look at the visitor but froze when he spoke. He knew the voice. It was Vorn, the sheriff, and he could tell by his tone that this was not a friendly call. The sheriff was tall and quite stout, with a look of confidence that he could take on any man in the kingdom and live to tell about it. He had sandy-brown hair, flecks of gray reflecting in the lantern's light, with hazel eyes and a scar that ran from above his left eye to the corner of his lip. He had obviously seen his share of battles and was content with finding more.

"It has been reported that your son, Tammuz, assaulted a town guard today while at the butcher's," he told him. Kèlris glanced back up the stairs with a tense look on his face. "It began as a verbal confrontation that escalated into a physical one. Were you aware of this, Kèlris?"

"This is the first I have heard of it," he replied. "Who made the report?"

The sheriff's lip twitched, only for a moment, hinting at a wicked smile. "My very own son. He is the guard that was assaulted."

Tamm leaned over the railing to get a better look at the men outside. Standing behind his father was Alred, with a tight-lipped grin, relishing in the idea of Tamm's punishment.

"Were there any other witnesses?" Kèlris asked. "Not that I believe your son to be a liar," he added.

Vorn folded his arms behind his back and let the silence linger before answering. "Holden verified the events. He reported that he was cutting meat in the backroom, and when he returned, the two aforementioned were arguing. As your two sons were leaving, Tammuz shoved Alred with his shoulder. This was done in sight of Holden, and he has testified to its validity."

"What then, now?" Kèlris asked, taking a deep breath and squaring his shoulders. "Our law is clear. There are at least two witnesses. Will he be taken into custody until his trial?"

"Oh," Vorn said with a deep, low chuckle. "There will be no trial. At least, not this time."

Kèlris raised his eyebrows in questioned concern. "What do you mean no trial?"

"Just this once, I will let you handle the situation," Vorn said. "See to it that it never happens again. If it does, I will not be so merciful next time." Alred looked up at his father in disgust that no punishment would be handed down tonight.

"I understand. Goodnight," Kèlris said, closing the door. He turned and looked at Tamm, wrinkles of disappointment in his face.

"Father," he said. "It didn't occur as he said…."

Kèlris let out a drawn-out sigh. "Speak no more of it tonight. Just go to bed."

Tamm stared at his father in disbelief. He was sure that he would get the rod after the sheriff left. Instead, Kèlris looked up at his son, and for a brief moment, Tamm thought he saw a look of sympathy in his father's eyes. Then, it was gone, his father turning to walk back into the kitchen.

THREE

†

Tamm rose early the following morning, intent on proving to his father that he could be responsible. The sky was still dark with only a hint of pale orange in the distance, the stars still faintly visible. The air was crisp, and a slight breeze made the hair on his arms stand as he exited the house. Instead of heading off to explore some cave or other stretches of wood as he was accustomed to, he set out to gather firewood. Once he was satisfied with his haul, he headed to the forge.

The flames roared as he pumped the bellows. He ensured his father's tools were set out and ready and even swept the area clear of debris. However, Kèlris had still not arrived. He noticed an order for a new set of horseshoes for Cardin, the stable master, sitting on a nearby table. Tamm was not exceptional at crafting a blade or shield, but he could make a remarkable horseshoe. It was one of the first things he had been taught to craft.

He selected a piece of steel and placed it in the forge. As he pumped the bellows, the warm air blew across his face, the smell of hot metal making his nose tingle. Tamm squinted as he stared at the color of the metal. Satisfied with its bright yellow-orange glow, he retrieved it and forced it onto a rounded piece of steel to obtain the basic shape of the shoe. Every time the shoe would cool and become difficult to shape, Tamm would toss it back into the fire and begin the process again. Once the steel had taken the basic shape of the shoe, he could now begin the difficult part, the hammering.

Tamm took the vibrant red-orange shoe from the forge and placed it on the anvil. Tap, tap, tap. Tap, tap, tap. The repetitive sounds lulled him into a calm, and for once, he understood what his father found so alluring about smithing. After several hours, Tamm had all four shoes completed and packaged, ready to be delivered.

It was already mid-morning, and Kèlris had yet to arrive at the forge. It was very unlike him. Tamm had not eaten breakfast in his rush to get to the shop and hunger was beginning to nag him, so he decided to head over to the kitchen to grab a bite to eat and check in on his mother. Maybe she would know what was taking his father so long.

He grabbed the shoes, intending to deliver them after he ate, and left the forge. He entered the house on the opposite side of the forge and placed the shoes on a small, wooden table by the door. When he entered the kitchen, his mother was preparing a large pot of potato soup. She greeted him with a kiss on the cheek and sat a loaf of bread and a few slices of cheese on the table in front of him.

Mariah was a lovely woman who cared dearly for her family. She had a darker complexion than many people in the village with dark hair and dark eyes. She used to tell Tamm and Echao stories about her family's history, how her grandparents had migrated to this area from a desert land in the west many years ago, and before that, her ancestors had dwelled on a small island in the Western Sea.

It is the story that had sparked Tamm's fascination with adventure and exploring. He could not fathom the perilous journeys to be had and amazing sights that could be seen sailing across the sea and exploring an unknown land.

"How was your morning?" Mariah asked.

"Fine," Tamm mumbled, his mouth full of bread. "I've been making horseshoes all morning. Where are Father and Echao? They haven't been at the forge all morning."

Mariah smiled. "Your brother had to go into town and speak with Anryn. He had to get a list of supplies to pick up to prepare for his apprenticeship."

"And he wanted to see Lily," Tamm said, swallowing the bread. "But where is Father?"

"He had to run an errand or two in town also," she told him, placing a bowl of hot soup in front of him.

"Thanks," he said with a smile as he shoveled the soup into his mouth. The soup was hot and burned his tongue, but it was delicious, as was everything his mother made. Once he finished the soup, he kissed his mother goodbye, grabbed the horseshoes and headed into town. He hoped that he would meet his father on the way there to let him know he had prepared the forge and crafted the horseshoes. But then again, he was in no hurry to see how last night's events would carry over to today.

Tamm had already made it past the first few stores and had still not seen his father. The village was not very big, and most of the shops were densely placed near the center of town with the homes surrounding the market area. There was no fence around the village, allowing it to grow, although it never did. It was the same old village that Tamm had grown up with.

He made his way past the center of the village and drifted toward the lake. Old man Cardin owned the stables and had for as long as Tamm could remember. He would be expecting the new set of shoes, so Tamm quickened his pace.

When Tamm reached the stables, he peered inside and knocked loudly. Horses neighed and snorted at the sudden sound. "Who is it?" called a high pitched, elderly man's voice from inside the stables.

"It is Tammuz, son of Kèlris," he said. "I have the new horseshoes you requested."

"By the gods, that was quick," Cardin said. "I wasn't expecting them for at least a week. Just leave them out there. Your payment is in the box there. I would come out, but I am knee-deep in manure at the moment. Good day."

"Good day," Tamm said, picking up the money and heading back the way he came. With his tasks completed for the day, he wondered how he would spend the remainder of his time. He had a few hours to spare, so he walked to the outskirts of the village, to the edge of Lake Aleesia.

The lake was the largest in the realm. It was said that it was even larger than the whole of Rakx'den, the capital city. If it were not for the lake and the fishing business that it provided, Aleesia would be no more than a ghost town. Tamm recalled hearing that Aleesia was the old High King's favorite place to vacation. He thought it would be a perfect place to escape the confines of city life, beautiful and open, but rather boring.

As he walked along the lakeshore, he could see someone coming toward him in the distance. He could recognize her strawberry-blond hair anywhere. It was Adina. "Hello, Tammuz," she called out, still a little way off.

He jogged up to meet her. "Well met." He dropped his head. "About yesterday…"

Adina interrupted with a giggle and shoved him in the arm. "Don't worry about it. You were obviously dealing with something, and I would have only gotten in the way."

Tamm smiled at her, and they walked back toward the village side by side, talking and laughing. She always knew how to cheer him up and make him feel better. Plus, she was easy to talk to, perhaps because she was such a good listener, or maybe because he could get lost staring in her deep blue eyes. They talked about many things, a few new books she had read, but most of all, the upcoming Spring Festival.

The Spring Festival was always a joyous time in the village. The entire town came together to celebrate the new year. She told him about the new dress she had found at Cevi Tailor's shop and about her favorite desserts that Bethel the baker would make. But the thing that caught Tamm off guard was when she told him that she had already received several requests for a dance.

It did not surprise him that someone had asked her to dance. She had become an attractive young lady, though rather thin, and was of age to begin being courted. What surprised him was the way he felt when she told him. At first, he had a hard time distinguishing the feeling, but the more he thought about it, the more he understood. He was jealous. And the jealousy was not just because Cyris and Zaech were two that had offered to dance with her. Well, it was partially because it was those two but mostly because he had not asked her himself.

They entered the edge of the village, and he offered to walk her home. She smiled and wrapped her arm into his. Tamm swallowed hard as he gathered his courage. He could not believe what he was about to do. His hands were sweating despite the slow pace of their walk. They reached her home just as the sun began to set over the horizon. "Adina," he said as she traipsed toward the house.

"Yes," she answered, turning around at the door with a hint of a blush at her cheeks.

He kicked at the dirt, sending dust over his boots. "I hope you were planning on saving a dance for me," he said.

"Of course," she said, smiling wide. "You can even have the first dance if you want."

Tamm's lips pulled into a nervous smile, and he wiped his sweaty palms on his pants. "The last also?"

She walked up to him, almost gliding, and placed a gentle hand on his cheek, smiling at him. "That depends on if you bring flowers. You remember my favorite, right?" She turned and walked into the house.

Tamm sauntered through the town streets, confused about his feelings. He had never felt this way about Adina. She had always been a good friend, but discovering that other young men were interested in her had awoken feelings he had not realized he had. He felt dizzy, giddy even, and meandered through the town trying to focus his thoughts.

He rounded the corner by the apothecary and saw movement just ahead by the healer's hut. His father was speaking with Linsyn, and the sight snapped him back to reality. Why had Kèlris sought out the healer? Was someone ill?

The two men noticed him approaching and rushed their goodbyes, parting ways. Tamm caught up with Kèlris and inquired about the encounter with the healer, concerned his father may be ill. Kèlris told him it was nothing, just two old men catching up on current events and then changed the subject, asking him about his day instead.

Tamm told him about getting to the forge early and making the horseshoes and delivering them. He handed him the coins he had received from Cardin for the horseshoes. They talked about meeting up with Adina, but he left out the part about asking her to dance. Kèlris clapped his hand on Tamm's shoulder and smiled at him. They continued the walk home, talking about their day, but neither mentioned the healer again.

FOUR

†

The following weeks passed by in a blur. The coolness of winter was fading, and signs of spring were peeking through the scattered clouds and occasional snow. Tamm had developed the habit of arriving early to go to the forge to prepare for the day. If any orders were waiting, he would begin them before his father would arrive each morning. Tamm found delight in his duties the more he did them. Plus, he enjoyed the fact that Kèlris was finally seeing him as reliable.

They stayed very busy in preparation for the Spring Festival. The celebration would begin with vendors lining the streets in less than a week and culminate in a town-wide party in a fortnight. It was common to have visitors from Delocia, but the number of revelers from other towns in the region had dwindled over the past several years. New orders were coming in faster than they could complete them. It was difficult to keep the pace with only the two of them. Echao had been spending more and more time preparing for his training with Anryn.

Kèlris was leaving a few times a week to go into town, which placed a heavy responsibility on Tamm at the shop. His father would never tell him where he had gone; instead, he would change the subject by complimenting Tamm on the progress he had made at the forge or discussing the Festival. Tamm had improved to become quite adept at the forge since devoting almost all of his time there recently.

As the Spring Festival and the boys' birthday grew closer, Tamm would try to lose himself in his work. He was nervous about the dance with Adina. He was still confused about his feelings and worried about how things would play out with the other suitors. Both Zaech and Cyris, Alred's best friends, had accepted apprenticeships as town guards also. Both were interested in Adina, and that did not bode well for Tamm's future. The last time he had seen the sheriff, he had told his father that he would arrest Tamm if he caused any more trouble, yet Tamm had never been one to back down. Besides, he did not want to upset Adina by not delivering on the dance or the flowers.

He rolled out of bed before sunrise this morning to hike to the foot of the mountains north of town. He knew that her favorite flower bloomed there, the snowdrop flower. There was still a light layer of snow on some of the lower cliffs, and he saw the flowers pushing through as he approached.

REBORN

The petals were pure white with a bright green center. They were not the most beautiful flower he had ever seen, but they were remarkable all the same. The way that they could bloom through the snow was incredible. He had asked her once why she liked them so much, and she had told him that they were a symbol of hope, that even through the harshest winter, life could start anew. He scrambled up a hill to the lower cliffs and plucked a few of the prettier flowers before sliding back down into the valley.

When Tamm made it to the forge, his father was not there yet. He was sure that Kèlris would have beaten him to the shop this morning after making his hike to the mountains. Tamm decided that since his father was not in yet that he would take the flowers home and put them in some water. As he rounded the shop, he saw his father in the front yard. He was talking with Linsyn. What could they be up to? He jogged up to the two men, but this time they did not conceal their conversation.

"You remember Linsyn," Kèlris said.

"Of course," Tamm replied, reaching out to shake the man's hand and raising an eyebrow at his father.

The old man shook Tamm's hand with more strength than a man his age should possess. "Well met, young Tammuz," Linsyn said, his voice steady and deep, ripe with wisdom.

Tamm looked to his father in concern. "Is everything alright? Mother is not ill, is she?"

"No, no," Kèlris said. "Your mother is fine. We were actually discussing you."

Tamm let out a nervous chuckle. "Am I ill then?"

"Actually," Kèlris said, "the Spring Festival will be within the next fortnight, as is your birthday. You have yet to choose a profession. I know you have noticed my being absent from the forge lately. I have been arranging your apprenticeship."

Tamm's mouth went slack; he tried but could not speak. He knew where this was going. His father had chosen an apprenticeship for him, but Tamm had no desire to be a healer. He could already see himself as an old, stooped man like Linsyn, who had never once stepped foot out of Aleesia. The thought made him cringe inside. He wanted to see the world, not rot away in this dying town.

"I...I...thought I could stay and work with you," Tamm said, wringing his hands.

Kèlris looked at the ground, avoiding Tamm's eyes. "No. It is done. You had not chosen an apprenticeship yet. So, I had to. You begin your training today. Look at the bright side, son. You can't cause much trouble as a healer." Tamm stared blankly back at his father, pleading him with his eyes.

Linsyn coughed, breaking through the awkward silence. "Come, young Tammuz. You have much to learn." He turned and walked away without looking to see if Tamm was following him.

Tamm gave one last look at his father. "It's for the best. Go, and I will see you home for dinner," Kèlris said before walking back to the forge alone.

Tamm followed behind Linsyn but did not speak. His arms swayed as they hung at his side. He had assumed, hoped, that his father knew him well enough to know that this would not have been a choice that he would make for himself. He wondered if this was his father's way of punishing him for the dispute he had with Alred. There was one thing for sure; he would not be arrested for being a healer.

"Snowdrop?" Linsyn asked, glancing back at Tamm and the flowers he still held in his hand.

"What?" Tamm asked, absorbed in his thoughts. "These? Yes. They're for a friend."

"Hmm. A very peculiar flower," Linsyn said. "They have medicinal uses also. They can be used to create a potion that will aid in healing wounds. I can show you."

Tamm pulled the flowers in close to his chest, as to protect them from Linsyn. "As I said, these are for a friend," he said, a little harsher than he had intended.

"Well then," Linsyn replied, ignoring Tamm's tone. "When we get back to the shop, I will show you how to preserve them. I assume you will deliver them during the Festival. We can keep them as fresh as the day you picked them."

Tamm relaxed his grip on the flowers, and they journeyed on in silence for the remainder of the trip into town.

They reached the shop, and Linsyn set about showing Tamm where everything was located. There were a few chairs to the right of the doorway as he entered the room. A cot dressed with white linens was set up in the middle of the room. To the left were several racks of powders and liquids that Tamm could not begin to comprehend, along with a small table used for mixing ingredients. Toward the rear of the room was a fireplace nestled in the back corner and a door that must have led to a bedroom, along with a chest and a small shelf of notes written by Linsyn. To the right were a writing desk and chair and a large bookcase that was overstuffed with books with topics that ranged from *Fungus Among Us: Identifying Mushrooms and other Fungi* to *Dragon's Thorn and Other Rare Ingredients*.

He looked around the room, taking it all in. Everything had a place, and there was not a speck of dust anywhere. There were so many books. Tamm was astonished at the complexity of it all. How could anyone expect to master even a quarter of the information in this tiny hut? He did not belong here, of that he was sure. He was an adventurer, not a healer. He desired to be outdoors, not cooped up behind a desk, studying old tomes. He did imagine, however, that knowing how to make a healing salve from plants found in the forest would be invaluable to an adventurer.

"Now to show you how to preserve these flowers," Linsyn said, pulling him back to reality. He walked over to the shelves of ingredients and picked up a glass and filled it with water from a basin. He searched the rows until his fingers found a white powder in a small vial. "This is salicyn. It is harvested from the willow tree." He popped a small cork top from the vial and tapped it against the glass pitcher, and a pinch of white powder fell into the water. "Place the flowers."

Tamm did as he was told. "Is that all?" he asked.

"That is all," Linsyn said. "It only takes a tiny amount. You will see. On the day of the Festival, they will remain as fresh as when you picked them. It will not preserve them forever, only extend their life. Now, for your first task. I need you to take this list and go into the forest and collect these ingredients."

REBORN

"What?" Tamm asked. "I have no idea what any of this stuff is. You haven't taught me yet."

"Take the list, and this book," Linsyn said, shoving a book into Tamm's arms. "There are pictures in the book and none are difficult to find. I would not test you so…yet. Each of these items is abundant in this area. You have seen many of these in your journeys through the forest already. You just never knew what you were seeing."

Tamm slammed the door in frustration on his way out of the clinic. He was relieved to be out of the stuffy hut and in the open air. He looked forward to being back in the forest, even if he did not know what he was looking for. There were simple things like clover, but there were also things he had never heard of; valerian root, fireblood petals, and sap from the moon-song tree.

Tamm explored the woods, following the diagrams from the book to find the items. Most of them were relatively simple to locate. There was another root listed to gather that grew among the rocky hills of the mountains. He headed there to find them. Once he had collected them, he headed further into the forest to find a moon song tree. There were several large oaks and other smaller trees scattered about, but nothing that looked like the picture he had been given. He followed a trail northward and discovered an odd-looking track in the dirt. It was large, too large to be an animal, but it was definitely not human; it had six toes. He knelt to investigate the footprint closer and heard a low, guttural growl from deeper in the trees, near the mountains.

Tamm's heart pounded in his chest, and he realized he was holding his breath. He had never heard a sound that struck fear in him like that. He backed away slowly, keeping his eyes focused in the direction of the sound. He did not hear it again, and once he believed he was far enough away, he turned and sprinted back out of the forest.

He slowed his pace only once he was out of the woods and could see the town in the distance. It was almost time for dinner, and he could see the sun setting in the distance. He would need to hurry back to the clinic, or he would not be home until well after dark. A squeezing sensation gripped his stomach at the thought of being outside after the sun went down. He hoped he had time to discuss the growl and footprint with Linsyn.

He entered the hut right at sunset. Breathing hard, he tossed the sack of supplies on the table and bent over, hands on his knees. Linsyn jumped from his seat in front of the desk. "By the gods," he said, eyes wary, his stance as if he was prepared to attack. "You nearly sent me to the grave, boy!" He leaned his staff against the wall, taking a deep breath, and straightened his robe before hobbling over to the satchel. "Did you get all of the items?"

Tamm paced the floor. It still gave him chills to think about it. "No," he said. "I still lacked the sap. But something strange happened."

"What do you mean something strange?" Linsyn asked. "What could be stranger than you barging in here all in a fit?"

He held his arms over his head, trying to slow his breathing. "Hopefully, you can explain this, or maybe I'm losing my mind."

"Calm down, boy," Linsyn said. "For all that is holy, just spit it out!"

He slid a chair out and gestured with his hand. Tamm did not hesitate to plop down in it.

"I was in the woods searching for the items you asked for," Tamm told him. "I was looking for the moon song tree and couldn't find it. Never mind that. I saw an odd track on the ground close to where the trees thinned out near the pass to the mountains. It was different than anything I had ever seen before."

"What did it look like?" Linsyn asked.

Tamm stretched out his hands, demonstrating the size of the print. "It was big, at least twice the size of my foot. Huge. It was not any animal I have ever seen but not human either. There were indentions for six toes. What kind of beast has six toes? It looked like whatever it was had been coming there frequently and then heading back toward the mountains."

Linsyn stroked his beard. "Hmm, that is interesting. Six toes, you say? Did you notice anything else?"

"Oh, yes," Tamm said, his eyes wide. "There was this growl. It was evil, chilled me to the bone. I have never been so frightened in my life."

"A growl? Like a bear?" asked Linsyn.

"No," he said, shaking his head. "This was no bear. It was more fearsome, more savage than any mere bear. It felt as if my heart had turned to ice."

"Draw what you saw," Linsyn said, handing Tamm a piece of parchment. Tamm grabbed a charcoal pencil and sketched the image of the footprint. Linsyn stood in disbelief. "This is impossible. They have not been seen since the Great War."

"What is it?" Tamm asked, dread bubbling in his stomach.

"This is not good, not good at all," Linsyn said, his eyes looking around worrisome and his hand mindlessly stroking his beard. "That is the print of a Kapre.

FIVE

Tamm parried the blow from the Kapre's blade with his own. His eyes burned as sweat dripped from his brow into them. It seemed as if the battle had raged for hours. His muscles ached, and he could barely raise the sword in time to block the next blow. The Kapre was massive with gray skin and biceps the size of Tamm's thigh. The beast lumbered forward and followed with another thrust and then a kick to the ribs.

The sword flew from Tamm's hands as he was thrown to his back. He laid there in agony, trying to catch his breath, but the pain in his side was so severe, he could only gasp. He splinted his ribs with his hand, and the crepitus he felt against his fingers told him the bones were broken. Glaring up at the Kapre, Tamm gathered his strength to rise to his knees. He resigned that this was the end. He no longer had the strength or the will to fight. This would be how he would die.

The monster rushed to his side, snarling, the blood-lust obvious in its eyes. Tamm met his gaze for only a moment and then lowered his head in defeat. It brought the blade high above its head and released a deafening roar, the same roar Tamm had heard in the woods. The Kapre swept the blade down towards Tamm's neck as the world around him lit up in bright white light.

The blanket flew to the floor as Tamm sat upright in bed, drenched in sweat, his breaths coming in heaves. Echao stood over him, pale as a ghost, a deep fear in his eyes.

"Tamm…What was… Are you well," Echao stammered. "I thought you had passed into the void."

Tamm tried to catch his breath, drawing them deeply in his nose and out his mouth. "It was a dream, only a dream," Tamm whispered, more for his own assurance than Echao's.

"What sort of dream could cause that?" Echao asked. "You were thrashing about in the bed, screaming and grunting, and then you went deathly still. I was sure you had come down with a fever and had succumbed to illness."

Tamm took a slow, deep breath, still trying to quell the fear and calm his nerves. "I did die," he said. "In the dream, I mean." He wiped the sweat from his brow. He felt as if he had sprinted to the lake and back. Once he was certain he was calm enough to continue, he recounted the dream to Echao, in all its gory detail.

REBORN

They sat in silence for a moment after Tamm finished the story. Echao cleared his throat. "At least it was only a dream, a frightful one at that but a dream all the same."

"Speak no more of it," Tamm said. "The sooner I am rid of it, the better off I will be."

Echao nodded his head in agreement and gave Tamm a sideways look with a crooked smirk. "Besides, today is a day for celebration."

Tamm's spirit began to rise with the thought of the day's festivities. "Yes, the Spring Festival. I have been looking forward to it for weeks."

"Actually, I was speaking of you finally getting the nerve to ask Adina to dance," Echao joked, shoving Tamm and knocking him off the bed.

Tamm looked up from the floor, his brow creased. "Not funny," he said, cutting his eyes at his brother. He leaped up and seized his brother by the foot, pulling him into the floor also. The brothers laughed heartily before quieting to a snicker, fearing they would awaken their parents. The two continued to joke and laugh as they prepared to enjoy the short holiday.

◆◆◆◆◆

Tamm rushed out through the front door after kissing his mother on the cheek. He had finished his breakfast late and had to hurry along to Linsyn's. The healer had a few tasks for him to complete before he released him from his duties for the day. Tamm had been upset about having to report today. The

Spring Festival was considered a holiday. Most shops closed all day for the celebrations that would take place but not Linsyn.

Earlier in the week when Tamm had mentioned being off the whole day, Linsyn had only clucked his tongue and scolded him. "A healer's work is never finished," he said. "We must always remain vigilant, lest those in our care suffer."

Tamm attempted to convince him that the work would be waiting when they returned the next day. Linsyn, however, was not so easily persuaded. He had leaned into Tamm's face and stared deep in his eyes. "It is our sacrifice to make for the greater good of those around us," Linsyn told him. "Being a healer is a work of compassion. We must lay our desires aside for those around us. There is no greater compassion than to sacrifice our desires, ourselves, for others. You would do well to remember that."

Despite not being able to persuade the healer on the issue, Tamm did not want to appear fickle by showing up late, so he quickened his pace. He had gotten used to all the tasks Linsyn would throw at him. The last few weeks had flown by in a frenzy with all the knowledge Linsyn attempted to pack into Tamm's brain. He had gone home more than one evening with a headache. Sometimes he felt as if his head would explode.

As he entered the town, the decorations were already placed. Colorful streamers full of wildflowers draped the top of the buildings. The smell of apple pies baking and hogs roasting on a spit wafted in the air. Tamm paused to take a

REBORN

deep breath and soak it all in. It was pleasant, the sun providing just enough warmth and a mild breeze blowing in from the lake. The sky was bright blue, a few clouds hanging about the mountains.

Tamm felt a slight pang of guilt over his desire to leave the small town. He had longed for adventure his whole life, had always seen himself leaving the comfort of home for the great unknown. But seeing the little lake town in all of its beauty made him miss it already. In that brief moment, he could see himself growing old here, marrying Adina and raising children. It would be a peaceful life, a comfortable life. He shook the thoughts from his head, as he reminded himself that he did not want comfortable. He had to know what lay beyond those waters, across those mountains.

He tamped the feelings down and continued on his journey to meet the healer. He had spent most of his time in the hut recently, researching tomes and learning what he could from Linsyn, which he had been content with. To be honest, he feared entering the woods again, especially after this morning's dream; however, he was curious as to the errand that the healer had prepared for him.

When Tamm entered the hut, the old man was seated at his desk, writing on a piece of parchment. Linsyn looked up as he entered the room, folded the note, and placed it gently in a book. He stood from the chair, stretching his back before walking over to Tamm as he placed his satchel on a stand by the door. He drew up to his full height, his face melancholy, and gripped each of Tamm's shoulders with strong hands.

Tamm froze, taken aback by the sudden predilection from the old man.

"I beg your pardon for the seriousness during this hour of celebration," Linsyn said. "I do not wish to burden you." He paused for a moment, continuing to stare into Tamm's eyes. "Alas," he sighed, his voice weary, "I am an old man, and many heavy thoughts have plagued me of late. It grieves me to share this burden with you." He cleared his throat before continuing. "As you have likely deduced in your short time here with me, I do not have one to call my heir, no family to call my own."

Tamm swallowed hard. Surely, he did not wish to appoint Tamm as his heir. Tamm had a father, a mother. True, he was his apprentice and could carry on the clinic in his honor but not his heritage and lineage.

"I will not be around forever," Linsyn told him. "You are my apprentice now, and therefore my closest companion. When my time comes, and I enter into a kingdom not of this world, I will need you to handle my affairs, ensure I am properly interred."

Tamm released a sigh of relief. This he could do. In the few weeks that he had spent with the healer, he had grown to respect him. He could see that Linsyn received a proper burial and that the knowledge he left behind would continue to serve the people of Aleesia. He deserved at least that, and more. He was a good man, an honorable man. Tamm pitied him that he did not have kin to call his own.

"When I am gone from this world," he said, "I have left a set of instructions for you here." He pointed to an old book that he had placed the parchment in. "It will have my last wishes, what to do with my belongings, and where to inter my body."

Tamm nodded his head, suddenly saddened by the thought of the old man not sitting at the writing desk when he would walk in. He had never even thought to ask if Linsyn had ever been married or had any children.

Linsyn walked back across the room and picked up the book, whispering under his breath. He shuffled back across the room as if his strength had fled him. Tamm noticed the book title, *The Inerrant History of Iradell: The Birth of a Kingdom*. He placed the book on the bookshelf then hobbled back to Tamm.

"I have but one task for you today," Linsyn said. "You will prepare your first treatment. Once it is complete, you are released to enjoy the rest of the day."

"What am I to prepare?" asked Tamm.

"This concoction will ease the stomach. You can imagine that many young people have a nervous stomach today as they begin courting one another." Linsyn handed him a pestle and three ingredients. "You are holding up quite well considering your new courtship," Linsyn said, a half-smile tugging at the edge of his lips. "She is a nice girl."

"She is," Tamm said. "But let's not speak of it, lest I need this remedy also. Who will I be delivering this to?" Tamm focused his attention on blending the correct measurement of ingredients.

Linsyn walked to a small closet. He opened it and stared inside for a moment before retrieving something on a hanger.

Tamm looked up curiously. The clothes were new and fit for nobility. The pants were black with a white collared shirt and a matching black tunic with ornate gold-threaded trim.

"I hope that you will accept this gift," Linsyn said, holding the clothing up near Tamm as if to ensure it would fit. "I remember when I was your age and attending the Spring Festival." Linsyn stared off as if he could see it all unfolding before him. A slight frown crept across his face for a moment before he turned his attention back to Tamm. "However, this is not about me. If you are to properly court this young lady, you cannot expect to do so in smithy leathers. These should suffice."

Linsyn handed the finery to Tamm and reached back into the closet, bringing out a new set of boots. Tamm took the clothes from him and looked in amazement between the clothes and Linsyn.

"These are the clothes of nobility, Linsyn. I do not deserve these. I am a commoner. I don't know what to say."

"You do not have to say anything, young Tammuz. Rather, show me your gratitude with your character. Wear them well and display yourself as if you were royalty."

"I will," Tamm said, running his fingers across the soft, smooth fabric. "Thank you!"

"Go get dressed. You have done well preparing the medicine." Linsyn began to collect the medicine and place it in a small tin container as Tamm rushed to dress behind a curtain. "Now comes the difficult part," Linsyn called to him from across the room.

"What do you mean?" Tamm asked.

REBORN

"You must deliver this to Alred," he replied. "His father ordered it earlier this week as a precaution.

Tamm's heart sank as he laced the delicate cord of the tunic. Alred was the last person he wanted to see today. Tamm finished dressing, sliding the leather belt through the scabbard of his dagger. He gathered the medicine from Linsyn, thanked him, and headed for the door.

"Do stay out of trouble, won't you," Linsyn implored. "Oh, and don't forget the flowers."

Tamm made his way north out of the village in the direction of Rhys Castle. The sheriff and his family resided in a manor house nestled in the foothills of the mountains, just below the castle grounds. The castle had been initially constructed as a retreat for the old King, seated high in the mountains, overlooking the town and lake; however, King Tzelder did not fancy Aleesia. He also did not fancy the old King either; hence, it was illegal to speak of him.

It was common knowledge among the kingdom that Tzelder usurped the throne from Riehner and destroyed the Battlemages, but no one spoke of it. They knew better, or at least they feared one of the king's agents hearing of it. Say a harsh word about the king, and you may never be seen or heard from again.

The empire was divided into provinces; the Aleesian province being the territory north of the King's Road and east of Rakx'den, the capital city. Rhys castle had most recently become the home of the province's overseer, although he rarely lingered in the castle, instead choosing to travel the cities he governed and dine with the elite of other provinces.

Tamm adjusted his tunic, trying to get used to the feel of the finery as he neared the edge of the town. He hastened his pace, realizing that many of the townspeople had already begun to gather at the city center. He dreaded the meeting with Alred and was inadvertently twirling the container of medicine between his fingers. He secretly hoped that Alred's nerves had already gotten the best of him, confining him to his room with sickness. Tamm smirked at the thought, all the while, feeling slightly ashamed, knowing that a healer should not wish illness on anyone, even an enemy.

The manor house was visible in the distance. It was much more lavish than the homes in town. It was two stories and made of stone, ivy trailing down the front of the home. Servants tended the gardens and pools around the property, and he could see them occasionally appear around shrubbery as they worked. Tamm felt a nagging in his chest that he recognized as jealousy.

Vorn did not boast of his station, unlike his son. He was very straightforward and conducted his business as such. Vorn had been knighted by the king after some heroic action during a battle as a young man and then placed as sheriff over the town of Aleesia, though he was not originally from the province. He and Tamm were not on the best of terms, but he had never been overly harsh with him.

Alred, on the other hand, was the epitome of how Tamm viewed nobles, arrogant and regarding those of a lower station as a mere nuisance. Shaking the thoughts from his head, Tamm stepped up to the front door and drew a deep breath to calm himself. "Let's just get this over with," he whispered, knocking on the door.

The knock echoed throughout the great room, and a servant promptly responded. Tamm stated his business, and the servant turned on his heel, closing the door and leaving Tamm outside. Tamm waited, rocking back and forth on the edge of the steps. He had almost decided to leave when the door flew open, and a cool wind hit him in the face.

Tamm snapped around toward the door expecting to confront Alred. Instead, he was face to face with the sheriff. "Staying out of trouble, I hope," Vorn said.

"Of course, sir. It seems it's quite difficult to find trouble to get into when Linsyn has my nose crammed into a book describing the different species of mushrooms and their medicinal purposes."

"Yes, I'm sure it is," Vorn said, obviously not finding the retort amusing. He reached into his pocket and retrieved a small coin purse. "Please see this to Linsyn."

Tamm accepted the money and provided the man with the vial. The door was shut without another word. All business as usual. Tamm turned to head back down the road, glancing back at the house one last time. Something caught his eye in the upper window. Alred, in the upstairs window, was standing in a solid black outfit with bright blue trim, hands folded behind his back, sneering at him.

Tamm could not hold back a quaint smirk and waved his hand over his head as if greeting an old friend. Alred snatched the curtains closed. As Tamm continued down the road, he checked the small satchel once more to ensure the preserved flowers were unharmed, and once out of sight of the house, broke into a jog

SIX

Tamm arrived at Adina's house around mid-afternoon. The day was beginning to cool, a soft orange dancing off the lake as the sun traveled further into the western horizon. He approached the door, hiding the flowers behind his back, and knocked. Adina appeared at the door in a long, flowing blue dress, her strawberry blond hair in a bun with strands of curls outlining either side of her face.

He tried to speak, mouth parted, but no words came out. He had never noticed just how beautiful Adina was. "Good evening, Tamm," she said with a shy smile, brushing the curls away from her eyes with the tips of her fingers.

He stuttered, unable to find the words to say. "Well, well, well met," he stammered.

Adina giggled. "You remembered," she said, pointing at the flowers hanging awkwardly at Tamm's side.

He shrugged his shoulders, realizing he had been standing like a fool with his arms hanging at his side. "Yes. Your favorite," he said, handing her the flowers, finally comfortable enough to talk with her as he always had. "And just wait until I tell you what I found while in the woods."

They walked closer to the center of town, and people were already gathering near the well and dancing. Streamers hung from poles, while vendors and artisans had stands lining the streets. A stage had been built, and musicians played an upbeat tune. Tamm halted outside the congested square and took a moment to breath in the excitement. He squeezed Adina's hand and took a step into the crowd as he told her all about hiking to the mountains and picking the flowers, all the fascinating things about healing that Linsyn had taught him, finding the footprint, and having to take medicine to Alred.

"But what was it?" she asked.

"It was just a tonic to ease his stomach. Must have been too nervous to see me here with you," he joked as he smiled and took her hand. She did not pull away at his touch, and he was relieved.

"Not the medicine," she said, a look of concern on her face. "The footprint, what did Linsyn say that it was?"

He did not want to alarm her. "It was nothing," he said, but from the look on her face, she did not believe him. "Linsyn said it sounded like it could have been a Kapre print."

She gasped, and Tamm pulled her in closer to himself, whispering in her ear, "Peace." She looked up at him, her ocean blue eyes lost in his, and he could feel her relaxing in his arms. He hoped that she knew he would protect her, no matter the danger.

"Kapres have not been seen since the end of the Great War. There's no reason for alarm. It was probably just a few bear tracks mixed together. Let me get you something to drink." She smiled at him and squeezed his hand before letting him go. Tamm returned from the vendor stand with two mint lemonades to find Adina talking with Lily and Echao. Tamm walked up, handing Adina her drink, and slapped Echao on the shoulder.

"Hail, brother," Echao said as Lily hugged him. "Or should I call you Your Majesty?" He dipped his head in an exaggerated bow. "From the look of your attire, I expect everything is going well."

"The evening has just begun, but I can't complain," Tamm said. "Linsyn gave me these as a gift today." He rubbed his hands along the smooth lapels. "To say I was surprised would be an understatement. Have you two been here long?"

"Not long," Echao said. "Come, let the women catch up, and you can tell me all about it." Echao leaned in and kissed Lily on the cheek before walking away.

They walked in silence around the different vendors. The mixing smells of the variety of baked goods and the cacophony of those celebrating, dancing, and playing games was intoxicating. He felt as if he were in a bigger city with a much busier and exciting lifestyle.

Echao shot down a side street towards a row of houses and away from the festivals. "What are we doing?" Tamm asked. "The festival is back that way."

"I knew we would have privacy here," Echao said. "Everyone will be at the festival. I needed to talk with you alone."

"What's the matter?" Tamm asked, concerned. "You have me worried."

"Still yourself," replied Echao. "I have something I wanted to tell you. Surely you've noticed I have been working quite a bit recently." Tamm nodded his head, unable to hide the curiousity on his face. "I have been putting back the money that I have earned, and I bought this today." He reached into a bag tied around his belt and withdrew a clenched fist. He held it out to Tamm and slowly opened it. The sun was setting, but even in the faint light, the diamond sparkled.

"Lily?" Tamm asked.

"I plan on asking her tonight," Echao said. "I spoke with her father today, and he gave his blessing. I know we're still young, but I will save most of my earnings this year to purchase a small plot of land to begin building a modest little home. Of course, I will not even complete my apprenticeship for nearly two more years. It will still be a couple of years before we can wed, but I cannot imagine living without her. I had to make it official."

"I'm happy for you," Tamm said. "I'm sure Lily will be overjoyed."

"That's not all," Echao said, his face solemn. "There is no need for another tanner here in Aleesia."

"Oh," Tamm said, the smile fading from his face.

"Anryn tells me that the tanner in Delocia will be preparing to retire in the next year or two. I plan to look into that possibility, but we may have to move further. I'll know for sure later in the year."

Tamm forced a smile, "I'm happy for you. Truly. You are my brother, no matter where you go."

Echao wrapped his brother in a tight hug. "I knew you would understand."

"Have you told mother and father?" Tamm asked.

"I will address that in the morning. There is too much to be concerned about tonight. My hands are so sweaty I will likely drop the blasted thing before I can get it on her finger."

Tamm laughed, patted his brother on the back, and led him back toward the city center where the girls awaited them. They were still a way off, but Tamm could see the concern on Adina and Lily's faces, although he could not make out what bothered them so. The crowd had swelled with the setting sun, and it was difficult to make anything out in the distance. Flickers of light and shadow danced around from the torch lights.

Once they were closer, he could see past some of the crowd. Standing in front of the two young ladies were Alred, Cyris, and Zaech, dressed in all black with diamond shapes of padded leather across their chests. Each man's outfit was trimmed in a different color thread; Alred in blue, Cyris in silver, and Zaech in red. They each wore a broadsword belted to their side.

Tamm could see the anger flare in Echao's eyes and knew he must act fast if he were to prevent bloodshed. Tamm jogged to get in front of Echao and cut him off before he could speak. "Well met, sirs."

They sneered at him without giving a response and turned their attention back to the women. Adina flashed a pleading look to Tamm. Tamm cleared his throat, and Alred gave him a sideways glance. "So Alred, how is your stomach?" he asked, an impish smile spreading across his face.

"Mind your tongue, fool, or you will find it cut out," Alred snapped.

Adina made a squeaking sound as she backed away. Tamm smiled at Alred, reaching behind him to place his hand on Echao's, who had reached toward his dagger. "What a shame," Tamm said. "Town guards harassing women, and in public too. And making threats against villagers? And here I thought you were supposed to protect us."

The three of them turned on Tamm in unison, Cyris and Zaech's hands reaching for the pommels of their swords. "It would be a shame," Tamm said, "if when next I deliver medicine, I happen to mention this to the Overseer. I'm sure he would be interested in hearing the concerns of a healer." Tamm's right hand slowly slipped to his dagger.

Alred raised an open palm to his comrades, staying their hands. "This is not over, Tammuz," Alred said. "It is only the beginning. One day. Soon."

"I look forward to it," Tamm said with an exaggerated bow. "Make sure you have the *stomach* for a fight." The guards stormed off into the night.

REBORN

Tamm turned to the others with a grin. "Well, that went well," he said. He could see that Echao was still raging mad, and both ladies were shocked that the encounter ended without bloodshed. Adina's lip was trembling. "Peace. They are gone, and we are here to celebrate." Echao nodded his appreciation to Tamm before wiping his hands on his pants and grabbing Lily's hand, leading her out to dance.

Adina rocked on her heels, her hands behind her back, glancing up to Tamm past her curls. "May I have the honor?" Tamm asked her, bowing and reaching out his hand.

Adina hesitated, then smiled at him, taking his hand and allowing him to lead her into the throng of other dancers. They danced and spun and twirled for what must have been hours. Adina rested her head on Tamm's shoulder as the music slowed, and Tamm rested his cheek against her head. He had never imagined that their relationship would grow this way. He glanced up and noticed the crowd had thinned considerably, and they were one of the only couples left dancing.

"Oh, dear," Adina said. "It's getting late. I should be getting home before Father gets too worried."

Tamm nodded, took her by the hand, and led her down the street. He almost walked into the well as he stared at her while they walked, making her giggle. They turned down a side street toward her house.

"I had an amazing time tonight," she said, smiling at him.

"As did I," he said. "Maybe we can spend more time together?" He wiped his sweaty palms on his pants leg. "I understand if you don't want to. I will be with Linsyn quite a bit and…" Tamm trailed off.

"I would love to," she said and kissed him on the cheek as she flitted inside. His fingertips traced the area of his cheek where her lips had been seconds before, and he marveled at how the evening had turned out. Emotions he had never felt before ran to and fro inside his stomach. The night had been perfect. It could not have gone any better. He headed back towards the town center to take the road home. The town was empty now, the revelers dispersed and gone home. Ribbon and bits of trash still littered the square. He meandered down the road, reliving the night again in his mind.

He heard a commotion up ahead but could not make it out. It sounded like men arguing and possibly scuffling. He assumed one of the villagers had a little too much to drink and was being tossed out of the tavern. As Tamm got closer, he could hear the sharp snapping of skin hitting skin and someone exhale sharply. This was more than someone getting tossed out of the tavern. He hurried down the road, peering down the dark rows of side streets for any clue as to what was happening. The further he went, the louder the sounds grew.

On the last side street, he could see shadows moving about and what appeared to be two men holding another man while a third assailant struck him hard in the face. "Hey!" Tamm shouted. They all turned toward the sound, and the man being held used this to his advantage.

He threw his legs back against the building and thrust himself forward, knocking the two men off balance and flipped past them. Tamm ran down the street to help the man.

REBORN

As he got closer, he noticed the man had drawn a dagger and was performing a flurry of blows towards the three, now armed, men. He recognized the style immediately. It was Echao.

Tamm rushed down the street and realized that the three men attacking Echao were Alred, Cyris, and Zaech. Echao was skilled with the dagger, even more than Tamm, but he could not hold out long against three trained fighters. The guards proved to be skilled in their own right, dodging and parrying Echao's attacks as quickly as he could throw them.

Echao swiped the dagger at Cyris's left arm, slicing through his tunic and into the flesh. The young man grabbed his arm and retreated a few steps back. Echao then turned his attention to Zaech in time to dodge a blow to the face, following with an upward thrust to Zaech's chest with his dagger. Zaech blocked the blow and wrapped his arm around Echao's throat and pulled him back against himself.

Tamm was almost there. He lowered his head and sprinted down the road. Echao squirmed in Zaech's arms, but could not free himself. Tamm lowered his right hand and drew his dagger. He was nearly within arm's reach of the two men when someone's foot flew out of nowhere and connected with his chest. Tamm soared backward through the air, landing on his back, his dagger somewhere in the street.

Through blurry eyes, Tamm raised his head to see Alred standing beside the other two men, Cyris approaching him, sword pointed at his chest. He was not sure what to do. He was afraid of what they may do to both he and his brother. They were in a desperate situation now that someone had noticed the assault. The guards could not just let them go. Tamm needed the upper hand to get control of the situation.

Cyris stood before him with his sword to Tamm's neck. "Leave him alone," Echao screamed. He was quickly silenced by Alred's fist to his mouth. Echao snarled as blood dripped from his lips.

Suddenly, Tamm had an idea. He lunged forward and grabbed Cyris's hands and pulled the sword toward himself, only barely missing his own head with the blade. As Cyris attempted to maintain his balance, Tamm jumped to his feet, blade still in his hands, pushing the sword over Cyris's head until he was thrown to the ground, and Tamm had full control of the sword. He held the sword at Cyris's throat. "Let him go," he shouted.

Alred raised his sword to Echao's neck. "This is not going to turn out well," he said. "Surely, you know that."

"I said, let him go!" Tamm cried, pushing the blade into Cyris's soft throat until blood began to pool at the tip of the blade. "I am in no mood to be tried!"

"Please…please don't," Cyris begged.

"Oh, shut up, you babbling fool," Alred said. "He is not going to kill you. Be a man for the gods' sake." Alred lowered his sword and motioned Zaech to do the same as he began to creep toward Tamm.

"Stand," Tamm said to Cyris. "Run away. Tell no one what's happened here, and I may spare your life."

Cyris glanced back at Alred, his face riddled with shame. Alred returned his look with one of utter resentment and disgust. Cyris scurried down the street and out of sight. "Release him," Tamm said.

Alred nodded his head, and Zaech loosened his grip around Echao's neck. Echao rubbed his throat and stretched his neck as he walked toward Tamm without even glancing back at the guards. Echao froze, wide-eyed, a look of pain spreading across his face. Tamm looked at him, puzzled, before noticing the fresh blood running down the corner of his mouth. Alred withdrew the dagger from Echao's back, and he slumped to the ground, gasping for breath. Alred stared back at Tamm, pure evil in his eyes as he wiped the blood from the dagger onto his pants leg.

Tamm flew into a rage, instincts reacting before he could think about what happened, running straight to Alred. Zaech stepped up to guard Alred, swinging his blade in an attempt to behead him. Tamm ducked, slicing through Zaech's thigh with the sword as he slid by. In one fluid motion, he brought his leg up, kicking Zaech right below the chin, knocking him out cold. He rolled forward, landing near Alred. Kèlris's lessons had served him well.

Alred's elbow connected with his jaw as soon as he landed, knocking him sideways into the building. Tamm's vision flickered with yellow and red lights as he shook his head to regain his focus. Alred was on him before he had time to respond and grasped him around his neck, lifting him high off the ground. He could not breathe and began to panic. He dropped the sword and began tugging frantically at Alred's hands. His grip was too tight. He could not get loose, no matter how hard he tried. His vision blurred as tiny lights flashed before him. In one last desperate attempt, Tamm gathered all his strength, and kicked, catching Alred between the legs. With a loud gasp, Alred's grip failed, and Tamm fell to the ground.

He could hear Alred retching beside him. He gasped for breath as he scrambled to his feet and began to stumble toward Echao's limp body. The boy was barely breathing now, lying in a pool of blood. Tamm noticed his dagger lying near Echao's body and picked it up and slid it back into the sheath. He was about to pick up the body when he heard a sword being drug across the street.

Tamm spun to see the blade flashing by his face. He leaned out of the way just as the sword missed his face and shoulder. Wasting no time, he slid the dagger from the sheath and slashed at Alred's gut, barely missing. Alred brought the blade back with both hands. Tamm had just enough time to duck under the blow, then brought his knee into Alred's stomach, causing him to drop the sword. Tamm slashed the dagger back across his body, connecting with Alred's face, gashing him from ear to chin.

Alred howled, snarling with rage, blood dripping from his chin. Tamm glared back at him before dropping the full force of his weight into his left hand as he struck Alred in the jaw. Before Alred could even flinch, Tamm lowered a blow with the pommel of the dagger just behind Alred's ear, rendering him unconscious.

Tamm scooped up Echao's limp body and ran to Linsyn with all haste. If anyone could save Echao, it was him.

SEVEN

The door blew open from the force of Tamm's kick, splinters scattering across the floor. He rushed into the familiar room, taking Echao's limp body to the cot that sat in the middle. He rushed across the room to a shelf full of bottles and vials containing potions, tonics, and powders. He snatched a bottle of a tan colored powder off of the rack and dug through the drawers snatching at dressings.

Tamm rolled Echao over to his stomach, cut off his tunic, and poured a disinfectant on the wound to clean it. Blood continued to ooze from the hole left by the dagger. Tamm dabbed it dry with some gauze before sprinkling the powder over the wound. Linsyn had taught him that this powder would clot the bleeding on most injuries. As Tamm pressed the clean dressings over the wound, still bleeding despite the powder, the door to Linsyn's bedroom flew open, and the old man stood there holding his staff at the ready as if poised to attack.

"What on earth?" Linsyn asked. His eyes scanned the boy before becoming wide and his jaw going slack at the sight of the blood pooling on the floor next to Tamm. He rushed to Tamm's side, patting down his torso and arms. "Are you wounded? Who did this?"

Tamm shook his head, tears beginning to flood his eyes. "Not me. You have to help him. I've tried. I can't stop it." Tamm stepped aside, revealing Echao's limp body lying on the cot, the blood continuing to drip onto the floor. He fell to his knees and began to sob.

Linsyn came to Echao's side and placed his fingers on his neck, just below the jaw. "He may still be saved," Linsyn said, more to himself than anyone else. Echao's skin was pale and small beads of sweat gathered on his forehead, like dew on a blade of grass just after dawn. Linsyn gathered additional dressings and began to apply direct pressure to the wound. "The purple tonic on the shelf there, I need it. Tamm, there! Post haste!"

Tamm shook himself out of the despair and scrambled to the shelf, scanning it for the vial. A foggy voice called out to him from across the room as he stared at the various glass bottles. "There, second shelf. No, to the right, there." Tamm grabbed the vial and rushed back to Linsyn's side. "Hold pressure here," Linsyn said, unstopping the cork of the vial with his teeth and pouring its content onto the wound, saturating the dressing and Tamm's hand. "Keep holding pressure for a few more minutes. With hope, this should stop the bleeding."

"He was going to ask for Lily's hand," Tamm muttered. He stared down at the wound, applying firm, steady pressure. He could taste the salt from his tears as they streamed onto his lips. "He was so focused on making a new life for her. He was planning on leaving this town. He was going to get out of here, see all the things that lie beyond these waters."

"You speak of him as if he is no longer here. You did well to get him here quickly. You have given him a chance."

Tamm shook his head, his eyes closed as the tears continued to fall.

"What happened? How did this happen?" Linsyn asked.

Tamm laid his head down on his hands, which were still pushing on the wound, his arms beginning to tremble. Lifting his head, he inhaled deeply before telling Linsyn all that had occurred that night. There was a silence following the story before Linsyn quietly spoke, his words soft. "You did the right thing. You were right to come in defense of your brother. You acted honorably."

Tamm looked up, surprised at his words. "I think that I probably caused more harm in the long run. He still did this to Echao. And once his father finds out that I'm the one who cut him, I'll be in chains."

"Remove the bandage," Linsyn said. "I believe you have held it long enough. We should have staunched the bleeding by now."

Tamm eased the dressing away and stared at the open wound, amazed that there was no more bleeding. He smiled in relief at Linsyn, who shared his smile. Tamm looked back at the wound again and stood in disbelief as a spray of red liquid splattered across his face. He stumbled backward before landing on his backside. The wound pulsated rhythmically with a steady flow of blood onto the floor beside him.

Tamm's ears were ringing, and he could not decode the words being called out to him by Linsyn. He sat on the floor, wiping at the blood on his face. Linsyn scurried across the floor, pressing his bare hands against the gushing wound as he mumbled to himself. "Must have been an artery. Why didn't I suspect this?"

Linsyn's eyes darted back and forth as if running through all the possibilities in his mind. He glanced at Tamm, a painful sympathy on his face. He turned back around to the boy on the cot, removed a necklace from under his nightshirt, and took a deep breath in preparation.

"*Leigheas!*" he commanded, and the small translucent gem on the necklace began to glow. Tamm was pulled from his shock as a soft glow began to fill the room. Linsyn stood with his back to Tamm, hands firmly over the wound, mumbling to himself. "*Leigheas*," Tamm heard him say again, more firmly this time, and a light began to emanate from around the old man's hands.

Tamm stood in disbelief. The old healer was attempting to use magic. So many thoughts ran through his mind, grasping at each one for clarity. Could it work? What if he were caught? Magic was banned by order of the king. What would Echao think if he could see this?

REBORN

The buzzing in Tamm's head faded, and he heard Linsyn calling his name. "Tammuz," he said, gasping for air. "Come, I need your help."

"What do you need me to do?" Tamm asked. "Do you need me to hold pressure while you…"

"No," Linsyn said with a gasp of air. "I am no longer strong enough…His wound is too great. You must be the one to heal him."

Tamm shook his head and backed away from the cot. "I can't. I'm a blacksmith's son. I'm no mage."

"You are more capable than you know, boy. Come and give me your hands. I will guide you."

Tamm crept over to the table, hands trembling. Echao was so still, his breaths coming shallow and slow. He looked as if he were sleeping, if only he had not been so pale, the crimson flow slowing with every breath."

"Quickly now," Linsyn said. "He doesn't have much time. Place your hand to the wound. Yes, like that."

Tamm laid his left hand upon the wound. "You can do this," Linsyn told him, placing his hand upon Tamm's. "You must believe it with all your heart. Believe. Now, repeat after me. *Stad an fhuil!*"

As Linsyn said the words, a faint light appeared below his hand, a white light. Tamm could feel the warmth flowing from Linsyn's hand through his own skin, and it began to tingle. He felt the magic flow through him as real as the air he was breathing. He knew he could heal him. Tamm took a deep breath and straightened to his full height. "*Stad an fhuil!*"

A bright silver light emanated from his hand. He could feel the power flowing through him, from him, and into Echao's lifeless body. He turned to look at Linsyn, who stared back with a determined grimace as if he would faint if he became the least bit distracted. "Focus," he told Tamm and turned back to Echao. "Feel your desire, your need to save him."

Linsyn removed his hand, and the white light faded. He stumbled back, panting, and fell back into a chair. Tamm followed suit, pulling his hand away, and the light that had been there seconds ago dissipated.

He stared down at the wound. It was gone, the skin completely healed over, only shiny, smooth skin where the wound had been only minutes before. "How?" he asked, walking around to look at Echao's face. "He still looks so pale."

"I must rest now," Linsyn replied. "We have done all that we can do. I just hope that it is enough." Linsyn rose and walked back to his bedroom, patting Tamm on the back as he walked by.

Tamm was exhausted, but he could not allow Echao to lie in that state. He went outside and drew some water, then washed the blood from Echao's body. Satisfied with his work, he placed Echao on his back, a pillow under his head, and covered him with a sheet and woolen blanket. He then cleaned the floor and the surrounding area. He slid a chair over to the cot and sat down. Within seconds he was fast asleep, his head resting on the cot beside Echao.

EIGHT

†

The aroma of sizzling meat pulled Tamm from sleep. He was so tired and fought the urge to open his eyes, but the savory smell of bacon was winning the battle. He glanced around the room, puzzled, rubbing the sleep from his eyes as he tried to remember the events of the night before. He jerked awake, remembering the fight and Echao's near mortal wound.

"He lives," Linsyn said from across the room. "You saved him. I cannot yet say if he will awake today or at all. He suffered a great wound and nearly bled out. It is difficult to discern the consequences so soon after the injury."

Tamm rose from his seat to look closer at Echao but wobbled and fell back to the chair. "My legs feel like water."

"You must eat," Linsyn said. "You performed a great feat last night, one that I could not have done on my own. Eat and we will discuss it more once your strength has returned."

"But how did I…" Tamm began to ask.

"Shh, shh," Linsyn scolded. "I said eat, and then we will discuss it further."

Tamm did not waste any time. He devoured the eggs, bacon, and hot oats that Linsyn had prepared, washing it down with fresh juice. Once he had eaten his fill, he turned to Linsyn with a questioning stare, patiently awaiting his explanation.

"Echao is stable for the moment," Linsyn said, lifting two fingers from his wrist. "I will need to notify his mother and father. I am certain they are quite concerned about both of you. Minds tend to believe the worst when left to wander. I will explain a few things now, but then I will need to speak to Kèlris and Mariah."

"I understand," Tamm said. Feeling his strength return after the meal, he walked over to the cot where his brother laid motionless, all but the slight rhythmic rise and fall of his chest with each breath. The wound was completely healed, a thin red line was left where the dagger had entered his body. Tamm was thankful that his brother still lived, but at the same time, he felt a deep nagging fear of what would happen to him once Alred reported how he had gotten the gash to his face. He knew that Alred would spin the story to suit himself and ensure he appeared to be the hero while leaving Tamm public enemy number one.

REBORN

He sighed, reaching out and brushing the hair from Echao's eyes. "What exactly happened last night? I am glad we were able to save him, but everything is still a blur. It feels like it all happened a thousand years ago."

The corner of Linsyn's lip twitched into a knowing smile. "Much has changed since yesterday morning. And much will continue to change, as it always does. The biggest question is, how will we let it change us. Tell me your concerns. Ask your questions."

Tamm shook his head, unsure of where to start. Confusion from the flurry of events unfolding overwhelmed him. "I have so many. I don't really know where to begin."

Linsyn looked at him, his expression teeming with empathy. "I have been in your shoes. Not with having a brother near murdered and suddenly discovering I can use magic, mind you. But I have seen my share of trials and tribulations. I have stared death in the eye and refused him his prey. I have discovered the mystery that is magic and marveled as I unraveled new intricacies daily. I have felt lost and undone, not knowing if I had anyone to confide in." He reached out and placed a hand on each of Tamm's shoulders. "You are safe here. I am here for you, Tammuz. I will instruct you; I will guide you. If required, I will give my last breath to protect you."

A small tear welled up, and Linsyn blinked it away. "Before we can go any further, you must calm yourself and clear your mind. Magic can be perilous if not respected and given your full attention. In order to learn more, you must search deep within yourself. There you will find the truth. There you will find power. Now, sit!"

The sudden command startled Tamm. He had been so embroiled in what he was being told and his racing thoughts, he was not expecting the sudden change of tone. He fumbled behind him, feeling for the chair he had sat in all night.

"Not in the chair," Linsyn said. "Sit on the floor." Tamm nodded, confused, and lowered himself to the floor, crossing his legs once seated. "Close your eyes, and just breathe. Inhale; now exhale. Again. Again."

Tamm breathed deeply, slowly, as Linsyn continued his instruction. "Focus," Linsyn said, whispering now so low Tamm strained to hear. "Focus on my voice. Let it guide you. Feel for the power deep inside you."

Tamm grimaced as he strained to hear, focus on his breathing, and search for whatever power Linsyn believed was inside him.

"Relax," Linsyn whispered. "You are not constrained by the rules of this physical world. You are spirit, and within that spirit lies power. Search for it. You must look deeply. It may only be a spark, a glimmer of what it is to become."

Tamm felt completely weightless as if he were no longer sitting in the old hut but floating above his body. He dared not open his eyes to look, desperate not to break the rhythm of his breathing and tempt banishing this feeling. For once, he felt at peace. The concerns that plagued him only moments ago were gone. There was no concern as to what might happen to him when the Sheriff comes. There was no concern about his brother's health. He was experiencing a peace that he could not even begin to comprehend.

Something flickered in the distance, and a tiny ember danced in the cold darkness. He did not see it with his eyes as they were still closed. He sensed it as if seeing it with his mind. He shivered and felt himself float closer until he was only a breath from it. He felt it calling for him, pleading for him to accept it.

A sudden tingling danced across his left hand, and he was reaching out to touch it without realizing it. The ember throbbed as he got closer. His hand was nearly on it when the tingling began to intensify. In his mind, it was as if the ember was asking for permission to touch him, asking if he would accept it. He nodded, and an excruciating burning sensation rushed through his hand as the ember turned to a flame, licking out touching his hand.

The flame called out to him. *Be consumed. The old shall be purged, the silver refined, the spirit reborn.* He could not hear it with his ears, but he sensed its intent. The words rushed all around him at once, as if hundreds of voices were speaking to him in a small room.

He did not fear the blaze or pull away from the heat. The flame continued to grow until it encompassed him. He was engulfed in the flames, and the burning in his hand moved through his entire body. He felt the pain; it would have been overwhelming had it not been for the peace that surrounded him. He knew in his heart that the flames would not destroy him. He welcomed them. He could feel the change occurring not only in his mind but in his body. He reached out with his mind to the flame and whispered, "Consume me and make me new." The fire surged in agreement.

Suddenly, the flames were gone, and Tamm was sitting back on the floor. Linsyn was standing there when he opened his eyes, staring at him with squinted eyes as if he were too bright to see. "What do you feel?"

Tamm did not know how to answer him. He felt a lot of things. The burning sensation subsided, but he still felt a tingle in his left palm. He looked down at it and noticed a small pink scar where the flame had first touched him. As he looked closer, he noticed it looked similar to the sun with outstretched rays, but in that symbol, he could feel something stirring.

"What do you feel?" Linsyn asked again.

"I feel power, and at the same time, peaceful," Tamm replied. "I know it sounds strange, but I feel renewed. I have never felt anything like this before."

"It is only the beginning, young Tammuz," Linsyn said. "I have much to teach you, and you have much to learn." Tamm stood from the chair and walked closer to Linsyn, staring at him, his eyes hungry, begging him for the knowledge. "What do you know of the world you live in, Tamm? Specifically, the creation of it."

Tamm shrugged his shoulders. "Much of the world was built by the great warrior god Brynjar. He had many siblings, Sylvi, a sister who dug the oceans and streams and planted the gardens that flourish the land today. His brother Halvar constructed the mountains and climbed to their heights to create the sky and clouds and give us light. Derwyn created all the animals. And finally, Brynjar's wife, Asta, created all the races who inhabit the earth."

"And where did you learn this?" Linsyn asked.

Tamm stared at him in confusion. "Surely, you know this already. You have been around longer than I. You know our legends and beliefs."

"You speak truly," Linsyn replied. "I have been around much longer and have heard these tales and many more. But where did these beliefs come from? Hmm?"

"They have been passed down for hundreds, maybe even thousands of years," Tamm said. "I don't know where it originated. I know it didn't originate in this land. Our people are refugees here. But, I do know that our people worshipped these gods long before coming to this land. You ask as if you don't believe."

Linsyn let out a deep sigh. "I mean to cause no confusion, Tammuz. I did not bring this up to argue or have you second guess your beliefs. I mentioned it to make you think. You have now felt this power. It must come from somewhere. But where? Ah? It is alive. It is everywhere around us, in everything we see, and in everything we do. As you travel, you will meet others who have different beliefs and ideas than you. Learn from them. From henceforth, being a scholar will be your greatest task. In order to become stronger with the magic, you must know the magic, must study it, must live it, must breathe it. Do you understand?"

Tamm blinked, overwhelmed with all he had been taught in such a short time. "This is a lot to take in. I'm not sure that

I will ever understand a portion of this power, much less all of it. However, I am willing to try."

"That is a very good attitude," Linsyn said. "That is all we can do, continue to try and continue to learn. With that said, I believe I have kept the blacksmith waiting long enough. In the meantime, keep an eye on Echao, and do try to keep him alive. There is some valerian root by the hearth. Fetch some water and make a tea. Do try to get him to drink a little something. The poor lad will need rest. I will give you something to practice while I am gone. The tea will need to heat. Sit by the hearth with a fresh log and try to light it. Focus on starting the fire, reach deep for the power that lies within, and speak the word *Lasair*. Do not be discouraged; it takes time and practice to bring forth the elements."

With a wave of his hand, he was out of the shack and on his way to deliver the news of Echao's wounds. Tamm sat back in the chair and stared at the hearth, overwhelmed with the events of the morning and slightly intimidated and frightened to be attempting to start a fire without Linsyn nearby. What if he burned down the clinic? He brushed the thought from his mind. Determined, he grabbed a pitcher and set out for some water to make the tea.

NINE

†

Linsyn hobbled through the town on his staff, ignoring the townspeople as he hurried toward the blacksmith's house. It was not a far walk, but he began to feel winded. He stroked his beard as he pondered it. It could have been all the excitement and stress over the past evening, or he could finally be showing his age.

As he approached the blacksmith's shop, he noticed Kèlris and Mariah were already standing outside speaking to someone. He was still too far off to make out the words, but he could sense that the discussion was not going well. Mariah was waving her arms around and raising her voice to where he could almost make out a word or two.

Despite the pain in his back and legs, he sped up to see what all the commotion was about. He arrived just as Sheriff

Vorn told the two, with very little enthusiasm, "I'm sure they are both fine. They are young and probably had a little too much fun and more ale than they could handle last night. I am sure they will be home anytime now."

"No!" Mariah yelled. "You do not know that they are fine, and neither do I. You would do well to remember the duties of your position, Sheriff."

"Mariah," Kèlris interjected. "I apologize for my wife's bluntness, Sheriff. As you can imagine, she is quite upset. Neither of our boys has ever done anything like this before. This is very unlike them."

Vorn's eyes cut back to Mariah, and he forced a smile. "I understand your concern. I will do what I can to assist."

Linsyn walked up to the group just as Alred jogged up to his father, a bandage dressing the side of his face and scattered bruises peeking out from the bandage. "Father," Alred said. "There's something important that I need to report to you."

Vorn held up a hand. "It can wait. Can't you see? We have more pressing matters at the moment."

"But Father," Alred said.

"We must remember the duties of our position," Vorn said, flashing a mock smile to Mariah.

Linsyn cleared his throat to interrupt. "This is quite important, Sheriff." Everyone turned to look at the healer, puzzled. "There have been some grievous actions taken last night." Alred flashed a panicked look to Linsyn.

"Kèlris, Mariah," Linsyn said. "Your children are with me. There was an incident last night." He glanced at Alred and saw that the boy's breaths were becoming more shallow and rapid, his eyes darting between the healer and his father.

Mariah gasped. "Are they well? Please tell me they are safe."

"They are alive," Linsyn assured her. "Thanks to Alred." Alred jumped at the sound of his name. The group all turned to him, and he shrugged his shoulders. "Well, not Alred only, Cyris and Zaech had a hand in it also." Alred wiped sweat from his brow and avoided meeting the eyes of anyone.

Linsyn chuckled. "Cat seems to have gotten Master Alred's tongue. In that case, I will relay what happened. Tammuz and Echao were on their way home last night. They heard a growl from the direction of the tree line. Being the brave young men that they are, they went to investigate." Alred's mouth hung open at hearing the healer's lies.

"Once near the tree line, some sort of monster attacked. Tammuz does not recall what it looked like, as it was quite dark, but said that it was large, taller than any man. They attempted to fight it off, concerned that it would attack the village. Echao was severely wounded. It would have likely killed both of the boys had Alred and his companions not showed up and fought the monster off, each receiving wounds in their efforts. The beast fled into the forest, and Tamm rushed Echao to my hut for much needed medical attention. I can only assume that Alred gave chase to the beast."

For a moment, everyone stared at the healer, soaking in the fanciful tale. "Alred?" Vorn asked. "Is that true?"

Alred looked to Linsyn, who gave him a nod. "Yes, father," Alred replied. "We gave chase, but the beast eluded us. It was significantly wounded itself. I don't believe it will return."

Vorn clapped him on the back. "You may make a hero after all. My boy, the monster slayer." Alred gave a half-hearted smile and shrugged.

"What of my boys?" Mariah asked. "I want to see them."

"There is much we need to discuss," Linsyn told her. "As I mentioned, Echao was severely wounded. He is alive but only barely. Let's go inside and discuss it more."

Kèlris placed his arm around Mariah and turned to walk to the house as Mariah sobbed softly. Linsyn turned to the Sheriff before following Tamm's parents into the house. "Thank you both for your assistance. I will see to them for now. I need to let them know that, though alive now, Echao is gravely injured and may still perish. Only time will tell. Good day."

♦♦♦♦♦

Tamm focused on the log in the fireplace. He placed one log, concerned about the damage he could cause with more should the flame catch. He quieted his mind, searching for the flame he had felt inside him only a short time earlier. He could still feel the tingling in his hand, but the inferno that consumed him previously was nowhere to be found.

"*Lasaír,*" he whispered, but nothing happened. He shifted his position on the floor, sliding closer to the fireplace. "*Lasaír,*" he said, louder this time but still nothing. He leaned closer, his nose a breath away from the log. "*Lasair!*" He stood and paced around the room, glaring at the fireplace. It had seemed so easy to heal Echao last night. Why would it not work today? He looked down at his left hand and noticed he did not feel the tingling any longer. He stroked the red skin with his fingers, but that did not elicit a response either.

He walked over to the chair beside Echao's cot and sat down. "Why won't it work?" he asked, knowing Echao would not answer him. "I don't understand. All I have ever wanted was a life of adventure. Last night was more adventure than I could stand. Maybe I'm not cut out for adventure. Maybe my place is here as a healer. Or even a smith. I'm not particularly good at this healing thing, either."

He walked to the cabinet and began arranging and sorting powders and tinctures, taking an inventory of what needed to be replaced after last night's imprudent use of supplies in the furious attempt to heal Echao. Nothing physical seemed to work last night. Nothing that Linsyn had taught him to stop the bleeding had actually stopped the bleeding. Maybe the word that he had taught him would bring fire, *Lasair*, would be like the medicines; perhaps it would not work either.

Tamm thought about what Linsyn had told him earlier, about where his beliefs came from, believing them because that is what he had always been told, and seeking to learn from others who may not believe as he does. He slid across the floor, coming to a stop in front of the bookcase, his eyes scanning from book to book. He needed to find one that would have information about magic in it, preferably from another race. There were so many books; it was hard to focus on just one. But there it was, tucked away between two larger bound books, a thin book with a green cover. There were no words on the spine, nothing exceptional that should have caught his attention.

He took the book from its place on the shelf. It was slick from the accumulation of dust. He blew the dust away to find a small tree etched on the cover with a sword pointing down in the foreground. He opened the book, and a musty smell made his nose wrinkle. He flipped through the pages, finding eloquent, flowing script in a language he did not recognize. He continued to flip the pages until he saw a flame drawn at the top of the page. He perused through the unintelligible words but discovered nothing he could understand. He turned the page and found notes scribbled in the margin of the page in his language. He read the text and found many words that described fire, each being able to elicit a slightly different reaction. *Lasaír* was there but was a word that described the flame itself. He found a word that, from what he could understand of the scribbled notes, would cause something to burn, *Sruthán*.

Echao groaned, and Tamm jumped, tossing the book onto the writing desk. He was beginning to stir but still needed to rest. Tamm needed to get the tea brewing quickly. He walked across the room and knelt at the fireplace. He closed his eyes and focused on his breathing. He searched for the fire inside him, a tiny ember that could burst into a rage. He could feel it, just in the distance, heat radiating onto his face. His left hand began to tingle. He stretched his hand out to the log resting in the fireplace. "*Sruthán!*" The flames licked up from the wood, nearly touching Tamm's hand. He did not pull his hand away, unafraid of the fire. He smiled and hung the pot of water over the fire to boil.

TEN

Tamm readjusted Echao's pillow. He was resting well after the tea. The tricky part had been getting him to swallow it while not fully awake. The fire was still roaring in the hearth, and he smiled at the thought of it. So much had changed in such a short time. All he had ever wanted in life was adventure, and now that he had experienced it, it was overwhelming.

The door creaked open behind him, and he turned to see Linsyn hobble through the doorway. He rushed over to steady the old man. "Are you alright?"

Linsyn coughed. "I'm fine. Just old is all. It is a fair journey to your home. Too much for these old bones."

Tamm snickered at his attempt at a joke and helped Linsyn to a chair. "How did it go?"

Linsyn told him how his parents were faring and how Vorn and Alred were present and the look on Alred's face when he made him appear to be the hero rather than a murderer.

"But why would you do that?" Tamm asked. "You should have made the report to his father, made him out to be the reprobate that he is."

"I could not. I was protecting you. Who would Vorn believe? You and I? Absurd. As long as Alred believes he is viewed as the victor, and others believe he received the gash to his face from a Kapre, he has no reason to tell his father the truth and place blame on you."

Tamm shook his head, knowing that he was no match for Linsyn's wisdom. "I trust your judgment."

Linsyn noticed the fire, and the corner of his mouth twitched. "I see you got the fire lit. And Echao seems to be resting well."

Tamm walked to the bookcase and took a book off of the shelf. He recounted to Linsyn about his multiple attempts to get the log to light and his numerous failures until he remembered what Linsyn had told him about being a scholar and examining things for himself. "Why couldn't I light the fire with *Lasair*?"

"It is a powerful word, more difficult to control than others. Words have power, some more than others. Keep the book, study its contents. Do not try to use the words without knowing how to control them. It can have dire consequences."

Tamm thumbed through the book. "How does it all work? How do words have power?"

Linsyn shifted in his chair and attempted to stand but tipped back into the seat. Tamm rushed to his side, but Linsyn brushed away the attempt. "I am fine." He tried again, and this time was able to stand. He ambled over to the bookshelf. "I apologize. It was not my intention to be so rude when you only offered to help." He reached to the top shelf and slid out an old book.

"You didn't offend me," Tamm said. "I know this has been difficult for you too. I am just eager to learn."

Linsyn pointed to a page in the book. "We can manipulate the elements. Never create, only manipulate."

Tamm stared at him, confused. "What do you mean by creating and manipulating?"

Linsyn raised an eyebrow. "Is it that difficult to understand? We can manipulate the elements, the energy around us. We cannot create something from nothing. There is nothing new under the sun. We can only alter and change what already exists."

Tamm pointed to the fire. "So how did I make that?"

"You made nothing," Linsyn said, hobbling over to the fire. "The word only allowed you to manipulate the heat in the air and cause the fire to begin. You harnessed its power and allowed it to be brought forth. You could do the same with wind, or ice, or even light, with enough study. The words guide your will, give the elements guidance as to what to do, that is all. The power to do that is inside you. The words are the keys that unlock that power."

REBORN

Tamm rubbed his temples. "So, what you are saying is I can manipulate most anything around me with the right words?"

"Yes and no." Linsyn flipped to another page. "Just because you cannot create energy does not necessarily limit your power. You are only limited by the words you do or do not know and your imagination on how to use them."

Tamm dropped his head into his hands. "I don't think I am cut out for this. Honestly, Linsyn, how did you ever learn any of this?"

Linsyn chuckled. "In the eyes of a mage, you are old to be beginning to learn the ways. In the days of the Battlemages, most trainees your age had already been training for years and were preparing to take their trials. You are getting a late start."

Tamm moved closer to Linsyn. "Well, let's get started. I have a lot of catching up to do."

"Very well. Let us begin."

◆◆◆◆◆

Tamm spent the next several days in Linsyn's hut, studying ancient tomes and learning which words could perform certain tasks. He thought he was gaining some insight on a few of the words and their uses until he tried to use the word for wind, *Gaoth,* to cause a broom to slide over to him and accidentally tripped Linsyn as he was walking across the floor. Luckily, Linsyn had gained some of his strength back over the last couple of days and was able to steady himself, preventing him from crashing down upon the floor. Tamm shrugged at him when he glared back over his shoulder at him.

Linsyn shook his head. "I feel it is time for a break."

"But, I was finally getting the hang of it," Tamm said. "I'm just getting started. There are a few more things I want to try."

Linsyn walked over to the shelf containing bandages and tinctures and potions. "We need to restock. You have had ample time to study today. You can't stay cooped up inside all day." Linsyn jotted some items onto a piece of parchment and handed it to Tamm. "Go into the forest and get these items. When you return, we will practice something new."

Tamm nodded, took the parchment and folded it up, and slid it into the pocket of his trousers. He grabbed his satchel and tossed it across his shoulder. Pulling the door open, he turned back to Linsyn. "Where did you learn all of this?"

Linsyn chuckled. "That is a story for another time. First, the supplies. One day we will discuss history, but today is not that day."

Tamm made his way out of town and towards the forest. The thoughts of magic and controlling the elements danced around in his head. He had never imagined he could find so much awe and adventure in the small fishing village where he grew up. He pulled the list from his pocket and read over it. The items should be simple enough to find and should not take long. Since his last encounter in the woods, he no longer craved his daily trips to the mountains to watch the sunrise. The growl he had heard during his previous trip still sent shivers down his spine when he thought about it. It will be a quick trip, just a few items. He would be fine.

When he entered the edge of the woods, the trees were sparse, and sunlight penetrated between them, lighting the ground around him. The further he went in, the denser the trees and the darker everything became. Now deep in the forest, he stopped to listen. All he could hear was his own rapid breathing. He had been moving more quickly than he realized. He knelt beside a tree and collected a group of tan mushrooms from the base of the tree. He secured them in his satchel before proceeding on.

The sun was beginning to go down, and it was becoming more challenging to see. He still needed to gather some moss. He knew that it typically grew on the north side of trees. He walked closer to the mountains in the north, glancing at the side of the trees facing the mountains, but he was having difficulty finding the moss.

The base of the mountain was now in view and he had yet to find any moss. In the distance, he noticed an opening in the side of the mountain. The cool, dank air from the cave provided a better climate for the moss to grow. It was getting quite dark now, and he was left to rely on his other senses to find the moss. He was determined to not go back without all the supplies on the list. He found a tree next to the opening of the cave and leaned against it. He sniffed, and a musty breeze emanated from the cave. There was almost a rotting smell mixed in the air. He blew the smell from his nose and reached his arm around the tree. He felt the soft tickle from the moss against his fingers and smiled. He grabbed a handful and secured it in his bag.

He leaned his back against the tree and pulled the plug off his waterskin, and gulped the cool liquid. A branch snapped from inside the forest, followed by rustling noise. He froze, then squatted behind the tree. He recapped the waterskin and could feel his heart thumping in his throat. His eyes found it difficult to focus in the dark. He saw movement everywhere but knew it was his mind playing tricks on him.

He could definitely hear movement now. Someone was coming toward him. He could see them now, more so their silhouettes. There were three of them. He made a quick decision to scamper up the side of the rock wall and perch above the entrance to the cave. He laid flat against the stone, trying to become one with it. His breaths came in shallow gasps as the three beings came closer to the cave. They were close enough now where he could begin to make out their stature but not their features. They were much taller than a human with strong arms and a barrel chest. Their legs were long and sat upon two enormous feet. They looked as though they could crush him with one hand.

They stopped just in front of the cave opening and were speaking emphatically to one another. Their speech was composed of grunts, growls, and clicks. Tamm had never heard anything like it. He could not understand any of it and did not really care to. He just wished they would go inside so he could flee. He did not want to spend the night lying on the cold stone with no cloak.

REBORN

One of them sniffed the air. Tamm slid further back away from the edge of the cliff. A pebble rolled from the top and clicked against the wall on the way down. The other two beasts growled with excitement and pointed near to where Tamm was hiding. He held his breath and closed his eyes, willing himself not to be seen. The first creature made its way to the edge of the rock wall and sniffed as it ran its hand along the stone that Tamm had climbed moments ago.

He could hear its grasp secure on the stone below him and begin to climb. Tamm panicked, eyes flashing around for a way to escape. His right hand grasped the hilt of the dagger at his waist. He knew he did not stand a chance against one of these monsters, much less three of them, but he did not know what else to do. He sensed the creature getting closer and could smell its fetid breath. He closed his eyes and tried to steady his breathing. In and out. In and out.

His left palm tingled, and he almost moved to scratch it but knew it would mean certain death. As he breathed in and out, he felt the flame rising up inside of himself. He focused on the fire and willed it to take over him the way it did when he first felt its power. He could feel the power throbbing inside of him and knew with complete competence that it would obey any request he made.

He turned his head away from the creature, who was almost at the crest of the rock and would soon be within reach of him. He squinted his eyes and found a large tree at the edge of his vision. He focused on one limb near the bottom and whispered, "*Gaoth.*" He felt the power attempt to surge from him, but he restrained it. He could barely hear the snap of the limb over the grunts and growls of the three creatures near him, but they heard it and became silent. They stared in the direction of the tree. The one that had been climbing up to Tamm scampered back down the rock face and grunted to the other two.

They stepped closer to the sound, glancing around them. They stopped near the tree and searched around. Tamm closed his eyes, knowing this would be his only chance. He focused back on the tree and felt the power thrumming inside him still. "*Gaoth.*" But this time, he did not restrict the power. The tree buckled under the force of the wind and tipped over towards the creatures with a crash. As they jumped away from the tipping tree, Tamm rolled to the edge and slid down the cliff. He stumbled, exhausted from the release of magic, but could not take the time to rest. The Kapre would soon find him if he tarried. He broke into a sprint, his satchel slapping against his back. He ran all the way back to Linsyn's without looking back.

ELEVEN

†

Tamm parried the blow and thrust back at the Kapre's gut, the large ax effortlessly deflecting his feeble attempt. The Kapre's laugh bellowed over the battlefield. Its gargling speech lifted above the cacophony of the battle. "This is the best your humans could send? You are pathetic."

Tamm lifted the sword back to the ready and summoned the beast to himself with his other hand. "Less talk. I would like to still get to bed early tonight. I have much to do tomorrow."

The Kapre growled as it whirled the ax over its head and charged at Tamm. He was able to deflect the first two blows, but the third sliced through the leather wrappings across his abdomen. The cut was not deep, but it burned like fire. Tamm felt the blood begin to trickle down his belly, and the beast smiled when he saw the stain appear.

Both warriors flung themselves at each other, a flurry of blows traded between the two. Tamm fatigued quicker than the Kapre. He brought his hand to his abdomen, checking to see if the bleeding had slowed, and cursed the crimson flow. The Kapre roared a deafening war cry and charged Tamm again. Tamm was barely able to block the blow before he felt a massive foot catch him in the ribs. His breath squealed as it burst from his lungs, and he rolled on the ground before coming to a stop. He gasped for breath as he reached out, searching for his sword. It was out of his reach, and the Kapre was only an arm's length away, lip quivering over his fangs.

Tamm clambered to his knees and looked up at the monster raising the ax above his head before he bowed his own in defeat. He heard the ax blade as it whistled toward his neck.

There was a bright flash of light, and he jumped upright in his bed with heaving breaths. It was only a dream. He looked around and was alone. His stomach ached like it was in knots. If only Echao were well, he could confide in him about the haunting dream.

Tamm dropped back into the bed as he willed his heart to slow its rapid, erratic pace. Last night had been the closest he had ever been to death. Those monsters, the Kapre, almost discovered where he was hiding, and he had no way to protect himself. What were they doing so close to the village? When he had gotten back to Linsyn's last night, he had difficulty recounting what had occurred. Linsyn had told him he wanted to sleep on it and would discuss it further in the morning. Tamm tried to protest, but it fell on deaf ears.

He pulled on his clothes and ran down the stairs three at a time. He grabbed an apple from a basket in the kitchen and was out on the road before his mother could tell him good morning. He ate the apple as he hurried down the road. The sun sliced through the clouds, painting splashes of light on the roofs of the surrounding buildings. He marveled at the simple beauty of the village while danger lurked just outside its borders.

He opened the door to the healer's hut, and Linsyn was sitting at his writing desk with multiple books lying around him. He was in deep study and did not look up at Tamm as he entered. Tamm hung his satchel up on the rack by the door and slid a chair across the floor to sit near Linsyn. "Did you get to sleep on it? It looks like you were up all night."

Linsyn still did not look up from the book. "I did sleep on it, but I have been up for some time. It was, without a doubt, a group of Kapre that you encountered last night. But why are they here? I was not aware there was even any of their kind left in this land."

Tamm thumbed through one of the books on the desk. "What do we do now?"

"We do not do anything. I am old, Tamm. I am no match for one Kapre, much less three. What do you think we should do?"

Tamm leaned back in his chair and stared up at the ceiling. "I don't know. I'm not comfortable with them being this close to the town. I couldn't understand what they were saying to each other, their language is quite strange, but I have a feeling that they are up to no good.

Linsyn grabbed one of the books and handed it to Tamm. "It's interesting that you say it that way. I was studying this morning and came across this." He pointed to the open page.

Tamm scanned across the script until he came across a section that discussed a mage who used magic to gift someone with the ability to understand and speak other languages. "How is that possible? Wouldn't that be considered creating something?"

"It is not necessarily creating something," Linsyn said. "I would simply be transferring my knowledge of the language to you. It would seem new to you as you did not know the language previously, but I do know the language. I studied it many years ago."

Tamm stood and paced the room as he read more of the book. "How do we do this? It seems difficult." He tossed the book back onto the desk with a thud.

Linsyn reached across the desk and closed the book. "It is difficult, but I believe that I can do it; although, it may take me a few hours to prepare. Afterward, it may take me a few days to recover."

Tamm walked over to the old man and placed a hand on his shoulder. "We don't have to do this."

"Yes, we do. Do not worry about me. I know I do not look like much now, but I have performed magic in the past much more difficult than this. I recommend that while I recover, you sneak back into the woods and listen in on the Kapre. Try

REBORN

to learn about their plans. You will need to be careful; they rarely travel alone."

Tamm shook his head. "You sound like you know quite a bit about the Kapre."

Linsyn now placed a hand on Tamm's shoulder. "More than you know. Go for now. I need time to prepare. I am sure you can find something to get into. Find a nice quiet place and practice. Just do not get caught."

Tamm bid Linsyn farewell and left the hut and strolled through the town and toward the lake. It was mid-morning, so not many people would be there, other than the local fishermen, and they would be out by the docks. He found a quiet spot by the water and plucked a sheath of grass and laid it upon the ground. He cupped his hand around the grass and looked across his shoulder, ensuring no one else was around. Pleased that he was alone, he closed his eyes and began to search for the power that lived inside of him now.

He could sense it deep in his soul, a flame hungering to be released. He opened his eyes and focused on the small leaf of grass and whispered, "*Gaoth.*" The grass began to tremble as he felt the power flow from his hands. Dirt began to swirl, and he fought to restrain the power trying to escape. He closed his eyes and focused on what he wanted the wind to do, only to lift, not to blow.

He opened his eyes and focused on the thin sliver of green in front of him. It swayed back and forth, just slightly above the ground. He smiled to himself, pleased at how he was learning to control the magic. He focused again and cut the flow of magic, and the grass fell.

Next, he collected a few small stones, nothing too large; he did not want to bruise his confidence should he fail. He sat back on the ground with his legs crossed and spoke the word for wind. The stones began to twitch and roll along on the ground. He allowed a little more of the power to escape, and the stones started to lift up from the ground. He kept his hands cupped around them, afraid someone might sneak up on him while he was focused on controlling the flow of the magic. He squinted and willed the wind to spin, and the stones began to circle each other. With a thought, he caused the stones to begin to undulate, up and down, while continuing to spin. He turned his focus to the lake. He glanced at a stone, then to the lake. He shifted his will, providing the power with a command, and the stones shot forward and skipped across the crystal waters.

He stood and looked for other items he could use to practice. He gathered some small twigs lying around and made a small pile. He glanced over his shoulder again to be sure he was not being watched. People were moving about closer into town, but none that were close enough to see what he was doing. He knelt down by the twigs and spoke the word, *Sruthán*. Small sparks danced between the twigs followed by a flame springing up in the center. He noticed there was very little smoke with the fire. He smiled at all he had accomplished in such a short time.

"What are you doing?" a voice asked over his shoulder. He spun around to find Adina standing there, her arms folded behind her back, rocking back and forth on her heels, smiling.

REBORN

Tamm quickly stomped out the fire. "Good morning, Adina. Linsyn gave me a little time off this morning."

Adina raised an eyebrow. "So, you decided to build a fire on such a warm day?"

He shrugged and smiled at her. "I was bored, so I was just practicing my skills. It's always a good skill for an adventurer to have."

She gave him a puzzled look. "A healer, you mean?" Adina asked. "You are a healer now. And a fine healer from what I hear. How is your brother?"

Tamm blushed and stared at the ground. "He's quite frail. He has not woken up yet. I couldn't have done it without Linsyn's help."

"Still, quite a feat from what I understand. They say he was gravely wounded. What kind of beast could do such a thing?"

Tamm wanted to tell her the truth. He hated lying, especially to her. But, it was for her own good. Should she let the truth slip that Alred was responsible, there is no telling how he would react. No, he had to keep with the story that Linsyn devised. And it was partly true. The Kapre were in the forest and would likely attack any human that entered the forest.

"Do you remember when I told you about the footprint in the forest?" Tamm asked.

"Of course, I do. It chilled me to the bone. Although, it was the last thing on my mind by the end of the night," she said, smiling at him.

He felt heat rise into his cheeks. "Me too. Until Echao was attacked. I've had nightmares about those things, Adina.

They're horrid beasts. I have spoken to Linsyn about them. The stories he told would terrify a marine. They smoke pipes with sweet-smelling tobacco that lures and disorients men, and then they attack, devouring the men they capture."

Adina gasped. "That's terrible."

"Promise me you will stay far away from the forest. I couldn't bear it if something happened to you."

She closed the gap between them and took both his hands in hers. "I promise. But you must do the same. Don't try to be a hero, Tamm. Don't go seeking revenge. Things will work themselves out. Echao will get better. I really believe he will."

TWELVE

†

Tamm walked back to Linsyn's after leaving Adina by the lake. She was a sweet girl; he really liked her, but things were changing so quickly. After dropping her off on the night of the festival, he could not wait for the next time he would get to see her. It all changed in a whirl of blades when Alred attacked Echao. Now, every time he saw her, it felt like he was living a lie. It was all for her protection, but he got a knot in his stomach every time he was near her.

He cracked the door open to the hut and peeked inside. Linsyn was seated at the writing desk with an old, dusty book open in front of him. "Come in, come in. Shut the door behind you and drop the latch in place. We shouldn't be disturbed during this."

Tamm did as he was told and bolted the door. "So, you've figured it out? Do you think it will work?"

Linsyn chuckled. "You doubt my abilities, do you? I have been doing this for much longer than you can imagine," he said as he drew the curtains closed, blocking any passersby from seeing into the hut.

"I'm sorry. I didn't intend to insult you. What must I do?"

"No apology needed. Come. Stand here," Linsyn said, indicating the center of the room. "Now, close your eyes and focus. I need you to focus on the desire to know, to understand. Search deep within yourself. As I speak the words, you will need to repeat it along with me and let the power flow from you. This is a transfer of knowledge. We will both need to activate the magic."

Tamm nodded, waiting while Linsyn placed the book on a stand near them. Linsyn smoothed the pages and laid his hand on Tamm's head. "Now close your eyes."

Tamm closed his eyes and felt the power thrumming from Linsyn. He was in awe at how much power this frail, old man had surging inside him. He shuddered as the power washed over him. He could hear a rhythmic humming in his ears.

"Repeat after me, Tammuz. Free the power within and let it flow. Do not hold back."

Tamm nodded his head.

"*Tòg eolas ar kieli. Seilbh eolas ar kieli.*"

As Linsyn spoke the words, a cool sensation rushed through Tamm's mind, followed by a desire to release the power inside him. He wet his lips and repeated the words. As the last sound fell from his lips, he released the power. He did as Linsyn had told him and did not restrain the power. He let it pour out of him like lava spewing from a volcano. He sensed Linsyn's medallion blaring with a white-hot light and squinted his eyes tighter. Beads of sweat began to drip on his forehead from the heat in the room emanating from him and Linsyn.

Without warning, the flow of power ceased, and he opened his eyes to find a pale Linsyn standing in front of him, bent forward and breathing hard.

"It is finished," Linsyn said in Elvish.

Tamm wobbled, weak from the release of magic, his thoughts foggy. Something seemed odd about the way Linsyn was speaking, maybe the inflection of his words. "You sound different," he said unwittingly in Elvish. "There is something different in the way I'm talking."

Linsyn smirked at him. "As well it should be. You are speaking in Elvish, as am I."

Tamm looked at him in confusion. "How can that be? I understand everything you're saying as if I've spoken Elvish my entire life."

"That is because I have passed my knowledge to you, and I am fluent in the language. That is why you easily recognize the words and can speak without effort. You will see with other languages that it is not always this easy. I chose Elvish because I am fluent, and it would be an easy language for you to practice. It should be like second nature speaking in this language. However, I am not as skilled in Kapresee, which was one of the things I was studying earlier today in an attempt to pass a little more knowledge on to you."

Tamm pulled up a chair. "So, what you're saying," he said, switching back to his native dialect, "is that when I next run into a Kapre, I may or may not understand what they are saying?"

"That is a possibility. You should be able to glean enough from their conversation to get an idea of their plans. The more you are exposed to the language, the more you will learn."

"So, when do you recommend I go back to the cave?"

Linsyn nodded and gestured to the door. "Unfortunately, yes. There is no time like the present. I would suggest changing your clothes so that you are not as easily detected in the woods. Maybe choose something dark green or black. After that, you should pack some food and plan on making a night out of it. Get as much information as you can, and we will discuss our options when you return."

Tamm ran his fingers through his hair, overwhelmed with the changes his life had undergone.

"Do take care, Tammuz. The Kapre are bred to be killers of men. Even one or two of them could overwhelm you. Should you find yourself in an unwelcomed predicament, feel free to use some of what you have learned."

Tamm departed the hut and made his way home. He took care not to make eye contact with any of the other villagers so as not to be delayed. Once he reached his home, he made a quick change of clothes, picking tones that would blend in with the forest, and tossed a dark cloak over his shoulder before bouncing back down the steps to the kitchen. He dropped a couple of apples and half of a loaf of bread into his satchel, making sure to top off his waterskin before exiting the house and making his way to the forest.

He entered the woods in the late afternoon, the sun was still up, but dusk would be settling in soon. The muted light would help him to stay hidden. He first headed to the old training grounds that he, his father, and his brother had constructed. He checked inside an old log and felt a deerskin bow sleeve. He pulled the bow from its sleeve and tested the string. It was still in good shape. He reached further into the log and retrieved five arrows. If he needed more than five, then the situation was already more dire than a few arrows could fix.

He threw the bow across his shoulder and strapped a small quiver around his waist. He made his way deeper into the woods toward the rock face of the local mountains. He had always heard that the mountains stretched the entire northern border of Iradell. Looking up at the masses of stone, he imagined that could be true.

He wanted to get as close to the mountain's edge as possible before turning west and making his way to the cave entrance. He did not want to take a chance of being discovered by those beasts. He came to the edge of the mountains and latched on to a small cleft in the rock and pulled himself up. If he could get to a stable ledge, that would allow him to sneak closer to the cave entrance and listen in from the outcropping he had been on a few nights ago and minimize his risks of being discovered by staying above the Kapre's line of sight.

He made for another handhold, but it was just out of reach. He looked down, which was a bad idea. His vision blurred as he stared at the ground below him. He dug his leg into the rock wall and took a deep, calming breath before attempting to jump. He closed his eyes as he pushed off the wall. His fingers cramped as he barely secured the small sliver of stone. He felt he was going to lose his grip but made for another hold with his right hand and stabilized himself.

He pulled up to a ledge and rested for a moment. The sun was now hidden despite his elevated vantage point. He looked down again, and mist was settling on the ground below. He removed the stopper from his waterskin and sipped. He did not want to drink too deeply, as he may be out all night and would need to ration his water. Once he had caught his breath, he traipsed along the ledge toward the cave opening. As he neared the opening of the cave, he crouched low to the ground and pulled the hood over his head.

He could hear murmurs and gurgles coming from inside the cave but could not make out what was being said. He laid on his stomach and eased toward the edge. He slid his upper body over the edge of the cave and peered inside. Barrels of supplies lined the walls, and a fire blazed toward the back of the cave, illuminating an open room. A large makeshift table made from a plank of wood atop four of the barrels serving as the legs sat near the fire. Several Kapre, at least ten, were seated around it. They appeared to be arguing about something. One of the Kapre towered above the rest and was jabbing his meaty finger at something on the table, commanding the attention of the others.

REBORN

Tamm slid back onto the ledge. He was going to have to get closer in order to hear what they were planning. Whatever they were arguing about, he knew it involved Aleesia. He scanned the area for any other Kapre. The outside of the cave was clear. He worried there could be some guards roving the area, but he had not heard any since arriving and decided to risk it.

He slid down the side of the rock wall, trying to make as little noise as possible. Once he was safely on the ground, he slipped behind a tree and appraised his surroundings; still, no sight of enemies. He pulled his cloak closer to him and crept through the shadows. He reached the edge of the cave and peaked in. The argument was heated. He used the opportunity to slip into the cave and ducked behind a group of barrels. The bow restricted his movement in this confined space. He risked sliding it off of his shoulder and unlatched the quiver from his waist. He quietly slid a lid from one of the barrels and glanced inside. It was full of grain. He took a lid from another, and it was full of beans. The Kapre were supplied well enough to hold out in this cave for quite some time. He found a barrel that was half full of what looked to be black powder, and he hid his bow and quiver in it. He left the lid ajar so that he could distinguish it from the other barrels.

He made his way deeper into the cave, staying hidden behind the barrels. There were weapon stands along some of the walls in the cave that held claymores, battle axes, and spears. These Kapre were not here for a simple raid. They were prepared for a long siege and were armed for war.

Tamm settled in behind a group of wooden boxes and barrels. He could easily see the group of Kapre while remaining hidden. He could make out their conversation now. It was not as easy as it had been with Elvish. Theirs was a strange, guttural speech.

"I say we attack tonight, Uskang," one of the Kapre said. "I'm sick of waiting, and my gut is tired of this meal. I need meat."

"Silence, fool," Uskang growled. "We will attack when I say we attack. It will not be long now. I received word today from a scout. The reinforcements are only a few days out."

Uskang was the obvious leader of the group. Tamm was not familiar with the hierarchy of the Kapre and how their leadership functioned, but the others fell in line at his commands. He was at least three heads taller than Tamm and was barrel-chested with thick muscular legs.

"I grow bored with waiting," another said. "I haven't had a kill in over a week. I was so close when that human was snooping around the other day. I could smell him, but he eluded me. I hope he's there so I can rip his flesh from his bones when we are finally set free on that miserable town." He chomped his teeth at his comrades as they all broke into harsh laughter.

Tamm saw enough of his face to recognize him as the beast that had scaled the wall and nearly caught him during his last visit to the cave. He felt in his gut that this Kapre would do everything in his power to fulfill his boast.

"Silence," Uskang demanded. "We must finish tonight. Everything needs to be in place when our brothers arrive. I

REBORN

say we launch the assault in a fortnight. This will give us time to equip our brethren and break into assault teams."

"How many will we have?" another asked.

"That should have our number to just around one hundred," Uskang said. "That should be plenty to dispose of them. They do not have weapons. It will be a slaughter."

The Kapre cheered and pounded their fists against the table. Heat flushed Tamm's face as he listened to how little they thought about his people. He would not let them have their way. He would protect his people. He leaned closer to them with his hand grasping and releasing the handle of his dagger. *I'll show them no weapons*, he thought.

Uskang slammed his fist onto the table, calling the group's attention back to him. "Every night the lamplighter goes out at dusk to light the town's lamps. This will be the signal for us to launch the attack. When the first lamp is lit, the townspeople will begin to make their way indoors. That is when we will wipe this town from the map. All the land will know the power of the Kapre has returned."

Tamm's knees ached from being crouched behind the barrels. He shifted his weight and lost his balance, bumping into one of the casks. The Kapre became silent and looked in his direction. Tamm held his breath, not moving a muscle. The Kapre that had almost caught him the last time stood from the table and sniffed the air. He drew a short sword from his waist and stalked toward Tamm's hiding place.

Tamm's heart raced, pounding against his chest. He knew he was cornered by beings much stronger and more proficient in swordsmanship than he was. He drew the dagger from its sheath without making a noise. He looked around to find a way out, then remembered what Linsyn had told him. If he gets in trouble, feel free to use some of what he had learned.

"Looky what we have here," the Kapre said, peering over the top of the casks at Tamm with murderous intent. "I don't have to wait until the assault to taste blood after all."

Rather than show fear, Tamm smiled up at the Kapre and winked at him before plunging his dagger through its foot. The Kapre bellowed in pain. Tamm withdrew the blade and shoved the barrels toward the remaining Kapre.

He darted toward the cave entrance. His eyes searched the other barrels for the one with the lid ajar. Recognizing the correct cask, he reached deep into the power inside him and allowed it flow out. "*Gaoth.*" The barrel flew forward, spilling the contents onto the cave floor. He let the power continue flowing forward, pushing the bow and quiver closer to the door and leaving a trail of the black powder.

The Kapre had recovered from the initial shock and were chasing Tamm through the cave. They all had their weapons drawn and roared a battle cry that echoed off the walls of the cave. Tamm's ears rang from the roar. He glanced over his shoulder and had some distance between him and the Kapre, but they were closing the gap.

Tamm scooped the bow and quiver from the ground. He tossed the quiver over his shoulder and knocked an arrow as he ran. He could hear the warriors closing in on him, but he dared not slow to look over his shoulder. He slid to a stop just outside the cave and turned toward the charging Kapre, drawing the bowstring to his ear. They slowed their pace and growled at him.

"You expect to defeat us all with only a bow?" Uskang taunted in Tamm's native language. "You humans are pathetic."

"You are wise," Tamm said in Kapresee. "Able to speak my language. That's impressive. Do you know any other languages? Maybe the language of the ancients?"

Uskang looked surprised. "You speak mine language? Alas, you do not frighten me, boy. Magic is dead. Your king ensured that. The elves and dwarves combined could not defeat us before. Your pathetic race will fare no better."

Tamm chuckled. "We will see about that." He loosed the arrow at the feet of the Kapre. "*Lasair.*" The arrow burst into flames as it struck the black powder on the floor of the cave opening, sending flames rushing into the cave. The Kapre dove to the ground as an explosion rang out from the cave. Tamm sprinted back toward town with the war cries of the Kapre still ringing in his ears.

THIRTEEN

Tamm arrived at Linsyn's just after midnight. He tried the door, but it was latched from the inside. He imagined the latch in his mind and whispered the word, and the latch lifted, allowing him entrance into the hut. He sat the bow, quiver, and satchel on the ground by the door and drank a long swallow from his waterskin. His breath was still racing, but he tried to rein it in so he would not frighten Linsyn awake.

Tamm knocked softly on Linsyn's door. "Linsyn, it's me. I'm back. I need to tell you what happened. I did what you said and used what I've learned. It was amazing!"

The door cracked open, and Linsyn peered through it. "I am pleased to see that you made it home safe. It would have been more polite if you had waited until morning."

REBORN

"This can't wait, Linsyn. I was able to gather quite a bit of information."

Linsyn hobbled over and took a seat at his writing desk. "Go on. You have woken me already. You might as well tell me what you have learned."

Tamm recounted the story of sneaking into the cave and learning about the plans the Kapre had to attack the town. He explained the expected day and time of the attack, how many warriors they would bring for the attack, and how well they were supplied. Lastly, he told him about his escape and being able to use the word *Lasair* for fire and igniting the cave with the black powder.

Linsyn released a breathless laugh. "I am impressed. You have learned much in such a short time. The information you gathered will prove to be invaluable in defending Aleesia. You did well using magic. Even if you had not gathered any information, you at least set them back by destroying some of their supplies."

Tamm smiled. "Thanks, Linsyn. That means a lot."

Linsyn did not speak for some time, stroking his beard as he stared out the window. "We need to discuss what else must be done. There is much to do if we are to ensure this town is properly defended. I doubt you will be pleased with my recommendations; however, I feel that it is the best course of action at this time. We need to notify the sheriff. We will need his guards and some soldiers to defend us."

"You're right," Tamm said, shrugging his shoulders. "I don't like that idea, but I do see the wisdom in it. We can't particularly defend ourselves. Those Kapre are well outfitted and could easily wipe out this entire place."

Linsyn pushed himself up from the chair. "Go home, Tammuz. Get some rest; you deserve it. Meet me here after you have slept, and I will go to the sheriff with you."

Tamm nodded and bid the old man farewell. As he walked back to his home, he appreciated the serenity of the town at night. No one was stirring; the town lamps had already died out. The only sound was a gentle breeze blowing in off the lake. He entered his home and eased up the stairs. He did not want to wake his parents but doubted that even if he did, they would ask him any questions about where he had been. They had not asked about much of anything Linsyn had him doing. As long as he was staying out of trouble, and he was as far as they were aware, they were content.

He opened the bedroom door and crawled into his bed. He looked over to the empty bed across the room, missing his talks with Echao. He hoped he would awaken soon. There was so much to tell him. Knowing Echao, he would want to jump right back into working as soon as he woke up. Tamm rolled over, away from the other bed, and closed his eyes. He was asleep in seconds.

◆◆◆◆◆

Tamm arose mid-morning, not feeling rested. He had dreamt of the fight with the Kapre again. This time he recognized the face. It was Uskang.

REBORN

He rolled out of bed and threw his clothes on and headed down to the kitchen to grab some food. His mother was cleaning the kitchen. "Long night?" she asked.

"Yes. Linsyn had me scouring the woods well into the night last night."

She slid a bowl of hot oats over to him. He gratefully took the bowl and devoured it. He thanked her with a kiss on the cheek and hurried out the door to find Linsyn. He made his way through the town, which was quite busy today. He looked around at all the people going on about their lives without any idea of the danger looming just inside the forest. He wondered how things would change if everyone knew that the town was about to be attacked in a fortnight.

He found Linsyn in front of his home, tending to his small garden. Linsyn looked up as he heard Tamm approaching. "Good morning. I trust you slept well."

Tamm rubbed his eyes, still tired from the previous night's events. "Actually, I didn't sleep much at all, but I suppose we should get going."

Linsyn gestured his hand toward the door. "Come inside for a moment. There is something we need to discuss."

Tamm looked at him, concerned, but walked into the hut. Linsyn closed the door behind him, then tossed something to him. Tamm caught it out of instinct and recognized it immediately. It was his bow. He had not taken the time to drop it off at the training grounds last night in his flight back to the town.

"I am so sorry, Linsyn. I must have been in such a rush last night that I just forgot."

"I know it was a mistake, but it is a mistake that could have dire consequences. If the sheriff had come by or another person from the town even, they would not have hesitated to turn me in. Just be careful in the future. And get this thing put away, please."

Tamm slung the bow across his shoulder and fastened the quiver at his waist. Linsyn shook his head. "Plan to go out in town like that, do you? You can hide it here for the time being, but once it is dark, you will need to sneak it back into the forest. It is dangerous to have it in town."

Tamm looked around but did not see any good hiding spots. He shrugged his shoulders at Linsyn, who took the bow and quiver from him.

"Here," Linsyn said. "*Oscail an chloch.*" A sound of scraping stone emanated from the hearth. The center stone in the foot of the fireplace slid back and exposed a hidden chamber inside. Linsyn placed the items inside. "*Sulje.*" Tamm winced as the grating sound of the stone sliding back into its original place. "Now, we can go to the sheriff."

Tamm and Linsyn left the house and made their way into the town. The sheriff could usually be found making rounds in the town; however, they walked the entirety of the town proper without finding him. Tamm recommended they check at the manor house. Maybe one of his servants could tell them where he would be.

They made the trek out of the town and up to the manor house. Tamm knocked on the door, and a servant in extravagant garb promptly answered the door. Linsyn announced that they were looking for the sheriff, and the servant motioned them in with a wave of his hand. Tamm thought it was odd that he did not speak. The house was immaculate and beautifully designed. It was more suited for someone in Rakx'den than in the quaint fishing village. The floors were marble and trim lined the ceiling. For a moment, Tamm was jealous of Alred for growing up in such affluence, but he stamped the feeling down.

The servant led them to a large open office with an oak desk, a suit of armor decorating each side. The sheriff was knelt beside a group of chests and was securing a lock to one of them. The servant stomped his foot on the ground, and Vorn stood and turned to the visitors. "Linsyn, to what do I owe the honor?"

Linsyn gave a slight nod of deference. "My apprentice has alerted me to some important information that I believe you should hear. It involves the safety of this town."

Vorn raised an eyebrow but did not appear to be impressed. "Tammuz has information that would protect this town?" He suppressed a laugh. "What could he possibly know that I don't already know?"

"This has to do with the attack on him and his brother the night of the Spring Festival," Linsyn replied.

Vorn rolled his eyes. "If this is about his so-called monster that attacked them, I have had my men check the woods, and they found nothing. Alred told me that it was dark, and he was not confident what he fought off to save the boys. In all honesty, I would more likely believe that they were arguing among themselves and got into a fight with one of them getting accidentally injured more than I would that some monster attacked this town. That is utterly ridiculous."

Tamm's face turned red. Not because he was angry that Vorn thought he was a liar but that it was Vorn's son and his cronies that had attacked Echao and caused his injuries. "Actually," Tamm said before being cut off by Linsyn, who gave him a stern look.

Linsyn rolled the staff around in his hand. Tamm knew he was frustrated, but he did well to keep it hidden. "I know you believe the boy to be hot-headed and a bit daft. I can assure you that he is quite intelligent and has proven to be an excellent asset to my work. His brother would not have survived without his efforts."

Vorn shrugged his shoulders. "I assume you are going to make a point eventually. The sooner, the better. I have been summoned by the king to the capital and need to be on my way."

"Very well," Linsyn said. "The boy went into the woods, seeking revenge on the beast that had nearly killed his brother. He stumbled across a cave near the mountains. He is fond of exploring and decided to go deeper into the cave. In it, he found several casks of food and supplies and racks of weapons. He did not know what to make of it at first, but then he heard some commotion outside the cave. On his way out, he made contact with several beasts that, by his description, I can only assume were Kapre."

"That is impossible," Vorn said, interrupting Linsyn. "They were eradicated decades ago. There have been no reports of them in at least one hundred years."

"Be that as it may, this is what he reports. The most concerning bit of information was that they appeared to be armed for a battle. He also reported that they were well supplied and could live in the forest for quite some time before needing to resupply. All we ask is that you request additional guards or maybe some soldiers to guard the town for the next few weeks."

"You realize that if I petition the king for a group of soldiers to defend Aleesia from an army of Kapre that I will be laughed out of court?" Vorn asked. "You do understand that it would be political suicide?"

Linsyn sighed. "Is the safety and security of this town not your number one priority? Is this not your sworn duty?"

Fire flashed in Vorn's eyes. "Do not lecture me on duty, old man! I would remind you of your own words just now. I am the sheriff, and I will not be disrespected."

"My apologies," Linsyn said. "I did not mean to cause offense. Whether or not you choose to believe him is up to you. I felt it my civic duty to notify you of what had been reported to me. Thank you for your time. We will see ourselves out. Good day."

"Good day," Vorn replied gruffly.

Linsyn led Tamm out of the house and down the street back toward the town. Tamm could tell by the pace the old man was keeping that he was angry. They did not speak for some time on their journey, but just outside of reaching some of the first stores on the path, Linsyn stopped and pulled Tamm to the side. "I feel we will not be getting any help from the sheriff or the one who currently sits on the throne. We are on our own."

"I'm sorry," Tamm said. "It's my fault. He doesn't trust anything I say."

Linsyn shook his head. "No. He is a stubborn, power-hungry man who does not want to look like a fool to the nobility. We will have to defend this town ourselves."

"I have felt the power inside you," Tamm said. "I have no doubts that you are a strong mage, but I think it's going to take more than the two of us to defend against over one hundred Kapre."

"You are correct. It is going to take an army. But the question is, where do we find one." Linsyn stroked his long, white beard. "Ah, go and see Kèlris. Tell him of all that you were able to discover about the Kapre's plans. Ask him if we gather an army, will he arm them. He has defied the king before. He will not fear to do so again."

"Even if he agrees," Tamm said, "where are we going to get an army?"

"That comes next, my good boy. That comes next. We shall defend this town. Do you feel the shifting? There is change coming. I feel that the attack on Aleesia will set many more things in motion, things that will change both of our lives drastically."

Tamm looked at Linsyn with wide-eyed surprise but also in fear of what he was implying. "I've always wanted to find adventure. I was so desperate to leave this town to get it. Now it seems it has found me."

REBORN

Linsyn put his hand on Tamm's shoulder. "Are you ready? Go find Kèlris. Once that is settled, find me, and we will move on to gathering our forces."

Tamm bid Linsyn farewell and took the road that bypassed around the town center and towards the blacksmith's shop. He went directly to the forge and found Kèlris hammering out a glowing orange piece of steel. He did not look up as Tamm walked in. Tamm knew better than to interrupt him while working a piece of steel before it had been quenched. He had received several severe scoldings as a child while learning the basics of the forge.

Kèlris thrust the steel back into the forge to heat back up, then turned to acknowledge Tamm. "What brings you by today, son?" He tossed his gloves on a table and slid his apron off before embracing Tamm in a tight hug. Tamm had not spoken with his father much recently. Linsyn had been keeping him so busy. Kèlris was usually in the forge before Tamm left in the morning, and his parents were asleep by the time he arrived home.

Tamm returned the embrace and pointed to a chair next to them. There was only one chair in the forge. It was where Kèlris would sit when sketching out ideas for new swords or when writing up invoices for his customers. Kèlris looked at Tamm with concern. Tamm gave him a half-hearted smile in an attempt to put him at ease.

Kèlris took a seat and waited for an explanation. Tamm cleared his throat and recounted his recent adventures involving the Kapre, leaving out the parts that involved magic. He went into detail regarding the impending assault, when it would likely take place, and the need for arms and armor to defend the town.

Kèlris leaned back in his chair and took a deep breath, considering all the information. "So, the king is willing to send soldiers to help protect us?"

"Well, not exactly," Tamm said. "Linsyn and I spoke with the sheriff, but he didn't believe us. He's been summoned to court by the king, but it is unlikely that he will broach the subject while in court. We need local men to stand and fight."

Kèlris stood and slid his apron and gloves back on. "Our people were once warriors. I did my best to train you and Echao in our ways. Unfortunately, not many of our men still feel this way. This king has weakened us as a people." He took the steel from the forge and examined the hue before sitting it on the anvil and grabbing the hammer."

"So, you won't help?" Tamm asked.

Kèlris chuckled. "I never said that. This is my home. I will defend it to the death. I can't answer for the rest of the men, but you have my hammer. As many as agree to fight, I can assure you they will have a capable weapon to use."

"Thank you, Father." Tamm approached to embrace him, but Kèlris just held up a hand and showed Tamm the hammer. Tamm nodded, understanding the gesture, and thanked him again as he left the forge.

By the time Tamm made it back to Linsyn's hut, the sun had gone down, and the air was crisp blowing in off the lake. The lamplighter was out lighting the lamps around town. Several of the townsmen were making their way into the tavern. Tamm pushed the door of the hut open, and Linsyn was already standing near the doorway, his staff in hand. "Shall we?" Linsyn asked as he pointed his staff to the door.

Tamm held the door open as Linsyn threw on a cloak and walked out into the brisk evening. Tamm pulled the door closed and followed after him. "Where are we going?"

"I could use a drink. You are of age now if you feel you need one also."

"I think I'll pass," Tamm said. "Thanks."

They entered the tavern. No one looked up from their drinks as they weaved between tables. Linsyn plopped down in a stool at the bar and ordered a drink. Tamm sat beside him and waved off the bartender as he looked to him for his order. Linsyn looked to Tamm and raised his eyebrows. "Are you sure you don't want to reconsider? You may need some liquid courage shortly."

"What do you mean?"

Linsyn gestured to the patrons in the bar. "These are the men you will need to recruit to your service. They may not look like much, sitting here drinking away some sorrow or another; however, I can assure you that if you can persuade them, they will faithfully stand with you through any command."

Tamm nearly tipped backward off of his stool. "I have to recruit these men? How do you suggest that I do that?" He lowered his voice to a whisper. "If I mention fighting or using weapons, I will be in chains before we can make it out of this tavern."

"I think you would be surprised. There is a reason these men are in here drinking. They are not content with their lot in life. They dream of an opportunity to change the hand they have been dealt. This could be the dream they have been waiting for."

Tamm looked around the room. He recognized all of these men; he had grown up with them his entire life. Some of them were not much older than he was, some were his father's age, and a few others were not much younger than Linsyn. In one of the corner tables, he saw Adina's father sitting quietly with a pint. Beyl was a stout man. He had served as a soldier in the king's army for a short time but had an injury that resulted in his discharge. Adina did not speak of it often, but Tamm had gotten the feeling that Beyl spent much of his time in the tavern.

"What am I supposed I say to earn their trust?"

"That is up to you, my boy. I am here and will help when needed. He took a swig of the foamy, yellow liquid and rose from his stool. "Ready?"

Linsyn walked out to the center of the pub before clearing his voice, bringing silence into the room. "My good fellows, you all know Master Tammuz, son of Kèlris. He is now my apprentice and is progressing splendidly in his knowledge of the healing arts. Due to this, he spends much of his time in the forest, searching for herbs and molds and the like that we use for our craft. He has made a significant discovery during his recent trip that I believe you all must hear." He motioned his arm to Tamm to give him the floor.

Tamm ambled to the center of the floor as Linsyn slipped back to his seat. He glanced around the room, many of the eyes were on him, but some of them had gone back to sipping their drinks. A nervous cough escaped when he tried to speak. "Men of Aleesia, I am in need, no, this town is in need of your assistance." The men who had gone back to drinking lifted their heads at the words. "As Linsyn said, I have been spending a lot of time in the woods of late. I came across a cave on my latest trip. In that cave, I discovered enough supplies to adequately outfit a small army. There were weapons, food, and even black powder."

Several of the men gasped, and many began murmuring to each other. "That is not the most distressing of the finds. As I was leaving the cave to report the discovery to the sheriff, I was confronted by the owners of the supplies. A group of Kapre have set up near our lands and are planning an attack on our beloved town."

Many of the men laughed and scoffed at him. Tamm tried to regain their attention. "I tell you the truth. I requested an increase in troops from the sheriff, but he scoffed at me also."

"You jest. Linsyn, have you been training him in comedy too?" one of them called out.

Tamm trudged back to his seat and sat down. Linsyn gave him a half-smile as he stood and patted the young man on the back before taking the center of the floor. The raucous laughter and talking from the men made Tamm want to hide in shame.

Linsyn raised his staff in the air, then struck it against the floor three times. The sudden silence caused Tamm to look up at Linsyn in amazement of the respect he commanded. "Before anyone says another word, I want you to listen. Sit back, enjoy your drink but listen. Everything the boy has said is true in its entirety. Now prepare for another truth that I feel many of you have forgotten."

The men looked around at one another but stayed silent. Linsyn glanced over at Tamm and winked before he continued the story. "Our people are warriors. We came to this land as sea voyagers seeking asylum from a tyrannical king. We arrived in this land seeking a home, and instead found a land that was already fraught with a war of its own. We settled in these hills and mountains that we now call home but were pulled into a war that was not ours to fight, but we made it our own."

"Although we fought against all the races in the beginning, King Riehner saw that the Kapre were the true enemy. He secured alliances with the elves and dwarves and founded the Battlemages. He brought magic together with our skill with sword and shield and ushered in an unprecedented period of peace before being overthrown by the usurper that now sits on the throne."

There were gasps among the men. Tamm's eyes felt like they were bulging. He had never heard someone speak of the king in this way, and so openly, without any fear of retaliation. He had always felt similarly, although he had never spoken it out loud. Kèlris had always told him to watch his tongue, as the king had agents throughout the kingdom.

Linsyn was now wringing his staff in his hands. "We have been softened by laws and regulations set forth by a false king, and now we are left vulnerable and unable to defend ourselves against an old enemy. The Kapre have returned my friends. If you sit idly by, everything and everyone you know and love will be destroyed in less than a month. This land, our people, need you. Reach deep inside and find your warrior heritage. Stand and fight. Tammuz and I will stand and fight regardless of your decision, and we will gladly give our lives in defense of this great land. Can we count on you?"

The silence in the tavern was deafening. No one moved. Tamm could hear the breathing of those around him. Beyl stood, holding onto the table for support. "Even if we wanted to fight, what would we fight with? Sticks? Pitchforks?"

Kèlris walked forward to stand beside Linsyn. "I testify today that I will stand with the people of this town. Anyone who stands with me can rest assured that they will be armed as well as any soldier in service to the king. You will not defend this town with any less."

Linsyn placed an arm around Kèlris. Tamm walked across the floor to join them. "What say you, men?" Linsyn asked. "Will you stand with us? Will you fight our ancient enemy and rid the world of them once and for all? Will you defend our people, our home?"

Silence. That is all Tamm could hear, a deafening silence. Then, Beyl limped forward and stood before them. "I may not be able to fight as I once did, but you will have my sword all the same."

Linsyn placed a fist across his heart, and Beyl returned the gesture, bowing his head. Beyl came and stood beside Tamm. Other men in the room began to look around to each other. Slowly, in twos and threes, the men began to stand and walk forward to join the others in the center of the room. The bartender poured drinks, and all the men made toasts to Linsyn, Tamm, and Kèlris.

Most of the men drank well into the night. Linsyn insisted that they stay with the men. Many times through the night, men would come by and clap Tamm on the back and mention how brave he was to stand up to the Kapre and make it back to town alive. He would smile politely and thank them.

Linsyn and Kèlris discussed among themselves for a while before calling Tamm over. They explained that many of the men were considered leaders among the town and could be trusted to pull in some of the other citizens to stand and fight without alerting the guards. Kèlris recommended that Tamm take Beyl out to the training grounds and show him around and that he and Tamm could begin training some of the men in private.

Tamm agreed. He was thankful that Kèlris had shown up to the tavern. Tamm learned that Linsyn had sent a note to him earlier in the day, inviting him to meet him tonight.

Tamm walked over to Beyl and discussed the idea of touring the training grounds with him. Beyl wanted to get started as soon as possible and suggested they meet the following afternoon so that he could assess the area before summoning the men. Tamm verified the time to meet and then notified Linsyn of the decision.

Tamm was having a hard time staying awake. The hour was late, and several of the townsmen had already passed out and were sleeping in booths and on the floor. Tamm bid goodnight to Linsyn. Kèlris had left already to not raise suspicions and to be able to rise early to get to the forge. He had much work ahead of him with less than two weeks to prepare the weapons. Tamm left the tavern and headed home. He was asleep before he could pull his blanket up to his chin.

FOURTEEN

†

Tamm woke just before lunch. He rubbed the sleep from his eyes and stumbled down the stairs. The house was dead quiet. He called out for his mother, but there was no answer. He snatched an apple from a basket on the kitchen table. It was sweet but soft, a little too ripe for his liking. He searched the pantry for something else to eat, but it was bare. His mother must have gone to the market to purchase some food.

He gathered his things and made his way to Linsyn's hut. Linsyn was standing over Echao and appeared to be busy doing something. Tamm rushed in, afraid Echao may have become worse. He had been so involved with everything going on around town recently that he had not given much thought to Echao and his wounds over the last few days. He felt ashamed at the thought.

He leaned around Linsyn to see what he was doing. Echao was sitting up on the cot. His eyes were open, and he was drinking a cup of tea. "Brother," he said. "How good it is to see you."

Tamm's vision blurred behind the tears welling up in his eyes. He rushed to his brother and wrapped him in a fierce hug. Echao grunted, and Tamm loosened the embrace some, then Echao returned the hug. "It's alright. Just still a little sore."

"I was afraid I would never get to speak to you again," Tamm said. "I'm so sorry I wasn't able to protect you."

"You don't need to apologize. If it weren't for you and your quick thinking, I wouldn't be here today. You'll make a fine healer, Tamm."

Tamm wiped his eyes. "Linsyn did most of the work. I just had to carry you here, which was no small feat."

They all three laughed, but Echao flinched a little, which caused Tamm and Linsyn to cease the laughter.

Echao slid down from the cot and tested his legs. He wobbled from side to side at first but did not fall. "I will heal. I would like to see Lily. Could you arrange that, Linsyn?"

Linsyn shook his head and comforted him with a light touch. "I do not believe that is a good idea at this time. Tamm, can you fill him in on our current situation? I will make some tea and a little something to help with the pain."

Tamm explained about the Kapre and the pending attack, the sheriff leaving them without any assistance, and having to recruit men from the town who were willing to stand and fight to defend the city. Echao appeared angry but did not interrupt. Tamm went on to explain that Kèlris was taking a considerable risk in outfitting the men for the town's defense and that, even with the number of men that had volunteered so far, it would be difficult to repel the attackers.

"This is why I do not believe it a good idea to speak with Lily yet," Linsyn told him. "As far as Alred knows, you are on death's door. We still have the upper hand as long as he feels you are still near death. He will be concerned that if you die, an official inquest will be conducted, and he may be implicated for the death. Once you have healed, that no longer hangs over his head, and he is free to do as he wills, even investigate and report us for mustering men and arms for a battle. He will likely not assist in the fighting either way. Deep down, I believe he is a coward."

Tamm smiled at hearing how little Linsyn thought of Alred. "Where do we begin? This is all so overwhelming."

"You will have my bow and daggers," Echao said.

"No," Linsyn retorted. "You are weak and still need to rest. The battle is still at least a week or two away. Much may change by then. I think it best if you can assist with the planning for now. You need to stay here until you have recovered."

Echao looked at Linsyn with disappointment and then back to Tamm, his eyes pleading him to interject. Tamm shook his head. "Linsyn is right. I will need your help with planning. Once you have recovered, you may help with training the men. Don't be so willing to rush back into battle."

Echao acquiesced. He and Tamm discussed strategies for training the men and preparing for the attack. Tamm had an idea that would stage the town in a way to not disrupt normal activities so that Alred would not catch any trace of their plans, but more so that the Kapre would think them none the wiser and still launch their attack as planned. When the lamplighter begins his nightly duty, he would have an ambush waiting for the beasts when they launched their attack.

Echao agreed with Tamm's plan to not disrupt day to day activities; however, he wanted to ensure the women, children, and elderly were safely away before the battle began. He recommended that Tamm speak with Lily and Adina and have them set up transport for the women, children, and elderly to take boats to Delocia before the battle.

Tamm sat on the floor as they bounced ideas between them. Echao was getting tired and kept dozing off while Tamm was brainstorming. He left Echao to rest and went to find Adina and Lily.

Tamm wandered through town, looking around, hoping to find the ladies in town. He searched in several of the shops he knew they frequented, but they were nowhere to be found. He explored the lakeshore; Adina would sit there and read some afternoons, but they were not there either. He went by Adina's home, but her father was not in the mood to talk at the time, grunting something about her not being there and having a headache.

He jogged through the streets, heading back in the direction of his home. Someone was standing by the split in the road that went toward his house. As he got closer, he could make out that there were three of them, a man and two women. He picked up the pace when he recognized Alred, waving his arms wildly. His voice boomed at the two girls, his tone raging.

Tamm raced up to them and placed an arm around the shoulder of each of the girls and ushered them back towards his house as he whispered to them. "Come with me; we must speak privately." Adina and Lily fell in line and allowed Tamm to lead them away from Alred.

"Where do you get off interrupting nobility when the lessers are being lectured?" Alred roared at Tamm as he walked away. "I thought you would have learned your lesson by now, boy. I am not one to be played with. Your brother found out the hard way. I suppose you will also."

Tamm's lip curled into a snarl. Adina tried to grab his hand, but he had spun away, and her hand grasped empty air. He drew the dagger from his belt. "You want a scar on the other side to match?" he asked, pointing the blade at the scar on the side of Alred's face.

Alred drew his sword, and Tamm heard the girls gasp behind him. Tamm glanced back at them, his eyes narrowed. "Go, I will deal with him quickly." The girls backed away, and Tamm's eyes locked with Adina's, and he winked. He turned back to Alred, who was spinning the sword in his wrist.

Alred smiled wickedly. "I'm going to enjoy this more than I did running your brother through"

REBORN

Tamm rushed at Alred, dagger held downward in his hand with the spine of the blade resting against his forearm. Kèlris had taught him that this was the most effective grip when fighting, leaving his lead hand to deflect and parry other blows. The sword whirred at his neck; Alred was going to try to kill him immediately. Tamm felt the power well up inside him, and he wanted to release it, but he pushed back the feeling. He could not allow anyone to know he was able to use magic. It would mean an instant death sentence, and it may implicate Linsyn as his teacher.

Tamm slipped around the blade as he pushed it to the side with his left hand. He stepped into Alred, placing his leg behind Alred's, and brought his elbow into Alred's teeth. He drove his elbow forward, causing Alred to stumble over his leg and fall backward to the ground, the sword spilling from his hand, clanging against the street. Tamm followed him to the ground, pinning his arm against the ground as he brought the blade up to Alred's throat. He stared him in the eye; Alred tried to hide his fear, but Tamm could sense it, and he felt empathy for the boy.

"You killed him," Tamm shouted. "I should kill you right here and now, rid the world of your foul soul." He pushed the blade forward against Alred's throat, and a small drop of blood trickled onto the blade. Adina shrieked behind him, and Lily started crying. He glanced over his shoulder and then back to Alred. "But I'm not like you. I don't run around killing people because they make me angry."

Alred narrowed his eyes at Tamm, and he could feel the hate emanating from him. Tamm pushed close into Alred's face. "You killed him, but I'm going to grant you mercy, for now. But if you ever cross me again, I will make sure that not only all of Aleesia knows but that all of Iradell knows that you are a murderer. I will see you tried, and I will see you hanged. Do you understand me?"

Alred stared back at Tamm, not blinking. The corner of his mouth twitched, but he said nothing. "You would do well to answer me," Tamm said as he slid the point of the dagger between a rib, just above his heart. "Or, I could just end it all now and be home in time for dinner." He pushed on the hilt of the dagger.

Alred gasped with pain as the dagger tip penetrated the skin. "I, I understand." He twitched under Tamm's weight. "I understand," he said, louder this time.

"I thought you would see it my way," Tamm said, rolling off the boy and standing up. He picked up Alred's sword and ran through a series of maneuvers with it that Kèlris had taught him. "This is a fine weapon. It's a shame it spends much of its time on the ground." Tamm tossed the sword back to Alred, and he caught it by the hilt, sliding it into the sheath at his waist. "Go now, let our family mourn in peace."

Alred turned on his heel and trudged back toward town, his head hung low. Adina rushed up and wrapped Tamm in an embrace. Tears ran down her cheeks, and Tamm could feel them against his cheek. He hugged her back and could smell the lavender in her hair. He closed his eyes as he breathed it in but was thrust back to reality when he heard Lily sobbing.

REBORN

She was on her knees, tears pouring down her face. He and Adina ran to her and knelt beside her. "What's wrong?" he asked. "The fight is over. He's gone."

Lily wiped her eyes and nose on the lace sleeve of her blouse. "He is gone? He is truly gone?"

Tamm nodded at her. "Yes. I sent him away. He can't hurt you now."

Lily looked up at Tamm, and he saw such sadness in her eyes. "Echao is truly gone? Alred killed him?"

Adina sniffled and wrapped her arm around Lily. Tamm cast his eyes to the ground. He had been trying to help. It was the first thing that came to his mind. He thought that if Alred believed Echao had died and that Tamm had evidence that he was the killer, that he would tread lightly around his family and friends and not cause any more trouble. He had not planned on hurting Lily. It had not even crossed his mind that she was not privy to the fact that Echao was alive and was healing in Linsyn's hut.

Tamm stood and reached a hand out to Lily. She took it, and he helped her to stand. She leaned in and wrapped her arms around him, sniffling in his ear. "What am I going to do, Tamm? We had so many plans; I'm so lost without him. These last few weeks have been misery. I have been coming to spend time with your mother just to feel closer to him."

Tamm patted her back. "Lily, he's not dead."

She pulled away from him, confusion flooding her face. "Do not jest with me, Tammuz!"

"I tell you the truth. He lives. He is with Linsyn now. I only told Alred that to get him to leave us and hopefully not bother you two again. I am sorry, Lily. I didn't mean to hurt you."

"He lives? He truly lives?" Lily asked, bouncing on her toes in giddiness.

Tamm nodded and saw that Adina's smile stretched across her face as she wiped a tear from her eye.

"Come, Adina. We must go to see him now." Lily grabbed Adina by the hands and spun her in circles.

Tamm cleared his throat, interrupting the girls' celebration. "That is not going to be possible. We don't want anyone else to know he is well. I have discussed this in length with Linsyn and Echao, and it's just not the right time."

Lily's arms dropped to her side in disappointment. Tamm rushed to her side. "I didn't say you couldn't see him, just not right now. I will tell him I saw you, and I can give him a message, or a letter if you would like."

The smile returned to Lily's face, and she grabbed Adina's hand. "That would be lovely."

"Consider it done. In the meantime, there is something I need to speak with you two about. It's actually what brought me here. Come with me to my house. I'm sure mother will have something we can snack on while we talk."

Tamm led the girls back to his home. They sat at the kitchen table and nibbled on some fruit, bread, and cheese his mother had set out for them. Mariah called Kèlris in from the forge so that they could all be privy to the discussion. Tamm started by telling them about finding the footprint and then told them the details of the fight with Alred. Adina and Lily sat close and comforted each other when the details of the fighting and Echao's wounds were mentioned. He told them about the difficulty they had in healing Echao and how he and Linsyn were finally able to stop the bleeding but leaving out the parts about magic. He concluded the tale with his most recent venture into the woods and discovering that the Kapre were planning an attack on the town.

Kèlris stood in silence as the tale concluded. Mariah's face was slack, her mouth hanging open. "You knew about this?" she asked, pointing at Kèlris. "I can't believe it. My husband, keeping secrets."

"My love, it was for your own protection. You know I wouldn't deliberately hide anything from you."

Mariah crossed her arms and huffed at him. "Well, at least my boy is better. When will he return home?"

"About that," Tamm said, dropping his arms to his side. "As I said before, it's best if the sheriff and Alred believe him to be dead, or at least still very ill. We don't want them snooping around more than needed. There is a hard fight ahead of us. They are not willing to help. So, the less they know, the better."

"What about us?" Adina asked. "How can we help?"

"You have one of the most important jobs," Tamm said. "You must convince the women and children to load boats in the night and flee to safety in Delocia."

Lily shook her head, but Adina shot to her feet. "I will do nothing of the sort, Tammuz. What makes you think that I would flee my home like some coward while those dear to me sacrifice their lives? I can do more to help here. I may not be a fighter, but I can be of service."

Tamm stood and brushed a lock of her strawberry blonde hair behind her ear. He had to admit, she had a fierce spirit, and she was cute when she was determined to get her way. "I cannot fight while worrying about something happening to you. If Echao is spending his time worrying whether Lily got to safety or not, he can't effectively plan. We don't want there to be anyone here that is not going to be on the battlefield. We don't need to be distracted when so much is on the line."

Adina plopped back into her seat, crossing her arms. "I suppose you make a valid point. We will do as you ask. When do we leave?"

"I will get a more specific time after I've spoken with Linsyn and Echao. There is still planning to do, but I would guess by the end of the week. We need to have everyone out in time to ensure a safe distance before the battle but not so early as to raise suspicion among the Kapre."

"Very well," Kèlris said, moving toward the door. "If there is nothing else, I must get back to the forge. Supplying a group of farmers with military-grade weapons takes some time." He elbowed Tamm in the shoulder playfully as he slipped out of the room.

"I must go, also," Tamm said. "Unfortunately, it takes quite a bit of time to train a group of farmers to fight like soldiers, too." He passed Adina and brushed his hand against hers as he strode out of the room. She smiled at him and looked away, blushing.

Tamm made his way back to Linsyn's, where he and Beyl stood outside the hut talking in hushed tones. The men greeted him as he strolled past and took a seat on the steps. Beyl tilted his head, looking at Tamm as if he had two heads.

"What is it?" Tamm asked.

"I am trying to see what my daughter sees in a lazy boy like you?" He laughed and clapped Linsyn jovially on the back. "Am I right, Linsyn? Get your things, Tamm; we have work to do."

Linsyn chuckled, then coughed to hide the laughter. Tamm cut his eyes at the old man as he entered the hut. Echao was sleeping on a pallet against the wall. He must have been tired of sleeping on the cot. He walked closer to Echao and called his name softly a few times, but he did not answer. Faint snores escaped his partially open mouth.

Convinced that he was asleep, Tamm turned his attention to the fireplace. "*Oscail an chloch*," he whispered, and the hearthstone rolled away. He reached inside and collected the bow and quiver resting near the top. "*Sulje.*" The stone slid back into place. Tamm slung the bow over his shoulder and pulled a dark cloak off the rack, carefully obscuring the bow and then slipping the hood over his head.

Tamm led Beyl into the woods and down the old game trails until they arrived at the training grounds. Beyl appraised the hay-stuffed torsos placed around the grove. "Your family did well, Tamm. This is quite impressive."

Tamm smiled at the compliment. "There's some weapons hidden in the stumps. Do you think it's good enough?"

"Aye," Beyl said, shaking his head. "I can work with this."

They walked back to the treeline, but stayed hidden in the brush, watching as several of the men from town walked toward the woods. They entered by twos and threes. "We are going to have to work on that," Beyl said. "Before you can fight, you must first be able to use common sense. Walking to the training ground like that is sure to get us all caught and strung from a tree."

"Let's just go," Tamm said. "Looks like we are going to have our work cut out for us."

They entered the treeline and split up, taking a different route to the training ground as to not raise suspicion. It was late afternoon, but enough of the sun was still up that they could easily make their way through trees. They entered the training grounds with at least fifty men. Most huddled up in the middle of the grove while a few more straggled in.

Tamm went to the fallen trees and collected the weapons; swords, long axes, spears, and bows, and passed them out in the crowd. The men seemed eager to get a weapon of their own, but most held them awkwardly. Several times, Tamm had to stop training to tell one of them to get their sword tip out of the dirt. To have come from such a long lineage of warriors, some of these men appeared hopeless.

Beyl and Tamm trained them well into dark and then had them return to the town in groups no larger than two. Tamm exited the woods near his house and gave Beyl, who was hiding in the treeline, a signal to let him know it was clear to send out another small group.

He was exhausted and just wanted to get in the bed. He had not been getting enough sleep recently with all the planning and training. The men worked hard, but it was going to take a lot to get them in fighting shape. He did not see himself getting much rest until after they secured a victory in the upcoming battle.

The moon was high overhead by the time all of the men were out of the forest. Beyl clapped him on the back with his big, meaty hand. "You did good, kid. You may make a decent warrior one day.

"Thanks, Beyl. That means a lot."

"Don't go getting soft on me, kid. Go get some rest. We have to do this all over again tomorrow."

FIFTEEN

The next two weeks passed in a blur. Tamm was continually running between the clinic, the forge, the forest, and the training grounds. He could barely recall any of the conversations he had. Echao had been healing well but was still not back to full health. He had proven invaluable in the strategy meetings, providing ideas and recommendations that were brilliant compared with some of the other ideas that were tossed around.

Tamm had recommended keeping their everyday life as normal as possible and then launching an ambush as the Kapre attacked. He felt that would give them the upper hand and limit the risks for casualties. Echao had come up with an idea to line the rooftops with archers and to scatter hay at the town entrances so that when the Kapre attacked, the archers would light arrows and ignite the hay, trapping the Kapre inside the town and hopefully cause panic in their ranks.

There were only a few men who could accurately fire an arrow, so Tamm was tasked as an archer, as was Echao. Echao was an outstanding archer, and although he was not back to full health, he had agreed to stay on the roof and not directly engage in the fighting. Beyl had been given command over the infantry. Their warriors numbered less than one hundred and comprised of a few rows of pikemen followed by light infantry with swords. Some of the men had also been trained with small axes, which could be thrown during a charge, should the need arise.

Adina and Lily had done well getting the women and children to Delocia. It had taken longer than expected to transport them all by boat. Too many boats leaving in the night would have been suspicious. Adina and Lily had stayed behind despite pleas from himself, Echao, and Linsyn. When Tamm had asked Beyl to have Adina go to Delocia, he only said that she was a headstrong woman like her mother. They were leaving this morning, and Tamm was glad for that. If his understanding of the Kapres' plan was correct, they would attack tonight as the lamplighter lit the lamps around the town. Unfortunately, he did not know from where they would launch the attack. He assumed it would be from the north, near the entrance to the forest that was closest to their cave, but he did not know much about Kapre military tactics. He had tried reading some of Linsyn's books that documented some of the battles from the Great War but found little that was useful.

Tamm had stayed the night at Linsyn's the previous night to be near to Echao. He found comfort being near his brother, knowing he supported him in his decision to stand and fight. Despite being exhausted, he had a hard time sleeping. He and Echao laid awake talking about all sorts of things, from what they thought would happen and how things would change after the fight, to Echao's feelings for Lily and Tamm's budding feelings for Adina, to their fears of going into a real battle for the first time. Tamm wondered if his ancestors had felt the same way before a battle, if they had the same feeling he did in the pit of his stomach. He knew he could just as easily die as he could survive, and he accepted that fact, as long as his sacrifice meant that his family and friends survived, and he was able to protect the town.

He was also afraid to go to sleep. He did not want to have the nightmare again. It had haunted him more frequently over the last several days, and it unnerved him. Now that he had been face-to-face with the Kapre in the forest, he recognized their faces in his dream. He was unsure if they had been the same before he had seen them in person or if they took on the faces of the ones who had attacked him. Either way, he died in his dream, and he was determined to do everything he could to prevent that fate.

The sun had only been up for a short time. Linsyn had not yet come out of his room, so Tamm assumed he was still sleeping. Echao was snoring, but he would awaken soon. The sun slipped past the shudders and scattered light along the floor. Tamm sat up on the side of the cot and stretched. He was still sleepy but could not will himself back to sleep. He had too much to do today. He wanted to make sure that everything went as planned.

He slid his boots on, still covered in dry mud from spending so much time in the forest. Early spring rain saturated the ground. He hoped it would dry enough for the hay to burn tonight. He traipsed over to a table and picked up an apple, then eased the door open. A low squeak escaped as the door freed itself from the frame. "Where do you think you're off to?" a voice asked from behind him.

He turned to find Echao with his head propped in his hand. His head slipped, and he almost fell back to the pillow before correcting himself. "You were leaving without saying goodbye," he joked. He sat up and rubbed the sleep from his eyes.

Tamm eased the door back shut, careful not to wake Linsyn. "I was going to the forge to help father stage the weapons before everyone starts moving around the town. Best to do it before Alred and his goons start snooping around."

Echao bent and pulled his boots on. "Well, why didn't you say so? That sounds like a perfect way to start the day. To be honest, it will be nice to get out of this shack. Besides, Mother will probably have breakfast ready, or soon will, and I have not seen her in a while. You never know, this may be our last day to live."

Tamm shook his head. "If you come along, you have to stay hidden. Alred still does not know that you have healed. He believes you're dead. But, I know the real reason you want out of here. You know that Lily is leaving for Delocia today, and you want to see her before she leaves."

"Do you blame me?" Echao tossed his hands in the air. "I haven't seen the girl in over a month. I know you think this is just young love, but mark my words brother, I will marry her someday."

"I don't doubt that you will." He tossed a cloak to Echao. "And put this on. We don't want anyone seeing you out. Hopefully, things will be different after the battle." Tamm hoped that if he could show his worth in protecting the town, that the sheriff would no longer see him as just some trouble maker and would have Alred and his fellow guards ease up on his friends and family.

The boys walked to the forge and found Kèlris already there. He was scurrying about the large room, loosening lids on several casks. He peeked inside and smiled. He withdrew a sword and tossed it to Tamm. "Try that out."

Tamm twirled the sword in his hand. It was one of the most balanced swords he had ever held. It was a steel longsword with a basic steel crossguard and pommel with simple black leather wrappings on the grip. It was plain but lethal. He could tell that it was an excellent weapon, made for war and not for show. He tried to toss it back to Kèlris, but he waved him off. "You use it. I think it fits you well. It was made for great things, but others may not see its worth because they assume it's plain." He took a leather scabbard off the table and presented it to Tamm. "I know you were a little jealous of Alred getting that blade for his birthday, but I tell you, it is no match for the sword you carry now. You may have grown up a commoner, Tammuz, but your soul is pure nobility."

Tamm stared at the sword. "Thank you, father."

"You deserve it. Your mother has breakfast ready. Go eat. Then we will move these weapons." He reached back into the barrel and tossed a linen wrap to Echao, who flinched as he caught it. He bounced the wrapping in his hand, measuring its weight. He flashed a smirk at Kèlris and tore back the wrappings, exposing two new curved daggers. The flame from the forge flickered in the reflection of the polished steel. Tamm could see his reflection in the curved blades from across the room. A delicate green fabric wrapped the grips, and ornately carved pommels topped each.

"They are amazing," Echao said, able to speak at last. "Thank you."

"You also deserve them. You have been through a lot lately, more than a man your age should endure. Yet, here you are, stronger than before. They are twin daggers to remind you that you and your brother are there for each other and will always be there for one another."

Tamm slid the sword in the sheath and hid it behind a jumble of scrap metal. Echao slid the daggers into their sheaths and attached them to his belt. He wrapped the cloak around him to disguise their presence. They ate a quick breakfast with their parents before heading back to the forge to grab the weapons. Before entering the forge, Tamm noticed Cyrus skulking nearby. He was searching for something, his head swinging from side to side. Echao ducked inside the forge to escape being discovered. Tamm jogged toward

Cyrus, but when Cyrus saw him coming, he looked alarmed and ran back towards the town.

Was he up to something, or was he afraid to see him after their last confrontation? Tamm decided to follow behind him. He kept his distance, trying not to alert Cyrus that he was being trailed. When he entered town, Zaech was snooping around Linsyn's hut. Tamm lost sight of Cyrus while trying to see what Zaech was doing. Zaech noticed him and doubled back behind the clinic and out of sight. Tamm sped around the building in time to see Zaech running back toward the outskirts of town. He sped up, breathing hard, trying not to lose sight of him.

As he neared the edge of town, the two men were speaking to a third. He ducked behind a tree and strained to hear what they were saying. He could not make it out, but they were definitely reporting to Alred, who grimaced as he barked back at the guards. Tamm did not dare to get any closer lest he be discovered. It was evident from the areas they had been patrolling, then running back to Alred when they were discovered, that they were gathering information on him. Alred must have sensed that something was going on under his nose and sent them out to spy for him. This was going to make it much more difficult to move the weapons into place.

Tamm raced back to the forge and reported what he had seen to Kèlris and Echao. Echao scowled and made for the door. "Where do you think you're going?" Kèlris asked, raising an eyebrow.

REBORN

Echao pulled up short at the door. "I will stay hidden. Lily will be leaving for Delocia soon, and I would like to tell her goodbye."

Tamm looked to Kèlris, waiting for his rebuttal, but the unimpressed look on his face told him that he did not believe Echao's excuse. "The town population is down some due to the battle preparations," Kèlris said, "but do be careful. Being seen will only make things more difficult."

Echao peeked out the door, checking for any other spies. "Understood." He darted out the door without pulling it closed.

"I don't have a good feeling about this," Tamm said.

Kèlris sighed. "Neither do I, Tamm. Neither do I. But, he is a man now. I can't stop him. But, you can keep an eye on him."

"Understood," Tamm said in a mock voice of Echao and left Kèlris and the forge behind. He made his way to the pier. It was almost time for Adina and Lily to sail for Delocia. He was in no hurry. He wanted to give Echao enough time to say goodbye properly before being interrupted. When he arrived at the pier, he found Adina and Lily there, loading their luggage into a small skiff, but Echao was not there.

Tamm waved at the two girls, and they waved back. Lily's eyes searched past Tamm. "Ready to go?"

"No," Adina said. "I don't want to leave my home and have these beasts run me out from the place that I love."

"I am not leaving until I see Echao," Lily said, her arms crossed. "You will have to tie me up and toss me into the boat."

Tamm chuckled. "No one is going to throw you into the boat, Lily. Echao wants you far from the battle so that you can be protected. And Adina, I don't want you to go either, but I also don't want you here where you can be hurt."

Adina blushed and gave him a half-smile. "We have everything packed. The oarsman is not very patient. He wants to be far from here when the fighting begins." She glanced back at him and smiled sweetly, then turned back to Tamm and looked nauseous. "Coward." The oarsman was propped against the oar and smiled back at her, obviously not hearing her whispered insult.

"It is not his fault, Adina," Tamm said. "Our way of life has changed. Our people are not the warriors they used to be." He brushed a strand of hair from her face. "You seem different. You have been awful fierce lately. What's the matter?"

Adina sighed. "I'm worried, Tamm. You are going to be fighting a beast that the elves and dwarves couldn't defeat alone. The Battlemages were established to defeat them and restore peace. My father is going to be in the heat of the battle. What will I do if something happens to one of you?"

"Your father is a strong warrior," he said.

"My father *was* a strong warrior. Now he is a drunk and a cripple. How is he going to stand in battle? He can barely walk."

"I assure you, Adina, I have seen your father with a blade, and he is a formidable opponent for anyone. He trained in the king's army. You shouldn't worry."

REBORN

"But I do worry. About him, about you." She grabbed his hands in hers. "I will worry every day until I hear from you again."

"This will all be over in the morning. I will see you in a few days." He wrapped her in his arms and pressed his forehead gently against hers. She squeezed him tightly in return.

"Did you think I would let you get away so easily?" someone asked from behind him. Before he could turn around, Lily had jumped out of the boat and ran past him. He turned to see her jump into Echao's arms. Echao was breathing hard but smiled as he embraced her. He still had the hood over his head.

Echao and Lily spoke in whispers to each other in front of the boat. Tamm noticed the position of the sun. "Echao, we need to go. There is still much to be done."

"Very well," Echao said and scooped Lily in his arms and passionately kissed her lips.

Tamm kissed Adina on the hand and assisted her into the boat. She wiped a tear from her eye and turned away from him. Echao carried Lily to the boat in his arms and signaled the oarsman to cast off.

They trudged back in the direction of the forge. Tamm tried to see Echao's expression, see how he was taking being separated from Lily again so soon, but he had the hood over his face. "We still need to figure out how to get the weapons in place without alerting Alred and the other guards to our plans."

Echao chucked. "I don't think that will be a problem."

"What do you mean?" Tamm asked, stopping in the middle of the road.

"Do you think I have just been traipsing along the countryside? I've taken care of it."

Tamm spun him around to look him in the eye. "How?"

Echao looked around to make sure no one was listening in. "When I left the forge, I found Alred, Cyrus, and Zaech in town. I was able to hide and overhear what they were saying. They were assigned to watch you and Linsyn. Alred knows something is going on but can't put his finger on it. He would have surely discovered our plans if he had been left to run amuck. But once they separated, I took them out one by one."

"Wait," Tamm said. "What do you mean you took them out?"

"Those new daggers are quite useful."

"Echao! Stop speaking in riddles. Tell me what happened."

Echao smirked. "I waited until they were alone and then tiptoed behind them. A quick pommel strike behind the ear and nighty-night. I tied them up and stuffed them in the hayloft of a nearby barn. They'll wake up in the morning with a headache, but by then, the fighting will be over, and they'll be none the wiser."

Tamm arched his eyebrows. "Wow! I'm impressed."

"Thanks," Echao said, starting to walk back down the road. "Now let's go get those weapons in place. It will be dark soon."

SIXTEEN

†

Tamm and Echao rushed around the town to get the weapons placed in time. If Echao had not incapacitated Alred, Zaech, and Cyrus, they would not have gotten finished before it was dark. The townsmen were all in place, the women and children safely away in Delocia. Tamm was perched on a rooftop with his belly flat against the thatched roof, peering over the gable to see the northern entrance of town. This was where the Kapre were most likely to launch their attack.

He glanced over to the roof next to him, and Echao was lying in a similar position. He was difficult to make out, dressed in all black with his hood pulled over his head. He tipped his bow to him in salute. Echao returned the gesture, then pointed toward the street. Tamm slid forward to get a better look over the rooftop. The lamplighter was on the road with his torch and trudged toward the town center. Tamm shook his head, irritated at how obvious the lamplighter was being, swiveling his head around like a pendulum on an old clock.

Tamm nocked an arrow, and it clacked against the bow. He looked over to Echao, who was doing the same. Rain started to fall, first in a drizzle, then more heavily, fat drops splashing against the roof. The lamplighter's torch flickered, and Tamm feared it would fail. He would have no way of knowing when the Kapre would attack if they could not get the lamps lit. If the rain kept up, he would not be able to set the trap by lighting the hay that had been left at the entrances.

The lamplighter stopped in front of a lamp in the center of town. He tried in vain to protect the flame as it was fading and sputtering out. Tamm could not let that happen and jeopardize the entire ambush. The man lifted the torch to the lamp, only embers blinking in and out. The sparks from the torch were not strong enough to ignite the wick. The lamplighter looked up to Tamm and shrugged. He cupped his hand over the torch as he touched the wick and blew on the darkening torch. Tamm focused on the torch and reached for the flame within. "*Sruthán.*" The lamp burst to life, a little stronger than he had anticipated.

A vicious roar pierced through the silence. The lamplighter dropped the torch and bolted for a nearby barn, where the infantry stood by waiting in the darkness. The torch bounced against the ground, still blazing. The Kapre stormed into the town, mud splashing as they ran. They were enormous, some larger than the ones Tamm had seen in the woods, at least a hundred in number, maybe more. Unfortunately, the men of Aleesia barely matched their number. If the ambush was not successful, they did not stand a chance.

Two of the Kapre broke in front of the group to chase the lamplighter. Tamm looked over to his left and saw Echao struggling in vain to light the arrow tip. He rolled to his other side and saw the only other archer, a young boy named Jeffrey, who was only around fourteen years old, likewise struggling with his arrow. The cursed rain was unraveling all they had planned. He had to set the ambush, or the lamplighter would never make it to the barn, and they would fail.

He whispered the word for fire, and the tip of the arrow flickered to life, casting a small shadow of his face on the roof. Now was the time; he had to make this one shot count. He cursed, wishing Echao could use magic to light the arrow. He was the better shot.

He slid to the apex of the roof and peered over. The two Kapre who had run ahead of the others were almost to the barn. The remaining Kapre had broken into two groups and searched around the town in confusion. He recognized their leader, dressed in blackened armor with red paint streaking in lines down his face. He pointed the arrow just over the chieftain's right shoulder, took a deep breath, and released the bowstring.

The string thrummed in his ear as the arrow soared past chieftain, scraping his cheek as it found its target. Tamm did not wait to see if the flames would catch. *"Lasaír,"* he breathed, allowing the power to flow from him. The hay erupted in flames, blocking any chance of an escape. The two Kapre that were chasing the lamplighter slid to a stop in the mud, both glaring back at the flames.

The chieftain focused his gaze in the direction of the arrow's assault, and Tamm stared back at him in defiance. The chieftain roared, and Tamm released a battle cry as he nocked another arrow and sent it directly at the beast's heart. The chieftain swatted it away with a massive war ax. Echao and Jeffrey joined the assault, launching arrows of their own. A few of the Kapre had spears and hurled them towards the snipers atop the roofs. They had plenty of time to dodge the spears, given the distance between them.

Tamm, Echao, and Jeffrey launched volleys of arrows at the Kapre, but they were spreading out and trying to surround the buildings where they made their nests. The Kapre were so tall, heads cresting the eaves of the roof, one could nearly scale the building without a ladder. A sinuous arm grasping an ax snatched hold of the roof Tamm was on. He risked a glance at the barn, wishing Beyl would send out the men already. If he waited any longer, they would be on the roof with them. Tamm released an arrow, striking the hand, and the body slid back to the ground. He peered over the edge, and the beast hurled the ax at his head. He flung himself onto his back to avoid having his head split in two.

He nocked another arrow and tried a different angle. He released it, striking a Kapre in the neck, blood splattering his comrade in the face. Tamm heard a screech and turned to see Jeffrey being pursued by two Kapre, who had succeeded at scaling onto the roof. "Jeffrey, to me!" Tamm shouted. The boy looked at Tamm, and he waved his arms, beckoning him to come. "Jump!"

The boy turned back to the Kapre, who were almost on him, and flung the bow at them. He turned and ran towards Tamm. The gap between the buildings was too far for the boy. Tamm knew he would not make the jump. He ran to the edge and held his bow out for him to grab. The boy turned to look back just before he got to the edge, and Tamm knew he was not going to make it.

He was too slow. The moment he took to look back gave the Kapre the extra distance they needed. The beast released the ax with deadly accuracy. Tamm closed his eyes just as Jeffrey pushed off for the jump and heard him scream, the ax slicing into the back of the leg. He only made it a few feet before his body began to sink back to the ground. Tamm reached as far as he could with the bow, the boy's fear-filled eyes glued to his. He could not let him die, even if it meant his life in return. "*Gaoth!*" He focused the air under the boy and behind him, carrying his thin body closer to the bow. He knew better than to unleash the power. It would be too obvious to the boy that magic had been the cause of his flight to safety.

Jeffrey's hand grasped the end of the bow, and Tamm wrestled him up beside him. He panted, the continued use of magic draining his energy. He readied another arrow, ignoring the boy's whimpers, and rolled to his side, aiming at the charging Kapre. The one that had hit Jeffrey with the ax had already picked it back up and had it cocked behind his ear, targeted directly at Tamm. He released the string and prayed his aim was true. Before looking to see if he had struck his target, he had another arrow flying straight at the second Kapre. As his vision expanded to take in the scene, both Kapre dropped in tandem and rolled off the roof.

He stole a glance at the other roof to check on Echao. He was rolling and ducking all over the roof as if he had not just been at death's door, his arrows wreaking havoc, easily finding their targets. Bodies of Kapre littered the ground below, but their numbers were still too powerful for the men of Aleesia. They could not keep this up and would run out of arrows soon.

Tamm turned his attention back to Jeffrey, who was rolling around in agony, hands wrapped around his right lower leg. Tamm drew his dagger and cut a strip from the boy's shirt and wrapped it tightly. "Shh, Shh," Tamm said, trying to calm the boy. "You did well, Jeffery. You have made your ancestors proud."

He examined the wound. The tendon had been cut, and his foot was dangling. He would have Linsyn mend it later, should they survive.

There was a roar behind him, and he turned to see a massive Kapre barreling toward him, teeth bared in an evil snarl. He reached for his bow, but it was out of reach from where he had tossed it while tending to Jeffrey's wound, and there was no way he would reach it before the Kapre would get to him. He sheathed his dagger and drew the sword his father had made him. He prayed to the god of battle that he would be up to the challenge.

REBORN

He held the sword in a defensive posture and stepped in front of Jeffrey, who had fainted from the pain.

The Kapre chuckled. "Awe, the little man, with a little sword, trying to protect the little boy. Give up now, and I will kill you both quickly."

Tamm wanted to send a fireball right into the Kapre's face. His mouth twitched into a tight smile. "You are sadly mistaken if you think I will go down without a fight." He waved his hand, summoning the beast closer.

He stumbled back as blood sprayed his face; he blinked, trying to clear his vision. What had happened? Had the Kapre attacked him that quickly? He wiped his face with the back of his sleeve. The Kapre stood there, twitching, with an arrow where his eye used to be. It dropped to its knees before sliding off the roof, and Echao stood behind it, bow still extended. He held up an empty quiver. "I'm out. You?"

"I've got a few more. Not enough. Jeffrey's hurt pretty badly. We can't stay up here. Where is Beyl?"

As he asked the question, he heard the men roar in defiance as they charged out of the barn, silver glistening in the firelight as they brandished their weapons. The boys looked at the men and then back at each other. "Go," Tamm yelled at Echao. "It's about to get ugly."

Echao nodded but then drew the twin daggers from his belt. "I wouldn't miss this for anything." Before Tamm could protest, Echao had slid off the back of the roof.

Tamm looked back to the injured Jeffrey. He was slipping in and out of consciousness. Tamm knelt and covered him with his cloak. "Rest now. All will be well in the morning."

Tamm ran to the front side of the house and found a stack of crates. He leaped onto one before jumping down to the yard. The Kapre had turned their attention away from the houses, no longer seeing them as a threat, and had begun to fight the men of Aleesia in close combat. Tamm had to get to them; he had to help.

He rushed toward the center of town, where the fighting had erupted in earnest. He could see flashes of Echao as he darted in and out, slashing and stabbing, before slipping back into the darkness. Tamm was relieved at seeing this. If he was determined to fight, at least he was being wise and sticking to the shadows and striking unseen.

Tamm reached a group of fighters. He was behind the Kapre and could not see over them to see how the men were faring. If they had used the tactics they had been taught, the pikemen would be out in front, hopefully keeping some distance between them and the Kapre.

Tamm slid the sword between the ribs of an unsuspecting Kapre warrior. He was dead before he could even shriek. He continued to dispatch them one by one as they were scrambling to get to the front of the attack. He had slain five before their compatriots were aware of him. Two turned to face him. He lunged at them, not giving them time to react. He swept the sword at the largest one's leg, amputating it at the calf. The beast roared and tipped over. He then parried the blow from the second and rolled to his side, bringing the sword around in a wide arc, slicing into its back.

Tamm was impressed with the lethality of the new sword. It was far sharper than any blade he had used in the past. The

REBORN

Kapre with the missing leg was wailing as it thrashed about in the mud. Tamm stood over it and dropped the blade into its face, ceasing its misery.

"I will enjoy sucking the marrow from your bones," a guttural voice called out over his shoulder. He spun around to see Uskang, the Kapre chieftain, within a few paces behind him. He was large but not quite as large as the others. His greasy black hair hung in locks down the side of his head, congealed blood coated through it. Tamm only hoped it was not the blood of his kinsmen.

The beast twirled a large battleax. "You will not escape from me so easily this time. I will add your ears to my collection." The chieftain's meaty fingers stroked a group of ears tied to the haft of the ax. "An ear from each of your people I have killed." He was ruthless, Tamm knew that. Tamm had no doubt he could fulfill each of his promises with ease.

"You chose the wrong village to attack," Tamm said in the Kapre's native language, his voice shaking. "As you can see, we don't fear the king's rules. We don't fear you." Tamm angled his eyes in determination, lifting the sword in the ready. He could at least look fearless on the outside. His palms were sweating against the leather grip as fear bubbled inside his stomach, threatening to make him vomit.

The Kapre charged, ax held high. Tamm held his ground, grinding his foot in the dirt to steady himself. The ax plunged at his head, threatening to slice him in half. He rolled to the side, narrowly missing the blade.

"You have to be faster than that," Tamm taunted.

Uskang growled and charged again. Tamm parried and dodged the flurry of blows. He gulped air as fast as he could. He could not keep this pace up for long. He hoped Uskang could not either. He rolled away from two successive blows and darted further away from the main horde. He needed to give himself some room to maneuver. He was a dead man if he got cornered.

"Don't run from me!" Uskang yelled. "You will only die tired."

Tamm slipped behind a large wooden crate. The ax cracked against the wood, splinters flying into Tamm's face. The Kapre was relentless. It heaved its massive foot onto the box, tugging to free the ax. Tamm snuck from behind the box and drew the sword back to strike the beast. The ax broke free of its prison and the Kapre spun, the ax aimed at Tamm's throat. Tamm twisted away from the blow, throwing the sword out as he did, catching the chieftain in the thigh. The beast roared as Tamm backed away, preparing for the onslaught to come.

It grabbed the wound and then flung the blood from its hand as if it was of no consequence. It charged Tamm again, throwing blows faster than Tamm was able to parry. He twisted away from a blow, but the ax sliced through his tunic and into his upper arm. The pain forced a sharp inhale as blood seeped from the gash. Crimson flowed down, dripping down his fingers and into the soil. He did not have time to check the wound as the beast continued to hurl attack after furious attack at him. He was relegated to using only his right arm, but he could not hold onto the sword against the maelstrom of attacks with only one hand. The next blow caused the sword to fly from his grip, but before he could flee, the ax was brought back in the opposite direction, slicing into his stomach.

He dropped to his knees. The cut was not deep, not into the muscle, but it was excruciating. He glanced over to where the sword had clanged against the ground, but it was too far away to grab. The beast towered over him and barked a coarse laugh. Tamm stared up at the beast, immediately realizing the similarity between this battle and the nightmare that haunted him of late. There was no pity in the Kapre's eyes. Tamm knew his life, along with the newly awakened flame inside him, would be snuffed out in a matter of seconds.

The beast hefted the ax above his head. "Time to die, little one. Do not cry. You fought with honor. Go knowing that the bones of your comrades will feed our conquest of your country." Tamm closed his eyes and bowed his head, too angry to shed a tear, as the ax hurled for his neck.

A bright flash of light. Tamm was surprised that his death was that quick, that there was no pain from the ax biting into his neck. But there was pain, pain in his arm, pain in his abdomen. If he were dead, then why was he still in pain? He looked up, and the Kapre was staggering around blindly, its hands rubbing at its eyes. He searched around and saw Linsyn standing nearby with his staff outstretched, a sly smile on his face. The old man had used magic in the open to save him. No one likely saw what he did due to the confusion of the battle, but he would know what Linsyn had risked to save him.

"Finish it," Linsyn yelled across the battlefield.

Tamm spun back to the fight, and the beast was regaining its vision, snarling at him. Tamm was still out of reach of his sword. The Kapre charged him, swinging the ax at Tamm full of fury. Tamm stumbled backward away from the blows. The Kapre was overconfident, taking no caution to his balance or preparing for any form of counter. Tamm slid the dagger from his belt and charged back at the Kapre, angling himself towards the sword lying nearby. The chieftain smiled at him and slowed his attack, putting more force rather than speed, into the strikes. Tamm slid underneath the blow and stabbed straight down into the top of the beast's foot as he slid by, pinning it to the ground.

Uskang roared behind him as he rolled out of the slide and snatched the sword from the ground. He spun to see the Kapre bent forward, grasping at the dagger. Tamm sprinted, and Uskang looked up and met his eyes just as the sword sliced through his neck, its head rolling across the ground, unblinking eyes staring forward.

Tamm blinked in surprise as blood spattered across his face. There was a strange feeling in his gut as he stared at Uskang's empty gaze. Was it disgust? Anger? Remorse? He leaned back against one of the houses as the realization struck him like a stone. It was pity. Despite his desire to protect his home and his friends, despite his will to live, he felt pity for the creature. He wiped the blood away from his face, not knowing what to think. The one thing he knew was that to snuff out the spark of life from another living being would forever haunt him.

REBORN

The sounds of battle snapped him back to reality. He recovered his dagger and rushed toward a group of villagers that were pinned against a building, fending off a large contingent of Kapre. He joined the fray, attempting to drive them back. "Your chieftain is dead," he yelled at them in their language. "Surrender now or join him." His fellow men looked at him in surprise but quickly turned back to the fighting.

The Kapre were not ones to surrender. On they fought throughout the night despite the loss of their leader. Eventually, the last Kapre fell, and the men of Aleesia celebrated. It was nearly dawn by the time the fires surrounding the village had been put out, and the bodies of the dead Kapre had been hauled out of town and left to burn. The men gathered them into several carts to remove them from the town center. They had slain every last one. Several of the Aleesian men were severely injured, but Tamm had heard of none that perished. The ambush had worked. He could hardly believe they had all made it out with their lives. He would not have been so lucky if Linsyn had not have risked everything by using magic to save him.

He and Linsyn would be busy over the next several days, tending to the wounded, but Aleesia was saved. The sun had begun to rise, gold dancing off the lake, as Tamm bid the men goodnight and left the tavern where they had all gathered to celebrate. He had offered to stay and help Linsyn tend to the wounded, but Linsyn refused.

He was so tired. The adrenaline had long faded, and he could no longer hold his eyes open. Today as he slept, he would not have the nightmare of fighting the Kapre chieftain. He had lived that nightmare and survived to see another day

SEVENTEEN

†

Tamm rolled out of bed and stumbled downstairs to the kitchen, hoping to grab some breakfast. The sun shone brightly through the shutters, scattering light across the kitchen table. It must be at least midday by the look of the sun. He splashed some water on his face to wipe the sleep away. He was still exhausted after all the fighting and use of magic last night and the hours of celebration that followed. It all seemed so unreal. Everything from last night was a blur. The throbbing from his stomach and left arm provided a quick reminder that the battle did take place.

His father was not at home. He must have stayed at the tavern last night. His mother was safe in Delocia, but she would be on her way home as soon as word reached her that the battle was a success. He grabbed a bit of food and changed the dressings on his arm and abdomen and headed into town. He did not want to tarry long. Linsyn would be busy tending to the wounded, and he wanted to help. He also wanted to properly thank him for risking his life last night to save his.

Linsyn had always been very careful about his use of magic. Tamm had lived in the village his whole life and never would have expected the old man to be a mage, not until he was forced to use magic to save Echao. The light he cast last night was so bright that it had blinded the Kapre. Had he not been there at the right time, and been willing to cast the spell, Tamm would not be alive today. Tamm's chest swelled with respect and affection for the old man the more he thought about it. Linsyn should have the day off, he thought. He could tend to the ill and wounded himself and let the old healer spend the day in leisure. It was the least he could do.

As he got closer to the healer's shack, he could see a throng of people gathered outside. At first, he thought it must be people coming to visit the wounded, but as he got closer, he could see several soldiers in armor bearing the king's symbol of a white withered tree on a black banner. They had a large cart with mules harnessed to the front and a scraggly old man tied to the back.

Tamm raced towards the shack just as the sheriff exited the hut. "Let's go, men. I loathe making this trip again today."

Tamm's eyes searched the area, looking for any clue as to what was going on. Linsyn's hands were bound in a thick rope and tethered to the back of the cart. "What's going on? What are you doing?"

REBORN

Vorn rolled his eyes. "Go away, boy. This is royal business. Go back to the forge."

Tamm ran in front of Vorn, blocking his way. "Where do you think you're taking him?"

Vorn turned to Tamm, unamused with his interruption. "He was witnessed using magic last night. He is being taken to the king to be tried for his crimes."

Tamm fidgeted in front of the sheriff, his head hung low. "You can't do this. He has done nothing wrong."

"I am the sheriff, and I can do anything I please. A witness has come forth claiming he used magic in the sight of multiple people in this village. I am sure that finding another witness to condemn him will be no great feat. There is also speak of a battle that took place last night. Do you know anything about this?"

Tamm looked to Linsyn. His face was bruised, one of his eyes swollen shut. He shook his head just enough for Tamm to see. "You cannot take him. He's our healer. You would leave our town without a healer?"

Vorn sighed. "You are right, Tammuz. There seems to be several of the men in town who have miraculously developed battle wounds without a battle occurring. How bizarre? Someone will need to see after them and investigate where the wounds came from."

"Thank you," Tamm whispered.

"You are very welcome. I only want what is best for this town. By the power ascribed to me by King Tzelder, I hereby appoint you, Tammuz, Son of Kèlris, as Aleesia's healer. Hopefully, the old man has taught you well."

Tamm's mouth gaped open as Vorn chuckled. "Did you think that I would just let him stay because more men of this village got themselves nearly killed breaking the law? You are a fool, boy. Go away before I get angry."

Tamm scowled as he stared at Vorn in disgust. "I cannot let you take him."

"Let me?" Vorn said with a chuckle. "You cannot *let* me? How exactly do you plan to stop me? I am the sheriff. I have killed more men than you have healed in your few years in this world. Soldiers of the king's army surround you. Don't do anything foolish. There is nowhere in this kingdom you could hide that I would not find you." He waved his hand, signaling that Tamm was dismissed.

Tamm's hand slipped to the dagger at his hip. He cut his eyes over to Linsyn, who was shaking his head violently. Tamm looked back at Vorn, his lip twitching. Vorn noticed Tamm's hand, and his lips curled into a smirk. "Do it," he whispered.

Tamm flicked his wrist forward, pulling the dagger from the sheath. Before the soldiers could respond and unsheathe their swords, the back of Vorn's armored hand struck Tamm hard in the temple. He stumbled sideways into the wall of the hut. His breaths were coming in short gasps, the pain too much to bear. Flashes of light danced in his vision and his ears roared, but he could hear the soldiers laughing and Linsyn shouting, but it sounded leagues away.

He was barely able to stay on his feet. He would have already fallen if the building was not holding him up now. The dagger fell out of his hand. He lifted his head, which felt like it weighed more than a blacksmith's hammer. Vorn wiped the blood from his bracers, oblivious to Tamm's pain. Tamm mustered all the strength remaining in him and threw himself toward the sheriff. The exertion was too much. He never made contact as his vision faded, and he landed on his face in the dirt. The coachmen snapped a whip, and the mules began to haul the cart away with Linsyn tethered to the back. He saw Linsyn's sandaled feet shuffling in the dirt as everything went black.

♦♦♦♦♦

Water splashed onto Tamm's face, and his eyes fluttered open. Echao was standing over him. "Are you alright? I saw what happened from over there, but I had to stay hidden." He pointed behind a building. "Vorn still doesn't know that I've recovered, and I didn't want to make anything worse by suddenly showing up. Can you stand?"

Tamm tried to push up, but the world around him spun like a top. He leaned to his side and vomited. His head was pounding, and he leaned back against the building and closed his eyes.

"Don't go back to sleep, Tamm. I know it hurts, but you have to stay awake. Here let me help you get inside." Echao took him under the arm and helped him to stand. Once on his feet, he leaned against Echao as he limped inside and was helped onto the cot.

His eyes were so heavy. He did not want to wake up. "I think I have a concussion."

Echao dabbed a wet cloth on his forehead. "I know you have a concussion, and I'm no healer."

Tamm kept his eyes closed but began to recite a number of ingredients for Echao to gather from the shelf. He had him grab something for pain and dizziness, then after vomiting again in a pail beside the cot, had him add something for nausea. He instructed him on how to mix it and then had him brew it into a tea. It would be more palatable as a tea.

He sipped on the tea and, after a time, was able to sit up on the side of the cot. "They took him, Echao. Vorn took him. What am I supposed to do?"

Echao shook his head and finally sat in Linsyn's chair. "Why did he arrest him? Where were they going?"

Tamm took a deep breath before breaking the news to Echao. "They arrested him for using magic. Someone from the battle last night saw him and turned him into the sheriff."

Echao's face scrunched in disbelief. "Why would they do that? Why would they think that he used magic?"

"Because he did."

Echao reached out and put a hand on Tamm's head. "Your concussion may be worse than I thought."

"It's not my concussion, Echao. He used magic last night. He used it to save my life."

Echao cocked his head to the side, unable to believe what Tamm was telling him.

"I was defeated. The Kapre chieftain had disarmed me, and I was wounded. I was about to be beheaded when there was a sudden flash of light that blinded the Kapre, and I was able to get to my sword and kill him. I looked around, and Linsyn was there and had cast the spell."

"Are you sure? Someone could have shot a flaming arrow at the Kapre."

Tamm slid down from the cot, the pounding in his head beginning to subside after drinking the tea. He waved a hand at the fireplace, murmuring a word under his breath, and the flames leaped to life. With a wave of his hand, he silenced them, and the light from the room faded.

Echao tripped as he scampered backward away from the fireplace. "How did you do that?"

"It's magic. Linsyn taught me. That's how I know he cast the spell and saved my life, and by doing so, forfeited his own."

Echao shook his head. "That's impossible. There are no mages anymore. They all either died out or were killed."

Tamm slapped his hands against the cot. "Do you doubt your eyes? I just gave you the proof, and you still doubt? Do you need another sign?"

"No," Echao said, walking over and placing a hand on Tamm's shoulder. "It is just hard to believe that my brother can use magic and that the crazy old healer taught him." He chuckled to himself. "Nothing is ever as it seems, I suppose."

"He risked his life to save me," Tamm said. "I can't let him be put to death on my account."

Echao plopped down in the chair and propped his legs on the writing desk. "What do you expect to do? You can't take on the king and the whole empire, magic or no."

"I can't just let him die, Echao. To you, he is only the *crazy old healer*. To me, he is more. He is my mentor, my friend."

Echao sat up in the chair and dusted the dirt from his boots off the desk. "I'm sorry. I know this must be hard. What do you want to do? I am with you, no matter what. If you want to charge the gates of the capital, I'll be by your side as we scale the wall."

"I don't know where to start," Tamm said, walking over to the writing desking and fingering the quill that Linsyn would use to scrawl out lists of ingredients for him to find in the forest. "He asked me to see to his affairs if anything ever happened to him. He left a will of sorts in one of these old books."

Tamm searched the bookshelf and pulled the book down. He flipped it open to the middle, and a folded piece of parchment was placed perfectly between the sheets. He put the book on the desk and sat down beside Echao.

"Do you want me to read it?" Echao asked.

"No. It's my duty. He asked me to see to his affairs."

Tamm unfolded the note and read the contents aloud for Echao to hear.

My dearest Tammuz,

If you are reading this, then I am no longer with you. I am sorry I had to take my leave so soon. There was so much more that I wanted to teach you. You are a magnificent pupil, and the rate at which you learn surprises even me, and I have witnessed many adept young students as they sought the ways of magic. I know that you may feel lost or in shock at my passing, but do not despair. I am in a much

REBORN

better place, free of the shackles of this old world.

Do not believe that since I am gone that your training must come to an end. There is still so much more for you to do. You already possess some skill with a blade. You are now seeking the secrets of magic. You will do great things. I believe that through you, the Battlemages will be reborn. You must seek out the elves. They will continue your training. I earned their trust many ages ago, as I feel you will also. Seek them out. Do not tarry. The empire grows more wicked each day. The Battlemages will restore order and will lead Iradell into new glory.

Yours Always,
*   Linsyn*

Oscail an chloch

As Tamm read the last words aloud, he felt a stirring in the fire inside him and a grinding emitted from the fireplace. He and Echao both jumped at the sound before walking over by the mantle. Tamm recognized the words that Linsyn had used before to open a secret compartment in the fireplace. He had hidden Tamm's bow here before the battle.

Tamm peered into the hole, but it was so dark he could not see anything. He looked at Echao, who shrugged. "He wouldn't give you words that opened a secret hiding place if he intended it to hurt you. Just reach in and see what's there."

Tamm looked again in the hole and sighed. He leaned forward and placed his hand in the darkness. He slid his fingers along the dusty stones below, not feeling anything of value until he brushed against something cold. He jerked his arm back, then, after a tense moment, eased it back in. He felt the cold once more on the tips of his fingers, then traced his fingers along it. It felt metallic, with maybe leather and thread. "I think it's a sword."

Echao huffed. "For the gods' sake, man. Will you just get it out of there, and let's have a look at it?"

Tamm arched his eyebrow at Echao, who stared at him impatiently. Tamm wrapped his hand around what felt like the grip of a sword and lifted it from its hiding place. It was a sword, and it was in an exquisite sheath that shone with the reflected light of the lamps in the room. Instead of a traditional pommel, a priceless diamond rested in its place.

The two boys looked at each other, mouths gaping. A sword like this was invaluable. How did a healer come into possession of a weapon of this caliber? Tamm slid the sword from the sheath, and the light danced along the blade. He could nearly see through the blade. It appeared to be made of glass, or maybe even diamond. He touched his thumb to the blade, and the skin split immediately. He let out a sharp inhale of pain as he pulled his hand away. It was sharper than any blade he had ever held. "Where does a sword like this come from?"

"I think the bigger question is how did Linsyn get it," Echao said. "He must have saved some rich man's life. Or maybe a royal or noble by the looks of it."

"Do you think he left it for me?" Tamm asked.

"Obviously. He addressed the letter to you. He gave you the words to say to access its hiding spot."

There was something special about this blade. Tamm knew it. Linsyn was not just passing the blade down to his successor. There was some story behind the sword. Any man who had owned a sword like this had a story, and Tamm was determined to hear it.

Tamm slid the blade back into the sheath, and it clicked as it locked into place. "I'm going after him. You can come along too, but there's not much time to pack. The caravan left at least a few hours ago, so they have a head start."

Echao looked taken aback. "You mean you're going to try to rescue him?"

"You can stay here. I'll not hold that against you, but I can't let him die for my sake. He risked his life to save me. Now, I'll return the favor." Tamm slid the sword over his shoulder and fastened a cloak around his neck to conceal it as best he could.

Echao leaped to his feet and snatched his cloak from the rack. "I'm not going to let you go alone. We'll need to slip out of here, though. Alred and his goons are not too pleased with me after I knocked them out and tied them up yesterday. They are watching for you to leave. They expect you to try and stop Vorn from taking Linsyn to the king. We will have to throw them off our trail."

"I have an idea," Tamm said. "Go home, quickly, and pack a bag. Just get a change of clothes or two, our waterskins, and some food. I'll slip into the storehouse behind the tavern and get a few sacks of grain. I'll leave the sacks out by the lake. Get a small skiff and put the bags on it, dressed in our clothes.

They'll think we're heading to Delocia to try to cut Vorn off. Then meet me outside the southern gate."

Echao stared at the ground, rubbing the toe of his boot across the floor.

"What's wrong?" Tamm asked.

"What if this doesn't work? What if I never see her again, and I left without saying goodbye?"

"Lily is a strong girl," Tamm replied. "She will understand. Besides, it's only a few days' journey. We will be back before you know it."

Echao nodded and slipped out the door, heading in the direction of their home. Tamm watched him from the door, then slipped out the back and made his way to the storehouse.

EIGHTEEN

†

Tamm saw Echao slipping past the buildings and rushing toward the southern gate. Tamm sat behind an old oak tree, out of view of the road. Echao waved as he approached. "It worked just like you said it would," he said, panting from the run. "I dressed the bags of grain and sent them out on the skiff. I climbed up to the roof of a house and watched as Alred, Cyrus, and Zaech rushed to catch the boat and then took one of their own to stop us. We should be in the clear."

Tamm staggered to his feet, still dizzy from the hit to the head. The sword did not help his balance. It was light but awkward on his back. "Let's go. It'll be dark soon, and we need to put some distance between us and this village."

Tamm had never left Aleesia before. He knew from Kèlris's trading trips that the road led south to the King's road that stretched east to west across nearly the entire country. Tamm hoped to make it to the intersection before dark. It would only be another day or two on foot from there to the capital.

They walked without speaking, both lost in their own thoughts, before Echao broke the silence. "Linsyn mentioned elves training you."

Tamm nodded.

"Well," Echao said, "are you going to go to them? How will you find them?"

"I don't plan to find them. I'll rescue Linsyn, and then he can complete my training."

"I don't mean to be a pessimist, Tamm, but what if we fail? You know I will stand by you in whatever you do, but you have to know that there is a chance we aren't going to make it back. For the gods' sakes, you are blatantly challenging the empire."

Tamm stopped. "I appreciate you coming along. I do. But you are not bound. You can return at any time. I'll rescue him, or I'll die trying."

Echao ran his fingers through his dark hair. "You would risk your life, and mine, to save him?"

"I would. I owe him that. He risked his life to save mine; he deserves no less."

"Very well then," Echao said, pointing down the road. "You lead, and I will follow."

Tamm started back down the road. The sun was just above the mountains in the west. It would be dark soon. He did not say another word to Echao the rest of the afternoon. He did not blame him, though. He had every right to be afraid. He was not wrong, either. There was a good chance that they would not make it back home. Actually, there was no chance that they would. Even if they succeeded in rescuing Linsyn, they would be fugitives on the run. Vorn had made that promise, that he would search him out no matter where he hid.

He took comfort in knowing Echao was with him and would have his back, but he also wished he would turn and go home. He did not want his brother to risk his life for him, a life that he almost lost not long ago.

"Put your hood up," Echao said.

"What?"

"Quick! Put up your hood. Someone is coming up the road. It may be soldiers."

Tamm had been lost in thought and not paying attention. He flicked the hood of his cloak up. It was still warm out, and hot air rushed up to his face as he walked.

They drew close to the newcomers, and Tamm could now tell that they were not soldiers. It was an old man stumbling along with a younger man trying to steady him, maybe an apprentice. The old man looked battered and was having difficulty walking, his short gray hair disheveled, and a hooked nose that was bent with dried blood around his nostrils. The younger man was tall and thin, with light brown hair cut close, and caring, brown eyes.

"Hail, kind sirs," the younger of the two said. "I am Terrance, and this is my father, Birger. We are traveling merchants."

"Where are your wares?" Echao asked, looking around suspiciously.

"Ah, that is a long story, but you look to be in a hurry, so I will give you the short version." Birger coughed and wiped spittle from his mouth with his sleeve. Terrance looked with concern at his father. "I beg your pardon, sirs. We are from the coast and are on our way to Aleesia and Delocia to do some trading." He coughed to clear his throat. "Were. We were on our way to do some trading. Unfortunately, we were heckled by some ruffians, and our wares were confiscated, and my father was given a good beating for trying to stop them."

"You don't seem any worse for wear," Tamm said.

"Well, you see, the ruffians I speak of were a group of soldiers. I tried to let them take what they wanted to avoid trouble, but my father was insistent that they would have none of our goods. So, they gave him a good trouncing and took all of our stock."

"I am sorry," Tamm said. "I have only met a few soldiers in my time, but they didn't seem to be the most patient."

"Aye, that is true, I suppose," Terrance said. "This pains me to ask, masters, but my father and I are a long way from home. That cart held our livelihood, and the soldiers took what few coins we had. Do you have a few coins to spare so that we can get a room for the night once we reach Aleesia?"

Tamm cut his eyes at Echao, who looked wary. "I don't have much." He reached into his coin purse and pulled out the only three draechs he had. "This should be enough to get you a room. The citizens of Aleesia are good people and may be able to help you more once you arrive."

"Thank you, sirs. Thank you kindly. You do not know how much you have helped us. May the gods bless you richly." Birger strained to give them a small smile, and Terrance crossed a fist over his heart.

"Best of luck to you," Tamm called to them as they went separate ways. Once they were out of earshot from the merchants, Echao spoke up. "You gave them all of our coin."

Tamm nodded. "I did."

"Why would you do that?"

He shrugged. "They were in more need than we are."

"Pfft," Echao huffed. "How do you figure? We are marching to our deaths. I would say we might need that money just as much."

"What do you think we would do with it, Echao? Bribe our way out of prison if we're caught? We have food, and we have clothes. There is nothing else we need at the moment. Besides, recent events have created a newly found hatred for the king's soldiers and the way they treat the people. That coin allowed us to right one of their wrongs."

Echao grunted his disapproval but did not argue. They marched on in silence, the light fading in the sky. The sun was setting behind the horizon, painting a pink and orange canvas across the sky. That is when Tamm spotted the torches ahead and reached an arm out to slow Echao. Echao swatted his arm away in frustration.

"Be still," Tamm whispered. "Do you not see those torches? Someone is camped down the road."

"Pull your hood back up," Echao said. "If it is soldiers, they may have been left behind to ensure you're not following Vorn."

Tamm flipped his hood up. As they neared the torches, he could see the armor of soldiers, torchlight flickering in the polished metal. These were heavily armed infantry. Tamm looked around to see if they could slip off the road and avoid being seen. Just as he thought it, a booming voice sounded from the camp. "What do we have here, fellas? More travelers? And so near dark. Didn't your mothers ever warn you about traveling so close to dark? There could be scoundrels about. Lucky for you, we're here to protect you."

"Play it cool," Echao said. "Limp like you're injured."

Tamm started to limp, hoping they had not seen him walking normally on the approach. He arched his back to give himself the appearance of an old man.

"And where might you be off to?" asked a large man with a barrel chest and dark hair. There was mischief in his eyes and filth in his teeth. He was the obvious leader of the small group. There were two other soldiers with him, one at each side. They smiled and egged him on.

"I'm an apprentice tanner from Delocia, and this is my master. As you can see, he is well on in age, and I am helping him get south to the port city of Balimòr. He is retiring and going to live with family there."

"Well, ain't that sweet boys? He's such a good apprentice. You're probably hoping he keels over on the way, so you can just head back home without making the whole trip," another soldier said while the other two laughed.

The leader pushed his way back in front of the other soldier. "You'll be safe camping near here for the night. We are on our way to Aleesia to garrison the town against revolt. We'll keep you safe. For a fee. How much money you got? We can make a deal."

Echao took a step back and wrapped his arms around Tamm as if to protect him. "We don't really have any money. We're just trying to make it south. We will be out of your way."

"Listen, fellas. I'm a lieutenant in the king's army. You can trust me. It's too dangerous to go alone at night. We'll watch over you."

"Like you watched over those two traders, right before you stole their goods?" Tamm asked from under the cowl.

The lieutenant flushed with anger. "This one's got a smart mouth, boys. You need to respect your betters, old man."

Tamm lowered his cowl, his face contorted with anger. "You can't treat people like that. You abuse your authority. You're sworn to protect these people."

The soldiers drew their swords, the leader pointing the tip at Tamm. "We are sworn men of the king. We owe you, peasants, nothing. Give us your coin, or we'll beat it out of you."

Tamm looked at Echao, who nodded at him as he slipped his hands around the twin dagger hilts at his waist. Tamm reached over his shoulder and drew the sword from under his cloak, and a whistle escaped one of the soldier's lips when he saw the blade.

"Don't be a fool, boy," the lieutenant said, staring at the pristine blade. "You can give us the sword, and we'll call it even. That thing is a beaut. Probably worth its weight in gold."

Tamm was disgusted at the soldiers' disregard of their duties, and their lustful greed fueled his anger. He lunged at the one in the center, the campfire light glistening off the blade. The man was, without a doubt, a trained soldier, parrying Tamm's blows with ease. The other two soldiers attempted to flank him, but Echao had drawn his daggers, quick as lightning, and deterred them with a flurry of attacks.

The skirmish did not last long. Echao had sliced the sword hand of one of the soldiers he was facing, forcing him to drop his sword in the dirt. Tamm spun on him as he stared at the wound in disbelief and struck him in the side of the skull with the pommel of his sword, knocking him out cold. The lieutenant went on the offensive, launching thrusts and slashes at Tamm in rapid succession. Tamm parried the blows but had to retreat at the ferocity of the attack. He brought his sword high above his head and brought it down, attempting to slice Tamm in half. Tamm braced himself to block the attack with the sword high above his head, and the soldier's sword shattered into pieces on the ground.

The now weaponless lieutenant gaped at the sword strewn across the ground. He tried to flee, but Tamm whispered a word that sent a small electric shock into the mule strapped to the trader's cart, and it bolted across the road, causing the soldier to run headlong into the cart and fall to the ground. The third soldier surrendered after they had dispatched the other two.

Echao searched the cart and found some rope. They gagged and bound the soldiers to keep them from following them or gathering reinforcements. Tamm walked over to the mule and felt for the power inside him. He did not know if trying to feed his words with magic would do anything to communicate with the animal or not, but he wanted to try. His knowledge of the words of power was limited, but Linsyn had taught him that it was the intent of the word that directed the magic.

He leaned into the mule's ear and whispered. The language was broken gibberish to anyone listening in; nonetheless, trying to communicate to the animal that it should continue north on the road until it entered Aleesia, and it would find its masters there. He used the words he knew and fed them with the power within. The mule stared at him for a moment, then turned and started in the direction of Aleesia.

"What was that?" Echao asked.

"I tried to tell him to go to Aleesia to find his masters," Tamm said, sliding the sword back into the sheath. "I don't know if it will work, but I hope it will."

Echao gave him a half-smile. "You have changed. You realize that, don't you?"

"We both have, I suppose," he said, shrugging. "And I feel it's only the beginning. Let's get to the intersection quickly. It will soon be too dark to see. We can make camp further off the road."

By the time they made it to the intersection, it was pitch black. Echao stepped on Tamm's heels numerous times as they searched for an area off the road to make camp.

"Can't you use magic to help us see?" Echao asked.

Tamm had not thought of that. Magic was still new to him, and he would sometimes forget that he could summon it for even menial tasks. He held his hand out and whispered the word for fire. He restricted the power, not wanting to draw any more attention to them. A small flame danced around in his hand, providing enough light to guide them.

"That's amazing," Echao said, his voice bright with wonder.

Tamm smiled but did not reply, leading them further off the road. They crested a small hill and found a flat field on the other side. "This should do. It will shield us from view from anyone passing on the road."

His legs were tired and fought against his every step. If he was this tired, then Echao had to be exhausted. He was still recovering from his injuries but had done well, considering he had nearly died only weeks before. He dropped his satchel and slid the sword from his back before checking the bandages on his arm and abdomen, relieved there was no new bleeding. He would change them tomorrow. He did not want to waste any of their drinking water on cleaning the wound now.

He chose not to make a fire, as it would just point out their location. He covered up with his cloak and used his satchel as a pillow. He slept with the sword under satchel and his hand resting around the grip. It did not take long before sleep overtook him.

◆◆◆◆◆

"Do you hear that?" Echao whispered.

Tamm's eyes opened, and he peered around, not daring to move. "I don't hear anything."

"Someone's moving around. Do you think the soldiers got loose?"

Tamm tightened his grip on the sword handle and strained to hear. Only crickets chirping. Then he heard it. It was faint, a shuffling in the grass. Someone was moving closer to them. It was not coming from the road, though. It was coming from the direction of the forest. The soldiers must have seen where they set up camp and moved in while they slept, trying to flank them.

Tamm leaned toward Echao so he could hear his whispers. "I hear it. Be ready to defend yourself."

The sound moved closer and was only a few paces away when Tamm leaped to his feet, drawing the sword in one swift motion while waving his free arm in a circle above his head. He fed the words with power, and a ring of fire encircled him and Echao. The light illuminated three figures walking toward them. One had a curved blade held out. Another had a bow drawn back to its ear, itching to let the arrow fly. The third led the way, a cowl hiding the face, but walking with an ornate staff tapping the ground with each cautious step.

Tamm held his sword at the ready as the beings approached the ring of fire. They halted just outside of the flames before the one in the middle pointed the tip of the staff at the flames, and they lowered, allowing it to walk into the circle.

Tamm was in awe that the mage was able to control his spell. Linsyn had never taught him that spells could be countered or controlled by another mage, but this mage did it effortlessly.

The figure strode within paces of Tamm but did not say a word, face shielded by the cowl. Echao cleared his throat to get Tamm's attention. "They're elves, Tamm. Look at the ears of the two in the back." Tamm looked past the mage warily and saw the pointed ears of the elves holding the sword and bow.

"What do we do?" Echao asked. "Legends say they're powerful."

Tamm did not take his eyes from the mage in front of him. He tilted his head, trying to get a look at its face. He still held the sword out in front of him, ready to strike if needed. "What do you want?"

The mage took a step closer. Tamm wanted to back away but did not want to appear weak. He puffed his chest out. "What do you want?"

It took another step closer until he could hear it breathing. An aroma drifted from it, something calming. Pine needles and flowers? It reminded him of home and wandering in the woods. "Greetings, Tammuz," it said in a sing-song voice.

It was female, or at least Tamm assumed it was from the tone of the voice. He had never met an elf and did not know if they all spoke in such soft, sweet tones.

She lowered the cowl, revealing first her golden hair and then eyes the color of honey. Tamm stared at her angled face. She was the most beautiful being he had ever seen. "Who? Who are you?" he stuttered.

"My name is Calla. You can lower your weapon, Tamm. We are not here to harm you."

Her voice danced around in his ears. He felt peace in her words, but he did not lower his weapon. "How do you know me?"

"I have known you for longer than you may realize, but we do not have time to discuss it now. Release your spell and follow me."

He shook his head. "I'm not going anywhere with you."

Calla looked down and took a deep breath, steeling herself. "Don't be so stubborn. I know where you think you are going, but you are only rushing into death. You cannot rescue him without help. I can help you, but you must come with me. Now."

He looked at Echao, who shrugged in confusion and turned back to Calla. "How do I know I can trust you?"

"You have my trust, and in turn, I request yours. Besides, you have already signaled your location to the soldiers with your flames. They will be here any minute. So, if you want you and your brother to survive, you will cease the spell and follow me."

Tamm moved toward the top of the hill and saw a group of torches making their way toward them. He closed off the flow of magic, and the flames faltered before going out completely. He rushed to his pack and snatched up their gear. "Echao, she's right. We have to go."

Echao scooped up the remainder of the gear in his arms and fumbled closer to the group of elves, flashing a nervous smile. "Shall we?"

They jogged toward the wood line, Calla leading the way, and Tamm running beside her. The other two elves and Echao brought up the rear. Tamm could hear the clatter of hooves storming down the hill behind them. He looked back and saw three riders closing in on them.

"Don't look back," Calla said. "It will only slow you down."

"They're closing in on us," Tamm said between panting breaths. "We aren't going to make it."

Tamm looked back again, and the horses were nearly on top of Echao and the other elves. Echao was a sitting duck. He could not get to his weapons because he had scooped his gear up and was carrying his pack in his arms instead of on his back. The elf with the bow nocked an arrow in preparation to defend himself.

"Make sure my brother gets to safety," Tamm said to Calla as he turned and ran at the horsemen, drawing his sword. He ignored Calla's calls that began to fade as he ran further into danger. Echao looked at him in shock as he sped past him.

REBORN

The lead horseman swung at Tamm's head with his sword, and Tamm rolled under the strike. He bounced back to his feet but was right in front of the next two soldiers. He threw his free arm out in front of him and shouted. *"Gaoth!"* A blast of wind hit the horses in the chest, causing them to buck and tip backward, spilling the soldiers onto the ground.

A growl behind caused him to spin, and the lead soldier had dismounted and was charging. Tamm parried the attacks. He ducked under another blow and swept out with his leg, tripping the attacker. He turned to see the other two soldiers had recovered from their fall and were now approaching him, swords drawn.

Tamm prepared for the onslaught. He doubted he would make it out alive, but at least he would buy Echao some time to get to safety. The soldiers spread out, encircling him. They launched their attacks in unison, and Tamm had to spin and twist to block the blows. It felt more like a dance than a sword fight. He managed to defend himself, but did not have time between blocking attacks to launch any of his own, and could not hold out much longer.

He spun to block two near-simultaneous attacks and noticed the third soldier moving in to join the fray. This would be the end. He was panting for breath and had difficulty keeping up with the pace of the battle. These were seasoned soldiers, and they did not show any sign of fatigue. He tried to focus his mind on the power inside himself. *"Solas,"* he said, and the sword glowed softly. The attacks slowed as the soldiers stared at the sword in awe.

"He's a mage," one of them shouted. "Kill him!"

Tamm fed the spell with more power, causing a blinding light to emanate from the sword. He had a hard time seeing past the glare himself. He reduced the flow of magic to lower the intensity. A shriek pierced the air. The lead soldier was wrapped in a soft, blue light that danced across his body. He looked past him to see Calla pointing the staff at him and bolts of lightning pouring from it. Smoke rose off the soldier's body, and a putrid smell of burned hair floated on the air. The soldier's body collapsed to the ground as the lightning retreated into Calla's staff.

The other two soldiers looked at each other in shock before fleeing. Tamm began to give chase, but Calla grabbed his arm, stopping him. "Let them go. They will not be able to follow where we are going."

"Did you kill him?" he asked.

"Not quite. But, he will wake up in a day or two with a terrible headache and muscle cramps."

"Did Echao make it into the forest?"

She smiled. "Of course. I told you that you could trust me. Let's go before more of them come."

Tamm nodded in agreement and followed Calla into the forest.

NINETEEN

Tamm, Echao, and the elves trekked deeper into the forest. Calla had summoned a small light at the end of her staff to guide them through the dark. The staff was made of ornately carved wood with an aquamarine stone perched at the top clasped with silver fingers. Tamm had been quiet, not knowing what to say after having been rescued by Calla and her companions. He walked near to her but not at her side. Echao and the other elves lingered a few paces behind them.

"You can be quite reckless," Calla said.

Tamm looked at her but did not reply.

"That was foolish what you did back there," she continued. "You throw caution to the wind, risk your life as if it does not matter."

Tamm scrunched his face, irritated at himself, and irritated at being lectured at by someone he just met. "I'm a healer from a small fishing village. I have wanted nothing more than to get out of there, to find adventure. Now I've found it. But at what cost? My mentor is captured. I am a fugitive on the run, and I have learned just enough magic to be dangerous and stupid. In the grand scheme of it all, why does my life matter?"

"It matters to me," Calla said.

Tamm cocked his eyebrow. "Why? You say you know me, but we have never met."

A faint smile passed her lips. "I misspoke before. I apologize. I am not the most comfortable around humans. My people have hidden within the walls of this forest since The Fall. I have watched your people from afar, occasionally mingling with the populace, and I am intrigued by your way of life. You differ so much from us. I can explain more later, but we are almost to Gaer Alon, the capital city of my people, and my home."

Tamm followed her in silence. The more she tried to explain, the more confused he felt. She was magnificent but in a strange way. She was beautiful, of that there was no confusion. But there was something else. There was power in her voice as if she laced every word with magic. The control she had over her magic was impressive. Linsyn had not even displayed that kind of power in front of him.

As they ventured further into the forest, he could see structures scattered among the trees. A shadow blurred between some brush, and he strained to see, unsure if it was an animal or something else. "Calla?"

"Yes."

"Could you increase your light some?" he said, edging closer to her. "I'm having difficulty seeing around me."

She shook her head. "I will not. I'm sorry. We are near the city, and what you see are homes. The elves inside are resting, and I do not wish to wake them."

Tamm nodded and sped up, coming alongside her. He felt drawn to her and wanted to learn as much as he could about her.

"We are here," she said, just as two elves slipped from behind a set of massive oaks, the tallest Tamm had ever seen. He stared up but could not see the top of the trees in the darkness. Calla crossed her fist over her heart, and the two guards moved aside, allowing them to enter.

"I have seen several people use that sign," Tamm said, crossing his fist over his heart. "Humans and now, elves. What does it mean?"

Calla paused her stride. "You do not know?"

Tamm shook his head.

"It is a salute, a sign of respect, a promise. Before The Fall, when King Riehner was the leader of Iradell and magic flourished, it was a sign among the people of Iradell. It began with the King, then the Battlemages, then the soldiers, then all of Iradell. It showed honor and love among others. The sign symbolizes a mantra. *My life for yours.*"

"My life for yours?" Tamm asked.

"Yes. King Riehner felt that if the people loved their neighbors as they did themselves, then there would be peace. No life was thought to be above another's. We were all equal and would sacrifice ourselves to protect one another."

"I know that Riehner was dethroned, but what happened?" he asked.

"Usurped is a better word. But that is a story for another time. For now, you must be introduced to the Council of Nine, our ruling house."

Tamm followed her through the city. His eyes were now able to take in its splendor due to small glowing lanterns scattered throughout the city. The lanterns were not lit with oil; they glowed with magic. He could feel it. Magic permeated this place. The trees themselves thrummed with it. There were structures built from wood, but many of the buildings were formed in and around existing trees and other flora. Branches and vines twisted and braided within each other to create walkways and stairs that, although appeared to be formed with magic, had a natural look to them.

They ascended a set of wooden stairs to a building formed in the base of a large pine near the center of the city. A tall, slender elf with jet black hair stood at the top of the stairs waiting for them. "Counsel Elion," Calla said, greeting him with a bow.

"Ah, you have returned with them," Elion said in a wise, hoarse voice. "You have done well, child. Greetings, Master Tammuz, Master Echao. We welcome your arrival." He crossed his fist over his heart. Tamm fumbled to return the gesture. "Calla will show you to your quarters. You will rest tonight, but tomorrow we have much to discuss."

"Counsel Elion," Tamm said. "Thank you for your hospitality, but we will not be staying. Calla rescued us from near-death by the king's henchmen, but my mentor has been arrested, and I must go and rescue him. If I tarry, he will surely be put to death."

Elion's eyes were filled with empathy as he looked at Tamm. "We are aware of his plight, and we wish to aid your attempt to rescue him."

Tamm looked surprised. "You do?"

Elion laughed a gentle chuckle, like a young barn owl hooting. "Why, yes. He is very special to us, also. We do not wish him to perish and will do everything in our power to prevent it. However, you are in no condition to continue your journey tonight. You are still wounded from your recent encounter with the Kapre. Rest tonight, and we will discuss it more in the morning."

Tamm looked at Calla, who smiled encouragingly at him. He looked at Echao for his opinion, but his eyes were almost shut while he stood. Deep down, he knew he could not continue his journey tonight. He and Echao were too tired. If they ran into any more soldiers, they would not be able to defend themselves. "Very well," he said with a sigh.

Elion nodded and pointed his hand back down the stairs to a building across the way. "Calla, do you mind?"

She bowed to Elion and summoned Tamm and Echao to follow her. She led them to a small structure nestled in a treetop up a short flight of stairs. He entered the door to find two beds, two trunks for their gear, and a small table in the center with water available, along with a writing desk against the wall and a few cedar chairs. Tamm dropped his gear in the trunk and placed the sword by the headboard.

"Goodnight," Calla called softly behind him, and he heard the door click shut. He sank into the bed and drifted off to sleep.

◆◆◆◆◆

Light slipped through the window, pulling Tamm from sleep. He stretched before sitting up on the side of the bed. Echao was sitting at the writing desk and finished a letter with a flourish before folding the piece of parchment and slipping it into a pocket. "Sleep well?" Echao asked without turning around.

Tamm poured some of the water in his hands and splashed it on his face. "I'm still exhausted, but I'll get over it."

A knock at the door startled him, and he hopped up to answer it.

"Good morning," Calla said as soon as Tamm opened the door. "Ready to go?"

Tamm brushed his hair down with his hands. "We've only just gotten up. We haven't even had time to eat or bathe."

She had a puzzled look like she did not understand his protest. "I will take you to the bathhouses, and I will have your breakfast ready when you return."

"By all means," Echao said, pushing past Tamm. "Lead the way. I'm starving, and I need a bath almost as bad."

REBORN

Tamm and Echao were led to a tented area near a river. There was a dressing area with benches that led into a long hall with short walls separating them. Large hollow logs ran along the top of the tent and had offshoots of smaller reeds. The tent canopy was constructed of leaves and vines woven together. Tamm stood in the stall but could not figure out how to get water. At home, he would just bring water in from the well and warm it for a bath. He tried to use magic, summoning water with a simple word. *"Struanna."* Water trickled from the reeds above his head. He yelled for Echao, who was further into the tent and shouted out the word to summon water for him.

"Whoa!" Echao said. "I could get used to this."

They finished bathing and made their way back to their room. There was a new table in the center of the room with two chairs around it loaded with a broad spread of bread, fruit, and berries. Cups of tea were placed out, steam rising in the air. Calla was not there. She must have set the table and left. Tamm and Echao devoured the food and left to find her. She was waiting for them at the bottom of the stairs.

She offered to finish showing them around the city. They followed her through the streets as she showed them where the Counsel of Nine met, where the mages studied, where the warriors trained, and multiple meeting houses and shops. The elves were social people and spent most of their day with each other, laughing and fellowshipping.

After showing them around the city, she took them back to Elion, who had prepared them a meal at his home.

"Greetings. Please come in. I expect you are hungry after touring our beloved capital. Come and dine while we talk."

Tamm followed Elion in and sat at the table. Calla sat beside him and Echao across from him, next to Elion. Elion made small talk as they ate, asking about life in Aleesia and the condition of Rhys Castle. He was very interested in the life of humans. He was specifically curious about the battle with the Kapre and how many there were and their capabilities. Tamm recounted the entire account to him but was becoming impatient.

Tamm folded his napkin and placed it on his empty plate. "Elion, you have been a most gracious guest, and I thank you for your hospitality, but I dare not delay any longer. If you would like to send some of your warriors with me on my quest to rescue Linsyn, I welcome their aid. Otherwise, I must take my leave. The king's evil has no bounds, and I refuse to let him carry out that evil on Linsyn."

"I am sorry," Elion said. "I am not trying to delay you. I feel there is more you need to know before you journey to rescue him. I have not been clear with my speech and have wasted time. Calla, will you please show him the Hall of Kings? You can go after you have visited there. I will send you with horses to speed your journey."

"Very well," Tamm said. "But, I will depart immediately afterward. Thank you again for your hospitality." He slid his chair away from the table.

Elion cleared his throat. "Once you have succeeded in your quest, please return here. I would like to catch up with Linsyn. It has been some time since I have spoken to him."

REBORN

Tamm exited the home and walked beside Calla. He waved to Echao, who was going with Elion to saddle the horses. They walked side by side and talked as they went. She was interested in human life and things that Tamm thought to be mundane. Tamm laughed at her. "The things I find boring about my life, you find exciting. I have always dreamed of leaving that village to see the world, and you would rather see my bland village."

"I find human life fascinating," she said. "I have lived my life closed off in this forest because Tzelder has persecuted and hunted my people. I have always watched you from a distance, your people from a distance. I want to know more about you and your people."

Tamm's fingers brushed hers as they walked, and he pulled his arm away in embarrassment. "You're different than the other elves here," he said. "Your hair, your eyes, your demeanor; it's all different."

She stopped suddenly, and he walked a few paces past her. "We're here."

Before him stood a solid glass building that stretched out away from them. They entered through glass doors. Suits of armor lined the hall. In the center of one wall was a suit of armor that was clear, like diamond. It matched the sword that Tamm had gotten from Linsyn's hut.

"This is King Riehner's Battlemage armor," she said. "He was the first Battlemage. When the humans first arrived in this land, the elves, dwarves, and Kapre were embroiled in a hellish war. No one made any headway, but the death tolls were devastating. Once the humans arrived, they were pulled into the battle. It was Riehner that brought the races together to defeat the Kapre and led Iradell into a time of peace and prosperity. He fell in love with a young elf named Beltia. She was the daughter of our ruling family. Before long, they were married and solidified an alliance among the humans and elves. Magic was given to the humans as a gift, and with it, Riehner created the Battlemages. There was peace for quite some time until Tzelder sought to overthrow Riehner. Beltia was set to deliver an heir to Riehner, but she was gravely wounded in the coup."

Tamm stood in amazement, listening to the story of Iradell's creation. "What happened next?"

"Beltia took a spear to the chest. Despite Riehner's abilities in magic, he could not heal her. He brought her here, hoping the elves could mend the wound. Unfortunately, we were not able to save her."

"You say *we* as if you were there," Tamm said.

She stared at the ground, avoiding his eyes. "I was there."

Tamm looked shocked. "How? You're no older than I am."

"We do not age the way humans do. I am much older than you think. You mentioned that I was not like the rest of my people. That is true. I use magic to change my hair and eye color to be more like the humans, to blend in when I enter their world."

"You said earlier that you were trapped in this forest," Tamm said.

She ran her fingers along the armor's glassy surface. "I am. Rarely do I leave this forest, but when I do, it is to check on you."

Tamm looked at her in surprise. "Why are you checking on me?"

"I told you that I have known you for longer than you could imagine. Come with me, and I will explain."

Tamm followed her through the back door to a mausoleum of polished marble. He ran his fingers along the smooth stone. "Is this hers?"

"It is," she said. "Hers and his." She wiped a tear away from her eye. "It is my fault."

Tamm looked surprised. "What do you mean, it's your fault?"

Calla placed a hand on the door of the mausoleum. "I was assigned as her protector. We lost many lives trying to save her. You can only spend so much of your power when using magic, and it will eventually deplete you of your life force, and you will slip away. We tried to save her for so, so long. But, she would not have wanted all of those lives to be lost to save her. We kept her in stasis, trying to heal her, until I suggested that we bring her out long enough to deliver the child, the heir to the throne. We were able to save the child, but she perished in the process. She was able to hold her son just before her spirit left her."

Tamm coughed, fighting back the tears that were welling up in his eyes. "That is awful. What happened to the boy?"

"He lived. After the queen passed, I was assigned as her son's protector, a position I have held until this day."

Tamm looked confused. "But the kingdom was overthrown so long ago. How could the boy still be living, and you be his protector?"

"We kept her in stasis for over one hundred years. We only delivered the child sixteen years ago."

"Could I meet him?" Tamm asked. "I would love to meet the rightful prince. Why has he stayed hidden so long and allowed Tzelder to continue his corrupt reign?"

Calla walked over and took Tamm by the hands. "Look at the sword you carry. That is the only piece of Riehner's Battlemage regalia that we are missing. And now, you have it. That is no coincidence. You are my charge, Tamm. I am your sworn protector. You are the prince, the son of King Riehner."

Tamm stumbled back away from her and sat on the ground, a thousand thoughts rushing through his mind. "That's impossible. I'm the son of Kèlris, blacksmith of Aleesia."

"Tamm, you know I speak the truth. Why would I lie to you?"

Tamm shook his head. "So, you're telling me that my parents aren't my real parents, that I have been a secret son of a king, and my actual parents are buried here?"

Calla sat beside him. "Mostly. Your mother is buried here. Your father still lives. He is a Battlemage, the last, and although human, the magic extends his life span."

"Why have I never met him?" Tamm asked in frustration. "If my father is the King and he lives, then why has he never come to me?"

"He has watched over you your entire life," she said. "You have grown close to him over the past few months, although you did not speak much to him before then."

He wrang his hands in frustration and sprung to his feet. "Calla, stop with the riddles. Who is the King? Who is my father?"

She stood and leaned in close to him as if to whisper a secret. "Linsyn is your father, Tamm. He is Riehner. He is the rightful High King of Iradell. He has lived in secret to protect you."

Tamm stared at her in awe, so many emotions rushing through him, before stumbling back on his rear-end. "Linsyn? Linsyn is my father?"

She nodded. "It is time, Tamm. Let's bring him home. You two have a lot to talk about. The horses should be ready."

Calla took him by the hand and helped him to stand. They journeyed back to the town gate in silence. He ran all the possibilities through his mind as he walked mindlessly beside her. He wanted to believe her, but how could he? The thought was outlandish. Although, he did have the sword and was able to use magic like the Battlemages.

Three horses were saddled and waiting when they arrived at the gate. Echao climbed into the saddle and turned to wave them closer. "What's wrong with you?" he asked Tamm. "You look like you've seen a ghost."

Tamm climbed onto the horse. "I'm fine. We need to hurry. Who's the other horse for?"

Calla scurried up into the saddle. "It is mine. You will not have to go anywhere alone. I am here to protect you. Let us ride; we have tarried long enough."

Calla led the way out of the forest. The horses were fast, and it was almost as if they steered themselves through the woods, following behind Calla and her horse with very little need of direction. The sun was setting as they came to the edge of the forest.

Calla pulled the horse to a stop at the edge of the trees. "There should be some food in your packs. You can eat during the ride if you need to. We will ride all night. Our scouts say Linsyn should arrive at the capital by tomorrow night. We have no time to spare."

Tamm nodded and spurred his horse forward to the road. They were going to have to stick to the road to make good time. Calla jabbed her heels into the horse's flanks, bringing the horse to a sprint and settling in alongside Tamm. Echao followed suit as they rode hard into the night.

TWENTY

†

Tamm, Echao, and Calla rode through the night without stopping, but at sunrise, they took a break by a calm part of the river long enough to water the horses but spurred them on without much rest. They were still half a day's ride from the capital, but the horses would not survive if they pushed them any further. The steeds foamed at the mouth and could no longer maintain a gallop. They dismounted and led the horses by a rope as they trudged along.

Tamm squinted and could see the outline of a city in the distance. It was mid-morning by the time it was clear enough to make out the city, Cartrice. Kèlris had mentioned it a time or two when discussing his trade routes. Homes and farms spread across the plains outside the sprawling metropolis. It was the next largest city in the empire after the capital and was well fortified by a high stone wall that encircled it. The gates were open, but there were not any guards posted.

"I say we stop here and rest the horses," Tamm said. "I want to get to the capital as soon as possible, but the horses won't make it any further. We can stable them and allow them to eat and drink while we speak to the locals. They may have heard news of the soldiers' movements and be able to tell us how far behind we are."

Echao grunted in agreement. "You two get us some food and refill our waterskins. I'll ask around for any information. And try to be inconspicuous. An elf in this city is going to stick out like a sore thumb. No offense, Calla."

"None taken," she said. "I'll be careful."

They passed through the gate into a bustling city, unlike anything Tamm had ever experienced. The streets crisscrossed here and there with buildings crammed in close and horse-drawn carts speeding past. The smell was horrendous. Manure lay on the roads, and several scraggly men ran behind the horses, shoveling the waste into another cart to deliver it to farms outside the city.

Tamm tried to shake the smell as he checked from side to side for signs of guards or soldiers, but he did not see any. They split up after entering the town proper. Tamm and Calla went to the city center, passing through the market district, to find the tavern and get some food, while Echao took the horses to a stablemaster near the gates to feed them and search for any information about Linsyn.

The tavern was full of patrons coming in for the midday meal. Calla lowered her hood so that she would not call attention to herself by keeping it up indoors. She adjusted her hair to cover her ears. The smell of pine trees and flowers wafted in the air from the flip of her hair. Tamm sniffed the sweet smell. He had to agree that she did blend in better with her hair and eye color. He could still tell she was an elf from the shape of her face and her slender body, but he was not sure if anyone else could.

He chose a table not far from the door. He did not want to be blocked from his only exit in case they were recognized. A bar wench stopped by the table and took an order for food and drink and took their waterskins to refill them. He left Calla at the table and went to the bar, searching the faces of the other patrons for any potential enemy.

"What can I do you for?" a large burly man behind the counter asked.

"We're traveling to the capital and had heard rumors of several soldiers moving through the area," Tamm said, using a coastal accent while trying to sound older. "My wife and I are looking to relocate to this area, but we want to live somewhere that is safe to raise children. It's not that dangerous around here, is it? Where soldiers have to run hither and tither arresting folks?"

The bartender looked to the booth where Calla sat, and then looked around the bar to see if anyone else was listening. "You're awful young to be worried about rearing children. Why are you so worried about soldiers?"

Tamm's heart started to race. The bartender was not buying his story. "Well," he said. "To be honest, sir, we ran away from home. Her father didn't like me much and wouldn't consent to our marriage. So, we thought the capital would be the last place he'd look for us."

The bartender looked at him more softly now but did not offer any information.

"So," Tamm said. "D'ya think you could help me out? Have you heard of any increase in soldiers in the area? Any whisper of them searching for a girl from the coast?"

The bartender gave him a gentle smile, softening his surly appearance. "Nah, boy. No one's looking for a girl." He looked around again. "There have been some soldiers around town. Got here last night, carrying some prisoner from across the lake. I hear they're taking him to the king for execution. Some mage, they say."

"They're here?" Tamm asked in surprise. "With a mage?"

The bartender gestured with his hands that Tamm sit down. "Calm yourself, boy. They ain't after you and your girl. They'll have the mage gone by morning."

Tamm's arms shook as he realized he was gripping the bar. He relaxed and wiped a streak of sweat from his brow. "Thank you, good sir. Your information has been invaluable. But, it looks like my gal is eating without me. I bid you a good day."

Tamm slipped back to the table and sat across from Calla, who was picking at some vegetables. "You know, the one thing I don't understand about your people, is why you insist on cooking everything," she said. "These vegetables, for instance. Why cook them? They were fine the way they were."

"Calla, they're here," he whispered, leaning in across the table.

REBORN

"What?" she asked, looking up from her food.

"I just spoke with the bartender. He said the soldiers have Linsyn here and are planning to move him to the capital sometime tonight. They're probably waiting for the cover of darkness."

She clapped her hands and bounced in her seat before looking around to see if anyone had noticed her reaction. "That is excellent news. We have to move quickly, but we must be wary."

Echao plopped down in a chair beside Tamm, startling him. "You'll never guess what I learned."

"Linsyn is here," Tamm said. "The bartender told us. We were just discussing our next step."

Echao arched his eyebrows. "Well, I see you've not wasted time. But do you know where he's being kept?"

Echao waited a moment in silence, letting the question linger. "No? Well, I do."

"Don't keep us waiting," Tamm said.

"There is a small castle in the northeast of the city. It's where the overseer resides when visiting but is otherwise unused. Vorn and his men have set up camp in there, and there's a dungeon below the castle. Rumor is that's where they're keeping Linsyn."

Calla adjusted in her seat and leaned closer to the two boys. "Eat quickly. A group of soldiers just entered."

Tamm and Echao peered over the table toward the bar. Tamm did not see any soldiers, no one in armor anyway.

"Don't stare," she said. "Look closer. The four men that just entered are wearing swords at their belts. No armor, likely an attempt to more easily blend in. We do not need to hang around here. Finish your food so we can leave. We can find somewhere else to finish discussing tactics."

They finished their meal and slipped out of the tavern. Echao recommended going back to the stables to discuss their next move. He had noticed a way up to the loft while stabling the horses, and they could sneak in through the back unseen and make their way to the top.

Tamm went first while Echao kept watch and was quickly followed by Calla, who flitted up the ladder without making a sound, like a crouching cat hunting prey. Echao crept behind them and lowered a hatch. They each slid a hay bale to the center of the loft and sat in a circle. Tamm wiggled, the hay poking through his pants.

"We could launch an ambush right outside the city," Echao said, not wasting any time. "If we catch them by surprise on the road to the capital, it could work."

"No," Tamm said, interrupting him. "Too much that could go wrong. What if they stay off the roadway or have added more soldiers to their ranks? Linsyn could be injured during the fighting."

Calla sat quietly for a moment, tapping her fingers on her knees before adding her thoughts. "Tamm is right. We need to have more control over the situation. What if we sneak into the dungeon?"

Echao shook his head. "Too dangerous. We don't know exactly where he's being held. Once we get in, if we're spotted, or another prisoner alerts the guards, we could be trapped inside. I don't know about you, but I would like to make it back home in one piece."

Tamm walked over to the ledge and stared out over the city. It was larger than Aleesia. Life here was so much busier. Merchants and citizens darted in and out of shops. Tradesmen rode in on horse-drawn carts piled full with stacks of wares. This was the first city, other than Gaer Alon, that he had been to outside of his hometown, Aleesia.

He searched around, looking for any clue that would tell him what to do, what the correct course of action would be. He could see the castle in the distance, but could not make out much detail. He could tell that there were multiple levels to the castle with another level below the first floor. "What if we can get in close to the castle to look around?" he asked, more to himself than anyone else.

"How do you suppose we do that?" Echao replied.

Tamm pointed toward the castle. "There's a lower level that's not quite all underground. You can see a piece of it from here. It's worth a shot."

Calla walked over beside him and peered out over the city. "I can see it. If there are any bars or doors nearby, we could sneak in from there or even listen in. It will be difficult to get in there without being seen. I would wager that the reason there have not been any guards at the gates is that they have been stationed inside."

"We all can't go," Tamm said. "It would be too suspicious. I'll go. You two can stay close by in case anything goes wrong."

Calla touched Tamm's arm softly. "I don't like you going alone."

Tamm smiled at her. "I appreciate your concern. I'll be careful."

"I think I saw an inn nearby," Echao said. "I'll walk you as close to the castle as I can without drawing attention, and then I'll meet Calla back at the inn. Don't take too long, or we'll come looking for you."

Tamm agreed. They sneaked back out of the stable and made the trek to the inn. It was a large three-story building, and except for a few cobblestone walls on the ground floor, made completely out of wood. Calla left to try to get a room on the top floor to have a better view of the castle.

Echao walked with Tamm to the outskirts of the keep. The walls were not very tall, just above Echao's head. They sneaked around to the far back corner, and Tamm looked around to make sure they were not being watched.

"What's going on with you and Calla?" Echao asked.

Tamm looked at him, confused. "What do you mean?"

"Tamm, don't take me for a fool. I see the way she touched your arm, the way she looks at you."

Tamm shook his head. "We don't have time for this. It'll be dark soon."

Echao's face softened. "The elves are fascinating. They aren't called the fair folk for no reason. We left home so abruptly without saying goodbye. I just wonder how Adina will take it."

Tamm's face fell flat at the sound of her name. "I will admit that Calla is beautiful, but there is nothing between us. She is here to protect me and help me free Linsyn. That's all. Now give me a boost."

Echao sighed and held out a hand to lift Tamm above the wall. Tamm pushed off and gripped the rough stone with his fingertips as he slid his body over and then down the other side. "I'm in. I won't be long."

"Be careful," Echao said, but Tamm barely heard him as he was already skulking along the side of the castle wall. The stones were marvelous up close, chiseled with precision. They were so finely cut that they did not require any mortar. How stable could the structure be against attack without any mortar? He shook the thought from his head, not having time to ponder it.

As he moved farther toward the back of the castle, the ground sloped down, not steeply at first but slanting deeper the further he went. The perfect walls of the fortress faded to a rougher cut, dark stone, small openings with bars covering them scattered along the rock wall. Wailing and moaning floated from some of the openings. He tried to peer inside, but the cells were so black that, even with the sun shining toward them, he could not see anything within.

He strained to hear as he passed the bars, but there was no sign of Linsyn. He had come to the back of the castle and thought Linsyn might be on the other side of the dungeon, although he did not remember seeing anything that looked similar to the rock wall and bars on the other side of the castle. He decided to crawl on his hands and knees so he could get his ear right next to the bars. "Linsyn," he whispered into each opening as he crawled along without any luck. He was almost back to the front of the dungeon when he heard a voice answer his call. "Tamm?"

It was only a whisper, hoarse and weak, but his stomach lurched, bringing him to a halt. "Linsyn, is that you?"

"You shouldn't have come," Linsyn said. A violent cough shook the old man. "I told you to go to the elves. Alas, you always were stubborn."

Tamm wanted to giggle at Linsyn's attempt to joke, but he could feel his pain emanating through the bars. "Hang on, Linsyn. We're going to get you out."

"We?" Linsyn asked, the weakness evident in his voice. "Who is with you?"

He reached his hand through the bars. "I didn't come alone. I brought help."

Linsyn wrapped his wrinkled hand around Tamm's and patted it. "Don't do anything stupid."

Tamm darted off in the direction of the wall. He was elated that he had found Linsyn, but thoughts overwhelmed him as he thought about how he could possibly break the old man out of prison. He was likely well-guarded and so weak. He would be unable to move with any haste. There was a tree near the inner wall, and he scaled it and rolled over the top of the wall to find Echao waiting on him.

"So?" Echao asked.

"I found him. Let's get back to the inn, and we'll talk more in private there."

They met Calla in a room she had secured for them on the third floor. It gave a good vantage point of the dungeon area behind the wall of the castle. Tamm peered out the window, staring at the small opening to Linsyn's cell.

"We have to find a way to get him out," he said. "We can't get in from behind that wall. The windows are too small, and I scouted the far end of the grounds as well and didn't see an entrance."

Echao had his head propped in his hands in deep thought, mumbling. "What if we... No, that's no good. Maybe if... No, that won't work either."

"We may not be able to enter through the front gate," Calla said. "But, there is a door leading to the dungeon."

"Enter through the door?" Echao asked, his face displaying his frustration. "Are you daft? Can your magic protect all four of us if we waltz up to the porter and ask to enter?"

Calla turned to him, her expression calm but puzzled. "No, I am not daft. And it could work. There have been soldiers moving through there all day, and they are not using the front gate. We just need to find the door that they are using. It is the path of least resistance and one that they will be least expecting."

"It could work," Tamm said, "if it doesn't get us killed. Echao, could you have the horses tethered and ready to ride?"

"I'm not letting you go in there alone," Echao said, pointing his finger at Tamm.

Tamm shook his head. "Not alone. Calla will come with me while you ready the horses. Once you have them ready, bring one back to the castle and meet us there. We'll never make it running through the streets, but if you have a horse ready, we can make it out."

Echao frowned. "I don't like it, but what other choice do we have?"

Tamm smiled at Calla. "Great. The sun has almost set. Let's get started."

◆◆◆◆◆

Night had fallen, and Echao had left to secure the horses. Tamm and Calla slipped into the dark and flitted between houses and shops on their way to the castle. Calla had spied a few soldiers moving in and out of the fortress, in what she assumed was the entrance to the dungeon, just before nightfall. The door was hidden from public view by foliage that had been planted there, likely deliberately, to hide the entrance. Their best guess was that there were at least five soldiers garrisoned inside by the numbers of those entering and exiting the compound.

Tamm poked his head around the corner of a nearby building to scout out the entrance. No soldiers were guarding the dungeon from the outside. He hoped there were none on the inside or requiring a password to get in.

They rushed across the street and parted the overgrown bushes obscuring the path. There were no soldiers there either. They crept down a sloping cobblestone path that ended abruptly at a thick iron-reinforced oak door. Tamm reached out and pushed the latch, and the door parted. He placed his ear near the crack but did not hear anyone on the other side.

He and Calla tiptoed into the hall, opening the door just far enough that they could slip through. The hallway was lit by torches lining the walls and the orange glow scattered shadows along the stone floor. The hall stretched the full length of the castle. There were no soldiers in the hall either, and this concerned him. "This is almost too easy."

"I agree," Calla said. "Tread lightly."

Tamm counted the cells as he passed them until he came to the one that should be Linsyn's. He peered inside, but it was too dark to see. He held his hand through the bars. "*Sruthán.*" A small flame sprouted in his hand, casting light into the cell, causing the shadows to flee. Linsyn was lying on the bed, his arm dangling into the floor. "Linsyn," Tamm called out, trying not to yell, but to be loud enough to arouse the old man.

His body stirred, and his hand twitched. "Water."

"He's too weak to move," Tamm said. "We have to get him out. Help me look for the keys."

Calla looked around but then turned back to the cell door. "We don't have time for this, Tamm. I can feel his energy fading from here." She pointed her staff at the lock. "*Sgaradh an glas.*" A soft light hummed around the stone on the end of her staff, and the lock fell away, dropping to the floor in pieces.

Tamm stared at her in surprise. "You'll have to teach me that someday." She smiled at him softly before he ran to Linsyn's side. The old man's eyes were closed, his breaths coming in gasps. "We have got to get him out of here," Tamm said. He scooped Linsyn under the arm and Calla followed his lead.

"I think you have gone far enough," a familiar voice said behind him, as the iron door slammed shut. He turned to see Vorn and a handful of guards. "It was fun watching you scramble around the city, trying to find a way to free the old bird. We pulled the guards away just to toy with you."

Tamm scowled at him. "Oh, come now," Vorn said. "No need to be so angry. It was all in good fun. I always knew you were trouble, and now I will put an end to your meddling.

Tamm rushed at the door, just as a soldier bolted another lock into place. "Don't think your little elf friend can remove this one," Vorn said. "We have ways to limit her magic. I'll not let you escape with him. The king has searched high and low for longer than you have been alive."

Tamm turned to see Calla kneeling, her brow furrowed in pain. "What are you doing to her?"

"It takes special precautions when you are holding one of the world's most powerful mages. See, this man is not Linsyn, not really. He has used that name for some time, cowering in fear rather than facing judgment. This is Riehner, once king of this great land until he was defeated by King Tzelder. He had us place certain protections in this cell to prevent the use of magic and slowly drain those who do use it. It won't be long until he fades into the next life, and the little knife-ear will be following him shortly."

Tamm turned to Linsyn, who was now lying on the cold, hard stone floor, and Calla was lying beside him, sweat beading up on her forehead, her staff lying at her side. Tamm felt confused, foggy-headed, but he did not feel weak or in pain as Linsyn and Calla did. The magic should affect him the same since he also had the same power inside of him.

He snarled at Vorn. "I will get out of here, and when I do, I will kill you!"

Vorn laughed, and the soldiers echoed him. "You will get out, that is the truth, but you will be the one to die. Once the old man and elf are dead, I will haul you off to the king to be tried for treason and, ultimately, put to death."

Tamm drew the sword from under his cloak, and Vorn's eyes lit up at the sight. "You carry his blade?" You are brave, indeed. Stupid, but brave. That is a powerful sword, boy. Lay it on the ground before you get yourself hurt."

Tamm closed his eyes and felt the flames inside him begin to rise. He fed the fire with his anger and felt it flow out of his hands and into the sword. He did not speak a word, but the sword glowed a soft white, then orange. Vorn and the soldiers stood in shock. The light continued to glow and change colors, and with it, heat emanated from the blade. Tamm could feel the heat on his face, but it did not burn him.

Tamm opened his eyes to see the soldiers on the other side of the gate, shielding their eyes. Vorn's face was stern, as always, but his eyes were wide in amazement. "How is he doing that?" Vorn asked. "He is so close to death, but is still strong enough to override the wards of this cage."

An arrow streaked in front of Tamm's face, striking one of the soldiers in the neck, and he crumpled to the ground, blood pooling on the floor beside him. Tamm looked up and saw Echao standing at the door, bow drawn, preparing to release another arrow. Two of the soldiers fled back up the stairs, but the other two drew their swords to stand their ground with Vorn. Echao released the bolt, but Vorn swatted it away with his sword. The three warriors moved to close in on him as Echao backed further away.

Tamm fed the sword with all the anger and fear he had pent up inside. The sword glowed so brightly, Tamm could barely make out its edges. He swung the sword at the bars, slicing through the iron like butter. He grabbed Calla first and drug her out of the cell. Once out, her strength began to return. He tossed her the staff, and she used it to push herself to a standing position.

"Can you get him out of the cell?" he asked her. She shook her head yes, still unable to use the strength to form words. He touched her on the shoulder and ran to help Echao. The first soldier fell quickly with a thrust to his back. The sword was no longer glowing, but it was still sharp as diamond and easily pierced the soldier's armor. Vorn turned to face Tamm as Echao drew his daggers and became tangled up with the other soldier.

Vorn feigned a few attacks at Tamm, playing with him, sizing up his abilities. "Ah, I always thought your foolhardy father was training you in secret. He never could quite let go of the old ways."

Vorn launched a series of attacks at Tamm. He dodged and parried, but it was apparent that Vorn was the more skilled swordsman. Tamm would not be able to continue evading the barrage of attacks for long. He danced away from several more blows, Vorn pushing him further away from the door.

REBORN

Tamm saw a slight opening on Vorn's left side and took advantage of it, thrusting at his exposed side. Vorn deflected the blow and spun Tamm around, trapping the sword against his neck.

Vorn laughed. "He didn't teach you enough, though. That was too easy. Leaving my side open drew you in like a bee to pollen."

Tamm squirmed but felt the sword bite into his neck. One wrong move and Vorn could behead him. "Let go of the sword, and I'll not kill you now. Bringing this blade to the king, along with Riehner's dead body, will buy you a few more days before you face the gallows, and should buy me a seat as an Overseer." He smiled slyly, and Tamm wrinkled his nose from the pungent smell of his breath.

Hundreds of possibilities rushed through Tamm's mind, but none of them feasible, each one ending with him losing his head from his own sword. Vorn pulled tighter on the sword's grip, and Tamm tried to bury his head further into Vorn's chest and away from the blade. A flame flew across the room and nearly hit Vorn in the head. They both turned to where the fireball had come from, and Calla was standing, pointing her staff, Linsyn staggering behind her.

The pressure from the sword on Tamm's neck lightened a hair's breadth as Vorn prepared to defend himself from another magical attack. Tamm used this opportunity and cut his eyes to the cuff of Vorn's tunic. "*Sruthán*," he whispered, and a flame erupted from the sleeve of Vorn's tunic. Vorn jumped away, swatting at his jacket. Tamm rolled away from Vorn and drew his sword back at the ready. Vorn backed into the wall, knocking a torch from its sconce and onto his pants, which burst into flames. He danced around the floor, patting and swatting at his clothes.

Tamm looked for Echao and saw the last soldier fall in a heap as Echao bent forward, gasping for breath. He was tired but unharmed. Echao waved his arm to signal it was time to go. Tamm slipped under one of Linsyn's arms, and Calla slipped under the other. They started to run outside, but Tamm stopped at the door. As Vorn rolled on the ground, Tamm looked to the stones that lined the ceiling and remembered the perfectly cut stones of the castle that did not require mortar. He smiled at Linsyn and handed him over to Calla. "Get him outside." He drew on his strength and muttered the word as he released the power inside him. "*Gaoth!*" Wind soared from his outstretched hand, hitting the ceiling in such force that the floor trembled and dust trickled down right before the stones tumbled down onto Vorn and the dead soldiers.

He stumbled out of the dungeon, exhausted from the use of magic, as the stones fell around him. He helped hoist Linsyn up onto a horse with Echao and smacked the horse on its flank, urging it forward. He and Calla raced between the buildings toward the stables, as citizens and soldiers poured out into the streets, drawn by the commotion of the castle collapsing.

Two mares were tied to a post outside the stables. Tamm and Calla swung into the saddles without slowing. Tamm flicked the sword, separating the ropes from the post before sheathing it behind his shoulder. He spurred the horse toward the gate, digging the heel of his boots into the horse's ribs. They did not slow until Cartrice was invisible in the distance.

TWENTY-ONE

Tamm paced outside the door of an elongated house formed from interwoven trees. They rode all night to get back to Gaer Alon while Linsyn drifted in and out of consciousness. Calla, although weakened from the ordeal herself, had to use magic on him continually to keep him from passing into the void. Elvish healers had taken over as soon as they arrived back to Gaer Alon and were in the longhouse with him still. Linsyn had not suffered many outward wounds, but the magic of the prison cell had been powerful to affect him and Calla the way that it did.

Tamm had not slept in a few days, his emotions keeping him going until now. He tottered side to side as he paced the forest floor, waiting for word of Linsyn's health. He physically could not stand any longer and plopped down onto a stump. He willed his eyes to stay open, but he was losing the battle. The faint sound of a door sliding open caused his eyelids to flutter open. He turned toward the sound as Calla stepped out from the longhouse. She looked weak, paler than usual, and a gray streak of hair outlined her face.

Tamm jumped to his feet. "Is he alright? Are you well? What happened to your hair?"

Calla waved him off and sat down on the ground near the stump where he had been sitting. He sat beside her. "I am tired," she said, lying back onto the grass. "We had to use strong magic to save him. The king had put some sort of hex on that cell, specifically for Linsyn, but it also targeted elves, though not as fiercely. That is likely why it didn't affect you. He didn't yet know of your abilities."

"But, Linsyn is alive?" Tamm asked.

She gave a slight tilt of her chin in affirmation. "Yes. He will recover. It will be a few days before he has the strength to stand, but you should not see him until then. Our people will continue to provide healing magic."

Tamm's shoulders slumped. He had only discovered a few days ago that he was the prince and that Linsyn, or Riehner as was his proper name, was the rightful King and his father. Everything had been a blur, and he had not had time to reflect on it all.

"Is that the natural color of your hair showing?" Tamm asked, pointing at the gray streak that had appeared.

"This?" she asked, running her fingers through the strand of gray hair. "No. My hair is like all the other elves, black. I change it magically to fit into your world more easily. This occurs from magic use. Or the overuse of it."

Tamm cocked his head to the side, confused.

"My apologies," she said. "My mind is not fully clear, as I'm sure you can tell. Magic draws on our inner strength. If we allow it to draw too much from us, it will drain us, even unto death. This is an example. I was already weakened from the hex and used magic throughout the night to save my King. I continued to help today, which resulted in my hair being changed. Once I realized how close I was to being consumed, I released the magic and came here to rest."

"Thank you," Tamm said, smiling at her.

Calla sat up, her brow wrinkled. "For what?"

"For saving him. For saving me. For being so kind. For taking the time to teach me, even when you are exhausted."

"That is what I am here for," she said, laying her head back on the grass. "I am your sworn protector. I will not leave your side." She smiled at him softly, her eyes closing.

He smiled back at her, though he did not think she saw him. "Calla?"

"Uh-huh," she murmured, but she was asleep before he could finish his question. He gathered some moss nearby and placed it under her head as she slept. He propped up against a nearby tree and watched over her until he could no longer hold his eyes open, and sleep took him.

REBORN

Tamm jolted awake, the smell of hot tea wafting on the air. He searched around him, confused. He was back in bed in the small tree loft he and Echao had shared before their ride to save Linsyn. Echao was still asleep but was stirring about in the bed. The sound of a chair sliding on the floor startled him. He turned to find an elf setting the table with breakfast and tea. He looked young, tall and thin with black hair, like the others, but with a sharp, bladed nose.

"What's going on?" Tamm asked.

The elf rolled his eyes. "Humans," he mumbled under his breath, Tamm barely able to make it out. "I am preparing your breakfast as I have been commanded. You were sleeping in the forest and were moved to more comfortable accommodations last night."

"Where is Calla?" he asked.

"She will meet you shortly. Do you require anything else before I leave you?"

"No," Tamm said, and the elf turned toward the door. "Thank you."

The elf turned toward him and gave an exaggerated bow.

"Wait," Tamm called. "I didn't get your name."

"Because I did not give it to you," the elf replied as he shut the door.

Tamm rolled out of bed and went to a basin of water on the desk, where he cleaned his face and hands before sitting at the table. There was a broad spread of fruit, vegetables, roots, and herbs. He wondered if this was a typical elven breakfast, or if they never ate any meat. As he ate, Echao waddled over to the table and poured a cup of hot tea, gulping it down.

"You look awful," Tamm said.

"I've been worse, I'm sure," Echao said. "I've not slept well, and riding a horse all night will do a number on a man's thighs. Besides, I'm worried about Lily. She should be back from Delocia now, and I am sure she is worried sick with me not being there to greet her. Her mind tends to wander, and she likely fears the worst."

"We'll be home soon," Tamm said between bites of an apple.

Echao shook his head. "I seriously doubt that, Tamm. We destroyed part of a castle. We killed a sheriff, whose son happens to be a town guard back home. We are never going home. If we do, we'll be arrested and put to death. The sooner you come to realize that, the better."

Tamm was taken aback by Echao's brashness, but deep down, he knew he spoke the truth. He had dreamed of getting out of Aleesia and going on adventures, but now that he could not go home, there was a longing for it in the pit of his stomach. He felt awful for Echao. Although he had always wanted to leave Aleesia, Echao never had those aspirations.

"I'm sorry, Echao. I never meant for any of this to happen."

"Alas, it did, whether it was your wish or not. I've written a letter, two actually, one to Lily and one to mother and father, explaining why we can't come home. I hope that wherever I go, Lily will meet me. I plan to ask Calla to have it delivered to Aleesia."

Tamm's thoughts had been so consumed with saving Linsyn that he had not thought much about his family. Thinking about it now, possibly never seeing his mother and father or Adina again, and Echao not being able to see Lily, made his eyes sting as tears threatened to spill out. "Maybe I should write a letter, too," he said as he shielded his eyes from Echao.

There was a rap at the door, and Tamm got up from the table to answer it. He wanted a break in the heaviness of the conversation and rubbed his misty eyes as he made his way across the small room. He opened the door, and Calla stood there, her hair a golden color again, although the strand that had been gray was lighter than the rest.

"Good morning," she said. "I hope you two rested well." Without waiting for affirmation, she stepped into the room and started gathering their things and tossing them fresh changes of clothes. "Eat quickly. We have things to do today, for each of you."

They scooped up the clothes and stared at each other in surprise.

Calla clucked her tongue at them. "Today, boys today."

After dressing, they left the treehouse behind and made their way through the city streets. Hundreds of elves were moving about their day as sunlight trickled through the branches. Tamm nodded in salutation at the elves he passed by. A few of them returned the greeting, but most ignored him.

"Don't worry," Calla said. "It's not you; it's me. I am not the most popular among my people."

"Why is that?" Echao asked.

She turned around and walked backward as they followed her. "For starters, I have changed my appearance to blend in with humans, which many elves despise. There are other reasons, but we must be moving on. Echao, I am taking you to the training grounds. You will train with some of our best assassins. Tamm, I am taking you to the School of Mages. You will be able to train with some of our warriors also, but first things first." She spun back around, facing forward.

Dust floated up as they both slid to a sudden stop in the road. "Training?" Echao asked. "I'm normally all for training, but we just rode all night, have barely had breakfast, and no one has even mentioned about how our parents are doing or about the possibility of going home. I would like some answers."

Calla paused as she looked both of the boys over, a look of sympathy on her face. "You both know that is not possible. As much as I would love to escort you home myself, it is too dangerous. You will stay here for now. If you would like, I can send a courier to check on your family and relay any messages you would like."

They both nodded. "Our families and friends, please," Tamm said. "Adina and Lilly. We'd like to know how they are also."

Calla arched her eyebrows at the request. "Of course. Anyone else?"

"What about Linsyn?" Tamm asked.

"He is still recovering," she said. "He is anxious to see you also, but you must wait until he is well."

After receiving no more requests, Calla turned and led them deeper into the city. They stopped by the training yards, and she introduced Echao to several of the elven warriors.

Before departing with them to begin training, he turned back to Calla. "Will you please see that these are delivered to Aleesia? One is for my parents; the other is for a dear friend."

She agreed and took the letters from him before parting ways. Tamm and Calla continued until they reached a high wooden tower that was surrounded by lush open grounds. There were scores of elves walking around the gardens carrying staves with various colored stones affixed to the top.

Calla approached a tall, bald elf holding solid black staff with a peridot stone at the top. He was speaking to a group of elves who were staring at him attentively. "Master Alhèrin," Calla interrupted.

Alhèrin dismissed the others and turned to greet them. "Calla, one of my most talented pupils. It is so good to see you."

She dipped her head in a respectful bow. "And you, Master. There is someone I would like for you to meet."

"Tammuz," Alhèrin said and crossed his fist over his heart. "I am overjoyed and humbled to finally meet you, my prince."

Tamm blushed. He had never been greeted with such honor. "It is my pleasure."

"Do I understand that Riehner has been teaching you the ways of the Battlemages?" he asked.

Calla nodded for him to speak freely. "Yes. He has taught me some, but it's still very new to me."

"We will continue your training here," Alhèrin said. "Riehner always wished for you to train here with us. This is where he was taught. And you are half-elf, so it is only right that you come here to learn."

Tamm paused to think about the statement. Calla had told him that his mother was elven, but he had not considered what all that meant until now. What did it mean? Would he be naturally adept at magic like the other elves? Would he live longer than those around him? He would have to remind himself to ask Calla about it later.

Alhèrin cleared his throat to call Tamm's attention back to the conversation. He blushed as he thanked him for the kind comment, and Calla left him in the hands of the mages. The next several days were a blur. He would get up early in the morning and travel to the mages' school to study with them. The lessons flooded him with new words and ideas, spells that he had not thought about before. Using magic, he discovered, was as much about being fluent in the language and being creative with its uses as it was learning to control the power inside him.

He rarely saw Echao anymore. They still slept in the same room, but Echao was out much of the night and was usually gone again before Tamm got up in the morning. He was able to spend more time with Calla, which he enjoyed. She was a mage and could come and go freely through the school and would visit him often. She would update him on Linsyn's health and any word from Aleesia. She also taught him about the general life of elves and magic.

He relished his time with her. She was kind and smart, and she showed genuine interest in him. He wanted to learn more about her and would try to pry little secrets from her. He learned that the reason some of the elves ignored her was that she had made the decision to stop the healing magic being performed on the Queen. She did so in order for him to be born, but it resulted in Beltia's death. Once shunned by her people, she began to take more interest in humans and would change her hair and eye colors to be more like them.

He felt sorry for her. She did not deserve to be treated so poorly by her people. She had been nothing but kind to him. He felt he could tell her anything and that she would understand. He told her of his wishes for adventure and, now that he had found it, his longing to be back in his home by the lake. He asked her why Riehner had been able to survive so long if he is human, and she explained that when he accepted the magic from the elves, some of their longevity passed on to him, and in turn, to all Battlemages. For some reason, this did not pass on to anyone who could use magic, just Battlemages, which puzzled him.

When asked about the origin of the Battlemages, she explained the Council of Nine and how they had come to rule over the elves and about the elves' homeland on a faraway island. A large group of their people set out in exploration to study other lands. They found Iradell and settled here, but the dwarves, who were not overly pleased with newcomers in their lands, and the Kapre were embroiled in a bloody war. They tried to stay neutral but were eventually drawn into battle as the other two races attacked them.

The elves were not warriors but scholars and mages and were not accustomed to taking another's life. They fought back out of necessity but were not able to gain any ground in the war. The fighting raged on for countless years until the humans, who were born warriors, arrived. The humans joined the battle without much provocation.

At that time, the humans were led by a chieftain, the elves by a queen, and the dwarves a king. The human chieftain, Brenin, had a son named Riehner, who did not crave war as his father did. He sought solutions rather than to conquer lands. On a visit with the elves to discuss a treaty, despite his father ordering him otherwise, he met his future wife, Beltia, daughter of the elven queen. This led to the passing of magic from elves to the humans and the start of the Battlemages. He later delivered the dwarves from near defeat and obtained an alliance with them. He was later crowned High King of Iradell and over all the races, and with the Battlemages, defeated the Kapre and led the land into an unprecedented peace.

Once Riehner was usurped, the dwarves fled back underground and the elves into the forests. Each had dissolved their governments in favor of Riehner's leadership and were required to devise new forms of governance while awaiting his return to power. With the Queen in stasis, teetering between life and death, the elves did not wish to appoint a new queen from a new line, hoping instead that Beltia's line would be continued, favoring the Counsel of Nine instead.

Tamm was overwhelmed with the knowledge she had shared during his time at the School of Mages. She had not only given him a glimpse into the history and political lives of the elves but also into that of the dwarves and even pieces of his own people's history.

REBORN

Today, he sat alone at the school, eating lunch and thinking over all he had learned and what life would have been like if Riehner had not been overthrown, if he were raised in the castle as a prince instead of in Aleesia as the son of a blacksmith with no knowledge of magic. Calla startled him as she sat down beside him, and he jumped. She put her hand on his shoulder and giggled. "I'm sorry. I did not intend to startle you."

He laughed, his cheeks flushing. "It's fine. I was just lost in thought."

She tapped her fingers on the table. "I know this is a lot to take in, but you are doing remarkably well. I do not believe I would have handled all this the way you have. You have truly impressed me."

"Thank you," he said, giving her a shy smile. "I assume that's not why you are here through."

She could not disguise her smile, and it stretched ear to ear. "I have been sent with great news," she said. "King Riehner is awake and is asking to see you as soon as you are able."

Tamm's eyes widened. He tried to speak, but the words would not come.

"You do not have to go right this moment," she said.

"No, I would like to see him. Can we go now?"

Calla's face became solemn. "Tamm, things will be different. He is no longer Linsyn. There is no reason to hide his identity any longer. Tzelder knows he lives. He is the one, true High King of Iradell, and the honors of such will be given to him, and you as his heir."

Tamm ran his fingers through his shaggy black hair. "I don't know what to say. I may have been born his son, but Kèlris has always been my father. I've always known him as the shy, awkward town healer, not some regal king ruling over a country. What am I to do?"

Calla moved as if to embrace him, then dropped her arms to her side. "I know this is hard. The people of Iradell will expect you to act like a prince, and to honor him as the King. The only advice I can offer is to get to know him. Just as you learned to know and love Linsyn, do the same with Riehner. I believe you will find that they are quite similar."

Tamm shrugged in partial approval. He grabbed his things and followed Calla out of the school, but to his surprise, they passed right by the healer's longhouse. She led him further into the city to the Council House. Hundreds upon hundreds of elves were lined up outside in a large square. Calla pushed past them to move to the front.

Several trumpets sounded from the steps, and red banners dropped, draping down the columns in front of the Council House as the double doors pulled open. Two lines of elvish soldiers marched out and bordered the stairs, drawing curved swords and arching them high above the walkway. A tall man in a flowing purple robe with gold trim strode out of the house with royal flair. His hair was shoulder length and pulled back, a jeweled crown perched on his head, a trimmed gray goatee framed his mouth. He looked so much like Linsyn, but at the same time, so different.

As he passed the doorway and descended down the stairs, the crowd of elves erupted into cheers. His face remained stoic as he stopped and waved at the elves, the applause deafening. Tamm stood in amazement at the welcome that Riehner received. Linsyn had rarely received more than a kind hello in Aleesia.

Riehner stopped waving as his eyes met with Tamm's. The crowd fell to silence, seeing father and son truly seeing each other for the first time. Tamm did not flinch. Calla gave him a slight push on his back, and he teetered. He cut his eyes back at her, but she only smiled and shrugged. Riehner stood with his arms folded behind his back, waiting.

Tamm looked at him, trying to see Linsyn behind all the gold and regalia. The hair and beard now trimmed, he looked younger and stronger than Tamm remembered. He reached over his shoulder and drew the sword before marching over to him, not taking his eyes away from Riehner's. He could feel the air getting tense between him and the soldiers lining the stairs.

He stood before Riehner without speaking a word, the sword still held out in front of him. Riehner did not move, his blue eyes piercing into Tamm's. Without warning, Tamm dropped to one knee and displayed the sword out to Riehner in open hands. "I believe this is yours."

Riehner reached out and took the sword from Tamm and turned it over in his hands as if being reacquainted with an old friend. He tapped the sword on Tamm's shoulders, then announced in a booming voice for all to hear, "This is my son, Tammuz, Prince of Iradell."

Tamm stood and faced the crowd, Riehner's arm around his shoulders. The elves cheered, causing his ears to ring. He looked up at Riehner, who smiled at him with admiration.

TWENTY-TWO

Another fortnight came and went in a blur. Tamm was no longer visiting the College of Mages regularly. He spent most of his time with Riehner, learning the ways of the Battlemages and discovering who his father was. So much of Linsyn was still present; the eyes, the joking demeanor of his voice sneaking past his seriousness, but at the same time, it was like he had met a new person. Riehner was more regal, his countenance displaying his kingship. He no longer stooped when he walked or relied on his cane. He carried himself with power, and the elves showed him respect. Deep down, Tamm felt the connection between them, the same way he felt it with Linsyn, but it was like looking at an entirely different person.

Riehner had taught him so much in the past two weeks. He told him of the founding of Iradell and how the humans came to this country, the way he had met Beltia, and how she had died. It made Tamm despise Tzelder even more. Riehner told him how much Beltia had loved him, her son, though she never met him and how she embodied the Battlemages motto "My life for yours," though she was not a Battlemage.

It was strange, learning about different parents when he had grown up knowing and loving two others in that role. His feelings toward Kèlris and Mariah did not change. He loved them just as much as always, and would always think of them as mother and father. He would also see Riehner and Beltia the same. Even now, not ever meeting his mother, he could feel her love around him, similar to the magic flowing inside of him. Riehner had suggested he visit her tomb and speak with her. It felt odd at first, speaking to her at her gravesite, but he tried. Over time, he looked forward to those talks. He would sit by her grave and talk with her as he would Echao or Calla. He could feel her love stronger there, near where she lay.

The dew was still moist on the ground; the sun barely visible through the trees as he sat down beside her. "I wish I could have met you. Riehner tells me all the time about how wonderful you were." Tamm cleared his throat, his facing flushing red. "Sorry, I have barely gotten used to calling him Riehner, much less father."

A light breeze passed through the branches, grazing his cheeks and making him shiver. "My mind is racing all the time. There's a whole other world outside the walls of Aleesia that I never even imagined. I knew Tzelder could be tyrannical, but tucked away in my little village, I never knew how evil he was. If not for him, I could be talking to you in person right now."

He plucked at leaves of grass and traced in the dirt with them. "I can't stay here forever, Mother. We'll have to venture out of the forest sooner or later. Tzelder will not sit idly by, knowing that Riehner...Father is just out of his grasp. Together, we will avenge you. We will remove him from power and restore this country to its former glory."

A soft voice whispered his name, and he spun around to find Calla standing behind him. Her gentle eyes gazed down on him in pity. "I'm sorry to interrupt," she said. "Your father has summoned you."

Tamm stood and patted the dirt from his pants. He was still not used to wearing such ornate clothing, but Riehner and Calla insisted he dress like a prince. He strode beside her back through the woods. They were side by side, and his hand brushed against hers. He blushed and eased his hand away. She glanced at his hand and then back down the trail.

"Tell me more about you," he said.

"What do you wish to know, my liege?" she replied in a serious tone.

"Drop the formalities, Calla. We're friends, are we not?"

She giggled. "Very well. I was only teasing. What would you like to know?"

He shrugged. "I don't know. Anything. Everything. You say you are my protector, yet I know very little about you."

She slowed her pace as she thought. "I was born here. I

have never seen my homeland. I have trained as a mage since I was a child. The war was already in motion by the time I was old enough to be a part of it. The battles were heated, but the humans had not yet arrived."

"You fought in the war?" he asked.

She nudged him in the side with her elbow. "Is that not what I just said?"

He was surprised. He knew she was old enough to have known his mother but not old enough to have fought in the Great War. "Then what?"

"Your people came along and made the war more difficult. They are warriors in every aspect, and it did not take long before they were fighting against us also. They claimed they only wanted peace, but their definition was not the same as ours. With our forces now divided among so many fronts, the Kapre took advantage and launched even more assaults. We lost many elves."

Tamm stared at her in amazement. He had seen her perform magic before and knew she was more advanced than he, but he never imagined she had fought in the war. "Go on," he said.

"The Kapre are evil. I had no qualms destroying them. The dwarves could be bad in their own right, though not as bad as the Kapre. But, the humans, they were different. Many of them did want peace; I believe that. But, their chieftain was a ruthless warrior and pressed them on. Had the mages not fought, the elves would have been lost."

She cleared her throat and sat on a nearby stump, motioning him to sit beside her before continuing. "I still remember when I first met Riehner. He was a young, ambitious boy, not much older than you. He wanted to please his father and was quickly made captain over a small warband. We had faced off on the field of battle, but the Kapre appeared and tried to flank us. We joined forces, if only briefly that day, and drove the Kapre off the field. Riehner was behind our lines, and that is when he saw Beltia. Her beauty immediately captured him. I could sense good in him. Unlike his father, who lusted for battle, he truly wanted peace and was willing to befriend our people."

"You and my mother were close?" he asked.

"Yes. Very. We had been friends all my life. She was older than I, but I have never met another friend quite like her."

She brushed a tear from her eye, and Tamm slid closer, putting his hand on hers. "I'm sorry. I didn't mean to upset you."

"I am not upset. I do miss her, but I pity you for having never been able to see how wonderful she was." She placed her other hand on top of his.

"It was my idea to bring her out of the magic to deliver you into this world. It is what led to her death, and for that, I am sorry. Many of my people despise me now because my decision is what brought about her death. However, at the same time, I do not regret it. It allowed you to be here."

A tear formed in his eye, but he did not pull his hands away to wipe it. He leaned his head down, resting his forehead against hers.

Her soft eyes met his before she leaned away slightly, her cheeks rosy. She blinked several times before continuing.

"She was holding you in her arms, the biggest smile on her face when she passed from this world. She loved you, Tamm, more than you will ever know."

Tamm stood, not letting go of her hands, then pulled her into his arms and hugged her. "Thank you. I know it was not an easy decision to make, and you have accepted the consequences with honor. I pray that our friendship can be just as strong as you had with my mother."

"I would like that," she said. "We should go. Your father is waiting."

They strolled side by side along the forest path until they entered the city. The streets were bustling with groups of elves talking and whispering. As they got closer to the House of Counsels, he could see Echao propped up on a column near the entrance. Echao noticed them approaching and jogged to meet them.

"A dwarf just arrived," Echao said as he came up to them. "A dwarf. Do you believe that? The elves are all flustered. Apparently, dwarves aren't common around here."

"What's going on?" Tamm asked.

Echao shrugged. "Beats me. They're waiting for you inside, though. I'm coming with you."

Tamm looked to Calla, who waved her hands at him, ushering him inward. She followed behind as he entered through the double doors and into a large foyer. Light twinkled, reflecting on the floor's polished stone. The building was beautiful, a work of nature and architecture. Tree trunks weaved around each other, forming pillars to support the corners of the domed ceiling.

Calla took him by the arm and led him further in, doors opening to each side. She turned into the last set of double doors, and Riehner was seated at a massive circular-cut oak table. Elion was with him, along with other elves that he did not recognize, and on the other end of the table, a stout dwarf was seated, smoke rolling from his nose as he passed a small pipe between his bushy, copper beard. He had a stern face, but caring amber eyes hid behind a strong brow. His eyebrows raised as Tamm entered the room. The sweet scent of the smoke tickled Tamm's nose.

"Ah, welcome," Riehner said, standing from his seat, calling him forward. "This is Tammuz, future Battlemage. This is Echao and Calla, his guardians. And this," he said, gesturing to the dwarf, "is Kadagan, emissary of the dwarven kingdom."

Kadagan nodded his head in acknowledgment of the others joining them but said nothing, continuing to puff on his pipe.

"Very well," Elion said. "Everyone has arrived. Please share your news, Kadagan."

The dwarf inched out of his seat like an old man who had sat too long. Even standing, he would only come to Tamm's chest, and Tamm was shorter than most other humans, but Kadagan was stocky and strong. He did not put his pipe down but continued to puff as he paced around the table.

"Our scouts have been watching the castle closely," he said, pausing to take a long draw from the pipe. "Especially after the hasty escape young Tammuz made with the King." He looked at Tamm, who blushed and lowered his head. "At any rate, it appears Tzelder has begun to mobilize his soldiers. More than we've seen since the King was usurped." He paused after saying this and looked to Riehner. "My scouts tell me that he plans to march on Aleesia."

Tamm sat up and leaned forward in the chair, his hands grasping the table. "But why?"

"Why?" Kadagan replied. "Partly because you made him look like a fool. And, partly because he knows it will draw King Riehner, and possibly you, out of hiding. He expects that neither of you will allow him to march unchecked into your homeland."

Tamm looked to Riehner, who was lost in thought, stroking his beard. "How long do we have?" Riehner asked.

"Maybe two weeks, three tops," Kadagan said.

Riehner looked to Elion, who nodded. "You know you have the support of my people, my King."

"And what of yours?" Riehner asked the dwarf. "Will the dwarves show their support?"

"That is left to be seen, my lord. Much has changed since you were on the throne. The dwarves feel stable now with their rulers. It was a tense alliance even in the olden days. I will do what I can to persuade them, but I don't know if that will be enough."

"Yours is a proud people, Kadagan, and mighty too," Riehner said. "We will not be able to do this without their help."

Kadagan tapped another pinch of something into the pipe and gave it a few quick puffs to keep it lit. "I agree, but they have never been fond of humans. They feel they are looked down on by them, are treated as a lesser species, even though you and I know that's not true. There was such animosity between us when you first arrived. There are factions that, should you retake the throne, would prefer to stay independent and not have anything to do with the humans."

"When," Riehner said.

"When? I'm not following," Kadagan said.

"*When* I retake the throne," he said sternly.

"Yes, my lord. *When* you retake the throne. Forgive my misspeech. I must be getting back to my lands. I assure you, I will do what I can to sway support for you." He bowed his head. "With your leave?"

Riehner nodded, and Echao jumped from his chair. "I will go with him," he shouted, startling Tamm and causing him to tip back in his seat. Everyone seated at the table now stared at Echao. "I will go with him. I will tell them of our plight and humbly request their assistance."

Riehner raised his eyebrows. "You understand that I can give you no promise of protection? You will be passing through dangerous lands, and as Kadagan has explained, the dwarves are not known for their love of humans."

Echao met Tamm's concerned gaze and nodded. "I understand. It may help if they see that we are not too proud to ask for their help. It's my homeland, too. I can't sit idly by as an army marches toward my home, my people. I will do what I must."

Riehner approached Echao and towered over him. "You are brave. Though I cannot give you protection, I can grant you courage and wisdom. Close your eyes, all of you."

Everyone at the table bowed their heads. Echao looked at Tamm, who reached up and squeezed his arm in assurance. Riehner laid his hand on Echao's forehead. "Echao, son of Kèlris, honorable servant to Iradell, I gift you with the courage to stand in the face of all dangers without fear and with the wisdom to discern when to fight and when to flee, when to be bold and when to be timid, when to destroy and when to show compassion. *Cróga ag gliocas.*"

A bright light shone around the room, causing Tamm to close his eyes tighter. He could feel the warmth on his face as he sat so near to Riehner and Echao. Just as suddenly as the warmth had kissed his face, it was gone. He opened his eyes, and the room seemed so much darker than it had before. The spell had been so powerful. He had expected to see Riehner hunched, catching his breath, but he was standing before Echao as regal as ever. Echao's face had a gleam about it, and Tamm could feel an air of confidence coming from him.

"Say your goodbyes. We must go." Kadagan snatched his pipe from the table and dashed for the door.

"You too, Tamm," Riehner said. "There is much to do with little time."

Tamm nodded before turning back to Echao. "Thank you. If anyone can persuade the dwarves to help, it's you."

"I can't let Aleesia be destroyed. Besides, what kind of guardian would I be if I let you run off to battle outnumbered? I'll be back soon."

"Do be careful," Tamm said as he wrapped him in a fierce hug.

REBORN

Echao hugged him back and then straightened, crossing his fist over his heart. "My life for yours."

"My life for yours," Tamm replied, returning the gesture. Echao turned on his heels and followed Kadagan out the door. Tamm stood in silence for a moment, staring at the doorway until he felt Calla's hand on his shoulder. "You should go. Your father is waiting."

Tamm squeezed her hand and left the room. He found Riehner standing outside, staring out toward the mausoleum where his wife was buried. Tamm stood beside him for a while before he recognized he was there. "Come," he said. "There is much we must discuss."

Tamm had to double his steps to keep up with Riehner's long, quick strides as he slipped through the streets. Soon they were off the roads and heading deeper into the forest. The trees were ancient, so high that he could not see their tops.

"Where are we going?" he asked.

"A little further," Riehner said. "Almost there."

Tamm wiped the sweat from his brow. The exertion of keeping up with Riehner in the woods was taking its toll, and he noticed he was beginning to pant. Tamm began to ask him again where they were going, but Riehner abruptly stopped.

"Here we are," he said.

Tamm looked confused as he stared at the side of a mountain. "Where is *here*?"

Riehner gestured to the valley where they stood and then back to the mountain wall. "We will come here every morning for your training. You must pass the trials before we go to Aleesia."

"What trials? What are you talking about?"

Riehner turned from looking at the mountain to face him. "This will not be an easy battle. Tzelder is likely to be there himself. I have escaped him numerous times, but I feel he will want to see to me personally this time."

He turned back to the wall and ran his fingers across the rough, cold stone. "This is where the Battlemages take their trials. All the training that you have been doing, it has led to this. In order to join the ranks of the Battlemages, you must pass the trials. Only then will you be awarded your medallion." He held a clear stone from his neck. It was the one that Tamm had seen glow so many times before when Riehner was using magic.

"What are the trials?" Tamm asked.

"That, I cannot tell you. It is different for us all. I will tell you that this cave is old and is infused with old magic. It will test the deepest parts of you. If you are found lacking, you will fail."

"What happens if I fail?" Tamm asked, tension building in his shoulders.

"In the height of our power, many did not make it through the training. If that was the case, they were released back to their families. They did not know much, did not have much magical talent at that time. Once they were trained in magic, releasing them could be dangerous. If they failed the trials, they were exiled to the Northern Wastes. They could not be allowed to live among everyone else, risk misusing their powers."

"So, I could be exiled?" Tamm asked, a tremor in his voice.

"It is unlikely, but yes, it is a possibility. There have only been a few who could not complete the trials. Tzelder was one. He was young and foolish. He cared more about his status and station, what others thought of him. He was weak-hearted. He was exiled, and you see what he is now."

Tamm sat down on a boulder and put his head in his hands. "This is all so new to me. I wasn't taken in as a child as they were in your day. How am I expected to pass these trials with a fraction of the training that Tzelder had?"

Riehner approached and sat beside him, wrapping his strong arm around his shoulders. "The amount of training you have had is irrelevant. It is what is in your heart that matters. And in that, you cannot fail. Now come, we have more training to do. You will know when you are ready for the trials." He tapped his fingers on Tamm's heart. "You will feel it here."

Tamm nodded, moving to a small clearing. "Let's begin. We don't have much time."

TWENTY-THREE

Tamm awoke, sitting in a chair in front of his writing desk. He had fallen asleep last night pouring over several of the books Riehner had given him. He rubbed the sleep from his eye and tried to stand to stretch his sore back. Instead, he fell to the floor. He could not feel his feet. A fierce burning and tingling coursed into his feet and legs as he squirmed to move them.

Someone knocked on the door. "Just a minute," he grunted, dragging himself near the bed to try to pull himself up.

"Are you alright?" Calla asked from the other side of the door.

"I'm fine. I'll be there in a moment."

"You don't sound fine. I could just..."

Tamm grabbed the blanket on the bed. "No, no. Almost there." The blanket slipped as he pulled himself up, and he fell back to the floor with a loud thump.

Calla opened the door to find him lying on the floor. "Oh my! Let me help."

He blushed with embarrassment, grateful he was not in his nightclothes. Calla scooped him under the arms and sat him onto the bed.

"I fell asleep in the chair," he said as he stretched his legs and rubbed them. "Apparently, so did my feet."

She giggled. "It's nice to know that the prince has flaws."

"Of course, I have flaws," he huffed. "Don't we all?"

"All except royalty," she joked. "You may have them, but you are expected not to show them."

"I'm no different than anyone else. I didn't grow up with any rank. I have always been a commoner. And now, I'm a fugitive, also."

Calla smirked at him. "I hope you never lose your humility. Your people will love you for it."

"Thanks," he said, testing the floor with his toes before trying to stand. Calla stood up to help him, but he waved her off. "I think I can stand now."

"I will walk with you," she said.

They strolled through the city, talking and laughing. Tamm needed to get to training; Riehner would be expecting him there, but he did not want to leave Calla. She stopped by a stream where a basket sat. "What is this?" he asked.

"I thought you might need some breakfast before you go," she said.

They sat down beside the stream and ate on honey and biscuits. Tamm could not remember the last time he had a bite of meat. It seemed the elves stayed far away from it. "Why don't the elves eat meat?"

She sat for a moment, thinking. "They strive to remain in harmony with all things. They detest the loss of any life, even that of an animal. They have learned that they can live abundantly with only what nature offers and choose to live this way. Why do your people eat meat?"

Tamm paused, then shrugged his shoulders. "I don't know. We just always have. Is one way right and the other wrong?"

Calla laughed. "Now you are thinking like a mage. That is a very philosophical question. What do you think?"

"Well," he said. "I don't think either is right or wrong. To your people, it may be wrong to eat meat, but just because my people believe differently doesn't make you wrong."

Calla nodded. "I believe you are learning more from your studies than you realize."

Tamm picked at some grass on the ground. "I'm afraid of failing," he said without raising his eyes. "Riehner believes I will pass, but I fear I won't live up to his expectations. What happens if I disappoint him? What happens if I let the entire country down?"

Calla slid closer to him. "I know there is a lot of pressure. I have faith in you. I have watched over you for a long time. You can do this. And if you do not, what then?"

"Exactly! If I don't, I will be exiled to the Northern Wastes. My father, who I have only known was my father for the last few weeks, will have to face Tzelder alone. He may be killed, and Iradell will continue to suffer under Tzelder's rule. He will seek out the other races and attempt to destroy them. He will seek you out for protecting me."

Calla stared into his eyes, letting him calm down before she spoke. "Fear is a liar. It will tell you things, make you doubt until you are paralyzed by it. Failure can be a gift. It can teach you the correct way and prepare you for your next journey. Squash your fear and face it. If you fail, pick yourself back up and try again, but never give up. That is the way of the Battlemage."

Tamm stared at her, his mouth parted. Her outward appearance made him believe she was around his age, but her wisdom showed she had lived for centuries. "Your wisdom amazes me sometimes."

"Wisdom comes from failure, Tamm. We all fail. I failed your mother. My own people do not accept me. But I learn from it and go on. There is something else I must tell you."

"What is it?" he replied.

"We will need all the help we can get in the battle against Tzelder. We cannot let Aleesia be blindsided by the attack. I have been tasked to go to Aleesia and prepare them for war."

Tamm's jaw went slack. He did not know what to say. He had grown accustomed to being with her each day and had learned so much from her. Their friendship had grown over the past few weeks, and he felt closer to her than anyone else.

"I understand why you must go," he said. "But understanding the reason doesn't put my heart to ease. I don't want you to go."

She frowned and lowered her head. "I would stay if I could, but the Council has ordered it. I leave in two days."

Tamm took her hand and squeezed it. "I would like to spend some time with you before you go. I may be gone when you return."

"I would like that," she said, a tear trickling down her cheek. "You should go now. You have trials to pass. I will see you this evening."

Tamm squeezed her hand before letting go and crossing the stream toward the cave where Riehner awaited. He glanced back before entering a copse of trees to see her packing the basket. He walked backward, watching her fade from sight as he trudged deeper into the woods.

Riehner was in a clearing near the cave when Tamm approached. He had the diamond-like sword in his hand, practicing fighting forms. Tamm dared not disturb him and sat on a nearby rock, watching him perform the moves. He moved with grace from one attack to another, parrying strikes from an invisible foe. Tamm was in awe at the smoothness of his form. It was as if the sword were weightless and he were gliding on air.

After a sweeping blow, he turned to Tamm and sheathed the sword. "Thank you for not interrupting my practice. It has been quite some time since I have had to use this sword. It was time we learn to trust one another again."

"Where did you learn to fight like that?" Tamm asked.

Riehner smiled. "I have studied with many fine warriors. My father first taught me. Later, I studied with the elves who taught me to use magic to focus and harness my skills. I also scholar. There will be plenty of time in the future to study and learn, but now is the time for war. You must pass the trials so that the Battlemages can be reborn through you. After Tzelder is defeated, I will teach you all that you desire."

Tamm shook his head. "I'm afraid. It's not only the trials. What if I fail the people of Aleesia. What if I fail you?"

Riehner put his arm around Tamm's shoulders, and Tamm could feel the calm and peace emanating from him. "Ah. There is the true cause of your fear. You must empty yourself. Nothing you can do would ever cause me to feel as if you have failed me. It is I who has failed you. I wish I would have been stronger and could have saved your mother. I wish that I could have been braver and raised you myself instead of whisking you away and watching you grow from a distance without you ever knowing I was your father."

Tamm wrapped Riehner in an embrace. His scent reminded him of the quaint cottage in Aleesia, where Linsyn had taught him to heal and taught him the secrets of magic. "You're here now. That's all that matters. Let's let go of the past, forsake our fears, and embrace the future. What do you say?"

"I would like that," Riehner said as he broke the embrace. "I do not have much longer here with you. Today will be our last training session. My presence is required with the Elders to prepare for the battle ahead. Calla will help teach you until she has to go to Aleesia. After that, I have arranged for some training with Tor'nys. He is an excellent bladesman."

"But," Tamm said.

had a dear friend, Iwan, who was General of Iradell's army. He was a magnificent warrior and could link attacks together with such ease that he made fighting look more like a dance."

"That's impressive," Tamm said.

Riehner motioned with his arm, inviting Tamm to join him. "Shall we begin?"

Tamm nodded and took his place across from Riehner. He picked up a training sword from atop a stone by his side and spun it around in his hand, testing its weight, before settling into his stance.

"There is no need for that," Riehner said. "Today, we will be focusing on the mind."

Tamm laid the training sword back onto the stone, and Riehner motioned for him to have a seat. Tamm sat on a log, and Riehner slid in beside him. "Do you remember when you first discovered magic? When you quieted your mind and felt the spark inside of you?"

"How could I forget?" Tamm said. "It was the most amazing thing I have ever experienced. I felt new like the old me had burned away."

Linsyn turned to face him and stared intently into his eyes. "It is not my will to make you feel pressured, but we are short on time. You will have to take the trials soon. When you enter the cave, remember that feeling, that spark inside you. Do you understand?"

Tamm twisted in his seat, his stomach in knots. "I do, but what if I'm not ready?"

"You are ready. I have taught you all that I can until you pass the trials. I told you this was a life of study, the life of a

REBORN

"I must petition you. In no later than two days, you must take the trials. Calla will assist you until then, but once she is gone, you must take the trials. Promise me."

Tamm let out an exaggerated sigh. "I promise."

Riehner tussled Tamm's shaggy hair, stood, and crossed his arm over his heart before walking back toward the village. Tamm sat quietly for a while before walking to the cave entrance. He stared into the opening, but it was like staring into a barrel full of pitch.

A cool breeze caressed his face, and the damp, musty air caused his nose to sting. He reached out his hand into the opening and whispered, "*Lasair*." A small flame sputtered to life in his outstretched palm, and he reached further into the entrance without stepping in. The light from his hand did not pierce the darkness. He released more power into the conjuration, and he could feel the heat against the side of his face. The fire pulsed in his hand, and he leaned forward, but the cave was as dark as before. Tamm scowled and released the flame from his hand, pushing it into the cave. A roar erupted from somewhere deep in the cave. The flame sputtered out, and a gust of wind struck him and knocked him on his backside.

"That was stupid," said a voice behind him. Tamm rolled over and peered up from the ground at the newcomer. He panted to catch his breath. "Who are you?"

The elf had a sly smirk on his face. He was about Tamm's height but was slender with sinuous muscles carving ridges in his arms, his black hair covering one of his eyes. "I'm Tor'nys. King Riehner sent me to retrieve you. He obviously thought you would be up to no good if left alone for too long. Lo and behold…"

Tamm stood and dusted off his clothes. He looked closer and recognized the elf. His arms were now bare in his tunic, and his hair slightly different, but there was no mistaking it. It was the elf that had prepared his breakfast in the treehouse shortly after arriving in Gaer Alon. "A little mouthy for an elf, aren't you?"

Tor'nys bared his teeth. "What does that mean?"

Tamm shook his head and took a deep breath. "Nothing. It means nothing. I think we've gotten off on the wrong…"

Tor'nys's angled eyes narrowed, and his nostrils flared. "First, you act as if my observations are of less importance because you are human, and now I am nothing?"

Tamm held his hands in front of him, his open palm toward Tor'nys. "That's not what I meant. You caught me off guard. Calm down."

Tor'nys drew a short sword from his side, the sound of metal scratching across the scabbard. "Who are you to give me orders?"

Tamm took a step back, and his face flushed with blood. "I am Tammuz, son of High King Riehner, Prince of the realm, and you would do well to remember your place." He reached his arm toward the sword that still rested on the stone. "*Dhòmhsa*." The sword flew into his hand.

Tor'nys snarled. "You are nothing but a blacksmith's son and nothing to me." He leaped at Tamm, his blade sweeping toward him.

Tamm threw his left hand forward and shouted, "*Gaoth.*" A blast of wind struck Tor'nys, knocking him to the ground. He was only down for a second before rolling back to his feet and hurling attacks at Tamm. He was relentless, and Tamm was having a hard time defending against the torrent of blows. He felt his breath come in shorter gasps, but Tor'nys showed no sign of tiring.

Tamm spun away from a series of quick slashes by Tor'nys. Why was he so aggressive? Tamm recalled his snide comment about his lineage and how Alred used to do the same thing to him. He hung his head and let the sword drop to the ground. "Enough!"

Tor'nys did not speak. He circled Tamm, spinning the blade in his hand. He shuffled toward Tamm as if to attack again. Tamm rolled to his side and flicked his wrist, causing a ring of fire to encircle him. As the flames danced around him, he saw Calla standing nearby, her mouth open.

Tamm yelled through the flames, "I'm sorry if I offended you. That was not my intention."

The flames parted as Tor'nys soared past them through the air, sword held high above his head, ready to strike. Tamm dropped to one knee, clawing for the sword he had dropped moments before, but Tor'nys was too close.

Everything else was silence as he heard Calla's voice pierce through the roar of the flames and Tor'nys's battle cry. "*Fós!*" Tamm could see, but he could not move. He tried to stand, but it felt like a boulder was lying on top of him. He forced his eyes to look up and saw Tor'nys suspended in air, a hazy, blue glow around him. He tried to speak, but the words would not come.

Calla knelt and stared into Tamm's eyes. "I'm sorry." She stood and turned to Tor'nys. "What are you doing? You fool! You would be wise to suppress your resentment towards humans. Whether you like it or not, King Riehner is back, and soon he will be seated on the throne again. If you ever try anything like this again, I will have you arrested and tried for treason. Understood?"

She turned back to Tamm and waved her hand; the power holding him vanished, and he fell to the ground. She reached out her hand and helped him to rise. "I'm sorry, Tamm. Get your sword."

He picked up the blade but did not sheath it. She turned back to Tor'nys. "I am going to release you now. You will immediately sheath your weapon. You will then lead us back to town. If you make any move other than those I have instructed, I will strike you with such a force that you will wish you were dead."

She waved her hand, and Tor'nys fell to the ground. He snarled as he scrambled to gather his footing, the blade still in his hand. Tamm summoned a flame in his hand. Tor'nys stared at him, the hate in his eyes fading away to humility, then hung his head and slipped the blade into the scabbard at his side. He spat on the ground. "Very well. Follow me."

Tor'nys walked in front with Tamm and Calla following a short way behind. Calla left the stone perched at the top of her staff pointed at his back as they walked.

"Do you think he's going to try anything else?" Tamm asked. "I didn't intend to insult him. His anger escalated so quickly."

"It's not your fault. He despises humans."

Tamm tilted his head as he looked at Tor'nys. "Why? What did we ever do to him?"

"A lot. But it's understandable that you don't know about it. It was during the war. The humans had recently joined in the fighting, and during one of the battles, both of his parents were killed by human warriors. Once Riehner was overthrown, more elves were slaughtered in the aftermath. He has hated them ever since."

Tamm lowered his voice to a whisper, worried Tor'nys would hear them talking about him and trigger his anger again. "I wasn't even alive then. I had nothing to do with their deaths. He could have killed me."

"He probably would have if I had not shown up. To be so young and arrogant, he is one of our most skilled fighters. To him, it doesn't matter if you knew about his parents' deaths. You inherited the sins of your ancestors by being born human."

Tamm huffed. "But I'm only half-human."

Calla shrugged her shoulders. "I don't think it will be a problem going forward. Just try not to goad him."

"He wasn't so aggressive the first time I met him. A little snide but not aggressive. Nevertheless, I'm going to avoid him at all costs."

She shook her head at him. "No, that will not do. Riehner wants you to train with him."

"True," he said. "But I'm sure he doesn't want me to die either."

"I recommend that you train with him. Just be careful. He will probably try to punish you at every opportunity, but maybe you can help him see that not all humans are bad. He could be a very formidable ally or enemy. The choice will be up to you."

Tamm grunted. Some of the buildings were coming into view between the trees. "Fine. I'll train with him. But I'm just doing it because you think it's best."

Calla smiled and grabbed his hand. "Wait here."

She called for Tor'nys and spoke with him briefly before he scurried off toward the city. She motioned for Tamm to follow her, and he jogged up to her side. "That seemed to go rather well," he said.

"I just reiterated our previous conversation. He will meet you after your trials to begin training. I do not think you will see him again until then."

Tamm stopped just outside of the city. "So, training begins bright and early in the morning?"

She smiled at him. "Of course. We will meet by the creek for breakfast. No going to the cave. We will do most of the training at the College of Mages. There is still a thing or two I can show you before your trials."

Tamm grabbed her hand. "I'm looking forward to it."

Tamm held her hand as long as he could before she slipped away as they parted to their respective homes. Despite being attacked and having to fight for his life, he was almost giddy that he got to spend so much time with her today.

REBORN

He wished he could tell Echao about it. He wondered how he was doing on his trip with Kadagan. He had been gone almost two days and should be getting close to Rothgaer. He hoped that Echao could assist Kadagan in rallying the support of the dwarves. They would need all the help they could get in the battle against Tzelder.

TWENTY-FOUR

Echao swayed in the saddle. He had strapped himself in some time ago to keep from falling out. His eyes burned from the sands of the Oseri desert, but he dared not close them should he fall asleep. He had dozed off several times on the trip already, but only for short periods. They had been riding for two days straight, only stopping long enough to feed and water the horses. He and Kadagan had traveled south from Arebel forest and past the port city of Trauss then westward toward the Oseri desert.

He moaned, thighs aching as if he had run across the kingdom. Kadagan chuckled and slowed his horse to circle around and check on him. "You humans complain too much. I assure you, we will be there before nightfall."

"Good. Hopefully, we will be able to rest first, because I don't think I could walk right now if I wanted to."

Kadagan angled his steed north and made a clicking noise with his tongue. Echao shifted in the saddle and followed him. The horses trotted on for several more hours until Echao could see two towering mountain ranges in the distance with a river flowing through the valley. "Is that...a mirage?"

"It is no mirage, my boy. That is a river flowing from Lake Ar'rad. We will hug the western shoreline and should arrive at Rothgaer just after dark."

Echao felt rejuvenated at the words and urged his horse forward. He craved a hearty meal and a good night's sleep; although, he would settle for just a good night's sleep right now. He had never traveled this far before. Taking the south road had been much safer than traveling on the King's Road. Kadagan was correct in telling him it would take longer but would keep them away from the watchful eyes of Tzelder. The false king was likely garrisoning troops in Rakx'den's outlying cities in preparation for the battle. There was no reason to put themselves in greater danger to save a few hours of travel.

Kadagan's timing was spot on. They arrived just after dark, which kept any spies from seeing their approach. The dwarves kept the entrance to Rothgaer well hidden. They had to dismount and lead the horses up a mountain trail, and Echao's thighs throbbed even more than before. They reached a crevice in the rock that did not appear any different from the surrounding stones. Had Kadagan not been with him, he would have walked right by it.

Kadagan drew his ax and slipped between the crevice. With the ax, he rapped on the rock wall in a peculiar rhythm. A few moments later, dust puffed through a crack as the wall opened to a large hallway carved into the stone. Echao stumbled back as the doors creaked open. Kadagan motioned him in, and two stout dwarves clad in armor took the horses and led them away.

"Follow me," Kadagan said. He turned to Echao and smiled. "Don't let those long, human legs slow you down."

He had a hard time keeping up with Kadagan. His short legs glided across the stone floor, boots clacking out a rhythm that echoed in the walkway. Torches lined the walls and gave off an oily scent. Ramps spiraled above and below, carved into the walls, leading to upper and lower levels of the mountain. The inside of the mountain seemed hollow, with a vast openness spreading out before him. Dwarves bustled around, some trading, others going to and fro with other business, staring at him as they went. Stone-carved doorways lined the walls, which Echao figured led to shops or homes. Merchants had tents lined up, creating the feel of streets passing through a market district.

Echao moved closer to the edge of the walkway and stopped for a moment to peer down. He could not see the bottom. A small light flickered in the distance, but he was unable to make out any detail. He looked up to find the same thing. This place could house millions of dwarves.

"Come, boy," Kadagan called from up ahead. "You don't want to be caught here alone. I can assure you of that. If you think it will be difficult to persuade the council to help you in battle, you have never tried to be the only human in Rothgaer and get caught out alone."

Echao ran to catch up with him, his stomach rolling with both hunger and nervousness. "How many of you live here? This place is huge."

"Not as many as you might think. We were once a great and mighty nation, but Tzelder rectified that. Once, there were cities throughout these mountains, and now, this is the main one. Most dwarves live here in Rothgaer. There are a few outlying settlements, some higher in the mountains, but none live in the open anymore. Too dangerous. We all live safely inside these walls."

"Most of our shops close at dusk," Echao said. "It seems you are just as busy after sunset."

Kadagan laughed. "Do you see any sunlight? Day and night are of no concern to us. We work and do our business when we please. There is no need for time. No one has to schedule when the next meal is. We eat when we're hungry, and we don't if we're not. Tis that simple."

Echao followed along in silence, soaking in the sights and sounds. They passed several booths that had meat and vegetables frying in a pan, and his stomach pained at the smell. Kadagan turned left, deeper into the mountain until he came to a large wooden door with iron bandings. He slid a key from his belt, and the lock clicked as he turned it and pushed the door open.

"This is my home," Kadagan said, gesturing around a large open living area hewn out of the stone wall. "You will be staying here with me during your time here. Your bed is through that door, and there is food set on the table."

Before he could finish, Echao rushed to the table and shoveled food in his mouth. He tried to mumble a thanks, but the only thing that came out was crumbs of bread and garbled words. Kadagan sat down on a plush chair and sparked his pipe, taking a long draw from it. A hearty dwarf woman came by and poured him a pint of mead. He guzzled it down and wiped the foam from his mouth. "Aren't you going to eat?"

Kadagan raised an eyebrow, and Echao nodded. "Right, right. No sun, no time, Eat and work when you want. Got it."

Kadagan leaned his head back and closed his eyes, still puffing on the pipe. "Now that you don't think you're starving to death, meet Brunda. She is my maidservant. She will assist you with anything you need and will be here to keep an eye on you when I cannot. You will find your bed through the door on the left. I suggest you go there as soon as possible. We will meet with the council first thing in the morning."

Echao reached his arm out to shake Brunda's hand. She stared down at his hand as if it were diseased and wrinkled her nose. He wiped his greasy hand on his pants and waved at her. "Nice to meet you, Brunda." She nodded and began to fill his cup. He slid his hand over the mouth of the cup. "No, thank you. I believe I'll be heading to bed now."

He walked to his room, and he could hear Kadagan whisper behind him, "Good boy." He laid in the bed and stared at the ceiling, thinking about the past few weeks, wondering what Lily was doing right now, and wishing she were with him. He had to get some rest. The council had to send their aid. He had to protect Lily. Her face was the last thing on his mind when sleep took him.

◆◆◆◆◆

The next morning was a rush to get up, snatch some fruit and a heel of bread from the table, and bathe off before Kadagan was already headed out the door. Echao slammed the juice glass back onto the table a little more forcefully than he had intended as he chased Kadagan out the door.

"I thought time didn't matter to the dwarves?" he asked.

"Typically, it doesn't; however, if you want the council's help, then I suggest we don't start with a bad impression. Keeping them waiting would not be in your people's best interest."

They strode past several groups of dwarves conducting business, and many of them stopped and stared. Some pointed and whispered. It made Echao feel odd. He disliked being the center of attention. After a while, he began to wave at the dwarves that were gawking at him. When he did, they would shuffle away, faces blushing.

Kadagan stopped abruptly at a set of large double doors guarded by two iron clad dwarves. "Kadagan, brother of Baridath, member of the council and Echao, son of Kèlris of Aleesia. We have an appointment with the council."

One of the dwarves pounded the haft of his long ax against the ground, and the door creaked open. Echao followed Kadagan through the door. The chamber was massive and lined with elegant stone statues of dwarves, some in royal regalia, some in armor and holding weapons. Kadagan slowed and allowed Echao to walk beside him. He tilted his head toward him and whispered, "Do not speak unless spoken to. When I tell you, you may address the council, but not until."

Echao dipped his head, his eyes stoic. At the end of the chamber were ten thrones carved from the surrounding stone, spaced out in an arch. Kadagan stopped so that he was lined on the left, front, and right by the dwarves in the seats. The dwarf seated front and center, in the most elaborate throne, stood and cleared his throat. "Welcome, brother and human of Aleesia. We were told you had an urgent matter that must be brought before the council." He projected his voice with an air of royalty mixed with a bit of sarcasm

Kadagan grimaced, but Echao was barely able to catch it as the look faded away just as quick. "Aye. I do."

Baridath sat back into the throne and crossed his short legs. He waved his arm toward Kadagan. "Then get on with it."

Kadagan was a skilled orator. Echao watched as his eyes flitted from dwarf to dwarf, making eye contact with them all as he addressed them. "Great council, I asked for you to grace us with your assembly today to address a most worrisome issue. As you are aware, our scouts have reported that Tzelder is rallying troops from across the country to march on Aleesia. King Riehner has resurfaced and is prepared to take back the throne."

A dwarf with a long silver beard tapped his fingers in annoyance. "We are well aware of this. Get to the point."

Kadagan's face flushed with blood. He cleared his throat before continuing. "Very well, your grace. Tzelder marches to Aleesia. Who knows where he will go next. The humans prepare for battle. If they are to survive, we must send aid. They will require the strength of the dwarves to win the battle."

The council sat in silence, not taking their eyes from Kadagan. Echao shifted side to side and pulled at the hem of his jerkin, impatient with how long it was taking them to respond. He looked at Kadagan, who stared at the council and avoided his glares. He looked calm, but Echao could hear him grinding his teeth. Echao leaned over to him. "Say something."

Kadagan hushed him with a look, and Echao rolled his eyes. A voice sounded from the council, calling Echao's attention. "Why does this concern us?"

Echao's mouth parted. Kadagan grabbed him by the wrist as he took a step forward, but he slung his hand away. "What do you mean by that? It is a war that concerns us all."

Baridath stood and held his arm out to the council, who had begun mumbling among themselves. "You have not been addressed by the council. I would remind you to hold…"

"You have been addressed by me," Echao said with fire in his voice. "My people need your help. I know we caused you much pain and heartache, but that was many years ago. King Riehner brought peace among the races before being overthrown by Tzelder. This is our chance to stand up to him, our chance to take this realm back."

"You young, naive fool," a barrel-chested dwarf shouted. "You are a guest in this mountain, and you address us so? How dare you? Has it occurred to you that we do not want things the way they were before, with you humans lording over us? Good riddance. I hope Tzelder wipes you from history."

Echao turned to Kadagan, tears welling up in his eyes. "You are just going to stand there?"

Kadagan did not move, his stoic eyes staring straight at his brother. Echao walked closer to the council, and the guards drew their weapons. Echao tore the jerkin away from his chest. "You think Riehner's wrath will not be terrible on Tzelder? That he will allow the assault to go unchecked? Then strike me down. Those are my people, and I will die with them. Just know that the Battlemages will be reborn. Should you choose to abandon us in our time of need, we will not rescue you in yours."

The council was silent, mouths agape at his outburst. Echao turned to storm out of the great hall. He heard Kadagan's voice boom behind him. "Brother, hear me." The hall was in total silence except for the echo of his voice reverberating off the stone walls. "You and your council may not wish to be involved, but as for me, I will not forsake this ancient alliance. I will stand with Echao and his people, and I will take as many dwarven warriors as would choose to follow me."

Baridath stood from his seat, his face red, hands shaking. "You dare defy the council? You wish to be ruled by these humans?"

Kadagan smiled. "I dare defy ignorance and hate. I will stand in battle with them, and should I fall, I will fall in honor. Can you say the same?"

Echao sighed as he marched out of the hall, Kadagan on his heels. He did not slow his pace until he was back in Kadagan's home. He grabbed his satchel and threw the few items he brought with him into it. Kadagan closed the door behind them. "What are you doing?"

"I'm leaving. I can't stay here. My people need me. What is the fastest way back to Gaer Alon?"

"I would recommend you retrace the path we took to get here," Kadagan said.

Echao looked up as he threw the satchel across his shoulder. "I don't want the safest route. I want the fastest."

Kadagan hung his head. "Very well. I will send for your horse and have Brunda gather you some food for the journey. Follow the lake north to the King's Road. Once there, you should be able to follow the road east and find your way."

"Thank you, Kadagan. You didn't have to support me back there. I know it cost you a great deal to stand up to the council."

Kadagan grabbed him by the forearm before crossing his arm over his chest. "Do be careful, Echao. I will be there as soon as I can, even if I come alone. You will have my ax. Ride fast."

Echao crossed his arm over his chest and left the dwarf behind. The dwarves in the common area were staring and gossiping again, but he paid them no attention. He rushed toward the hidden crevice and saddled his horse once down the mountain trail. He pushed the horse to its limit through the night. His only thought was getting back in time to save Lily from the battle ahead.

TWENTY-FIVE

Tamm rushed down the steps from his treehouse to the small clearing where he was to meet Calla. He woke up early, anxious to see her. He expected that she would have beat him there and would already have their usual breakfast spread out on a blanket, but the grove was empty. Some elves had been moving around the city on his walk to the grove but not as many as usual.

He noticed some twigs lying nearby on the ground and released the magic inside him, manipulating the wind, causing them to rise and fall, float away, then reeling them back. He thought about Riehner's reminder of the day he learned about magic, the feeling he had, and how he would need to find that feeling during his trials.

He lowered himself to the ground and crossed his legs. He closed his eyes and took a deep breath, in and out, focusing on the rhythm of his breath. He always felt the spark inside him now, it was a part of him, but it did not feel the same as the day he discovered it. The intensity was different. He searched deeper, but something nagged at the back of his mind.

He was pulled farther away from the spark with thoughts of Echao, wondering if he was successful in rallying the dwarves' support; thoughts of his parents back in Aleesia, hoping they would be safe; and for the first time in weeks, Adina. How could he have so quickly forgotten her? His life had been a blur since the Spring Festival, but that was no excuse. She had been so important to him just a few weeks ago. He berated himself for not having thought of her first when he heard of the attack on Aleesia.

A twig snapped behind him, and he leaped to his feet. Calla strode up behind him. She was in a long robe and carried a dark, wooden staff with a polished stone affixed to the top. She tossed him an apple. "Eat up. Sorry, I'm late. I had to meet with the Elders this morning."

Tamm polished the apple on his shirt and took a bite. "It's fine. Riehner had told me to do some preparation for the trials."

"Good. You need to be prepared. The trials are no easy task."

"I don't take it lightly," he said. "I'm glad you're here to help."

Tamm trained with Calla for the rest of the day, only taking a break to eat a few bites during a hasty lunch. He was surprised that she did not teach him any new spells, rather taking the words he already knew and having him experiment with different uses of each, including learning to coat his blade in flames and expounding on his healing ability. Once, before heading back to the city for the night, Calla climbed up a tree and jumped out; Tamm had to use *Gaoth* to maintain a gust under her feet to let her float to the ground. She glided down as if she were flying, her hair flowing in the wind. He almost dropped her once as he marveled at how beautiful she looked.

He wanted to spend more time with her, but it was getting late. He only had one more day with her before she had to go to Aleesia. She walked him to the steps of his treehouse and touched his arm as she told him goodnight. He leaned toward her, wanting to wrap her in an embrace, but dared not to. "Goodnight," he whispered before trudging up the stairs.

The next morning, Tamm made his way to the clearing and found Calla waiting on him. She had a large satchel with her. "What's that?"

She poked the satchel with her foot. "Provisions for the trip."

It felt like someone kicked him in the gut. "You're leaving now?"

"I leave this evening, but I will be here when you enter the trials."

He released a pent-up breath. "Good. I wouldn't want to do it without you."

They walked in tandem further into the forest toward the cave. Tamm was quiet for the majority of the trip. They crossed the stream, and Tamm could see the cave up ahead. "We're going to cave now?"

"Uh-huh," she said without making eye contact. "There are preparations to do."

Tamm stopped, but Calla continued walking. "No training today, then?"

She slowed and glanced back at him. "Come on. We have much to do. You must center yourself. You need to prepare."

"What do I need to expect?"

She shook her head. "I cannot explain the trials to you, even if I wanted to, I am no Battlemage. I don't even know what to expect when you get inside. You will do fine."

"Very well," Tamm said, kicking a stone into the creek before following Calla into the glade outside the cave.

Outside of the cave, there was a round oak table surrounded by five elves in flowing robes. Two of them were crushing some sort of leaf in a pestle, another goading the coals under a small cauldron, and the last two were chanting words that Tamm did not recognize as a faint green light shimmered around their hands. A cloud of acrid smoke rose from the cauldron, tingling Tamm's nose.

He coughed as he walked near the table. "What are they doing?"

Calla wrapped an arm around him and ushered him away from the table to a quieter place. "It is part of the ritual. You do not want to breathe the fumes in too much. It can be toxic in high doses."

He tried to turn back around to see the table, but she steered him away. "What are they going to do with it?"

"Well," she said. "You will have to drink it before going into the cave."

Tamm shook his head. "I'm not drinking that. You just told me it was toxic."

"In high doses. In small amounts, you will be fine. You are not the first to go through the trials, and you will not be the last. This is something that you must do."

Tamm ran his hands through his dark hair and paced in circles. Calla gripped him by his arms and stared into his eyes. "You must calm yourself. You will not be able to complete the trials while your emotions are controlling you. Remember what Riehner told you. Go sit under that tree and center yourself."

"It's just that…:

Calla shook his arms. "Do as I say, Tamm. You must take the trials today, and we have a long road ahead of us. Go over there and reflect on the future."

Tamm stormed off and plopped down under the tree. He closed his eyes and began his rhythmic breathing. After several cycles, he felt his fear and anxiety fade away. With each breath, he felt calmer, feeling the spark deep inside him, faintly at first, but then growing stronger.

A voice called him out of his meditation. A sound in the distance grew louder as he pulled himself toward it. It was Calla, but she still sounded far away.

His eyes snapped open and darted from side to side, looking around. He looked up, and the sun was already making its descent. He had meditated past lunch. He stood and stretched the stiffness from his legs.

"It is time," Calla said.

Tamm looked around. "Where's Riehner?"

"He will be here, but we must start. Now is the time. Come."

Tamm followed her to the cave opening. The elves that had been working at the cauldron were there with a chalice. The center elf handed him the cup. The fluid was steaming and smelled of mint with the hint of something rotten disguised. He curled his nose, and the apple he ate earlier threatened to come up.

"Drink," the five elves said in unison.

He held the cup away from his face, the smell nauseating. "What is this?"

"Drink."

He looked at Calla, who nodded at him.

He held his breath and turned the chalice up, drinking deeply. He coughed and felt the liquid bubble up into the back of his throat, and he forced it back down. He handed the cup back to the elf and was ushered toward the cave entrance. His vision blurred, which caused him to wobble as he walked. Was he poisoned?

He stopped at the entrance but could not see in, his vision unable to pierce the darkness. He glanced over his shoulder at Calla, who shooed him in with her hands. She said something, but he failed to make it out, a roaring buzz in his ears.

He took a step through the mouth of the cave, the darkness enveloping him like the water when he would dive into Lake Aleesia. It was cold and damp with a musty smell thick in the air. He stumbled further into the cave, his arms stretched out, grasping for the wall but coming up empty. How was he supposed to find his way around if he could not see?

His heart raced as the fear set in. Nobody had told him what the trials were. There could be some beast just outside of arms reach, wanting him for dinner, and he could not see it. The last time he had tried to look into the cave, he had used fire, but the cave rejected it and hit him with a blast of air in retaliation. Maybe he was not ready for the trials then.

He held out his hand. *"Lasaír."* A small flame sparked alive in his hand. Unlike the last time he tried to send fire into the cave, he could see some of what was in front of him. He fed more power into the flame, and it shone brighter. He could see a wall in front of him with what looked like a torch hanging on it. He dared not move, not knowing what else was around him, and instead released the flame to glide through the air toward the torch, leaving him in darkness.

The flame reached the torch, and it blazed to life. He could now see a few more torches to the sides of the first. He willed the fire to reach out to the other torches, and it obeyed his command. Light scattered across the room with shadows dancing around the ceiling and walls. The room was circular, and as he peered around, he could not find the exit. He ran his hand along the slimy wall, but the opening had sealed itself off.

"Tammuz," a gruff voice said behind him and, he jumped, spinning around to find a large grey Kapre with an iron helmet and armor standing in front of him. He reached to his side instinctively and drew a sword that had not been there earlier.

The Kapre slid the helmet from his head. "Did you think you had destroyed us? Your people have tried before and failed. What were one boy and a few farmers going to do?"

Tamm held the sword at the ready as the Kapre circled him. He thought back to the last fight with a Kapre this size and how he would have died if Riehner had not saved him. His breaths came in short gasps as he tried in vain to calm himself. He closed his eyes, and when he opened them again, the Kapre had drawn a battle ax and was banging the haft against the iron armor.

The beast rushed at him, swinging the ax wildly at Tamm's head. Tamm rolled to the side, the whooshing of the ax rushing past his ear. As he rolled back to his feet, the ax came down again, and he deflected it with the blade and slashed at the Kapre's ribs, but it leaped back to avoid the attack.

It cackled at him, not amused with his attempts. "You are weak, Tammuz. Lower your weapon, and let us end this now."

Tamm stood firm, his eyes hard set as he gripped the sword tighter in his hand. The Kapre spun the ax and charged at Tamm again. This time, Tamm summoned fire to surround his blade and stood his ground. As the Kapre closed in for the attack, Tamm slipped under the ax as he dragged his sword across the Kapre's abdomen. There was a booming crack like thunder, and the Kapre burst into ash and embers as the ax clattered against the ground.

Tamm ceased the flow of magic to the blade and looked around, expecting the door to open, allowing him to leave, but it did not. He sheathed the sword and walked around the chamber, looking for some sign that he missed. He found a small stone ledge with what appeared to be a table and chair carved out of the stone. He clambered up to it and sat in the chair.

Several moments passed, and he was beginning to think that he would be stuck in the cave forever. He propped his head in his hands and closed his eyes. Another voice spoke to him, and when he opened his eyes, Riehner was sitting across from him. "Giving up already?

"Is it not over? Are you here to get me out of here?"

Riehner leaned back in the chair. "I can let you go if you would like, but you would be forfeiting your chance at becoming a Battlemage."

"What else must I do?"

Riehner clapped his hands on the table. "Good question. Follow me."

Riehner walked over to the edge of the room with Tamm following behind him. He waved his hand in front of the wall, and Tamm stood perplexed as the wall faded away, and in its place, grass, mountains, a lake, and a town twinkled into view.

Tamm's voice was barely a whisper as it escaped. "Aleesia?"

Riehner smiled. "It is." He stepped past the wall and onto the grass. Tamm stepped over, feeling the soft grass on his feet, staring down in surprise to find that his boots were gone, and he was now barefoot. The rest of his clothes had changed also. He was back in peasants' clothing, his sword gone, a small hunting knife in its place. He looked at Riehner, who was back in robes, and had his staff as he did when he was the healer in Aleesia. He had a regal look about him. His hair was still shorter, but whiter than the last time Tamm had seen him.

Up ahead, Adina was lounging by the lake reading a book. Echao and Lily were dancing in town, decorated for the Spring Festival, his parents dancing beside them. A tear trickled down his face. "How are we here?" he asked, wiping the tear from his eye.

Riehner patted him on the back as he wrapped an arm around his shoulder. "Does it matter? The important thing is that we are home. All is well. There is peace and joy, and you can stay here. With us."

Tamm gazed around the town he grew up in, the town he always thought he wanted to leave, but now that he had been away for so long, he only wanted to be home. "I can stay?"

"Of course," Riehner said. "We both can."

He thought of Calla and the elves, the army marching toward Aleesia. "What about the war? We've promised the elves that we would overthrow Tzelder."

REBORN

Riehner shook his head and led Tamm closer to the town. "None of that matters here. You can live the rest of your life in peace. Your parents will be here, as will Echao and Adina."

"What about Calla?" he asked, his brow furrowed.

Riehner rolled his eyes. "What about her? You have everything you need here."

Tamm shook himself free from Riehner's arm. "No. I don't. I have a responsibility to my people."

"*Your* people?" Riehner asked.

"Yes. My people. Riehner's people. The people of Aleesia, of Iradell. Aleesia will soon be attacked, and I can't live in some fairytale land while that happens. I will save them. I will defeat Tzelder and return Iradell to its former glory."

Riehner looked angry. "I am giving you a gift. No more worry, no more sorrow, no more tears."

"Take me back," Tamm said. "Now!"

The sky darkened, and he could hear the screams of women and children in the distance. Storm clouds rolled through the sky, and lightning lit the countryside. Tzelder's army was on them, and the townspeople were being slaughtered. He looked to Riehner, his mouth gaping open.

Riehner shrugged his shoulders. "This is what you wanted." He placed the crystal helm on his head and raised his sword over his head as he rushed into the fray with a battle cry.

Tamm reached to his side, surprised that his sword was belted back at his waist. He was wearing a metallic armor that felt bulky and heavy as he tried to run after Riehner. Two soldiers confronted him, both swinging their swords at his neck simultaneously. He rolled under the attack and flung his arm around towards them, sending them flying through the air with a burst of wind.

He searched the battlefield for Riehner but could not find him. He saw another group of soldiers surrounding Kèlris. He traced his finger along the blade of his sword as it burst into flames, then rushed at one of the soldiers, his ears ringing as the metal from their armors crashed together. He swept his sword toward another soldier who fled at the sight of the fiery blade. Together, he and Kèlris were able to dispatch the last two.

A shriek pierced the discord of battle. He turned to the sound to find Adina and Lily crawling away with several soldiers in pursuit. Echao was lying nearby, blood pooling around his pale body.

"No, no, no," Tamm pleaded as he ran toward him. Calla jumped down from a nearby building, landing between the soldiers and the retreating girls. A spear replaced the staff she typically carried. She thrust, slashed, and stabbed at the soldiers while spells flew from the blade of the spear. The soldiers advanced, undeterred in their pursuit.

Tamm ran to help her but heard another cry from across the battlefield. It was Riehner's voice, and he sounded distressed. He spun toward the call to find Riehner hobbling away, blood flowing from a gash in his thigh as soldiers closed in on him. "To me, Tammuz. Help me."

Tamm sprinted across the battlefield before stopping and turning back to Calla, who was now surrounded. Lily was holding Echao's lifeless body while Adina had her eyes closed, and her hands pressed over her ears. Kèlris held a motionless Mariah slumped across his shoulders. The soldiers still came, and Calla was beginning to falter.

"Tamm, please," she called.

His heart ached. How could he choose between them and Riehner, the father he only just learned that he had? He turned back to Riehner, who was now on the ground, his crystal armor cracked and broken, blood pooling from several wounds. The soldiers had him surrounded, his eyes pleading with Tamm's, his arm stretched out toward him. "Please…"

Tamm looked back to Calla, and she had lost her spear and was now on her knees, her arms out, begging her attackers for mercy. The soldiers were now gone, and a solitary man in solid black armor stood over her, a sword with a blade as black as night prepared to strike. Tamm knew in his heart that it was Tzelder. He glanced back at Riehner. He reached for Tamm, a tear in his eye. The soldiers had their spears raised, prepared to impale him. He spun back to Calla and then again to Riehner.

"I'm sorry," he said.

A weak smile spread across the corner of Riehner's lips as the tear trickled down his cheek, and he stared at his murderers, forcing them to look into his eyes. Tamm turned away as the spears plunged into Riehner's flesh. He could hear the old man gurgle as he sped towards Calla and his family.

The sword was on its way down to cleave Calla's pleading body in half. Tamm was so close. He lowered his head as he raced toward her. He flung his body in front of her and held out his left arm and shouted. "*Sciath.*" A shimmering purple shield appeared on his arm. He could see through its astral form to the sword slicing down. The blade clanged off the shield, and Tzelder stumbled back from the force.

Tamm snuck a glance at his friends and family before turning his attention back to Tzelder, who was already marching toward him. He stared down at the shield in surprise. He had never learned that word before, *sciath*. He had only felt it on his tongue, and in his desperation, it urged its way out. The colors danced and shifted, but when he touched, it was as firm as if touching metal.

Tzelder closed in and slashed the sword wildly at him. He held the arcane shield out in front of him, deflecting the blows with ease. He fed the flames on his sword with more power and launched a series of counter-attacks. He threw the first blow aside, but the second shattered the obsidian sword in Tzelder's hands. Tamm rushed forward, thrusting the flaming sword into Tzelder's abdomen. His eyes widened as he tried to speak. "It will not be so easy next time."

Tamm cocked his head as Tzelder disintegrated into ash. He spun around, but Calla and his family were gone, the city slowly fading from his vision. He looked down, and the armor he wore had disappeared. When he looked back up, Aleesia had dissolved, and he was back in the musty cave. The torches along the walls had gone out, but there was a single torch flickering in the center of the cave.

He was not able to see the exit, so he walked closer to the torch. He tried to lift it to get a better look around, but it was immovable, rooted in the cave floor. He was exhausted and just wanted to sit and rest; he wanted to be back in his treehouse, but most of all, he wanted to be in Aleesia.

He knelt at the torch and closed his eyes. He focused on his breath, but a light pierced through his closed eyelids. He opened them, and where the walls had been, there were now mounds of different colored stones and crystals. They emitted lights of all colors that were hypnotic to watch dance throughout the cave. He tried to stand, but his legs felt like bags of sand.

A thrum reverberated through the cave, and the crystals began to vibrate. A red light pulsed from a group of crystals in the center. He heard a tinkling as one of the stones fell to the cave floor. He tried to stand again and found it much easier this time. He approached the crystal on the floor and found a small red stone lying near a puddle of water. It was beautiful. He picked it up and wiped the grime from the floor away. The clarity was flawless. Faint light from the torch hit it, and it scattered a ruby light across his chest.

A screeching of stone against stone sounded behind him. He spun to find the wall opened, revealing the exit. A tall figure stood in the entryway, torchlight behind him casting his silhouette in shadow. Tamm put the stone in his pocket and walked toward the figure.

TWENTY-SIX

Riehner waited on Tamm outside the cave. Tamm fiddled with the stone in his pocket as he walked toward the opening. Riehner was careful to not enter the cave but stood just on the outside with his arms outstretched. Tamm walked into his arms, and he wrapped him in a tight embrace. "Well done, my son. Show it to me."

Tamm pulled away and smiled as he dug in his pocket for the stone. "It's a ruby, I think."

He handed the stone to Riehner, but he waved him off, not taking it from him. "No, it's yours. You hold on to it. But it's garnet. Rhodolite, to be exact, and it is perfect. Congratulations, Battlemage Tammuz."

REBORN

Tamm stared at him, a smile tugging at his lips before fading away. "The trials...the things I saw in there...it was awful."

"I know," Riehner said knowingly.

"You were there. Calla was there. All of my family and friends from Aleesia were there. Even Tzelder was there."

"Obviously, it turned out for the best."

"No, it didn't. I had to watch you..." Tamm choked back tears. "I had to watch Tzelder's soldiers murder you."

"It was not real," Riehner said, patting Tamm's shoulder in sympathy. "Only in your mind. I am still here."

Tamm shook his head. "I know, but it was so real."

Riehner wrapped his arm around Tamm's shoulder and ushered him away from the cave. The oak table that had held the ingredients for the concoction he drank earlier now had small pieces of metal and leather. Riehner explained to Tamm how to shape the metal around the garnet and helped him to thread the leather through it, creating a necklace that he tied around his neck, the garnet sparkling in the torchlight.

Riehner explained the trials in more detail, and how when the Battlemages were first created, the elves had introduced him to the mind-altering drink made from caapri root and chotria leaves. The elves sang magic over the cave, allowing it to perform spectacular feats such as the trials while also protecting itself from those not meant to enter it. The concoction permitted the mind of the drinker to wander as the magic worked through them to produce some of their worst fears while allowing them to be cognizant enough to decide to overcome them.

He told him how the cave senses the strengths and weaknesses of the Battlemages and chooses a stone for them to create their medallion should they pass the trials. The medallion links them to the power of the cave and helps to enhance their magical abilities.

Tamm gulped water from his waterskin, suddenly realizing how thirsty he was as he tried to digest all the information that Riehner was throwing at him. "So now, I can use this medallion to draw on the power from the cave."

"Absolutely. Do remember that some spells are more demanding than others and will draw on your strength also. If it is too much for you to handle, it very well could kill you. You must know your strength, what you can and cannot handle."

Tamm nodded as he swallowed another gulp of water. As he capped the waterskin back, a silver-haired elf interrupted, his back so arched that he only came to Tamm's chin. "My lord, I must request a portion of Master Tammuz's time. I need measurements."

"Very well, Riehner said. "Go with him, Tamm. I will meet you later."

Tamm followed the elderly elf down a trail he had not taken before. He scurried along the path in the direction of the city but started curving away from the city center. He muttered to himself along the way.

"What's your name?" Tamm asked.

He mumbled something about too much work and not enough time as he hurried onward. Tamm had to open his stride to keep up with the old elf. Just outside the city, they came upon a building made from lumber and mud mortar. Smoke billowed from the chimney, and a familiar metallic odor made Tamm sniff the air. It reminded him of home and working in the forge with Kèlris.

The strange elf opened the door, and Tamm saw the anvil and forge and closed his eyes, remembering his last time at the forge when Kèlris gave him a sword that he made, the one he had used in the battle against the Kapre. "What are we doing at a forge?"

The elf stared at him for a moment, his face no longer tense and worried, but relaxed. He had no wrinkles, but there were faint age lines around his nose and mouth. "I apologize for the rush, Master Tammuz. My name is Lysanthir. I am not a Battlemage myself, but I serve the Order in other ways. I make the weapons and armor for all new Battlemages."

"It's a pleasure to meet you. So, I get my own sword? Like Riehner's?

"In a way, yes. All swords are special and vary among each Battlemage. Although they are all different. Typically, they all hold a stone that matches their medallion."

Tamm rolled the garnet medallion between his fingers. "Where do you get the stone? Does it help me to focus magic like my medallion?"

"Riehner explained the magic of the cave to you? Good. The cave gives us the stone. And yes, to my knowledge, it works very much in the same way as your medallion."

"Great. So, where do we start?"

Lysanthir chuckled, his high pitch voice cracking at the effort. "You may know your way around a forge, but *we* do not start anywhere. This is a sacred act that requires metals from the dwarves and magic from the elves. You will not be privy to the rite, but I do need to get your measurements."

He measured Tamm's arm and torso lengths. He asked him several questions about his fighting style and had him go through some forms with a sword hanging on the wall. He questioned him about what style of armor he preferred and had him try some on. Tamm did not like the weight of the armor. It felt bulky and limited his movement. Tamm asked for armor that would provide maximum protection while not limiting his mobility. Once he had the information he needed, he dismissed Tamm to return to the city.

The sun had long since set, and soft glowing lights lined the city streets. He wanted to find Calla to tell her about all that had happened before she left for Alessia. Everything had been so rushed after the trials that he had not been able to look for her. He had hoped that she would be waiting on him when he returned, but after making it back to his treehouse, he had not seen or heard from her.

The wooden stairs did not make a creak as he ascended them. He pushed the door open and sat at the writing desk, removing the dagger from his belt and kicking off his boots. They thumped against the floor as they fell. He tipped back in the chair and hit the floor when a noise sounded from behind him. He leaped back to his feet, scrambling to get to his dagger.

There was a man with shorter hair and a wild, confused look in his eyes. Tamm blinked, not sure what he was seeing.

REBORN

"You scared me to death," Echao said. "I must have been sleeping like the dead. I didn't even hear you come in."

Tamm jumped onto the bed with him and hugged him. "When did you return?"

"Just after dark. I rode hard. The poor horse was foaming at the mouth by the time I arrived, but I couldn't take a chance of missing the fight. They told me you were undergoing your trials. How did it go?"

Tamm climbed onto his own bed and ran his hand through his hair before letting out a long sigh. "It was amazing and terrifying all at the same time. I can't go into much detail, but I performed magic that I had never even dreamed of and saw things that will haunt me the rest of my life."

"So, you passed?"

Tamm gave him a confused look. "Did you doubt that I would?"

"Of course not," Echao said, laughing. "But, you did pass?"

Tamm held up the stone medallion around his neck. "Yes, I passed."

"That's amazing. It's just like Linsyn's. I mean Riehner's. Whichever. Congratulations. Now what?"

He cupped his chin in his hands and stretched his neck. "To be honest, I don't know. Tzelder's army has to be getting close. It can't be more than a few days before they arrive, and the war starts. I think it's best if we spend these last few days here with friends and as much time on the training grounds as possible. I wish I could have found Calla tonight. I'm sure she could tell us something."

Echao's head cocked as he looked at Tamm in confusion. "Calla? You didn't hear? Oh, Tamm. She has already left for Aleesia. I saw Riehner when I returned, and he told me where you were and that Calla had to leave shortly after your trials started. I'm sorry."

Tamm hung his head and dropped back onto the bed, staring at the ceiling. There was a gentle rap at the door, and Tamm cut his eyes to Echao, who shrugged. When he pulled the door open, he was surprised to see Counsel Elion.

Tamm dipped his head in a bow. "Master Elion, I wasn't expecting anyone at this hour. Forgive me; I recently returned from the trials."

Elion smiled. "My apologies for the late arrival. I have recently met with King Riehner and had to get the message to you." He peeked in the door at Echao. "And it warms my heart to see you have returned safe, Master Echao. I do regret the news from the dwarves. Alas, what will be, will be."

"What news from the dwarves?" Tamm asked.

Echao sighed. "They wouldn't agree to come. Kadagan swore he would be here, though. I like him, Tamm. He's honorable, and I believe he will bring as many as he can with him. I'm sorry I failed."

Tamm was silent for a moment. "It's alright, Echao. As Counsel Elion said, 'what will be, will be.'"

Elion nodded. "If I could speak with you for a moment outside?"

Tamm nodded and followed him outside, pulling the door closed on his way out. "Why all the secrecy?

"With the war starting soon and your now having passed your trials, your father has called for your coronation as prince to commence tomorrow."

Tamm leaned back against the door. "Wow. This is all happening so fast."

"I apologize for the inconvenience; however, it must happen. Should anything happen to the King during the battle, curse the thought. Well, there needs to be an official coronation. And, you need to explain this to Echao. He was not present when your father revealed himself as King Riehner and claimed you as his son. He needs to hear it from you and before the coronation."

Tamm had forgotten that Echao was training when Riehner awoke and claimed him as his son. He would have to tell Echao before he found out from someone else.

He bid Elion goodnight and returned to his room. He explained everything to Echao. He told of the usurpation of Riehner and how his mother was wounded, how elvish magic kept them both alive until sixteen years ago when, by Calla's recommendation, they stopped the magic to allow for him to be born. Unfortunately, it resulted in his mother's death.

Echao sat in silence and stared past Tamm. Tamm got up and sat beside him on the bed, but he did not move. "Echao. Look at me." Echao continued to stare at the wall, his arms limp in his lap. "No matter what, by birth or not, you will always be my brother. Kèlris and Mariah will always be my parents, as will Riehner and Beltia."

Echao turned to Tamm, looking at him for the first time since hearing the news, a puzzled look on his face as if he were seeing someone that he used to know but could not quite remember. "Why didn't you tell me before?"

"Everything has been so hectic. I just wasn't thinking. I'm sorry. Riehner made this big announcement, but you weren't around. I may be the son of the King, but this changes nothing between us."

Echao smiled. "I would hope not. Having family in the nobility could come in handy." He nudged Tamm in the ribs with his elbow.

"Well, there's one more thing," Tamm said. "They want to make everything official and have a coronation tomorrow."

Echao leaned back against the wall, pausing before responding. "This all seems so quick, but when you're on the verge of a civil war, I suppose time is of the essence. It's going to take a while for all of this to sink in, but we'll figure it out together."

"Thank you for understanding," Tamm said, climbing into bed. "Let's get some sleep. Tomorrow will have enough worries of its own."

◆◆◆◆◆

Tamm woke from a knocking on the door. Several elvish women rushed into the room and set the table with a light breakfast and hot tea. Tamm and Echao robed themselves and ate quickly as the elvish women hurried them along. As soon as they had laid their napkins down, the elves removed the table, and several elvish men entered the room as the women slipped out the door.

REBORN

They elves measured Tamm and Echao with rapid stretches of a tape, and then gave them several lavish outfits to try on, some velvet lined with silver and gold thread, others in some of the softest linen Tamm had ever felt. Echao arched his eyebrows, and Tamm laughed. "If this is what being the brother of the prince is like, I'm going to keep you around."

They laughed together, and it felt like the old times when they would laugh and joke in their room in Aleesia. Tamm's smile faded as he thought of the small village and the upcoming battle. He did not want anything to happen to the people there or his hometown.

"What's wrong?" Echao asked.

"Nothing. I'm fine. Just nervous about this morning," he said, avoiding Echao's eyes.

The elves finished their tailoring and had the boys dressed and ready. Echao wore dark pants and a white shirt with a dark green jacket equipped with a tail that flowed like a robe. Tamm was dressed similarly, though slightly more regal. His coat was a royal blue, and he wore a red braided cord that matched his medallion draped across his shoulder and chest. He had protested the cord initially, feeling it was too pretentious until one of the elves explained that it was an aiguillette and was a customary decoration of the Battlemages. It was typically worn to festive events such as a coronation or balls and sometimes worn into battle.

An elegantly dressed elf led Tamm into the House of Counsels through a rear door. He paced the hallway, glancing through open doors, but trying to stay out of view. A throne had been set out in front of the longhouse. Two smaller thrones sat on each side. The one to the King's right hand sat empty, prepared for Tamm to take his seat after he was crowned. The one to his left sat empty except for a single rose in honor of his mother.

Tamm spun on his heel and saw Lysanthir slip into the back of the building, something long in his arms wrapped in delicate cloth. He waved for Tamm to meet him in one of the side rooms. He laid the item on the table and backed away, signaling Tamm to unwrap it.

Tamm slid the cloth back with care. A garnet set in the pommel gleamed in the light from the room. The sheath was dark leather with ornately shaped designs etched down the full length of the scabbard. The hilt was wooden and stained a cherry color and wrapped in red velvet bound with delicate gold chain. He slid the sword from its sheath. The room's lights reflected in the perfectly polished blade with a fuller running the entire length of the sword. He waved the sword around. It was lighter than any sword he had ever held, except maybe Riehner's. It felt like when he and Echao would play-fight with sticks as children.

Lysanthir sidled up beside him and whispered in his ear. "It is a mixture of mythril and dwarven-steel mined from the deepest tunnels in Rothgaer and a garnet from the cave where you took your trial. It should serve you well."

Tamm choked back his emotion. "Thank you, Lysanthir. It's perfect."

Lysanthir nodded. "Your armor will be ready before you leave for Aleesia. You should strap the sword on and be on your way. It is time."

REBORN

Tamm slid his belt through the sheath. "Thank you again."

He took a deep breath and walked to the door. Riehner's voice resounded with authority as he spoke to the elves. He spoke of his dreams for the kingdom, and once Tzelder was removed from power, how he would restore the peace that they once enjoyed for so long before he was overthrown.

He stood at the base of the steps addressing the people. Echao was seated in the front row and smiled at Tamm as he peeked from around the door. Riehner motioned his hands for everyone to stand. "I now introduce you to my son, Prince of the Realm, and heir to the throne of Iradell, Tammuz."

Tamm closed his eyes, the spark inside calming his emotions, before marching through the door and down the steps, stopping at Riehner's right hand. Those assembled erupted in applause. Tamm blushed and glanced up to his father, who smiled at him. Tamm drew the sword and presented it to Riehner, then took his place in front of him.

Riehner looked the blade over, turning it to inspect both sides, before laying it flat in both hands. "This is a fine blade, fit for a Battlemage. May it serve you well," he said softly to Tamm before again addressing the crowd. "Tammuz, today, you kneel, relinquishing your old life and promising to lay it down for the good of your people." He took the sword and touched the tip to each of Tamm's shoulders. An elf brought a purple pillow holding a thin, jeweled circlet. Riehner took it and placed it on Tamm's head. "You rise Crowned Prince and future High King of Iradell."

Tamm stood, and Riehner handed the blade back to him. He sheathed the sword, and the crowd clapped and whooped. Tamm embraced Riehner, and the old man clapped him on the back. "I'm proud of you, son," he whispered in Tamm's ear. "You will do great things for Iradell."

They walked up the stairs, side by side. Riehner sat in the center throne, and Tamm took his place at his right hand. The crowd continued to cheer as servants brought around wine and a variety of foods. A band with flutes, pipes, strings, and drums played into the night. Before long, the chairs were removed, and many of the elves started dancing. Tamm noticed Echao dancing with a few of the younger elves. The celebration lasted late into the night, and Tamm was dozing in his chair when Riehner nudged him.

"Sorry," he said.

"You must be exhausted. I know all of this is overwhelming. I will call it a night. We both need rest. We ride to Aleesia on the morrow."

Tamm nodded, and Riehner announced that the party could go on, but that he and Tamm would take their leave. Riehner walked him to the steps of the treehouse and bid him goodnight. Tamm fell back onto the bed. He wondered what Calla was doing and how her preparations were going in Aleesia. He drifted off to sleep with her on his mind.

TWENTY-SEVEN

Tamm twisted the necklace around his neck, rolling the stone between his fingers as the elves formed up to march. He was not yet accustomed to wearing the jewel. The elvish warriors were dressed in elegant armor and carried exquisite weapons. Gender did not matter to elves when it came to fighting. Female elves were lined up next to the males and were just as fierce. The heavier infantry was lined in the front and flanked by cavalry followed by light infantry, then archers and mages. Another detail of light infantry made up the rear guard.

Riehner and Tamm led the formation. The elves provided all the able-bodied warriors they could while leaving enough to guard their homeland should their efforts fail, still only totaling around a thousand. Tamm hoped it would be enough. With any luck, Tzelder had been overconfident and not sent the bulk of his troops.

Echao fell in with the rearguard. He was skilled with a bow and with daggers for skirmishing. Tamm had spoken with him before taking his place at the front of the formation and wished him a safe journey. Tamm was more concerned with his marching in the rear guard with Tor'nys, the elf that Tamm had battled with earlier. He had told Echao about the fight and his dislike of humans. Echao assured him he would keep an eye on Tor'nys.

The formation marched out just before daylight. Fog spread across the land as they exited the trees and turned north toward Aleesia. The sound of their boots rhythmically slapping the dirt was relaxing, and Tamm's mind wandered as he marched. Riehner marched beside him, his face resigned and lost in thought. Tamm wondered what he was thinking. Was he contemplating strategy, or was he worried about the outcome?

Neither he or Tamm had yet donned their armor. Theirs was also of elvish make and would be light enough to travel long distances in, but Tamm declined to wear his, hoping not to have to fight on the way there, and Riehner had followed suit. Marching in formation with this many soldiers would likely slow them some, and he expected it to be a full day's journey. Tamm had not traveled much in his life, but he figured they would arrive at Aleesia just after dark. Riehner forbade them to use torches or mage-lights, not wanting to signal Tzelder's forces that they were on the move.

REBORN

Tamm agreed that it would be a bad idea, but with the cool morning air and all the fog, it would have been nice to have had the heat of the torches. He wished the sun would rise soon and burn away the mist and chill from the air, but then again, it provided them concealment as they moved.

A few hours after sunrise, the fog lifted, and it warmed up nicely. Tamm had already begun to sweat. They had been marching for some time and had not stopped to rest. This surprised him due to Riehner's age. Linsyn would have never been able to make this type of journey.

"How are you able to keep going like this?" Tamm asked. "Linsyn would have never been able to keep up this pace."

Riehner laughed. "Though we are different, we are one and the same. I believe several things played into my weakness as Linsyn. First, to be an old healer, I had to look the part. I do believe that the depression from your mother passing and your having to grow up without me led to stress and, ultimately, some premature aging. Battlemages, once gifted with magic from the elves, take on many elvish qualities, such as long life and slower aging."

"That makes sense," Tamm said. "But spells that I can now perform with ease would have drained you back in Aleesia."

Riehner nodded. "You are right in your assessment. It had been so long since I had used any form of magic, that when I did, it tested my abilities and required more energy to do so. Being back with the elves and having you know who I truly am has invigorated me. I feel as if now, I could lift a mountain and place it somewhere else."

Tamm nodded and marched on in silence, smiling, imagining Riehner lifting a mountain. Just before sunset, he could see Aleesia in the distance. He looked toward Rakx'den and saw clouds of smoke rising. Tzelder's forces had waited until nightfall to move. The army would be on them soon, and the battle would likely take place in the morning. There must have been a considerable number of troops to cause dust clouds that size.

They arrived just after nightfall and set up camp in the large valley below Aleesia with the lake bordering their western flank. Riehner, Echao, and Tamm entered the town together. Echao barely made it through the gates before he saw Lily and ran to her, wrapping her in his arms. Adina was right behind her and leaped into Tamm's arms and squeezed his neck, tears running down her cheek and onto his.

"By the gods, I've been so worried," she said. "I can't believe you've returned. Oh, how I've missed you." She grabbed his face and stared into his eyes before wrapping her arms around him again. Tamm blushed, a thousand thoughts running through his mind but could not make the words come. She pulled back away from him, looking him over as if she did not believe he was indeed there. "Aren't you going to say anything?"

He looked at Echao, who was entangled with Lily, then to Riehner speaking with Kèlris and Mariah. Riehner caught his gaze and shrugged at him. "I've missed you too," he said. "So much has happened since we last spoke."

"Well, I want to hear all about it," she said, taking him by the hand and leading him toward the place where they used to sit by the lake and talk. He glanced behind him, and Calla was watching him walk away, propped on her staff.

Tamm sat by Adina and recounted everything to her; how Linsyn was actually Riehner, how he is Riehner's son and heir to the throne, that he was trained in magic, and that the attack on Aleesia is his fault for rescuing Riehner from Vorn.

"It's not your fault," she said, pushing his shaggy hair back with her finger. "It was inevitable. About time that Tzelder's reign comes to an end if you ask me."

Tamm raised an eyebrow, unsure of how to respond. "I tell you all that, and all you have to say is that it's not my fault? I'm a Battlemage and the future king. Does none of this surprise you?"

She giggled. "Of course, it does. I'm just so happy you've returned. You could have told me you had changed into a wolf, and I'd believe it as long as it meant you were here with me. Besides, I've always known that you were special. Just a feeling I had. And as for your being the prince, well, it's almost like one of the books I would read has became a reality."

"Seriously?" he asked.

"Sort of. But, I met Calla when she arrived, and she told me who you really were. So, I've had a few days to let it sink in." She wrapped her fingers in his and squeezed. "I'm so glad you're back."

Tamm sat with her for a little while longer before bidding her goodnight. He explained that he needed to see his parents and make preparations with Riehner before the battle. She kissed him on the cheek before he walked away. Feelings for her rushed back, and his stomach felt queasy. He flitted down the road until he found Riehner, Kèlris, and Echao standing on the edge of town.

He jogged over to them, but they did not stop their discussion. Riehner was speaking with Echao and Kèlris. "Should something happen to me during the battle, I am leaving him in your hands again, Kèlris."

Kèlris nodded. "And the same with you. Should I fall, I know that you will take good care of our boys."

Tamm interrupted. "What's with all the doom and gloom? You act like we're going into war or something."

"This is serious," Riehner said. "None of us know what to expect tomorrow. Even with Aleesia's soldiers, we have only fifteen-hundred warriors at best. If Tzelder brings his main force, well..."

"Let's not dwell on it, tonight," Kèlris said. "Tomorrow has enough worries for itself."

Tamm nodded and crossed his arm over his heart. "My life for yours." The others returned the gesture, and he bid them goodnight before jogging into town to see Mariah then retiring for the night.

◆◆◆◆◆

Tamm stood on the field, looking out over Tzelder's army. They had at least twice their number formed up, all in black armor. Tamm took a deep breath, the fumes from the torches burning his lungs. He hoped beyond all hope that the dwarves would arrive with aid. If the battle was drawn out, they did not have the numbers to stand against Tzelder's forces.

Tamm adjusted the bracers on his arm; they were maroon in color and were light but durable. He wore a mythril chainmail chest piece and greaves to protect his legs with padded leather armor dyed red overlaying the mail. He had foregone a helmet, fearing it would limit his peripheral vision.

Riehner exited his tent dressed in his full regalia. He was adorned head to toe in an armor that shone like glass. A faint hue of orange and purple painted the eastern sky above the mountains, the sun not yet rising above them. The armor flickered with the colors as it scattered the light around. Riehner removed his helmet and placed an arm on Tamm's shoulder. "A glorious day for a battle, is it not?"

"As good a day as any other, I suppose," Tamm said.

"My general, Iwan, and I shared many battles. Even during times of peace, he thirsted for it. He was a staunch ally and an amazing friend. I wish you could have met him."

"As do I. It would have been nice to have his skill here today."

Riehner patted Tamm on the back. "If you get in a situation where the battle gets too tough, send up a flare of magic, and I will come to you. It will not matter how far across the battlefield I am; I will make my way to you."

"I will, and I trust you will do the same," Tamm said, crossing his arm over his chest.

"I realize that I have not had much time with you, especially as a father, but I want you to know that I am proud of the man you are becoming. You will make an excellent king one day. I love you, son."

Tamm looked away. He knew this man was his father. He did love him; as a father, a friend, and a mentor, but the sentiment caught him off guard. Riehner had never been so forthcoming with his emotions before. Tamm coughed back a tear at the thought of losing him. "And I, you, father."

Riehner patted him on the head as horns sounded from the formation below. "Come. It is time."

Riehner and Tamm took their places among the troops. Tamm's palms were sweating as he drew his sword. With less than half the number of troops as their enemy and no sign of the dwarves, any optimism he had previously had now left him.

Thump, thump, thump. The sound of boots padding against the ground echoed off the nearby mountains as Tzelder's troops marched forward. Tamm adjusted his grip on his sword as Riehner raised his blade in the sky and shouted, "For Aleesia! For Iradell!" He pointed the sword toward the enemy, and the throng started marching to their doom.

Tamm made a suggestion last night to hide a small contingent of troops in the forest to help flank the enemy should the main force be pushed back. About two hundred humans and elves laid in wait a short distance into the woods, just out of sight. It was not much, but it was all they could afford to separate from the main force, some skirmishers, archers, and a few mages.

Echao had shifted further up in the formation that morning

despite Tamm's pleas for him to stay in the rear guard. He told Tamm that he was not going to let Lily and his homeland be threatened without serving out punishment to those who wished them harm. Tamm understood his stance and relented to his desire.

Calla was near the center of the formation with the other mages. Tamm could not even think about something happening to her. She had been in war before and could take care of herself, but she was the one he worried about the most.

As they neared the center of the valley, Tamm could make out more detail of the enemy. A man in all black armor led them. He had on a helm, disallowing Tamm from making out any more detail.

"Is that Tzelder?" he asked.

"I don't think so," Riehner said. "It has been quite some time since I have seen him, but his armor was more elaborate and decorated."

"Any idea who it could be?"

"No," Riehner said. "And that is what concerns me."

The armies were closing in on each other. Riehner held up a hand, halting the formation. He signaled to his captains, and Tamm heard the bows creak as they bent with the tightening strings. Riehner looked to Tamm, his face hard. "Do not hold back. Use everything that you have learned. This is war. The goal is to survive."

Tamm nodded as Riehner dropped his arm. Mages whispered words of power, and the bowstrings thrummed, flaming arrows flying over their heads toward their enemies. The opposing side released arrows of their own. They must not have had many mages, as the arrows were not lit. The infantry raised shields over their heads to deflect the arrows coming in. Tamm whispered the words and summoned an arcane shield. He glanced at Riehner to see that he had done the same.

As the flaming arrows rained down on the enemy, they did not even flinch. Some of them fell as the bolts struck home. Some burst into flame and ran around before collapsing to the ground, but none attempted to raise a shield. If anything, they were well trained and disciplined.

Their leader made a motion, and the main body of the infantry marched forward. Tamm looked to Riehner for instruction, but he only stared back at the enemy. Tamm tightened his grip on the sword, waiting for a command.

Suddenly, the arrow fire from Tzelder's army stopped. There was a blast from a trumpet, and the infantry charged toward them. Riehner did not flinch. He made another signal, and Tamm heard marching behind him. Rows of heavy spearmen engulfed him as they moved past, humans interspersed with elves. He recognized several of the men he had grown up around in Aleesia. Some focused and angry, some their eyes wide with fear.

The spearmen took their places in front of the formation, locking their long shields together, spears extended out in front of them. Tamm could no longer see the advancing force., hidden behind a wall of shields and spears.

"Get ready," Riehner said. "Once the main force hits the spearmen, the infantry will deploy to hit their flanks. After that, the battle will descend into chaos."

Tamm nodded in assent.

"Don't forget to send the sparks up if you need help," Riehner said.

"I won't."

The clash of metal against metal caused Tamm to jump. He had not expected it to be so loud. The sound of wood snapping and men screaming drowned out everything else. The metallic smell of blood floated in the air and made him queasy. The thumping of hooves galloping roared behind him and around the formation of spearmen. The light infantry and skirmishers shouted behind him.

The spearmen took small, occasional steps back. The cavalry pulled up and reared around again for another charge. Tamm looked again to Riehner, but his eyes were closed. Suddenly, Riehner's eyes fluttered open. "Now, Tamm. The line isn't going to hold. Circle them."

He signaled again, and the mages and skirmishers charged forward. Tamm ran around with one side of the skirmishers as Riehner ran around the other. Blood soaked the ground, and it splashed against his legs as he ran.

A burly man with a two-handed sword spun on him as he attempted to approach his flank. The man thrust the sword at him, and he rolled to the side, easily avoiding the blade. As he spun, he flicked the feather-light sword at the man's face, nearly cleaving his jaw from his head as the man crumpled to the ground.

Tamm moved further into the battle. A group of skirmishers was tangled up with several of Tzelder's forces. Tamm took two of them down before a third threw his shield back, knocking Tamm flat on his back. He gasped for air and could hear one of the men let out a scream. Tamm rolled back onto his feet and swept his sword across one of the man's legs, separating it below the knee. Blood spurted as the man writhed on the ground grasping at the stump.

"You good?" he asked the remaining skirmishers.

They cheered, and Tamm ran deeper into the fray. The fighting was heavy, and Tamm weaved in and out, taking down soldiers and moving on to the next. He caught a glimpse of Echao from the corner of his eye. He had both daggers drawn and was slicing through bodies as if he were filleting fish. More soldiers moved in on him, and Tamm ran to assist.

He yelled out to Echao to signal him he was on the way to help, hoping he did not catch a blade in the ribs on the way. He reached Echao and pressed his back against his as the black-clad soldiers closed in, sword held at the ready.

"Long time no see," Echao said. "Glad you could stop by."

"Ha," Tamm said. "Always the jokester. What do you say we carve a way out of here?"

"I thought you'd never ask."

Tamm heard Echao's daggers swishing through the air, but he had three soldiers in front of him. He whispered the words for fire as he traced his finger along the blade. The flames followed his finger up one side and down the other. The soldiers faltered for only a moment, but that was all the time he needed. He swung the fire-blade at the soldiers, the fabric and leather within their armors bursting into flames as the blade sliced through them.

REBORN

Tamm felt Echao's back fall away from his, and he spun to find him finishing off a soldier. "What are you getting at?"

Echao shrugged his shoulders. "What do you mean?"

"You know you aren't supposed to break contact with me until they're defeated."

Echao bowed. "They are now. Sorry to disappoint, your majesty."

Tamm shook his head before running off. "I'll be around if you need me," he yelled as he left.

He continued through the battlefield, helping where he could. The main line faltered, and the spearmen had been pushed back towards the town. The rear guard had moved up to help them, but they were not able to gain any ground back. The townspeople were at the northernmost point of the village and had boats prepared to escape to Delocia should they fail at defending it.

Tamm rushed to the rear of the Black Army's line. Calla was there and was dispatching soldier after soldier. Still, she came under heavier attack as some of the soldiers had circled back since their line was easily breaking though Aleesia's. Tamm rushed to help Calla, but she waved him away. "The cavalry has fallen. Signal the reserves."

Tamm scanned the battlefield for Riehner but could not find him. He dared not send up sparks to discuss whether or not to signal the reserves from the tree line. He was the prince. He could make these types of decisions now; he had to. Tamm searched the ground and found a fallen elvish archer. He grabbed the archer's bow and three arrows. He aimed toward the hidden troops in the forest and ignited the arrows with fire and let them fly. He kept them in his sight as they soared across the sky. As they descended near the edge of the trees, he fed more power into the fire until the arrows were consumed, and the flames were flickering blue and white.

The reserve soldiers rushed out of the trees and charged directly at the army's right flank. They collided with Tzelder's forces and caught them off guard. It seemed for a moment that they would break through the line, but some of the lines performed a right-face and circled the reserves. Tamm had to do something, or they would all be slaughtered.

He rushed to the rear of the encircling troops, his blade slicing through the backs of their armor. They did not turn to face him, keeping their focus on the flanking soldiers of Aleesia. He heard a cry from behind him and spun to see an ax whirling toward his face. He dove to the ground, the ax plunging into a soldier behind him. He scrambled to his feet, but something struck him in the back. His face sunk into the bloody mud. He rolled over to see a boot coming down onto his face. He rolled out of the way, and the boot smashed down beside his head.

"*Gaoth!*" A blast of air blew the soldier off his feet and onto another warrior. Tamm stood as several more of the troops closed in on him. There were at least ten, with more breaking off the line and coming toward him. He fought with all his might, but every time he struck one down, another took his place. This was it. This is how he was going to die. Their numbers were dwindling, and the enemies seemed to be growing. If only the dwarves would have shown up.

REBORN

The soldiers were right on top of him now. He spun the blade around in his hand. If he were going to die, he would take as many of them with him as possible. He spun and rolled, sword twisting, spells flying, but nothing he did made a difference. There were too many of them. He was in the middle of the battle and surrounded. But the signal. He had forgotten the signal.

He thrust his fist in the air and released magical flares as high in the air as he could. Some of the soldiers started laughing. "Oh, the poor bloke. Celebrating his death with a light show. How pathetic."

Tamm pointed the sparks at him, scorching his face. The soldier coughed and spluttered before grabbing his throat and falling forward with a thump. He directed the magic back to the sky. "Come on, come on."

A blinding light cut through the stack of bodies, and Tamm snapped his eyes closed. When he opened them back up, the soldiers that had surrounded him were crawling along the ground, groaning. He looked across the field in the direction of where the light came from, and Riehner stood leaning, using his sword to help hold himself upright. Tamm felt terrible for calling for his aid. The fighting was obviously taking too much out of him.

Tamm mouthed the words, *thank you* to him. Riehner smiled and waved at him, but the smile fell from his face, a trickle of blood sliding down the corner of his mouth.

"No," Tamm yelled. A blade protruded through his abdomen, and his body went slack as he coughed up blood, his blank eyes still locked onto Tamm. The sword slid out of his body, and he crumpled to the ground. Behind him stood a man in all black armor with silver filigree laced throughout. He wiped the blood away from the blade, a dark green stone set into the pommel.

Tamm's sword tip dragged the ground as he trudged toward the assassin. Sweat trickled down his brow, but he felt cold inside. He snarled his lip as he closed in on the man who had killed his father.

"Remove your helm so I can look into your eyes as I kill you, you coward," Tamm said, spitting at the man's feet. As the man slid the helmet off, a necklace with a dark green medallion caught his attention. It was a Battlemage, but if not Tzelder, then who?

He tossed the helmet to the ground and held his arms out, bowing to Tamm. "Did you think you could get rid of me so easily, Tammuz?" Tamm recognized him immediately, the puckered scar running down his cheek, the salt and pepper hair.

"Vorn! How could you?"

"The king will reward me greatly, I assure you. I should have killed him in the beginning, and we wouldn't be dealing with all this foolery now. Tzelder is not a patient man, and he does not suffer failure. You caused me a great deal of hardship with your little prison escape, and now, you're going to pay."

He rushed at Tamm with a series of blows. Tamm retreated as he parried and dodged. It was evident that Vorn was the better swordsman. He was more experienced, and now, somehow, a Battlemage. A sweeping blow at Tamm's head forced him to roll out of the way, flipping right back to his feet.

Tamm sent a blast of air at Vorn, but he waved his arm and deflected it. Vorn then took a deep breath and flicked his wrists as if throwing daggers. Instead of daggers, shards of ice flew at Tamm. He ran, doing all he could to avoid the deadly missiles. One was headed straight at his face, and he summoned a pillar of fire, and the ice dissipated into steam. He absorbed the flame in his hands, forming a ball with it, then hurled it at Vorn.

Vorn raised his hand as he rolled his eyes, a sheet of water enveloping him as the fireball crashed into it and disappeared. "Is that all you've got, boy? Is that all he could teach you? You are pathetic. He was pathetic. Tzelder could teach you more in a week than that fool ever could."

Tamm scowled, his breath heaving, face burning with anger. He marched toward Vorn and felt the power rising up inside him, begging to be released. The angrier he got, the more the magic wanted to be released. Traces of lightning ran down his arms and danced down the sword, scattering across the garnet in the hilt. He closed his eyes and felt a tingle as the electricity sparked and danced across his body, arcing across his medallion.

"No, there is much Riehner could have taught you," Tamm said as he pointed the sword at Vorn and let the lightning fly. Arcs scattered and hit nearby soldiers as it ran through the air and ground toward Vorn. He held his sword out in front of him as the bolts hit Vorn full force, staggering him back. The stone in the sword's hilt displaced and absorbed some of the power while tendrils of lightning arced across his boots and into the ground.

Tamm could have killed him; he felt it. All he had to do was release the power that wanted so badly to escape him. He stood there with his eyes closed, and he thought of Riehner. He thought of all he had taught him. Standing outside the tent this morning, he remembered his words. *"I am proud of the man you are becoming. You will make an excellent king one day."* Tamm opened his eyes and let the magic dissipate.

As the last bolt flickered away from his sword, Vorn snarled at him. "You foolish boy. You should have finished me when you had the chance." He launched a flurry of blows at Tamm. As much as Tamm tried, he could not keep up with attacks. He was exhausted after releasing the blast of lightning. The next blow sliced into his left arm. He roared in pain and spun away from the assault. Before he was able to try to heal the wound, the sword slashed across his right arm, and he dropped his sword. Blood dripped down his fingers to the ground.

Tamm gripped both arms and panted as Vorn circled him. If he went for his sword, Vorn would cut him down. Even if he could get to it in time, his arm would not hold it. He glanced down at the sword, but Vorn clucked his tongue. "Give up, boy. You are defeated. Your master is dead, and your city will fall."

Tamm bowed his head in defeat. "I'm sorry," he whispered to Riehner. He glanced around the battlefield. His army was en route, fleeing back toward Aleesia. He looked up at Vorn in defiance. He reached for his sword, and Vorn sliced him across his back. Tamm sprawled onto his back, the dirt sending pain like fire into the gash.

Vorn stood over him, laughing. "You are too weak to have followed Tzelder. He has power you couldn't even fathom."

Tamm's vision faded in and out. In the distance, he could hear Echao yelling above the ruckus. "To me. To me. The dwarves have arrived. Defend your homeland."

A weak smile spread across Tamm's lips. The dwarves had arrived. Even as he died, his homeland would be saved.

"You will not win," Vorn said as he pressed the tip of the blade into Tamm's ribs. The pain was pure agony. His breath caught, and his eyes widened as the blade slid in deeper. He grabbed the blade and allowed the power to flow through him into the blade. The sword glowed red as Tamm continued to surge fire into it until Vorn had to pull away from him. Tamm pulled himself to his knees and grabbed his sword, using it to push himself up.

The heat faded once Tamm released the sword. Vorn steeled himself and charged, his blade held high for the death strike. The feather-light blade felt like a boulder in Tamm's injured arms, and he strained to hold the sword in a defensive posture. Vorn brought the sword down at Tamm's neck. Their blades glanced as Tamm blocked the attack and spun under Vorn's arm, thrusting the sword behind him. There was a sickening crunch as the blade slide into Vorn's chest, and he spewed blood onto the back of Tamm's neck.

Vorn's eyes were wide in shock as Tamm looked over his shoulder to meet his gaze. "I told you I would stare into your eyes as you died." Tamm jerked the sword from Vorn's torso and spun with the blade coming back across his neck. The dark green medallion tumbled to the ground as Vorn's head rolled across the battlefield, and his body crumpled.

Tamm fell to his knees, heaving and gasping for breath. He sheathed his sword and crawled to Riehner's body. His face and chest were covered with blood, congealing in his salt and pepper beard. Tamm put his ear near his mouth and listened. A faint breath blew across his face. Tamm put his hands over the wound to slow the bleeding.

"Help me," he cried. "Someone help me."

The battle raged on. The dwarves' arrival turned the tide of the battle. The elves and Aleesians were no longer fleeing but had returned to fight. Tears poured down his face as he stared helplessly at Riehner. He closed his eyes and breathed deeply, focusing himself. The magic called to him, begging to be poured out. It was overflowing inside of him. Despite his wounds and exhaustion, there was a well of power within him, desperate to be released.

He pressed harder onto the wound. "*Stad an fhuil.*" He let the power flow. The bleeding slowed and then stopped. The power surged against him, wanting to be released, no longer trapped inside his body. He ceased the flow of magic and checked the wounds. The bleeding had stopped.

He closed his eyes again. "*Leigheas!*" The power poured from him like a waterfall after a flood. Riehner's eyelids fluttered. Tamm poured everything he had into the spell. He thought he heard Riehner whisper something. Stop? His head swooned, and his vision flickered. His breaths came in gasps. He laid his head on Riehner's chest. The power still pouring

REBORN

from him as he slipped into darkness. The last thing he heard was Calla's voice whispering in his ear, but he could not make out what she was saying, then everything went black.

TWENTY-EIGHT

Tamm thrashed in the bed as Calla ran her fingers through his hair, trying to calm him. His muscles ached as he stretched and tried to sit up.

"Calla?" he whispered.

She continued petting his hair. "Mmm, hmm."

A smile tugged at his lips, her familiar voice soothing to his ears. He rubbed his arms and noticed there were no bandages there. Scenes of the battle flashed in his mind. His eyes shot open, and he bolted up in the bed. Calla jumped back. "*Síocháin a bheith ar do shon,*" she said, and Tamm laid back in the bed, a feeling of peace and comfort washing over him.

"Where am I?" he asked.

"You are in Aleesia. Back in your old bedroom. Lie still, let me get the healer."

"Linsyn," he mumbled

"No, Tamm. I will be back."

Calla left the room, and moments later, a crook-backed old man entered, hobbling on a wooden cane. He placed the back of his hand on Tamm's forehead. "Good, good," he said in a squeaky, high-pitched voice. "No fever, this is very good. How do you feel?"

"Sore."

"It is to be expected. You had some serious injuries, deep cuts to both arms, a rather large gash to your back that would likely have killed others, and your lung was punctured from the wound at your ribs. For all intents and purposes, Tammuz, you should be dead."

"Well," Tamm said. "Thank the gods I'm not. Where is Calla?"

"Ah, she is a good girl. She has not left your side but for brief moments. If not for her and her skill in magical healing, you would have perished. She shall return soon. I insisted that she get some rest, alas, she can be stubborn."

Tamm turned to the old man, who was hunched over the cane, a scraggily, short beard on his face. He wore a dingy, white robe, the hem muddy and worn.

"Who are you?" Tamm asked.

"I am Dimma. I am the healer from Delocia. When news of the battle reached us, I took a boat as soon as I could. The casualties were high on both sides. I received word that Vorn took Linsyn and that my services would be needed."

"Thank you, Dimma. You honor Iradell with your willingness to serve."

He released a sharp giggle. "You honor an old man with your kind words. Linsyn was an old friend of mine. It was my pleasure to help. I do miss him, though."

"What of Riehner?" Tamm asked. "Do you have news of the King?"

"The elves are tending to him. His wounds are grievous, far beyond my abilities. Magic is his only hope. I dare not trouble you with such things. You need to rest. Your wounds have healed, but you will be sore and likely to be weak for some time."

"What of my family? Kèlris, Mariah, and Echao? Are they well? And Adina, too."

"Ah," the old man said, his voice becoming low and fatigued. "They are well. Kèlris and Echao received minor wounds, but I patched them up right nice. They should heal fine. Get some rest, young master. You will need it."

The old man hobbled to the door, his cane clicking against the hardwood floor.

"Before you go," Tamm said. "When Riehner is better, you should go by and visit him."

"Why is that?" Dimma asked.

"He and Linsyn, they are the same person. The King hid here as Linsyn for many years. I'm sure he would like to see you."

The old man's face lit up in delight. He nodded and hobbled out of the room. Tamm struggled to sit up in bed and hung his feet off the side. His breaths were short and rapid as he tried to calm his racing heart.

REBORN

He sat on the side of the bed for several moments before he felt his strength return. There was a basin of water on a nearby table, and he wanted to wash his face. He stumbled when he stood from the bed and wobbled to a chair and sat down. He splashed the cool water on his face. As the ripples rolled to the rim of the bowl and the water calmed, Tamm saw himself in the reflection. He looked tired. Dark lines ran under his eyes, his hair disheveled. His hair…He squinted and saw a solid white streak of hair that draped over his right eye.

Tamm held the rail as he descended the stairs, nearly falling several times. He shoved open the front door and limped outside. He had to see his father. The town was alive, elves, humans, and dwarves intermingling, going to and fro. This was the type of town he had always dreamed of living in.

As he stumbled down the street, still in his nightclothes, an old man and a younger man approached him. He did not recognize them at first until he saw the old man's crooked nose. It was Birger and Terrance, the two traders he and Echao had met on the road while trying to rescue Riehner.

"As I live and breathe," Terrance said, running up to Tamm. "Would you look at that, pop? Our savior on the road and our hero of Aleesia. It's mighty good to see you, master."

"It's good to see you, too," Tamm said. "I'm glad you made it here safely. What about your mule?"

Birger let out a rolling chuckle. "Strangest thing, a couple of days after we arrived, she just pranced right in, pretty as you please. I don't know how we could ever repay the kindness you showed us in our time of need. Trading in

Aleesia and Delocia has been good to us. Here take this, your coin plus interest." He reached in a bag at his waist and handed Tamm several draechs.

Tamm waved him off. "Truly, thank you, but that won't be necessary. Keep your coin. Your gratitude is plenty." Tamm looked past the men, searching for signs of where the elves had Riehner. "I'm sorry to rush off, but I must find my father. Have you seen him?"

"I think he may be home with your mother," Terrance said. "She was worried sick about him after the fighting."

Tamm shook his head. "Not Kèlris. My birth father, Riehner."

They looked at each other in confusion. "Your pop is the King?" Terrance asked.

Tamm nodded, waiting for their answer.

Terrance straightened his posture, his voice no longer casual but respectful. "I'm sorry. I heard he was terribly injured, but I haven't heard where they're keeping him. Best of luck to you, your highness." Terrance wrapped his arm around Birger and led him away, whispering as they went.

Frustrated, Tamm wandered around the village, asking the townsfolk where Riehner was being kept, but no one seemed to know where he was. He searched the city for Calla or Echao but could not find them either. His back ached, and his legs faltered. Someone had to know where Riehner was.

He started yelling in the streets. "Where is he? One of you knows. Where are you keeping him?" Someone touched him on the shoulder, and he spun toward them. He recognized the elf but could not remember his name. He sat on the Council with Elion.

"Your majesty, is there something I can assist you with?"

"Do you know where they are keeping the King?" he asked.

"I do, but I do not think it wise…"

"I must see him right away," Tamm said.

"My lord, that would be impossible. I assure you, he is in good hands, but he has not been conscious since the battle."

Tamm felt dizzy, the exertion of the search taking its toll. "Where is he?"

"He is in his home. His old hut. Our best healers are with him now. Please, you do not look well. I must object…"

"Thank you," Tamm said as he limped deeper into town toward the healer's hut. He weaved in and out, slipping between people in the street. He panted and stumbled at times, his legs aching and no longer able to hold him up. He tripped and slid in the dirt outside the hut, his chin bouncing off the dirt path.

A man helped him to his feet. Tamm thanked him and dusted himself off before staggering toward the door. An elf with a spear stepped up, blocking the door. Tamm sidestepped him and almost lost his balance. The elf stepped with him to block his route and reached out with his other hand to help steady him.

"Step aside," Tamm said.

"Sire, I cannot. The healers must not be disturbed. They require complete concentration."

Tamm tried to push past him. "I said, step aside."

"My apologies, my Prince, but I cannot."

"That is an order," Tamm said, pointing his finger in the elf's chest.

The elf looked to his brother-in-arms, who shook his head. "I will not. I must protect the King at all costs."

Tamm's face filled with blood, his vision blurring with anger, hands balling into fists, relaxing and balling into fists again.

A sing-song voice called out behind him. "Tamm, are you alright?"

It was Calla. He knew her voice. He faced her, her features soft and peaceful but concerned.

"I need to see my father," he said, tears welling up in his eyes.

"You know that is not possible. If you want him to have a chance to recover, we must let the healers do their jobs."

Tamm shook his head. "I don't want to lose him. There is so much I still want to know, so much I want to say. I have had so little time with him."

"I know. Come with me, let us talk." She slid her shoulder under his arm and helped support some of his weight as they walked away from the hut. She took him near the lake and toward the gate. She stopped by the gate and stared up at the sky. The sky was dark with grey clouds blocking out the sun, the smell of rain on the air. "Do you think you can stand now? We can go slow."

"Sure. Thank you."

"Do you want to sit by the lake?" she asked.

"No. I'd like to walk the battlefield if you'll come with me."

REBORN

She shook her head. "I don't think that is a good idea. They are still clearing some of the dead."

"That's my hope. There is something I'm looking for," he said.

Calla reluctantly agreed, and they walked the battlefield together. The pungent smell of death was overbearing, and Tamm gagged several times. He saw several people he recognized from his home town. He directed her toward the place where he fell in battle then stopped by the trench where Riehner had fallen. The mud was stained red from his and Riehner's intermingled blood.

A clap of thunder rang through the air, and rain splattered the puddles of blood. Calla touched his shoulder. "We should be going."

"Not yet," he said. "One more stop."

He took her to where he had killed Vorn. He explained to her about Vorn being a Battlemage and recounted the fight to her. He found the patch of blood where Vorn's body had fallen, but his corpse and head had already been taken away. He searched the ground nearby for the dark green medallion.

"Help me look. It has to be around here somewhere. It doesn't need to fall into the wrong hands."

She joined him on her hands and knees. They searched until the rain became so heavy he could barely see. Calla urged him that they needed to head back to town, that they would not be able to find the medallion in this weather. Tamm stayed until his clothes were sopping with mud. Calla helped him up. He tried to stay but reluctantly gave in to her requests.

Tamm walked by several men digging a pit. There were hundreds of black-clad bodies laid out near the hole. Tamm called out to the men to stop their work. They dropped their shovels, looking at each other with puzzled expressions.

"What are you doing?" Tamm asked.

"Burying the dead, sire," one of the soldiers said.

Tamm looked into the pit. "That's an awfully deep hole for a body."

The soldiers laughed. "You are funny. It's a mass grave if you couldn't tell. I would dig it to Sheol and throw them in if I could."

Tamm's brow furrowed. "You will ensure they have a proper burial. Our men and theirs."

"You're joking," one of them said.

"I certainly am not. Enemies or not, they are our kin, and they fought honorably. Our ancestors will accept them today."

"But, Tamm…"

Tamm cleared his throat. "You have known me my whole life as Tamm. Today, I am your prince and heir to Iradell, and I have given you an order. Ensure that everyone who fell on this field receives a proper burial."

The soldiers snapped to attention, and each crossed their fist over their heart. "As you desire, Prince Tammuz."

He and Calla sludged through the mud back to the town gates. "You handled that well," Calla said. "You did the right thing, and you demonstrated that no one is above another in this world."

"Where have you been staying?" he asked.

REBORN

"One of the townspeople opened their home to me when I first arrived. Last night, I stayed with you, though I didn't sleep."

"Will you stay with me tonight?" he asked. "I don't want to be alone."

Calla blushed. "Umm."

"There are some things I'd like to get done tomorrow, and I would like your help. We can get an early start. I want to stay busy to keep my mind clear. Echao's bed is still in my room. I don't think he will mind if you use it."

She gave him a single nod of her head. "Of course, I will. I am your protector, and you tend to get yourself in trouble. I should probably keep a closer eye on you."

They laughed. It was not forced, but Tamm felt it was ironic with all that had happened over the last few days. Tamm wrapped his hand in hers as they took the long way back to his house in the rain.

TWENTY-NINE

Tamm scurried around the room, cleaning and straightening his bed. He had to keep his mind busy. Thoughts of the war, those they had lost, and of Riehner's wounds plagued him and were worse when he was idle. He and Calla shared a cold breakfast downstairs before heading out for the day. Mariah had been working with some of the other women in town, tending to the sick and wounded and preparing meals for the masses. Kèlris worked to improve the town's fortifications and to repair and replace arms and armor.

As Tamm and Calla left his home, a crisp breeze blew in off the lake, and a sprinkle of rain fell on the back of his neck, making him shiver. He pulled his cloak tighter and slid the hood up. Calla stepped in closer to him, their shoulders touching, and he could sense her warmth spread through him. They were on their way to Rhys Castle. Tamm had never been inside but had heard it was Riehner's favorite spot to vacation during his reign as High King.

Tamm hoped to tour the castle and assess it for any damages. He wanted to make sure that it was prepared to accept Riehner once he had recovered. For as long as he could remember, it had been the home of the region's Overseer, although he rarely ever stayed there. He preferred the bigger cities with livelier nightlife, or at least that is what Tamm had been told.

They passed by the cottage where Vorn, his wife, and Alred had lived. It was dark inside. Someone had removed the drapes, and the front door sat ajar. Tamm peered through the windows, but there were no candles or torches lit. He eased the door open with a creak. The furniture was all in place, but papers littered the floor near the desk, and the closets were bare. Vorn must have moved his family to Rakx'den while training with Tzelder to become a Battlemage. The door clicked as he pulled it shut. He could not help but feel sorry for Alred, receiving the news that his father was killed in battle. The near loss of Riehner was still fresh in his heart, and he could only imagine what Alred was going through.

They entered the gates of the castle and crossed a small drawbridge that straddled a moat surrounding the castle, fed by a river flowing from the mountains. The courtyard was large and open, with streams of sunlight shimmering through the clouds and dancing off the wet stone. Tamm pushed a massive door open with his shoulder, a groan vibrating through the stiff hinges. The air was musty, and a thin layer of dust covered most everything. Footprints tracked through the dust and down a hallway. He knelt to investigate the tracks. The size of the print indicated it belonged to an adult. He followed them to see where they went.

They led through the dining room with a long oaken table situated in the center of the room. The putrid smell of rotten food entered his nose before he noticed the plates and cups still on the table. Someone had left in a hurry. He continued to follow the footsteps further into the kitchen and through a door tucked away in the back of the room. A series of steps led down into a larder that still had stores of food and wine on shelves and racks that lined the walls. Tamm summoned a small flame in his hand to provide light. The footprints disappeared at the edge of the back wall.

He gave Calla a questioning look. She shrugged and motioned him to proceed, so he stepped forward and ran his fingers across the cold stone. The mortar between one of the stones felt rough and out of place compared to the others, the stone not flush with the others. He pushed on it, and a hidden door scraped against the floor as it opened. He sent the light from his palm ahead through the door and discovered a long hallway. They followed the narrow passage for quite a while as it turned and slanted, sometimes going downhill and sometimes uphill.

Neither spoke a word as they traveled the corridor, treading softly on the dirt floor as they went. Tamm noticed a light at the far end. As they drew closer to the light, the hallway opened into a large cave. Birds chirped outside, and he went to investigate. The cave opened into a meadow surrounded by thinly scattered trees. Faint sounds of people could be heard in the distance, a town, maybe. He and Calla jogged down a game trail that opened into a valley. He looked around and instantly recognized where he was. The path led to fields just past the western border of Delocia. It must have been a secret shortcut through the mountains to get to the capital.

Upon returning to the cave, signs of a recent fire and a pallet where someone had slept caught his eye. Scraps from a meal were scattered near the firepit. He and Calla discussed what they had found and decided it was likely from one or more of the servants that had left in a rush through a secret escape route. He made a mental note to seal the corridor or have it guarded once Riehner moved in.

They returned to the castle, and after finding some cleaning supplies in a closet, he started cleaning the castle. He cleaned well into the evening, he and Calla barely speaking a word to one another. He used the busy work to drown out his worries and fears. He was on the second floor, dusting the throne room when he decided to take a break, sitting on the hard, cold throne. He had just closed his eyes when he heard someone calling his name.

"Calla?" he called. But, no answer.

He walked out of the throne room and to a balcony overlooking the first floor. He did not see Calla but heard someone speaking in hushed tones.

"Calla?" No answer again. He jogged down the stairs, following the voices. He passed through the foyer and discovered Calla speaking with another elf. As he approached, the other elf stood at attention and crossed his fist over his heart, and Tamm returned the salute.

"What's going on?" he asked.

Calla stepped forward in front of the other elf. "This is Nieven, a young mage in training. The Council sent him." She lurched forward and hugged him. "Riehner is awake and is asking for you."

Tamm pulled away from her. "What are we waiting on? Why are you crying?"

A tear ran down her cheek, and she wiped it away, choking back her emotion. "Tamm, he is not well. He is asking to see you…one last time."

Tamm shook his head in disbelief. "No, that's not possible." He stepped away from her as she reached out to him.

"Please, Tamm. Nieven has been instructed to return with you with all haste. He will lead you there. I can come with you if you would like."

Tamm waved his hand at her and pushed past Nieven to get out the door. Tears threatened to burst from his eyes. He raced across the drawbridge and down the hill toward town. He could see the healer's hut in the distance as he sped through the streets, the tears falling at the sight of it. The memories rushed back of all the times he had spent with the healer. He stopped beside a nearby house and sat on an overturned log near a stack of firewood. He rubbed his eyes as a tear trickled down his cheek when he remembered Linsyn teaching him how to preserve a flower for Adina, the first time he used magic, and the way Linsyn would tease him with his refined sarcasm. He smiled at the memory of when he learned that Riehner was his father, and when before the battle, he told him he was proud of him.

He choked back the tears and steeled himself. He had to be strong; he was the prince. He stood with his head held high and marched toward the hut.

"Tamm," Calla called from behind him. He turned to her as she and Nieven ran up to him. She touched his face with the tips of her fingers. "I will be here waiting for you."

"I hope so." He gave her a soft smile and approached the door. The elf that had blocked his approach yesterday gave him a sympathetic look and bowed his head, sliding away from the door and granting him access. Tamm took a deep breath and pushed the door open.

The room was full of mages, the power of the spells pushing against him as he entered the room. Riehner's bed had been moved from his small back bedroom and was centered in the room where the medical cot had been when he and Linsyn had treated Echao and when he had first learned to use magic. Riehner's head rested on a soft pillow, and he was draped with clean, white linen sheets. What little color he had left in his hair had faded to pure gray since the last time Tamm had seen him.

Tamm approached the bed and touched Riehner's hair. "You're getting a little gray," he joked.

Riehner's eyes fluttered open, and he coughed as he tried to laugh. "So are you," he said as he stroked the gray streak in Tamm's bangs. "Magic is powerful but not always powerful enough." Riehner nodded to one of the mages, and they staunched the flow of magic and crossed their fists over their hearts before leaving the hut.

"Where are they going?" asked Tamm.

"It is my time," Riehner said. "Time to see your mother again. Oh, how I've missed her."

"You can't go, Father. We haven't had enough time." A tear fell from his eye.

"It pleases my heart to hear you call me father. I always wanted a son, but when Tzelder attacked and wounded your mother, I thought my chance of having children was destroyed. Alas, here you are, and you have fulfilled all my hopes. I could not have asked for a better son. And as for time, unfortunately, there never seems to be enough."

He reached up and grabbed Tamm's hand. "You must understand. When the elves tried to save your mother, many of them lost their lives using their last bit of strength to force the healing magic that was keeping her there. I cannot ask that of them, to forfeit their lives to save mine. I have always strived to live a life that proved no one life is greater than another."

Tamm crossed his arm over his chest. "Then take mine. Teach me the spell, and I will cast it."

"No, no. You have much more to do here. That was a noble gesture you showed on the battlefield, ensuring our enemies received the same honors as our warriors. You are a great man." Riehner struggled to cross his fist over his heart. "This life, I give to you, so that you can continue *our* work here. You will make a fine king."

Tamm shook his head. "I don't want to do this without you."

A weak smile spread across Riehner's lips. "You can, and you will." He coughed, and the pain was visible as it wracked his body. "The magic is fading, and I don't have much longer. I want you to promise me something. Say it."

"I swear it," Tamm said, tears falling freely.

"Continue your training. You will require it… in order to defeat Tzelder. He is cunning and strong, more so than Vorn. Return Rhys Castle to its former glory. I love this town and would have set up my reign here. I hope you will do the same."

"I will, Father."

Riehner gripped his hand tighter as his face squinched in pain. "My last bit of knowledge to pass on to you is this. There is no greater act of compassion… than to lay down your life… for another." He brought Tamm's hand to his lips and kissed it. "Your mother calls me, and I must go to her." His breaths were short and gasped. "I love you, Tammuz, High King of Iradell."

"I love you, Father."

"More," he said and closed his eyes forever.

Tamm leaned down and kissed his father's forehead as his body spasmed with sobs. He stayed by his side weeping until nightfall. He summoned faint blue lights to fill the lamps in the room before exiting the hut, his eyes red and puffy.

Calla was waiting right outside the door and wrapped him in her arms as he walked out. He did not have the strength to hug her back, only to sob. She held him for a long time before leading him back towards his home.

"Where are the men?" he asked, sniffling.

Calla continued to hold onto him as they walked. "Many of them spend much of the night in the tavern, drinking away memories and drowning their sorrows in ale."

"Let's go there."

"I don't know if drinking is a good idea right now, Tamm."

He slid from under her arm and straightened his tunic. "Not to drink. I need to announce that the King has died and request some assistance going forward. I will head there now. Summon everyone in town that will come."

She nodded and left him. He continued on to the pub. As soon as he reached the bar, the barkeep passed him a mug of ale. "On the house," he said. Tamm nodded his thanks and took a gulp of the honey-colored liquid to calm his nerves, and a smile lifted one end of his lips as he thought about the time Linsyn brought him to the pub to enlist the townsmen's help in the fight against the Kapre. He had never been much of a public speaker. A bell on the door sounded and one by one, men, women, elves, and dwarves poured into the tavern.

Tamm climbed onto a table in the center of the room as people continued to pour in. Once they all seemed to settle, he raised the mug of ale in the air in a toast. "Whether you knew him by Linsyn or knew him by Riehner, whether you knew him by healer or knew him by King, deep down, I believe you all knew him as friend. I know I did. Tonight, we lost one of the greatest men I have ever known in my short life, and I would have traded my own to save him if I could."

The crowd listened in captivated silence.

"Not long ago, I learned that the man I had grown up near which I knew as Linsyn the Healer, was actually Riehner, High King of Iradell, and the first Battlemage. Shortly after, I learned that he was actually my birth father, and I suddenly went from being an apprentice healer to a prince. And now, it pains me to announce that the father I only just learned I had, has passed into the void."

Gasps and cries carried through the tavern, and Tamm wiped a tear from his eye. "Do not weep, for he would not have wanted that. He is finally at peace and home with his love, my mother, Beltia, Queen of Iradell. Tonight, we celebrate his life and toast in his honor." He held his glass up, and everyone else did the same, mead sloshing onto the floor.

"But tomorrow," Tamm said, pulling everyone's attention back to him. "Work begins anew. There is still a war to be fought and a kingdom to restore. Iradell will be reborn and together, we will bring freedom back to this land. In Riehner's honor."

Tamm clambered down the table and back to the floor. People came and gave their condolences and bragged about his speech. He spoke with several of the able-bodied men and requested their help in renovating Rhys Castle. He did not have money to pay them, but as long as he ensured they had a hot meal and were protected from Tzelder's retaliation, they were agreeable. Echao hugged him and talked about how great a man Riehner was. Kadagan clapped him on the shoulder but stayed silent, only shaking his head and giving a grunt before walking away.

Tamm walked outside and found Calla seated on a nearby bench. He plopped down beside her.

"Great speech," she said.

He sighed. "I'm tired."

"I can walk you home," she said.

"No," he said, shaking his head. "Of war. It's only just begun, and I'm already tired of it. Why do people have to be so evil?"

"Unfortunately, I don't have an answer to that question, and in all my years, I have never met anyone who has. We can only hope that when all is said and done, Tzelder is defeated and that maybe, you can bring a little peace into this chaotic world." She put her arm around his shoulder. "Come. You need rest. Let me walk you home."

THIRTY

†

Tamm paced back and forth in the throne room, mulling over the events of the past few days in his mind. He peered out the window and stared at the lake below. The rain had cleared, and rays of sunlight glittered across the waves. Birds sang as they flitted past the window. He ran his fingers along the smooth stone of the window sill before turning away and walking deeper into the dark room. Everything outside seemed so cheerful. The world should be mourning the loss of such a great man.

He sat down on the throne and leaned his head back against the high seatback. He closed his eyes as the sorrow built up in his chest. He had been alone since Calla offered to walk home with him last night. He had gone home and grabbed a few things; some clothes, a pillow and blanket, and a little food, and went to the castle. He slept in one of the old beds and ate a cold breakfast of fruit and bread. He did not want any visitors either; he just wanted to be left alone with his grief. He could not avoid them forever, though. Some of the men from the town would be showing up soon to clean the castle and begin to furnish it. He hoped that if he stayed hidden in the throne room that he could avoid them.

He had not even seen Calla. He felt bad about rejecting her offer to walk with him to the castle last night. He always felt better when she was near, but he did not have the strength to be around others right now. He was afraid that he might break into tears at any moment and wanted to be strong in front of his people.

There was a knock on the door, but he made no move to see who it was. He leaned forward and placed his head in his hands, and the knock sounded again. "Go away," he called. The door creaked open, and a girl poked her head in, long strawberry blonde hair hanging down past her shoulders.

"Tamm," she said.

He looked at her, his face frustrated until he noticed the strawberry blonde hair. He leaped up from the throne. "Adina, what are you doing here?"

She stood just inside the door, waiting for his approval to enter. "I have looked for you all morning. No one in town seemed to know where you had gone. No one except Calla. She didn't want to tell me where you were, but I can be very persuasive."

REBORN

He leaned against the throne and stared up at the ceiling. "But what brings you all the way up here? I came here to grieve and wasn't expecting company."

She ran up and wrapped her arms around his neck, pulling him close. "I know your heart must be breaking. Just learning he was your father and then having him ripped from you. It's cruel."

He hugged her back. "Thank you, Adina. You have always been so sweet. It has been challenging. Thank you for coming." He pulled away from her and noticed tears streaming down her face. "Why are you crying?"

She wiped at the tears and sniffled. "I understand your sadness, and that you want to be alone, but I don't think that's best."

Tamm paced to the window and gripped the sill. "No. I don't think you understand. How could you understand what I'm going through?"

She walked up behind him and rubbed his shoulders. "I understand more than you realize. You are not the only one that lost a father on that battlefield."

Tamm stiffened before turning around to look into her sad eyes. "What do you mean? No. Beyl?"

She nodded and dabbed her nose with a linen kerchief. He hugged her tightly. "Adina, I'm sorry."

"That's why I wanted to find you. Neither of us needs to be alone. We're orphans now. I don't know what I'm going to do."

Tamm took her by the hand and led her to the throne. He sat down and let her sit on his leg, keeping his arm wrapped around her. "It's not much right now, but I'll have the castle furnished soon. You can stay here if you'd like."

She shook her head. "I couldn't impose."

"You wouldn't be imposing," Tamm said. "I would enjoy your company, and I couldn't bear knowing that you're staying in your home alone. As you said, we shouldn't be alone. We are all each other have right now."

She touched his face with the tips of her fingers. "You are so good to me, Tamm. You always have been."

She leaned in close to his face. Tamm's breaths were short. She closed her eyes as she leaned in closer. A knock on the door called Tamm's attention back to the room, his face flushing at the thought of almost kissing Adina. Someone knocked again, a little louder this time. "Enter."

The door slid open, and Calla entered the room. She wore a slim-fitting green robe with tan-yellow intricate designs sewn throughout. She carried a black, polished longstaff with an ornamental pearl mounted on the top. She had her honey-colored hair pulled away from her face and pinned in the back.

"She is stunning," Adina whispered.

"Yes. Yes, she is," Tamm said before glancing at Adina, then swallowing hard.

Calla gave a slight bow to Tamm. "Your highness."

Tamm jumped up from the throne, and Adina slid off of his knee. He returned the bow to Calla.

She straightened. "Your highness," she said again. "It is time. The preparations have been made, and we leave as soon as you give the word."

REBORN

"Where are you going?" Adina asked.

"My father will be buried beside my mother. We march to her homeland for the funeral."

Adina grabbed his hand. "I can come with you. You shouldn't be alone."

"He will not be alone," Calla said. She blushed as Tamm and Adina looked up at her. She coughed and lowered her head before continuing. "Um, what I meant was that my people would be marching with him."

Tamm touched Adina on the shoulder. "You need to be here, Adina. You need time to mourn your father, just as I need time to mourn mine. Prepare for his burial. I will return once I have done the same."

She sidled up closer to him. "I don't wish to part from you, but I will do as you say."

Calla rolled her eyes and crossed her staff in front of her face to hide her disgust, but Tamm noticed it from the corner of his eye.

"I will arrange with Lily to have her stay with you while I am gone. When I return, the offer still stands for you to stay here in the castle."

She smiled and grabbed his hands, pulling his head close to hers and kissed him on the lips. Tamm fell into the kiss. Before Adina broke the contact, he cut his eyes to Calla, who was looking on, her mouth agape.

Adina let go of his hands and flitted out the door. He could hear her shoes patter down the stairs, and the main doors close behind her. He looked at Calla, her face indifferent. He tried to look into her eyes, but she avoided his stare.

"Calla," he said.

She turned toward the door. "My lord, it is time to depart."

He reached for her arm, but she pulled away. "Calla, you have to understand…"

"What I understand is that you are grieving. Your father just died, and we are on our way to his funeral. I recommend that you grab your things for the journey, or we will not make it to Gaer Alon by nightfall. If you would rather I collect your things, please give the word, and you can make your way to town."

He sighed, dropping his arms to his side. "I'll get my things."

She turned to walk out the door. "Wait," he said, his voice only a whisper.

She paused at the door but did not turn to look at him, remaining silent. "Will you wait and walk with me?"

She turned, staring at him for a long moment. "No. I will not. I will not likely be good company. I will see you at Gaer Alon." She slammed the door on her way out.

Tamm ran to his new bedroom. He was still adjusting to having the master suite in a castle. The townspeople delivered some of his more stylish clothes earlier this morning. He browsed the clothes hanging in a large closet, the scant amount of clothing making it seem even larger. He chose an outfit with black trousers and a white shirt along with a gold-accented black tunic and shiny dress boots. It was the outfit that Riehner had given him the morning of the Spring Festival. He appraised the suit as the memories flooded him.

REBORN

It was suiting; a black suit fit for mourning that was presented on the day to celebrate rebirth and renewal.

He packed his things and skipped down the stairs two at a time and into the town. By the look of the sun, it was a little after mid-day. There was a long line of processioners outside the gates. He searched for Calla but could not find her. A young elf saw him wandering around and brought him to the front of the formation. He helped him load his things in a nearby wagon before assisting him onto his horse. The horse was chestnut colored and bred for long-distance trips.

He twisted in the saddle and looked back at the town. Kèlris and the other townsmen had done well on the fortifications. It would not stop an all-out invasion, but it would discourage smaller forces from a frontal assault. Soldiers of the elvish army were scattered throughout the formation to provide security should they be attacked along the way. Tamm thought that an attack would be highly unlikely, except by stragglers that been scattered after the battle, but he kept his sword belted at his waist, just in case.

He searched around for Calla again but still could not spot her among the formation. Mariah, Kèlris, and Echao came out to see him off. They were going to continue working on the town's defenses and repairing weapons and armor rather than making the trip to Gaer Alon. Tamm understood their intentions and honored their wish to stay.

Elion was on a horse a few paces behind Tamm. He gave him a quizzical look as if to ask if he were ready to depart. Tamm nodded at him and gave the horse a gentle tap with his heals. The horse was steady, but not very fast. Tamm set a relaxed pace as the mare trotted toward Gaer Alon.

THIRTY-ONE

†

They had been on the road for some time, the sun falling far into the westward sky. Tamm's backside ached from riding in the saddle for so long without a break. His sword and old hunting knife bounced against his hip with each movement of the mare. He wore Riehner's diamond and mythril sword strapped to his back. The swords were not heavy compared to the steel swords Kèlris would make, but it did make riding in the saddle more awkward and uncomfortable.

He led the procession, setting the pace of the trip since they had departed Aleesia. He slowed the mare and pulled alongside Elion. "Do you think you could lead them the rest of the way? I'm getting a bit sore from riding and would like to walk among the people for the remainder of the trip." Elion took the reins from him, and Tamm slid to the ground. "Thank you."

"It is nothing," Elion said as he tapped his stallion's side, urging him onward.

Tamm stood to the side, allowing the mass of humans, elves, and dwarves to pass him. Many of them waved and gave their condolences as they went by, and he accepted them with grace. After over half the procession had passed, he finally caught sight of Calla. She was walking alone among a group of elves that avoided entering her space.

He slid past the elves and changed his pace to match hers, drawing up beside her. "I don't remember the trip being this long the first time I made it," he said. Calla stared straight ahead and refused to reply. He grabbed her hand, and she pulled it away.

"Calla, you can't stay mad at me forever. I'm sorry. I didn't ask her to kiss me."

"You also did nothing to stop her either," she said, not looking at him.

"No, I don't suppose I did. But, you have to understand, she and I have known each other all of our lives. Something was starting between us before everything in my life was turned upside down, and I discovered I didn't even know who I was."

Calla frowned. "What is it to me who you kiss? I am your protector, and I will protect you no matter whom you love. It caught me off guard is all. You had never really spoken of her much before. I did not know that you two were so close."

REBORN

Tamm's heart ached at her words. She was *only* his protector? He had hoped that there was something more there, a friendship, maybe more. They had spent so much time together the past several weeks; he felt closer to her than anyone else.

"Is that all that you are? My protector?"

She straightened her shoulders, avoiding eye contact. "I will be your protector until I draw my last breath. It is my sworn duty, just as yours is to be High King over Iradell and rule its people honorably."

He grabbed her hand, and this time, she did not immediately pull away, just sliding her fingers away from his. "So, there is nothing more? No friendship? Nothing?"

"I pray that you will always count me as a friend," she said.

Tamm's shoulders slumped. "I hate this. All of it. This war. Being made to be king. Magic. All of it. I never asked for any of this. I was perfectly content being the son of a blacksmith, working the rest of my life in the forge."

Calla's eyes softened when she looked at him. "That is not entirely true. You may hate the war. You may hate the fact that you have been royalty your entire life and did not know it, but you do not regret having worked with Riehner, being taught magic, or becoming a Battlemage."

"Maybe I do," he said. "If not for all that, Riehner would still be here. Adina's father would still be here. Many of our people would still be here."

Her hand slid across his arm. "You want a friend? Then I will speak to you as a friend. You would still not be happy. Do not forget that I have watched you most of your life. You never wanted to stay in Aleesia. You were looking for the first opportunity to leave. You were destined for more. And, yes, if things had not happened the way that they did, all those people may still be alive. But, you know what else? Riehner would still be cowering behind those robes and staff as Linsyn. You would not be poised to overthrow Tzelder from his fallacious throne, and many more people would still be living under his persecution."

Tamm remained silent as she lectured him. She leaned in closer and lowered her voice. "Those people, Riehner included, knew what they were risking. And, they risked it anyway. They risked it because they counted the man's life beside them just as important as their own and wanted to ensure a better future for those left behind. It is what Riehner built his kingdom on."

Tamm nodded. "There is no greater act of compassion than to lay down one's life for another. He told me that before he died."

"And you would do well to remember it. Selfishness only leads to hate. Riehner had very high expectations for you. I have high expectations for you. Tamm, I…."

"What is it?" he asked.

"Nevermind," she said, shaking her head. "We are almost in the forest. We will speak more tomorrow."

The sun was setting; pink, purple, and orange hues spilled over the tops of the dwarven mountains. The large group slipped into the forest as if it were swallowing them up, all traces of them gone from the road. Tamm stayed at Calla's side, although they did not speak during their trek in the forest.

A messenger approached and summoned him back to the front of the formation. He met with Elion, who explained the plans to him. They were going to release the people once in the city. There would be servants waiting to usher everyone to their living quarters. Other than a very select few, there had not been any humans or dwarves in the elven cities in nearly one hundred years. Once the people were dispersed, Tamm and representatives from each race would assist him in placing Riehner's casket to lie in wait in the House of Counsels. It would be guarded around the clock until the funeral the following morning.

They arrived in Gaer Alon just after dark. After Elion released the processioners for the night, he led Tamm to a cart that was backed up against the stairs of the Council House. Tamm dropped the cart's back gate and grabbed a handle at the head of the casket and pulled, a scrapping sound echoing off the trees as the wood of the coffin slid against the wood of the cart. Next, two human men approached, one on each side of Tamm, to secure a handle as they continued to pull. Next were two dwarves, and then two elves. Lastly, Calla lowered the cowl of her robe as she grabbed the back handle.

Tamm led them through the large double doors and down the hallway. Elion had a set of doors open in the back near an exit that led to the mausoleum. They turned and gently placed the casket on a stand. Elion thanked them all and dismissed them. Before Tamm could leave the room, Elion called to him.

"I know that wood is common among your people for burial," he said. "But it is not fitting for someone of Riehner's rank and station. Permit me to have our people construct him another tonight. I will personally see it completed before the morn."

Tamm rubbed his eyes and yawned. "I permit it. Do as you wish."

"Thank you, your highness," Elion said before placing his hands on both of Tamm's shoulders. "Without Riehner here…Well, let me say this. Leading an army is no easy feat, much less while you are trying to rule a country. Riehner had complete faith in your abilities. If there is anything that I can ever be of assistance with, just send for me. I will help in any way that I can."

"Thank you, Elion. Now, if you don't mind, I would like to take my leave. My room is ready in the treehouse?"

"Oh," Elion said. "You may stay in Riehner's quarters. They are quite lavish, and you should find them most suitable."

"Thank you, but if it's all the same, and no one else is using it, I would like to go to the treehouse."

"Very well," Elion said and gestured to the door with his hand.

◆◆◆◆◆

Tamm awoke and splashed water on his face, took a blade, and shaved the stubble away from his chin. He donned the outfit Riehner gave him and headed downstairs. A couple of servants were waiting on him and whisked him away to the House of Counsels. Elion awaited him inside, and a large breakfast had been set out on the massive oaken table. Several of the elvish elite were seated but had yet begun to eat. Calla stood off by a side table collecting some sort of drink in a chalice from a fountain and speaking with another elf who did not look pleased to be talking with her.

Tamm made his way around the table and began to sit in the seat he had held when Kadagan addressed them about Tzelder's army marching on Aleesia. Elion took him by the arm before he could sit down and led him further around the table. "You are now the rightful King. You sit at the head of the table."

He slid Tamm's chair out, and once seated, pushed it back under the table for him. Tamm reached out and grasped the hem of Elion's robe sleeve. "I'm sorry. I'm not used to all the courtesies of being a noble."

"You will be," Elion said. "That is why I offered my help last night." He turned back to some of the other guests, and Tamm noticed some of the people from Aleesia who had been closer to Riehner. Kadagan was the only dwarf in the room, although several others had made the trip with them. He must have been the only one that knew Riehner well, or maybe the only one that cared for him. The elf Calla had been talking to slipped away when she turned her head for a moment, so Calla took a seat beside Tamm.

After everyone was seated, Elion raised his cup and toasted Riehner, his accomplishments as King, and to Tamm's good health and future as their leader. Once everyone had lowered their glasses, several elves in elegant attire approached the table and began to serve all the guests.

Tamm leaned over to Calla to whisper in her ear, and she leaned in to hear him. "I don't think I'm cut out for this. I feel odd. It's like I'm the center of attention when we should be focusing on Riehner."

She patted his arm. "You are doing fine. This is an elvish custom. We break our fast in honor of the dead with some of their closest family and friends. Afterward, we shall gather for the funeral. There will be a procession from the city center that will march to the tomb. You and I, along with the others from yesterday, will assist in bringing in the casket."

"Elion had some elven craftsmen assist in creating a new, more elaborate casket last night."

She gave him a soft smile. "I assumed that he would. We do not typically bury our dead in wood. It degrades very quick. We go to great lengths to preserve the bodies of the dead so that they appear as they did in life. You will see today."

Tamm nodded and took a bite of porridge. He whistled, and steam rolled from his mouth as it burned him. He and Calla giggled before coughing to disguise the laughter. He whispered to her, "I missed it here. It's so peaceful. I'm glad he'll be buried here."

"We must get back to Aleesia right after the funeral. There is much to do."

"We don't have to be in such a rush," Tamm said. "It will take Tzelder some time to gather his forces again."

REBORN

"No, we must be on our way." Her tone became serious. "We shouldn't delay the coronation. You need to act quickly to set up your rule before others start to use the opportunity to contend for it. Besides, we need to ensure that the castle is ready and begin building up the armies. We can talk strategy later, but ultimately, we will have to march on the cities throughout Aleesia. They will either surrender and swear fealty, or we will have to conquer them."

Tamm looked at with surprise. "What do you mean *conquer* them?"

"I know it sounds harsh, but it is the truth. You cannot defeat Tzelder without the rest of Iradell on your side."

Tamm sipped some tea before responding. "When did you become such a military strategist?"

"I have seen war, and I have lived much longer than you. I have experienced how politics work, and I am just stating the facts."

"You are being idealistic," he said. "Can we talk about this later? I've had enough of war and death for a while."

"Very well," she said, pushing the food around on her plate.

After the meal, Elion led most everyone back out to the front to join the funeral procession. Tamm, Calla, and the other pallbearers entered the room where Riehner lay in state. Tamm's mouth fell open when he saw the casket. It was transparent and shone like a polished diamond. He peered in at the old man and half expected him to breathe or open his eyes. He looked so alive, so much like he did before the battle.

"How did they do this?" Tamm asked.

"It is magic," Calla said. "He will not decay, either. Someone could pay homage in a thousand years, and he would still look exactly like this."

The lid was on the casket, but it was so clear that Tamm felt he could almost touch him. He slid his hand across the polished stone, and the hairs on his arm stood on end. He pulled Calla in close and whispered in her ear. She smiled and nodded in agreement. He called to the others and told them what he wanted to do in honor of Riehner. Since Riehner was the first Battlemage, Tamm felt he should not be carried by hand like everyone else. Rather, he and Calla would use magic to lift and float the casket in with the others flanking it on its sides.

A soft arrangement of strings and wind instruments floated through the air, signaling that the funeral had begun. He and Calla whispered the words in unison. "*Gaoth.*" The casket floated off the stand and hovered in the air. He turned and took a step forward, and the glass-coffin followed. They proceeded down the trail toward the mausoleum. When the crowd caught sight of them, there were gasps and whispers of surprise and approval.

Tamm stopped in front of the stand in the center of the garden. He and Calla eased the casket over the stand and let the magic fade as it lowered into place. They each took their seats in the front row of chairs. Each race had a representative come and speak of Riehner. The human priest spoke of his legacy as a warrior and leader. The elf representative told of his ability in magic and willingness to see the good in all. Kadagan was the dwarven speaker. He spoke of their exploits on the battlefield, and how, if not for Riehner disobeying his father's orders to attack the dwarves, and instead, coming to their rescue, he would have likely perished. But most of all, he spoke of his friendship.

Tamm was summoned next. He stood in the front and withdrew Riehner's sword from the sheath on his back. "I did not have the luxury of knowing Riehner as long as the rest of you have; however, I did have the pleasure to call him father, even if only for a short time. He was the epitome of a king, leader, and Battlemage. He lived out the Battlemages creed of 'My life for yours' by giving his life on the battlefield to save mine."

He wiped away a tear that had slipped past his lashes. "I remember when I first discovered magic. It was with his help, and without him, my brother would have died. He knew that by using magic, he would likely be discovered, but that is just the kind of man that he was. He always thought of others above himself. A good friend recently told me that if I wished to be half the king that he was, that I would do well to learn that lesson from him."

Tamm took the sword to the casket and whispered a word. The lid slid off with ease, exposing Riehner's face underneath. Tamm lifted Riehner's hand and placed the sword on his chest and laid his hands back over the grip, giving his fingers a gentle squeeze. "Where you are going, you will finally be in peace. You will not need this sword any longer, but I wish you to take it with you. Because soon, following in your footsteps, I will lead our lands back to peace and shall not need it either."

With a wave of his hand, the lid slid back into place. The band played again, and Tamm and Calla used their magic to guide the casket into the mausoleum and placed it beside Beltia, who was in a similar glass-like tomb. Tamm walked to the jeweled enclosure and peered into the polished stone. She was absolutely beautiful. Tamm had her eye shape, he realized, and her dark raven hair but had his father's strong chin. He kissed his fingers and placed them on the tomb.

The crowd dispersed, and Tamm sat on the stone floor of the mausoleum. He heard the shuffling of rocks behind him and turned to see Calla standing there. "Hey," he said.

"It is time to seal the tomb back," she said. "Are you ready?"

Tamm stood, and his joints popped from sitting so long. "How long have I been in here?"

"It is nearly nightfall. We must leave soon if we are to get back to Aleesia in time for you to get any rest."

"Can't we just stay here tonight?" he asked.

Her eyes flowed with empathy as he stared into them, willing her to say yes. "You could. You could stay as long as you want, but you are only delaying the inevitable. The people will eventually demand your coronation, whether you wish it or not. They have risked a great deal by standing up to Tzelder, and now they look to you for leadership and protection."

"I know. I'm just not sure I'm ready. Everything is happening so fast. Maybe I wasn't born for this."

She took him by the hands. "You are right. You were born for so much more. You were raised Tammuz, son of Kèlris.

REBORN

You have been reborn into Tammuz, the last Battlemage and rightful ruler of this land. The question is, what are you going to do with it?"

Her words stirred the power inside him. It fed him with strength, with resolve, as he felt its tingle run through his body. He squeezed her hands. "You're right. Let's go. We have work to do."

JAMES BLACKWOOD

Join Tamm and Calla in Rekindle: Book Two of The Battlemage Trilogy

REBORN

THANK YOU

I hope you enjoyed delving into Tamm's journey of discovering magic and what lay beyond Lake Aleesia. Don't worry. There is more to Tamm's story. Reborn is only the beginning. While you wait for the next book in the series, you can head over to Amazon and leave an honest review to let me know what you liked about the story and even what you didn't. Thank you again for embarking on this journey with me.

Want to stay up to date with my writing projects and upcoming novels? You can follow me on Facebook and Instagram @jamesblackwoodbooks and Twitter @jblackwoodbooks. Feel free to visit my website, where you can also sign up for my VIP list. You can find it at jamesblackwoodbooks.com. See you soon.

- James

ACKNOWLEDGEMENTS

†

This has always been one of my favorite sections to read in a book, and now, I finally get the privilege of writing one of my own. I'm sure you have heard the old adage "It takes a village" when talking about raising children. Well, it's true about writing books also. I could go on for days telling you about everyone that has a part in making this book a reality. But let's be honest, you just read an entire book and don't want to hear me ramble on.

First, I want to thank my wife, Rachel, and two girls, Addelynn and Avery, for their love and support. There were days sacrificed for the sake of writing. That is time that I will never get back in the lives of my wife and little girls. No amount of success is worth time lost with those you love. I only hope that when they read this story, they realize that it could have never been brought to life without their support and encouragement throughout the process.

To my mom and dad, you have always been supportive of my dreams, no matter how outlandish they seemed. Dad, you showed me through your actions what hard work and dedication can achieve. Mom, you have always been my biggest cheerleader.

Kathy, without your vast knowledge and expertise of the English language, I don't know where I would be. No matter how many times I read through this novel, there were still going to be spelling and punctuation errors, but you took this manuscript and polished it until it shined. Thank you.

Thank you to all who offered up their time to beta read Reborn, but one person really stood out. Crimsynn, you were a lifesaver. You were so dedicated to delivering specific comments and recommendations promptly. Without your help, this book would be a shell of what it is now.

And what would a book be without a spectacular cover? Les, or better known as germancreative, you did an outstanding job on this cover. I couldn't have imagined it any better. I look forward to working with you again in the future.

Last but not least, I want to thank a man who is no longer with us. To my uncle Roy: I don't know if you knew it or not, but I always looked up to you. You always encouraged me, whether it was me joining the army or going to nursing school . I still remember the day you told me you had written a book, first a children's book, then a fantasy novel. On the days when writing seems hard, I think about all you accomplished, and that gives me strength.

Thank you all. Without each of you, Tamm, Riehner, Echao, and Calla would still just be figments of my imagination, traces of a dream that I could only partly remember after waking. I love you all.

ABOUT THE AUTHOR

James Blackwood is a part-time writer. He has always been a storyteller and loves reading. He is also a husband and a father of two girls. He works full-time as a nurse practitioner and has served in the Army Reserve for the last 18 years. He is an active member of Center Point Baptist Church. He enjoys spending time with his family, playing guitar, and when time allows, gaming. You can find more information on his website at: www.jamesblackwoodbooks.com

GLOSSARY OF WORDS OF POWER

Cróga ag gloicas – Bravery by wisdom

Dhòmsa – (Come) To me

Fós – Be still

Gaoth – Wind

Lasaír – Flame

Leigheas – Cure/Be well

Oscail an chloch – Open the stone

Sciath - Shield

Seilbh eolas ar kieli – Take the knowledge of languages

Síocháin a bheith ar do shon – Peace be upon you

Sgaradh an glas – Break/separate the lock

Solas - Light

Sruthán – Burn

Stad an fhuil – Stop the blood

Struanna- Bring or flow the water

Sulje – Close

Tóg eolas ar kieli – Possess the knowledge of languages

Made in the USA
Las Vegas, NV
15 August 2021